Cutting it Neat for the Wedding

Margaret Amatt

LEANNAN
PRESS
INDEPENDENT PUBLISHER

LEANNAN PRESS

CHAPTER ONE

Hayley

October

Hayley McBride took the steps to her brother's flat two at a time. Running late was nothing new for her, but if that grumpy friend of Finlay's was there, then she didn't want to appear anything but the pinnacle of perfection. Heaven forbid she lost the right to throw stones, which she would if her own glass house came clattering down around her. And throwing stones was about all she wanted to do when it came to Oliver Wright.

She pushed open the door using the bags looped over her arms and burst into the hallway. One bag slipped, and she did a quick save, grabbing a tub of olives before they toppled out and splattered across Finlay's perfect cream carpet.

'Hello!' she called, giving the bags a shake so their contents were safely inside. At the end of the hall was the bright living room, lined with large windows overlooking the River Briar.

Even from here, she saw the water beyond, raging with autumn rain, threatening to burst its banks close to the riverside path.

'Come through,' Finlay said.

Hayley peeked around the open door, hoping to see only her brother and her friend Genevieve. *Yes, just them, please!* She held her breath, relaxing a little when she saw Finlay on the sofa, hand in hand with Genevieve. *Phew. Oh, and look at them!* How lovely for her friend and her brother to be so happy. A rush of warmth flooded through her. She'd love to stand here all day and smile goofy smiles at them, but a shuffling sound on the opposite side of the room yanked her attention from the idyllic scene. Slowly her focus shifted to the armchair in the corner.

A man, dressed in a black suit that would have fit in well at a funeral, sat there, slow-tapping the arm. His dark hair matched his attire perfectly and his thick eyebrows were knitted in the middle of his furrowed brow. Why did he always scowl? It could be one of the handsomest faces ever to bless planet Earth if it weren't for that ugly frown. And what was with the expression of distaste plastered across it from ear to ear? Had he trod on dog poo on the way up? As if hearing her thoughts, a little French bulldog peeked up from a basket in the corner. Spotting Hayley, she leapt out of the bed and bolted across to greet her.

'Hi, Mitzi.' Hayley gave Genevieve and Finlay's dog a one-handed pat, still keeping a tight hold on the shopping bags. When she straightened up, she caught sight of the grouch in the corner again. His jaw appeared even stiffer than before.

Hayley raised her eyes to the mirror, flicked her long hair over her shoulder, and took a deep breath. 'And hey, everyone else.' She swooped down on Finlay and Genevieve, giving them both one-armed hugs and kisses on the cheek. 'How are we?' Taking an empty chair, she briefly glanced at Mr grumpy face. He stared forward, seeming intent on taking in the view and determined not to notice her arrival.

'Great,' Genevieve said.

'Look what I brought for dinner.' Hayley lifted a bag from the floor as Mitzi sniffed around them. 'Don't worry, I have some treats for you too, but I've also got human goodies.'

She kept her focus on Mitzi, making sure her eyes didn't stray anywhere near the grump, sometimes known as Oliver Wright, frequently as Mr always-thinks-he's Wright, and usually as Mr Wright-pain-in-the-arse, but she sensed him bristle. She always thought it strange he didn't have a girlfriend, but maybe it was just as well. His potential partners had dodged a bullet.

'Ooh, what have you brought?' Genevieve asked.

'Loads from the deli – I love it there – and a few other things to celebrate the engagement of the year.'

'You mean us?' Finlay said.

'Obviously. Who else would I mean?'

'I thought maybe one of your favourite TV reality show people got engaged and this is the bulk-buy popcorn so we can watch as it goes south from now on.'

'Ha ha, no,' she said. 'Of course I mean you, you dafty.'

Oliver was now giving off vibes so bristly he may as well have transformed into a hedgehog, or maybe a bear-sized porcupine. Hayley ignored him and dived into the bag.

'Oh wait,' Finlay said. 'It's not the fourth sandwich toaster or a George Foreman grill, is it?'

'No, this isn't the nineteen-eighties,' she groaned. 'We have some Freixenet prosecco; just look at that bottle.' She held it up, so the light bounced off the cut glass surface.

'Not sure prosecco is good for us,' Finlay said, and Genevieve smirked at him. Hayley chuckled, knowing full well Finlay had initially proposed after a few too many glasses of the stuff. But that was all water under the bridge now and they were going to be the most amazing bride and groom ever.

'It's not good for anyone,' Oliver muttered. 'It's full of sulphur dioxide, which can give you all sorts of breathing issues and indigestion.'

What a party pooper! Hayley continued to smile, though she was grinding her teeth, and carried on like she hadn't heard him.

'Indigestion?' Finlay said. 'Do you mean it makes you burp or fa—'

'I got a few bottles of it,' Hayley cut in, and Genevieve slapped his leg, frowning. 'You can stick them in the fridge. Even if we don't drink them tonight, I'm sure you'll use them. I expect you'll have loads of people popping in and out.'

'I suppose it's almost Halloween,' Finlay said. 'We might get some posh guisers who only perform for prosecco.'

'Well, if you're offering prosecco,' Hayley said. 'I'll dress up and come knocking on the door. Now, we also have...' She pulled out some fresh sourdough loaves, olives, chutneys, cheese and cold meats, showing them one by one. 'And these. I couldn't resist.' She held up a heart-shaped box of handmade chocolates.

'Nice,' Genevieve said. 'But remember, I have a dress to fit into in six months.'

'One or two won't hurt.'

'I'll eat them if you don't want them,' Finlay said. 'Shall we put this stuff in the kitchen before Mitzi runs off with the salami?' He got up and lifted the bags, taking them over to the kitchen area, separated from the living area by a large kitchen island with barstools.

'Thank you for offering to provide food,' Genevieve said. 'Much as I love cooking, it's nice not to have to sometimes.'

'No bother.' Hayley sat back and clasped her hands, glancing around like an angelic schoolgirl. Oliver shifted in his seat, reclining to the corner furthest from her, despite already being on the other side of the room, and rubbed at his neck. Maybe he thought if he got too close, he'd get hives or something.

'So... What was the special reason you invited us then?' Hayley beamed at Finlay and Genevieve as he took his seat on the sofa again. Mitzi jumped up beside him, and he rested his hand on her. How sweet the way he'd taken to her, and the feeling was obviously mutual. She'd originally been Genevieve's dog, but she looked very content as part of a bigger family. Hayley blinked.

Was that why they'd invited her? Were they expecting? Being an aunty would be fun, but it seemed so quick. They hadn't even had the wedding yet... But she was getting ahead of herself.

'We wanted to ask you both something.' Genevieve smiled at Hayley, then Oliver.

'And it seemed fitting to have you both here at the same time.' Finlay shifted his gaze between the two of them.

'Yeah?' Hayley frowned at Oliver. His fingers flexed on the arm of the chair, but he didn't make eye contact. Did he know what was going on?

'We'd like you to be our chief bridesmaid and best man.' Genevieve grinned from ear to ear.

'Exactly.' Finlay squeezed her knee.

'Aw wow, that's amazing.' Hayley jumped up from her seat and engulfed them in a hug again. 'Of course I will. I'd love to.'

They laughed, patting her back, and Mitzi got to her feet, wagging her stubby little tail and panting.

When Hayley moved back to her seat, Finlay glanced over at Oliver. 'What about you, mate?'

Oliver pulled a face that was possibly meant to be a smile but looked more like he'd sat on a pincushion. 'Sure. If that's what you want.' He tapped the arm of the chair. 'But wouldn't you prefer your cousin, Aidan, to do it?'

'I'm asking you,' Finlay said. 'Aidan's too busy planning his own wedding and you're my best buddy.'

Hayley held her eyeroll behind a shared smile with Genevieve. Her brother had chosen a great partner, but his taste in friends... Well, what exactly did they have in common? She wished he'd pick Aidan too, though she understood Finlay's reasons.

'Then I'll do it,' Oliver said.

Finlay got to his feet. 'Let's crack open some of that prosecco and celebrate.'

'I assume you want us to do some organising?' Hayley clapped her hands together. 'Hen nights, stags, stens, that kind of thing.'

'I can't imagine anyone better for the job,' Genevieve said.

Hayley beamed, her imagination already running wild. Then her eyes landed on Oliver again. For the first time since she'd entered the room, he fully met her gaze. His dark irises were calm, but behind them she sensed a raging fire. How obvious was it that he didn't want to do anything that might involve seeing her? What she'd done to inspire such disgust and irritation she wasn't sure, but one thing was certain, she wouldn't be letting his grumpy moods ruin her brother's wedding – not to mention anything she was planning for in between.

Finlay handed her a glass of prosecco. She raised it in Oliver's direction and winked. She was doing this thing with or without him.

CHAPTER TWO

Oliver

Autumn sun filtered through the blinds, casting a pale glow across Oliver's ordered desk. Despite his perfectly arranged workspace, the office was small, and felt suffocating, much like Glenbriar itself. Divorce papers and bitter disputes were his daily diet. Over the years, he'd grown a thick skin, but it was tiring going over people's bitterness again and again.

As he reviewed his latest divorce settlement, his gaze drifted to a framed photograph on his desk: a picture of his late mother and him as a young child. He ground his teeth and picked at his shirt sleeves. The pain of her loss was never far away, a reminder of what happened when you let love get the better of you. What was love if not something to raise you up, only to slam you deep underground the next moment? The high wasn't worth it... Not when you understood the lows the way he did.

'You'd have hated this, Mum. The whole damn business,' he murmured, running his fingers through his jet-black hair. What would she make of his reputation for being thorough, relentless, and, some might say, unfeeling? Maybe she'd understand. It was a defence mechanism he'd perfected over the years. Or maybe she'd tell him to shake things up. His life had got so static.

He read through the case files, realising as he got to the bottom of the first page that he hadn't taken any of it in. His mind had drifted to Finlay's upcoming wedding. Why had he allowed himself to get embroiled in that? Only as a kindness to his friend – his only friend. The one who'd stuck by him like a brother. *God only knows why. I'm sure I don't deserve such loyalty.* But being best man was nothing more than a formality. These days, it wasn't like he actually had to do anything. Finlay's sister could arrange all the silly stuff she was rabbiting on about the other night and he could turn up at the wedding, hand over the rings and be done with it. Hopefully they wouldn't require his professional services any time after that. He wished them a long happy marriage, not like the sad cases he got through his doors.

Ugh. He threw himself back in the seat and tugged at the blind. A tree outside the window swayed in the breeze, and its constantly moving shadow was irritating. Weddings. He hated them. He'd never forget the first one he ever went to, dressed in a suit that trapped him like a straitjacket. His whole body was on edge, his nerves in tatters. People asking how he was, if he was pleased for his dad, if he liked his new 'mum'. Except he didn't have a new mum. No one could replace his mum, and his father remarrying barely a year after her death was a constant source of grief. It infuriated him more than anything in his life.

He shook off the memory, trying to focus on the legal documents before him. He couldn't afford distractions, especially not now, when the practice was busier than ever. If he had his way, he'd make so many changes, but it wasn't really his place.

The phone on his desk rang, jolting him from his thoughts. 'Sterling Family Legal, Oliver Wright speaking. How can I help you?'

'Hello, Oliver, it's Nathan.'

'Hi.'

'Listen, let me cut right to the quick. I've got a big opportunity sitting on my desk.'

'What opportunity?'

'We've got a potential biggy coming in. High-profile and the client is willing to pay a lot. I'm looking for someone good to take this on and I'm looking your way.'

'I've got a lot on here. My time for helping out will be limited.'

'I'm not talking about you helping us out. There's an opening coming up in our London office and the way I see it, your name is written all over it. It's time to get out of that backwater and get down to the city where you can really shine.'

'Wow, really? It sounds too good to be true.' Especially as he'd been thinking about moving on for some time now. His career was going nowhere while he was here. It was about time he at least had a partnership. A high-profile London job could be just the ticket.

'Well, you'd need to go for an interview, but I had an idea about that. You'll be heading to London for the annual conference anyway, won't you? I could see if the boss can arrange for the interview then. What do you say?'

Oliver took a deep breath and glanced out the window. Glenbriar had been his home forever, but did that really matter? It wasn't like he'd ever been happy or had any ties here. 'Go for it. Set something up.'

'Fantastic. I knew you'd be up for it. I'll let you know more details as soon as I have them.'

Oliver ended the call and refocused on his case. That little interruption was unexpected, but what perfect timing.

Determined to bury himself in work and not let anything else distract him, he turned off his phone and ploughed on until five o'clock. When his alarm went off, he still had work to do, but he stopped. *Must try not to let work rule my whole life.* It would be so easy to let work take over every hour, and if he succumbed, his life would be even more sterile. If he forced himself to leave at five, it left time for other things. He could cook himself a meal, work out in his home gym, on Friday he watched movies. Sometimes, very occasionally, he dated, but never in the town. He'd travel into Perth, even Dundee or Edinburgh, for casual dates or rare hookups, but they were getting fewer and further between. Nobody really appealed to him...

Well, except *her.* The one he forced himself not to think about. London would be an easier, more anonymous place. He wouldn't need to worry about running into women he'd hooked up with and face the ensuing awkwardness in a big city.

He switched on his phone, and it sprung to life with notifications. *What the...?*

His heart sank as he glimpsed the screen. A long line of missed calls and messages from Hayley. The very person he'd been trying not to think about. What the hell was her problem? And why had Finlay given her his number? He had no intention of engaging in discussions about her endless ideas for those extravagant sten parties. Sten! Honestly, what an utterly stupid name. When she'd first mentioned it, he thought she was talking about something to do with guns. Since when had combined stag and hen parties become a thing? Why were stag and hen parties a thing anyway? They were just frivolous distractions, a waste of time and money.

His hand hovered over the screen. *Block her and be done with?* But even her tiny profile picture had an effect on his body temperature. She was so picture perfect with the hair, the make-up, the smile. *God, that smile.*

He slapped the phone down, tidied his desk, and closed his laptop. After packing his case, he signed out at the reception area. Everyone else had already left for the day. The main door automatically locked behind him and he stepped into the paved parking area in front of the old Victorian building that housed the company offices. All this was very provincial, having an office in a building that was formerly a large family town house. The other buildings on the main street were a mix of old and new, but none of the older ones were houses anymore. They'd all been taken over by businesses.

A gust of cool autumn air greeted him and some leaves rustled across the empty parking spaces.

And then he saw her. What was she doing here? His intense effort to not think about her seemed to have summoned her here instead. How twisted could you get?

'Ah, you do exist.' Hayley got up from the low stone wall she'd been sitting on. 'I thought I'd hang about here for a minute or two and see if you emerged.'

'What do you want?' His jaw hardened, and he looked away, focusing on the tree that had been irritating him all afternoon. Its roots had outgrown the space it was supposed to be confined to and were cracking their way into the paving slabs. Not very interesting really but it saved him from seeing her. Because when he saw her, things happened. Uncontrollable things. Things he didn't like, didn't need, or want... Or maybe he did want them and that was the problem, because he couldn't have her. *Mustn't even try.* She was not for him. She deserved so much better.

'I want to know why you've been ignoring all my messages,' she said.

'I've been working. I don't have time to reply to messages.' He still didn't meet her eyes.

'I've been working too; I messaged during my break. Surely you have breaks too. You're a lawyer. Don't you know you have a legal right to a break?'

'Of course I do, but that doesn't mean I want to spend them reading and replying to messages.' He glanced at her in time to see her rolling her eyes. This was exactly why she didn't need someone like him in her life. She was all sunshine and rainbows, but his influence leached the smiles and joy from her. It couldn't be plainer that she found him irritating. *So be it. Safer this way.*

'Well, how about I save you the bother of reading them by telling you the ideas I had?' She clapped her hands together and smiled.

'Why don't you just do whatever you want? I don't really care.'

She blinked and took a step back. 'Wow, ok. That's pretty brutal. You speak your mind, why don't you? Don't hold back.'

'It's just the truth.' But he swallowed, his throat dry. He hadn't meant to be quite so abrasive.

'What exactly don't you care about?' she pressed. 'The ideas? The sten in general? Or my brother's wedding?'

He flashed her a narrow-eyed look, trying to ignore the jolt in his gut. Not again. It always happened. Always had. No matter how much he tried to ignore it – ignore her. That smile, her voice, her hair... such beautiful hair. The bolt struck him deep and low again, making him imagine things he really should not be imagining, like running his fingers through those chestnut locks, kissing those lips. *Christ, stop.* 'I don't particularly care about the sten.' He cleared his throat. 'It's nothing to do with me. Let Genevieve and Finlay decide what they want and leave them to it.'

'That isn't how it works. It's our job to arrange something for them.'

'Says who?'

'It's traditional.'

'Is it?' He gave a little shrug. 'I don't see how it can be traditional when these stens haven't existed that long.'

'Oh, don't be ridiculous. It's always been the best man's job to arrange the stag night and the bridesmaids' job to do the hen party. So when you put them together to make a sten, it means you and I have to work together too. Now that may be offensive to you, but let's be grown-ups and do this for my brother and my friend.'

'It's not offensive to me, it's just... Oh, never mind. Tell me the crazy ideas.'

'Who said they were crazy?'

'Are things like this ever sensible?'

Again, her eyes rolled as she pulled out her phone. 'This is the list I've made so far.' She threw him a look, presumably to check he was listening and hadn't wandered off. 'We could do a whisky tasting tour of local distilleries. My friend, Felicity, will help us with that if we choose it. An outdoor adventure weekend with hiking, canoeing and camping at Heather Glen. A murder mystery dinner at the Loch View Hotel. A ghost walk around the town or horse riding at a nearby farm.'

He gave a little shrug. 'How am I supposed to know what they want to do? Just ask them.'

'I will, when the time is right.' She pulled a face at him. 'But what do *you* think of the list?'

'None of them are my cup of tea and they all sound like a complete waste of time and money, but it's not me who's getting married.'

'Thankfully. A narrow escape for would-be Mrs Wrights all around the world.'

'Listen, we don't all need to subscribe to your romantic notions or ideas on what a "traditional" wedding should look like. I'm entitled to my own opinions.'

'And luckily we don't all have to sign up to being dour, stuck-in-the-mud, grumpy gits either.' Her tone was still light and breezy, but her brown eyes flashed. 'Just because you're a cynic who thinks every happy couple will end up in your office two months down the line doesn't mean we all have to think like that.'

The wind picked up, gusting across the small parking area. Hayley gathered her hair together at the base of her neck and rolled it over her shoulder. Dark chestnut coils looped over the lapels of her smart grey coat.

Oliver breathed in deeply and very deliberately. Her words may have been aimed to wound him, but watching her twist a loose curl around her little finger was more torturous than anything she might say. He forced his gaze away as a small bus stopped on the street beyond. A woman got on and Oliver watched her approach the driver and pay – anything not to look at Hayley. In some ways, she was right about him, but he wasn't a cynic. *I'm just a realist.* Why should he believe in everlasting love when he knew it was a lie?

'We'll just have to agree to disagree.' He sensed she was about to fill the silence with another snipe at his character. 'But I genuinely think we should butt out and let Finlay and Genevieve choose their own stuff. All our job should be is to make sure they don't spend too much money on a one-day event in what I hope is a long and happy marriage.'

Hayley huffed out a laugh, still rolling her hair between her fingers. That shouldn't be seductive, right? Was it normal to find someone's hair this attractive?

'That's almost progress for you,' she said. 'And I'm not planning on choosing something they'll hate. That's why I'm trying to find a list of things I think they'll like. All I wanted was some help from you.'

'What's the point? It's not like I'll be there.'

'Are you kidding?' She let her hair fall from her fingers, and gaped at him.

'No. It sounds like my idea of hell.'

She shook her head and glanced skyward. 'You are unbelievable. How can you even think about not going? You're the best man.'

'It's not my kind of thing. I won't enjoy it and I don't want to spoil other people's enjoyment.'

Her head tilted a little, and she eyed him like she was examining him or trying to mind read. Why was every inappropriate thought he'd ever had about her rushing to the surface? Try as he might, he couldn't stop them. If she really could read minds, she'd be getting an eye opener alright.

'Why do you think you wouldn't enjoy it? Is it because you're worried about being there on your own?'

'No,' he said, far too quickly. How had she come up with that? Maybe she'd hit closer to the mark than he cared to admit.

'It's not like you won't know anyone,' she said. 'I could set you up with someone if you want? You might enjoy it more if you had a date.'

'What? No—'

'Though you better lighten up a bit if I set you up with one of my friends.' Her voice was jokey again, and she raised her eyebrow in tandem with her coy smile.

'I'm perfectly capable of getting a date if I need to.' He tightened his grip on his laptop case and took a step forward. 'That's got nothing to do with why I don't want to go.'

'If you say so.' She dropped her phone into her bag with a sigh. 'Well, that was a happy waste of five minutes then. So, the bottom line is you don't care what we do as long as it doesn't cost too much and it's what Finlay and Genevieve want, because you won't be going anyway.' She flicked him a pointed look, almost daring him to contradict her.

'An excellent summary. Well done. Have a nice evening.' He hitched his laptop bag over his shoulder, held his breath, and walked past her. Setting eyes on her ignited his insides, her perfume messed with his head, and he couldn't risk even the slightest whiff. God only knew what would happen if he had to spend more time with her. That had to be avoided at all costs.

CHAPTER THREE

Hayley

Hayley lined up the bottles of conditioner on the hanging display shelves in the window of Cutting Edge, the salon she'd worked in for the last five years.

'I was thinking last night,' her colleague Amber said.

'Uh-oh, dangerous.' Hayley giggled, winking at Colette, the new salon assistant.

'Oh stop.' Amber flapped her hand. 'It was about this time last year we went to the National Hair Show, wasn't it?'

'Yes, you're right,' Hayley said. 'It's another salon's turn this year though, isn't it? I can't remember which one.' She made her way through the salon, which was a long narrow room with chairs and mirrors up both sides, a reception desk and a small waiting area to the front and a row of washbasins at the back. Behind them was the backroom that doubled as a small staff room and storage area. Hardly the salon of top stylists, but Hayley didn't mind. She loved this place and couldn't imagine working anywhere else. It was like a wee home from home and her colleagues were friends, almost like a family.

The faint scent of conditioner mixed with colouring solution lingered in the backroom as Hayley arranged a portable workstation ready for her first client. By the end of the day, she wouldn't notice the smell, but before the clients arrived, and the dryers started up, it was the signature scent of the place.

'Pity we couldn't wangle tickets for us too.' Amber rolled up a towel and placed it on the shelf. 'It was so good last year.'

'That was because we got to go together,' Hayley said. 'I don't think they'll allow that again. We had such a backlog afterwards.'

'Yeah, true. Shame.' Amber rolled up another towel.

'It sounds amazing,' Colette said. 'I hope I get to go sometime. Is it in Glasgow?'

'There is a salon show in Glasgow,' Hayley said. 'But this was the big one in London.'

'I'd love to go to London again.' Colette let out a sigh. 'My mum took me for my eighteenth last year, but I've never had a chance to go back.'

'I don't fancy doing it on my own.' Amber placed the final towel on the shelf. 'I'd get lost too easily.'

'Oh, same,' Colette said. 'What if I got lost or mugged?'

'London can be a scary place.' Hayley bobbed her head in agreement. 'But lots of fun too. I know my way around quite well.'

'You were great.' Amber patted Hayley's elbow. 'Remember when those two guys tried to pick us up last time?'

'Oh my god. I don't think we've ever run faster. They were so creepy.'

The door to the main salon opened with a tinkle of the bell.

'I think that's Felicity Swan, your first client.' Colette peered towards the door.

'Ah, yes, it is.' She'd been a friend for a few years now. Hayley wheeled her mobile workstation into the salon, smiling at Felicity. How lucky she was to have met lots of people here she now classed as friends. 'Hey Felicity. In you come and take a seat.'

'Hi.' Felicity sat down. 'I haven't seen you for ages.'

'It's been a while.' Hayley combed through Felicity's gorgeous long blonde hair. 'Far too long, in fact. That's what happens when you have such amazing hair. You don't need to come and see me so often.'

'I've just been so busy, but I've missed our chats.'

'We can catch up today.' Hayley winked at Felicity's reflection. 'So, just a trim?'

'Yes. That's perfect.'

'I'll wet it first if you'll come to the sink with me.' Hayley led her to the row of sinks. 'You know, I was just thinking about you yesterday.' She lifted Felicity's hair up and angled the sink to cradle her neck.

'Something good, I hope.'

'Of course.' Hayley started the showerhead. 'I was thinking about possible venues for Finlay and Genevieve's sten party. I thought with your distillery connections, you might have some suggestions. They might not fancy it, but I'm trying to think up some ideas.'

'We could lay something on, I'm sure. Maybe set up some tasting sessions or we could get you out to Inverbuie. We're making gin there now.'

'I can see Genevieve liking that, though I'm not sure about Finlay.'

'We could still do the whisky too if people preferred it. Just give me a call if they fancy it.'

'I'm not sure what exactly they'd like. I'm looking into options. What flavours of gin are you making?' She rubbed shampoo into Felicity's hair, listening as she recounted their gin range. When Felicity was ready, Hayley wrapped a towel around her head and took her back to the seat. 'And how are your own wedding plans going?'

'Pretty well.' Felicity sat back down. 'We've only got a couple of months to go. It's so difficult with my family living in London, trying to get dresses that fit. And you know what Gavin's mum is like. She's trying to stage manage in her own delightful way, though pretending to keep out of it.'

Hayley laughed. 'She comes in here sometimes and tells me all the gossip.'

'Oh no.' Felicity hid her face in her hands. 'I dread to think what she says about me.'

'Nothing bad. She loves you.'

'Really?'

'Gosh yes. You're the shining star of daughters-in-law.'

'I would never have believed that.'

'It's true.' Hayley slid a wide-tooth comb through Felicity's damp hair, aligning the strands perfectly. Felicity was naturally pretty and her cheeks glowed. She'd make a beautiful bride. Hayley took a shuddery little breath, trying to ease out a weird little sensation in her chest – if only she could run a comb through that too and straighten it out. But there was no easing the tension. Most of the time she didn't notice it, but it was always there, reminding her that everyone else was getting married. Ok, so *everyone* was an exaggeration, but it felt like that. People came in every week wanting wedding hair, and so many of her friends and family were planning weddings. Her lovely little cousin Willow was marrying super-handsome weatherman Marcus Bowman – she'd be a stunning bride, lovely Willow. Then there was her cousin Aidan. He was engaged to his gorgeous girlfriend Lilah. They were a jaw dropping couple any day of the week and would look a million dollars on their wedding day. Felicity was another. And there was Finlay and Genevieve, of course. *As for me...* She'd still be Bridesmaid McBride, chief stylist and organiser, but with no one for herself. *Mustn't complain.* She loved helping people get together and seeing them find love and happiness was so sweet and heartwarming, but when it came to her own romantic life, things never seemed to click.

'Now, let's see.' She separated some strands of hair and held them out to the side so Felicity could see in the mirror. 'This much off?'

'Yes. That'll be fine. Just tidy the edges.'

Hayley lifted her scissors and carefully trimmed a centimetre from the strands.

Felicity smiled at her in the mirror. 'What about you?'

'What about me?'

'Are you seeing anyone?'

'No.' She let out a sigh. 'I'm on my tod for now and it's ok. I quite like the freedom, you know. I can eat when I want, go out whenever I like, have the whole bed to myself.'

Felicity giggled. 'You're such a sweetie. I know you'll find the right person when the time is right. Love has a funny way of sneaking up on you when you least expect it.'

'You're so right.' Though it hadn't found her yet. 'Don't you worry about me. I'm not bothered.' Maybe if she said it enough, she could trick her brain into believing it was true and not panicking that every date would be yet another fail. It wasn't like she was unlikeable... She had loads of friends and nearly always got on with people. And she'd always found the dates pleasant enough. Except pleasant wasn't enough. Not really. She didn't want to settle for just ok. Where was the spark, the buzz? The sense of something big. Maybe she wasn't putting in enough time and effort. Was she expecting to be handed love on a plate?

Will I ever find Mr Right? Or am I doomed to be single forever?

Oh stop!

'Can you put on the magic oil so it won't fluff up if it rains, please?' Felicity asked.

'Of course.'

'What other ideas did you have for the sten, if Finlay and Genevieve don't fancy the whisky tasting?'

'Well, that's my main problem at the moment. They've left it to me to organise with Oliver.' She pulled a face. 'Finlay's best man. Honestly, he is so exasperating and makes no secret of how boring he finds the whole thing. I'd be quicker doing it all myself, but I feel like Finlay wants Oliver to help. I don't want to be the one to tell him his best man is the grumpiest guy on the planet and has no interest in his wedding.'

'Can't Finlay see that himself?'

'Apparently not. They've been friends for a long time.'

'He sounds maddening.'

'It's like he's allergic to anything even remotely related to fun.'

Felicity raised an eyebrow. 'Almost reminds me of Gavin when I first met him.'

Hayley paused for a moment, holding the straighteners poised behind Felicity's head. 'Really?'

'Totally. I thought he was a right stick in the mud until the office Secret Santa day when he turned up in a Christmas jumper. That was when I first started to notice there was more to him.'

Hayley focused on her friend's reflection in the mirror. 'That's hilarious, but truly there's more chance of Scotland winning the world cup than Oliver doing anything half as fun as putting on a Christmas jumper.'

'Oh dear. Sounds like you'd be better going ahead and organising something yourself.'

'Yup. Only it's such a copout for him.'

'If anyone can charm him, it's you.'

Hayley laughed. 'Charm him? I'm not sure I'd even dare attempt it.'

Later, as she went about tidying up the salon with the girls, her thoughts wandered away from the chatter about what they were doing after work or having for dinner and onto the sten. The road to it was like a mountain path meandering up into the clouds, the pinnacle obscured. What would she find at the top and how could she drag the grump up with her? With a wistful smile, she put the towels into the wash.

'Let's lock up then.' She took the keys from the hook.

Amber stifled a yawn. 'That was a long day.'

Hayley waved goodbye to her and Colette, then pulled out her phone. She strolled up the familiar streets of Glenbriar, passing the shops filled with autumn decorations or spooky Halloween displays. Posters in the windows advertised the Forest Light Show. Was it too late to get tickets for that? Was that something they could use as a base for a sten? Probably not. The timing was all wrong.

She typed a text to Oliver as she walked.

HAYLEY: So, had any ideas for the sten?

Without much hope of a reply, she pocketed her phone. On her way up the road, she passed the Drip Drop Coffee Shop where her mum worked part time. Hayley peered in, not sure if this was a day her mum was in or not. Lights were off and it appeared to be closed. A waving figure looked up from wiping a table and Hayley grinned as her mum rushed over to the glass door and unlocked it.

'Hey, sweetheart.' Hayley's mum, Lisa, embraced her as soon as the door was open and Hayley relaxed into her arms. Even after a day at work, Lisa seemed fresh as a daisy, her dark neatly bobbed hair sat almost as immaculately as when Hayley had cut it for her a couple of weeks ago. Her sweet perfume was like coming home, and Hayley forgot all the silly things that had been bothering her. Mum's hugs made everything better. Always.

'You're late today.' Hayley pulled back from the hug and looked around.

'Two people were off,' she said. 'I've been run off my feet. This is me just catching up on the cleaning. I'm not meant to be in tomorrow, but I can see myself being drafted in. Annoying really, I've got loads to do at home.'

Hayley smiled. Her mum was always busy but would never see anyone stuck.

'I'll give you a hand cleaning up,' Hayley said.

'Oh, don't be silly. You don't want to be doing that after a long day.'

'I don't mind. Are you going straight home after?'

'Yes.' Lisa locked the door behind Hayley as she stepped inside. 'I need to put my feet up.'

'How about we grab a carry out?'

'Love that idea.' Lisa beamed as she wiped down a table. 'You can stay over if you like. We'll have some drinks, watch a movie and enjoy a girls' night.'

'Perfect.' It would beat sitting at home alone and she and Mum always had so much to chat about. Hayley had always told her mum everything. As a teenager, when she'd brought friends around, Lisa had always been about, chatting, making food, and joining in like she was one of them.

Hayley had just started wiping down a table when her phone vibrated in her coat pocket. She pulled it out and glanced at it.

'Who's that?' Lisa asked.

'Oliver,' Hayley groaned. 'I asked him if he'd had any ideas for the sten.'

'And has he?'

'I doubt it.' Hayley read the message.

OLIVER: Oh, sure. I've been thinking about nothing else all day.

Sarky git. Well, two could play at that game.

HAYLEY: Great! I bet you've come up with some great ideas then. Let's have them.

'Finlay will be happy you and Oliver are sorting this together. He was worried the two of you would fall out,' her mum said.

'Wonder where he got that idea,' Hayley muttered as another text pinged in.

OLIVER: Sure, here you go... How about a seminar on the tax implications of marriage?

HAYLEY: Seriously? Come on...

OLIVER: No? A thrilling afternoon watching paint dry?

HAYLEY: Er, no...

But she smirked. What was he doing? Was this him trying to be funny? Or what? With him, she honestly wasn't sure.

OLIVER: Alright, how about we all gather to count grains of sand on the beach? Truly romantic stuff.

HAYLEY: You're impossible!

OLIVER: Just realistic. How about a thrilling game of 'Guess the Divorce Settlement Amount'? Winner takes home a free prenup.

HAYLEY: OMFG!!! You're awful!

OLIVER: Cutting too close? Maybe we need a new angle... perhaps a 'Best Excel Spreadsheet Design' competition...

Hayley shook her head, barely holding back a laugh. She glanced up to see her mum watching her.

'What on earth is he saying? Sounds like he has loads of ideas.'

'No, really, he doesn't. I think he's trying to be funny.'

'That doesn't sound like Oliver. Such a serious lad. So cruel that he lost his mum when he was little. I've never seen him smile since.'

'Yeah. That must have been hellish.' Hayley pulled a side pout. It seemed a long time ago to her. Something she hardly even remembered. She'd only been about eight, but it obviously wasn't something he could so easily forget. She couldn't imagine life without her mum. Maybe she'd been too harsh on him.

She returned her focus to the messages. How out of character were they? If she didn't know better, she'd almost call it phone-flirting. *Phlirting*. She giggled at the word. *I think I just invented that.* Or maybe it should be *flexting*? She sent another message.

HAYLEY: Those ideas are bollocks, BTW.

OLIVER: Excuse me? What's wrong with them? Not fancy testing any of them? I see you being an expert in the art of watching paint dry.

HAYLEY: Maybe, but you know I wouldn't be able to do it quietly, right?

OLIVER: I knew there would be a catch.

'He's got a lot to say anyway.' Lisa went back to wiping her table.

'Apparently so.'

HAYLEY: Not something you have to worry about, because you don't want to join in anyway.

OLIVER: I might make an exception for the thrill of seeing paint drying.

HAYLEY: Would you now? Isn't that straying into dangerous territory?

OLIVER: *Why? Is the paint toxic?*

HAYLEY: **string of laughing emojis* Haha. I was thinking more along the lines of you testing out a freshly painted venue with me. Sounds almost romantic... Next thing you know, we'll be falling in love.*

She chuckled out loud as she sent it.

'Hayley.' Lisa put her hands on her hips. 'I hope you're not teasing him.'

'Can't help it,' she said.

Lisa shook her head, but she was smiling. 'Just don't be mean.'

'When am I ever mean?'

'That's true. I've got good kids, that's one thing I can say for sure. The two of you have always done me proud.'

'Thanks, Mum.' Hayley glanced back at her phone.

OLIVER: *Zero chance, I assure you.*

Her thumbs raced as she fired back a response.

HAYLEY: *For once, I agree with you. Shocker! But got to admit that's progress. Tell you what I am going to do though...*

OLIVER: *Whatever it is I strongly doubt you'll succeed.*

HAYLEY: *I'm making it my mission to get you to crack a smile.*

CHAPTER FOUR

Oliver

Oliver let out a groan after completing his final round of dumbbell curls. He laid down the weights, straightened up and wiped sweat from his brow. Hard workouts were great and the buzz of adrenaline was pushing him to do more, but he knew not to push it too far. Not when he had work the next day. He'd converted half his garage into a home gym, not a workshop, which was what his dad would have used the extra space for. Just another reason for him to be disappointed in his son. After growing up on the family farm, Oliver had no desire to take it on or do anything remotely connected to agriculture. He'd chosen a different career and lifestyle. One his dad sure as hell didn't get.

Not that it mattered. Oliver rarely saw him these days. But a twinge of guilt always accompanied thoughts of his dad, a niggling sense that he'd forgotten to do something, or hadn't done enough of something.

He tossed his towel into the washing machine and headed for the shower. Finlay was always badgering him to join the gym so they could work out together, but Oliver much preferred the peace of his own home. He didn't want to socialise while he exercised, see other people, or have them see him.

After showering, he got dressed and checked his phone. More messages from Hayley. No matter what he did, there was no shaking her. If he ignored her, she messaged nonstop. If he engaged with her chat, she messaged nonstop. He could turn off the phone or ignore it, but knowing the messages were there set him on edge, like he had a very irritating nymph sitting on his shoulder, twisting his ear and prodding him continually. And the fact that nymph looked like Hayley in his mind's eye didn't help matters. Things had been so much easier when he didn't have to see her. When she'd just been there in the background, he could pretend she didn't exist. Kind of. This 'working together' situation was causing too many ructions in the neatly ordered caverns of his mind.

The quickest way to reply to all Hayley's messages at once would be to call her. Then he could answer all her questions, give his opinion on her suggestions and tell her not to bother him for the rest of the evening... Make that week.

His instinct battled over what would be worse, talking to her or not talking to her, and while he half hoped she wouldn't pick up, he also craved to hear her voice.

'Hello,' she said, putting on a posh accent. Just that one word sent a fizz of electricity through his veins. 'And to what do I owe this honour? I mean, it must be something rather large and important for you to call little old me.'

He chewed his tongue, waiting for her to finish. 'I'm replying to your messages in the quickest way I can think of. And once I've replied, please stop sending them to me.'

'Can't make any promises, but let's hear your replies.'

How did her voice have the power to soothe him, madden him, cheer him up and turn him on all at once?

'So...' He cleared his throat. 'These potential sten venues all look... fine.'

'Ooh, that's very good progress. I likey.'

'So, you go right ahead and book whatever you want.'

'Oh, Oliver! You ruined it. Don't you want to go and see any of them? It wouldn't take long. Just a couple of hours and we could nip around them and see what we think.'

'No can do, sorry. Not in the next couple of weeks anyway. I've got lots of demanding cases at work, plus prepping for...' He stopped. Maybe telling her he had an interview coming up in London wasn't smart. She'd tell Finlay, and Oliver didn't want anyone knowing just yet. In case nothing came of it. No need to bother anyone else on his behalf. 'A legal conference in London.' That part was true, no need for embellishment.

'And will that take all weekend?'

'A lot of it. Don't you work weekends anyway?'

'Only Saturday. I'm free on Sunday.'

'I'm not. Finlay and I are cycling in the Glenbriar Spin-Off.'

'Hmm. I forgot about that. Oh well, never mind.' She let out a sigh. 'I'll see if Genevieve wants to go while Finlay's cycling.'

'Sounds like a better idea.' Though a sharp little niggle stabbed him in the chest at the disappointment in her voice.

Oliver slugged back some water, then attached the bottle to his bike. Close by in the forestry car park among the cyclists taking part in the Glenbriar Spin-Off, Finlay was chatting to his cousin Aidan. Nice to see them talking again after they'd had a fall out earlier in the year. All caused by love. What else? They both thought they were in love with the same woman, only neither had been. They'd moved on and found other partners, and now they were both engaged. How quickly things changed. Hopefully it would work out for them both, but Oliver had serious doubts. Not that he was about to voice them. Thoughts like that were safer kept locked inside.

He wheeled his bike towards them, but before he was too close, he noticed they weren't alone. Three women were behind them, talking and laughing. One woman was a striking redhead he recognised as Aidan's fiancée. The one beside her was Genevieve, running her fingers through her sleek caramel coloured hair as the wind tried its best to ruffle it. And the third... Oliver half-closed his eyes before he started walking again. Hayley. Why was she here? As if in answer to his question, she looked over. She tossed her head to the side and her dark hair coiled over her shoulder in perfect barrel curls. Oliver gripped his handlebars like his life depended on it. That hair. How he loved that gorgeous glossy hair. He wanted to stroke it, knit his fingers into it... *Oh fuck, stop.* Her eyes travelled down him in a very definite once over. Normally, he didn't care about wearing his cycling clothes, especially at a bike event. Christ, it would look more stupid to be wearing something else, but under Hayley's scrutiny an uncomfortable heat in his gut developed. *Need to duck out.* This was like being found naked in public.

'Hi.' She waved with an overbright smile and everyone turned to look at him. His stomach did a backflip.

'There you are,' Finlay said. 'What kept you?'

'Nothing. I'm not late.'

'True, but you're later than us and that's not normal.'

'I... Um... Got held up.' He couldn't look at Hayley, but his skin prickled and the hairs at the back of his neck rose. Why did he get the sensation she was watching him?

'Shall we head to the starting point?' Aidan said.

'Think so.' Oliver forced his eyes anywhere but on Hayley. But they were fighting him, desperate to settle on her. Her face was magnetic, picture perfect, shining, and happy. She had the ability to draw attention to herself even when she wasn't talking or doing anything.

'Well, we're off to do some investigating,' Hayley said. 'Sten venues. While you boys razz around on your bikes.'

'That's your job, mate.' Finlay slapped Oliver on the upper arm. 'Why are you not doing the investigating?'

'Not my thing.' Though the pang of guilt struck again. Was he letting people down? Investigating venues and that kind of thing wasn't for him... but was he just being selfish and thoughtless?

'Never mind,' Hayley said. 'We'll have a lot more fun without you. All girls together.' She put her arms around the shoulders of the other two women.

'It definitely sounds like fun to me,' Aidan's girlfriend said.

'It will be.' Hayley beamed at her, then threw Oliver a see-what-you're-missing smile.

It hit its mark and, for a second, he desired nothing but to throw away his cycle helmet, drop his bike and go with her.

Finlay gave him a funny little look before kissing Genevieve goodbye. Aidan did the same with his fiancée. Oliver clung to the handlebars, trying not to notice the lovey-dovey scene unfolding before him. Needing to do something, he lifted the helmet he'd looped onto the bars and pulled it on. Without really meaning to, he caught Hayley's eyes as he hooked up his chin strap. She gave him a little wink and a cheeky wave. An unspoken thread lingered between the two of them. It strummed with pressure and a desire to join in with the fond farewells. To touch her lips with his, pull her close and embrace her would satisfy a deep ache inside him, but it was way too dangerous.

That road led to trouble at best and pain at worst.

'See you.' He pushed his bike towards the starting point.

Put distance between self and Hayley now! How the hell could he keep away from her with the wedding looming and her insistence on including him in everything? *Eyes on the London job.* If he got that, he would be hundreds of miles away from the peril and too far to be pushed into wedding planning. And that was good. Yes. He'd outgrown Glenbriar and was ready to spread his wings.

Why then did his soul ache rather than rejoice at the idea? No time to ponder that now. In fact, a gruelling cycle run was exactly what he needed to chase these irritating feelings away. If only it was a permanent fix.

CHAPTER FIVE

Hayley

'I've always loved this place.' Hayley pulled into the car park of The Loch View Hotel. Could have been the fact that it was painted pink. Anything pink was good. Even though no one seemed to know exactly why it was that colour, that unique feature made it a famous local landmark and locals always referred to it as the pink hotel. It was also beautifully situated on the shores of Loch Briar. The surrounding trees were popping with colour in their autumn glory, and it brought a smile to Hayley's face. Who wouldn't love living in a place as gorgeous as this? The scenery around Glenbriar was unrivalled and with the town itself being such an awesome little place, she never wanted to live anywhere else.

'I love it too,' Genevieve agreed.

'I haven't ever been inside,' Lilah said. 'But it looks cute.'

'Let's get you an education then.' Hayley smiled at Lilah. She was a real sweetheart, but had had a troubled past. Aidan was the perfect man for her, or more like they were perfect together, but Hayley still liked to keep Lilah under her wing.

'So, if we come here for the sten,' Genevieve said, 'what exactly would we be doing?'

'The owner, Briony, I don't know if you know her,' Hayley said. 'I've been doing her hair for a while now. Anyway, she said they could put on a murder mystery evening for us and we could all dress up in twenties or thirties costumes like we were in an Agatha Christie drama.'

'That sounds intriguing.' Genevieve shaded her eyes as she looked around. 'I like the sound of it, but you know I'll like anything you arrange.'

'Agatha Christie's books are great,' Lilah said. 'I always enjoy classic books and they're so well written, so clever.'

'I haven't even read them.' Hayley gave a rueful shrug. 'But I love the films and old TV shows. My mum and I love Hercule Poirot. He's so funny.'

They went inside and were greeted by a receptionist.

'Hi.' Hayley approached her. 'I wonder if I could speak to Briony. She knows we're coming. It's to chat about a sten party.'

'Sure.' The receptionist picked up a phone, and a few moments later, Briony appeared from a side door.

'Hi.' She smiled at them all, and Hayley embraced her. 'Good to see you. And which one of you is the bride-to-be?' She looked between Genevieve and Lilah.

'They're both brides-to-be actually,' Hayley said. 'But it's Genevieve we're having the sten for.' She pointed out Genevieve.

'Lovely,' Briony said. 'And you're both getting married. That's exciting. I can show you the function room where we would hold the dinner if you decide this is the option for you. You'd have to give me a bit of notice though, as I have to hire the group who put on the murder. It's a small group of actors. We've had them a couple of times before and they're great.'

They followed her through the main dining room to a side room.

'It's roomy enough for up to thirty people. If you needed more, we could always host it in the main dining room.'

'I think this would be brilliant.' Lilah's eyes widened.

Genevieve took Hayley by the arm and whispered, 'Maybe we should have a sten here for Lilah, and I could do something different.'

'That might not be a bad idea. I don't think anyone has done one for her. I'll speak to Aidan.'

Hayley looked around with Genevieve as Briony went over to Lilah. Lilah was clearly sold on the idea of a murder mystery, though Hayley wasn't convinced it was the right thing for Finlay and Genevieve. As Lilah chatted enthusiastically about her wedding plans to Briony, the words drifted into Hayley's consciousness and a strange sensation crept over her. A shadow of something she wasn't used to, something that made her a bit hot and slightly sick. Was it jealousy? How could it be? She was happy for Lilah. Just as she was happy for Genevieve and her brother and she wanted them to be happy too. A hollow ache inside grew heavier, like she was hungry for something, but at the same time nothing appealed.

'Aidan suggested we get married here,' Lilah said. 'But we both like the outdoors idea better. Even if it rains, it doesn't matter. Being outside is much more us. But maybe we could do the murder dinner before the wedding. We don't have a big budget, but it sounds fun.'

'I think you should,' Hayley agreed. 'I think it's perfect and we'll all chip in.'

'Totally.' Genevieve brought her hands together. 'And your outdoor wedding sounds very exciting.'

'And very Aidan.' Hayley flicked Lilah a little grin. 'I even expect him to invite the bees.'

Lilah chuckled. 'I think he might.'

Hayley patted her on the back, trying to stop the sensation rising again. She had no need to be jealous of either Genevieve or Lilah. She loved them both and knew they'd caught two amazing guys in her brother and her cousin. And really, she wasn't jealous of *them* – just their situations. It hadn't been plain sailing for either of them but they'd got there; they'd found their special person and they were happily planning their futures. Genevieve had been the champion of the single girl for a long time, but she'd cast off that mantel and was enjoying life as part of a couple. Hayley might insist she didn't mind being single, but she kind of did. She wasn't a loner. People featured heavily in her life and she loved having them about. But that one special person still eluded her.

Why, at that exact moment, did she have to think of Oliver? Seriously she did not need him cropping up anywhere near thoughts about special people. He may be special, but not in a good way. How irritating was he? And how rude to leave her doing this while he buggered off on his cycle run? Granted, it was more fun with the girls, but still infuriating. The vision of him standing by his bike in his cycle gear reared in her mind and she stifled a laugh. *Jesus.* Those outfits were hideous. She'd often chuckled at Finlay and Aidan in them, but Oliver... *Christ. Must stop this train of thought!* That Lycra hadn't left much to the imagination. Why had he hidden behind his bike? It wasn't like he had anything to be ashamed of... Though *she* did! Why had she even looked in the first place? This was the slippery slope alright. The door of denial was creeping open. How could she deny Oliver was hot? He might be a grumpy twat, but he was a hot grumpy twat.

'What are you laughing at?' Lilah asked.

'What?' Hayley glanced at her. 'Oh... I, er, can't remember.'

They had lunch at the hotel before driving to a local water sports centre around the lochside. The owner was a pleasant young woman called Eleanor. Genevieve recognised her and they all melted at the sight of her tiny little baby in a carrier at her chest. Hayley's insides turned to goo at the sight of the baby's little hands. How cute and itsy bitsy was she? One day Hayley wanted one of them for herself… though, of course, a vital part of the equation was missing.

Eleanor talked them through the various adventure sports they could take part in if they decided to hold the sten here. Hayley tried not to laugh at the expression on Genevieve's face – outdoor sports were so obviously not her thing.

'Is Logan doing the Spin-Off today?' Genevieve asked Eleanor, possibly in a deliberate attempt to steer the conversation away from white-water rafting.

'Yes,' Eleanor said. 'I'm a cycling widow for the day.'

'Me too.' Genevieve gave her a commiserative look. 'Or widow-to-be. So's Lilah.'

But not me, Hayley thought.

'If you want to see where we do the water sports, you can walk over the hill and then down the other side to the loch. The new centre is there.'

'Ok. We'll take a look. Thanks,' Hayley said.

'You know how I said I wouldn't mind anything you chose,' Genevieve said as they headed up the hill some minutes later. 'I don't think I was including adventure sports. Can you imagine me in a canoe? Or crossing a gorge on a rope?'

Hayley laughed. 'No, and I can't imagine doing it either. But I kind of fancied white-water rafting. It always looks so cool.'

'Not to me.' Genevieve pulled a face.

'I'd give gorge-crossing a go,' Lilah said.

'You're braver than me.' Hayley put her arm around her shoulder. 'And younger and more foolhardy.'

'Not that much younger.' Lilah pulled a face.

'Five years... That's pretty young.'

'The guys would love this.' Genevieve shielded her eyes and squinted at the view of the approaching loch. 'We could always do things in tandem with them.'

'And what about me?' Hayley asked.

'We could always strap you to Oliver and send you canyoning,' Genevieve suggested. 'Then you could attempt to drown him under the pretext of having fun.'

'Good god, no.' Hayley held up her palm. 'I never want to get that close to him. He drives me insane.'

Genevieve waggled her eyebrows. 'He may have other ways of doing that... but they all involve getting very close indeed.'

'Stop.' Hayley threw up her hand. 'I forbid you to say anything like that ever again. It's almost as bad as giving me TMI about your relationship with my brother. Anymore chat like this and I might have to shove you in the loch.'

Genevieve laughed just as Hayley's phone vibrated in her pocket.

'Oh heck. It's Andrew, the salon owner. He never calls unless it's something catastrophic.' An exaggeration maybe, but as the owner of a chain of salons across the country, he was a busy man and the Glenbriar salon didn't usually even register on his recognition scale, which was fine by them. The stylists there got by themselves with minimal interference but still enjoyed the security of being part of a chain, and they also got invited to large company functions in Edinburgh every Christmas. 'Hello.' Hayley tried to sound professional, not petrified.

'Hayley. Wonderful to talk to you again. I really need to make a visit sometime and catch up on the latest in person, but I'm so strapped for time.'

'Yeah...' Was this why he was calling? Did he want to arrange a visit? And why call on her day off if that was the case?

'So, just giving you a call to let you know there's a spare ticket going for the Hair Show in London. I know it's short notice, and it's the girls from the Musselburgh salon's turn this year, but there's an extra one. I remembered you and Amber had a wonderful time there last year and the ideas you've put into place since then have been excellent, so I wondered if either of you would like to go again.'

'Oh... That sounds great.'

'There's a slight downside. Whichever of you decides to go would have to get to London under their own steam and arrange accommodation. We don't have an extra flight ticket or hotel room, unfortunately, but if you could get a train or the overnight bus perhaps, that might work. I'll message you the maximum expenses claim amount and you can see if you can find something suitable.'

'Ok. I'll speak to Amber about it.'

'Perfect. If you can let me know by close of play tomorrow, that would be great.'

Hayley ended the call and pocketed her phone.

'Was it a catastrophe then?' Genevieve asked.

'No. It was quite a good call actually. I might be able to go to the London Hair Show after all, though I need to speak to Amber about it tomorrow.'

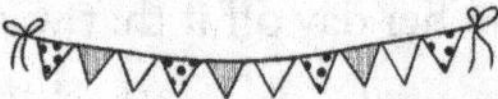

'Ah no,' Amber said when Hayley told her the dates of the hair show and the expenses budget over the phone. 'I'll have to leave it to you. That's my sister's birthday week. She'd kill me if I was away for her fortieth. And I'm actually petrified at the thought of going to London alone. You'll find it tricky getting a good flight and a decent hotel room at that short notice for that price.'

Hayley bit her lower lip, thinking. 'I wonder.' The salon didn't open on Monday or Tuesday, so if she was to be away from Wednesday to Friday next week, she'd need to do some client rearranging. That would take time, so she had to decide now.

'What?' Amber said.

'I'd love to go but this budget is rubbish.'

'Yeah. Such a shame. Let me know what you find.'

Hayley googled the trains again. She'd already looked at them several times, plus buses, cheap flights and budget hotels, but nothing really fitted, She wasn't so desperate that she wanted to subsidise it herself, not when she'd still have to eat and use public transport once she got there.

As she swiped through lists of far-too-expensive rooms, a message popped in.

OLIVER: How did the sten hunt go yesterday? You've succeeded in making me feel guilty and I therefore apologise for not doing my best man duty properly. Now I suppose I owe you something to make up for this, though I'm not sure what that might be yet.

She did a slow blink as she read it. Was that message serious, or more of his dry humour? But another thought flickered into her head.

HAYLEY: When are you going to London for that conference thingy?

OLIVER: What has that got to do with anything?

HAYLEY: Answer the question. Also, how are you getting there and where are you staying?

OLIVER: Seriously, why do you want to know?

HAYLEY: Answer me, or the price of what you owe me to get you to forgive me will go up and up until you do.

OLIVER: You're insane.

HAYLEY: That's the price gone up again.

OLIVER: Monday to Friday next week. Sleeper train. The Royal Saxon Hotel, Mayfair.

Hayley sucked on her lower lip. Could that be more perfect? Well, minus the part that he would be there too. She let out a laugh… like he'd agree to her going too. He wouldn't want her gatecrashing.

HAYLEY: Will you have a bunk bed cabin on the train and a twin room at the hotel? If you do, can I come with you? I need somewhere to stay for the Hair Show next week and the Royal Saxon Hotel sounds wonderful.

She added hundreds of smiley faces.

OLIVER: You are actually insane.

HAYLEY: Is that a yes?

She knew he was probably crapping himself round about now, trying to think up an excuse to fob her off and no way would he really let her go, but it was fun playing with him like this. Even a tiny false hope that she might get to London gave her the warm fuzzies. She loved a London trip.

OLIVER: You can't be serious. For all I know, it's a single room.

HAYLEY: Can't you change it? And consider your debt paid!

OLIVER: Er… How about no!

Hayley smirked. Well, it had been worth a try, but it looked like the Hair Show was off the calendar this year. As was a trip to London with Oliver, which on second thought was probably a good thing.

CHAPTER SIX

Oliver

The train rattled towards Edinburgh, crossing the Forth Rail Bridge, which never looked that impressive from inside the carriage despite the famous structural design. Oliver only glanced up from his phone to check where he was and make sure he hadn't been abducted to a strange planet where random women tried to invite themselves along for business trips to London. Maybe it was just as well those messages were there in front of him because otherwise he might have thought he'd dreamt the whole thing. She couldn't be serious, could she? Did she really want to go to London with him? Surely that wasn't a good idea.

His phone buzzed, and he ground his teeth at the sight of her name. What now? And did he really want to take this call in the middle of a packed train? But then if he didn't, he'd wonder all day what she wanted.

'Yes,' he muttered, swiping the green button to the top.

'Hola.' Hayley's chirpy voice seemed so loud he was sure everyone could hear her and he glanced up to check.

'What do you want?' he said quietly.

'Just checking that I can't persuade you to let me come with you.'

Oliver turned his head, so he was right in at the window and carried on in his quietest voice. 'Do you really think it's ok to crash my business trip like that?'

'I can hardly hear you. Where are you? Aren't you at work?'

'I'm on the train. I can't speak any louder.'

'You're on your way to London already? But you said it was next week.'

'It is. I'm going to Edinburgh today to meet a client.' Not that it was any of her business. 'Why do you want to go to London anyway?'

'It's the London Hair Show next week.'

'Ah... Ok. But why are you only just looking for accommodation and transport now? If it's next week, why haven't you had somewhere booked for months?' Stupid question. She'd probably forgotten when she was off chasing sunshine and unicorns, but then if the sten was anything to go by, she was an obsessive planner, so this didn't make sense.

'I only got the ticket yesterday. It was a last-minute thing. My boss said I could go if I find accommodation and transport, but everything is booked or out of budget.'

Oliver let out a sigh that came out like a groan and he winced and drew in closer to the window. 'I don't think inviting yourself to tag along on a business trip with me is a good idea. Do you?'

'Probably not. In my head, it seemed like a better idea than in real life. I thought we'd hardly see each other because I would have events to attend and you would have work. All we'd need to do would be sleep together.'

'Pardon?'

She giggled and the sound tickled his ear. 'You know what I mean. That's why I asked if you had a twin room. As if I'd mean, well, *that*!'

He rolled his eyes, but his stomach clenched. She'd used the phrase to deliberately tease him. Her tone had made that so obvious. Little did she know how much he wanted to do exactly *that*. Having her so close to him in a hotel room would be nothing short of torture. No way could he do it. Just no. She'd simply have to live with her disappointment.

'Look, I'm sorry, but no. It won't work.'

'That's ok,' she said. 'I knew you'd say that. I was just chancing my luck.'

Part of him hated himself for letting her down. Again. He'd seen the look on her face at the Spin-Off and didn't want to be the one causing that kind of disappointment. But how could he do this? The fire of desire burned low, as it always did. But he could never act on it. He didn't do relationships. Period.

She doesn't even like you!

And there was the rub. She wasn't inviting herself along because she wanted to spend the week with him. The hotel and transport were all she wanted. If she'd had any feelings for him, she wouldn't even risk asking, because the close proximity to each other might have dangerous consequences. He couldn't even chance a short fling with her. How would that affect the wedding plans? Finlay wouldn't be happy either. He wouldn't want Oliver toying with his sister. She deserved so much better. Roses, smiles, and happy endings. He didn't do any of them.

'Right, I need to go,' he said. 'I've got work to do.'

'Sure. Have a good day,' she chirped, and she sounded happy, but he thought he caught a twinge of melancholy. He laid down the phone with a sigh and rubbed at his cheeks, trying to dispel the sensation that he'd done something wrong.

When he arrived in Edinburgh, he took a taxi to the home of his client. She'd lived in Glenbriar when her case had started but had since moved to the capital. Oliver's boss saw her in pound signs and insisted Oliver went to meet her rather than her coming into the office. He hadn't argued, even though it seemed excessive.

He still couldn't get Hayley out of his mind, no matter how much he tried to distract himself. She kept popping up in his brain like her messages did on his phone. Reflexively, he checked it. Nothing. Just a two-day-old message from his dad he'd been ignoring. He had to psych himself up to read Dad's messages, as they usually infuriated him. Maybe this was the distraction he needed.

DAD: Just thinking ahead to Christmas. Got a big do planned and we're working out numbers. Should I include you?

Should he indeed? Because it wasn't exactly an invitation, was it? If he went, he'd be a spare part, as usual. Kind and well-meaning relatives of his dad and his stepmum were always present and would make conversation, but it felt so sterile and superficial. Mostly these family gatherings were more of a showcase for his two half-sisters, Ava and Sofia. First it had been ballet and dancing, then piano and singing or poetry recitals in French. Now, it was to celebrate university successes and discuss their grand plans – none of which had ever happened for Oliver. *Bitter much?* Well, why shouldn't he be? So, he couldn't dance, play the piano, or sing, but he had other talents and when it came to grades and qualifications, he could knock both his half-sisters into a cocked hat. But it had all passed by unnoticed and unmentioned, more expected rather than cause for celebration. Oliver didn't need that kind of shit in his life, so he kept away as much as possible. He could almost hear his stepmum's righteously indignant voice saying, 'There's not really any point in inviting him. He never shows up to anything anyway.' He let out a sigh and rested his head back. Reading that text had produced the desired effect. It had made him stop thinking about Hayley for five minutes.

The client's house was a nineteen-thirties style bungalow in Corstorphine, heavily alarmed on the gates and the front windows. Now he had to get his work head on and let everything else go for the next hour or so while he worked on this deal. It was a complicated case, especially as he wanted to get his client the best possible outcome. She supplied cake and coffee, which he was paranoid he would spill over her plush white carpet and sofa. The cloying air-freshener was really getting to him and he was glad to eventually leave and claim the fresh air.

He didn't really know his way around Edinburgh, but the taxi ride hadn't taken too long, so he decided to try to walk from here back to the station. He turned his phone back on to see a missed call from Nathan Shelby and a voice message. Raising his phone to his ear, he listened as Nathan spoke.

'Hi, just wanted to touch base re London next week. Interview all set up. And don't forget the corporate dinner on Thursday eve. Everyone will be there, so pack your top hat and tails. Also, can't remember if you said or not, but if you have a partner, bring them along; it's a plus one do. I'll forward you the link. See you there.'

A corporate dinner? Sounded like his idea of hell. He'd been to them occasionally and usually managed to arrange a date for the evening, but taking strangers and trying to pass them off as his partner was painful and going alone was a hideous thought.

Ask Hayley.

The words burst into his subconscious like a flashing neon sign. She wanted to go to London. If he agreed to her coming with him, she could surely spare him one evening. It would be a damn sight better than dusting off some long forgotten dating apps in the hope of finding someone suitable for the evening.

Of course it would open up all the cans of worms he'd wanted to sit on and never admit were there at all, never mind let them loose, but now the idea was in his mind, he couldn't get rid of it. Something fizzed inside him. Maybe a tiny bit of excitement. Not for himself, but for her. She'd be happy. Going to London was what she wanted.

Hiding the interview would be a lot trickier, but he was confident he could keep quiet about it. She wouldn't be any the wiser where he was during the day.

He steered his mind away from thoughts about having to share a bedroom or what might happen if he couldn't get a twin room. He opened his phone and scrolled for the email from the hotel. Should he call them first? Or risk it and ask her anyway? He'd also have to buy her a train ticket. He'd booked a bunk cabin, but he'd paid for single occupancy. Would her boss cover the expense of a cabin on the sleeper? Oliver suspected not; they didn't come cheap.

Ask her first!

His fingers flew across his phone, typing a message.

OLIVER: Still want to go to London?

He pocketed his phone and carried on walking as he waited for a reply. Barely a minute had passed when the phone vibrated.

HAYLEY: Are you kidding? Of course I do... Why?

OLIVER: I've been invited to a dinner in London, and I need a partner. If you come to that with me, then you can have the room and the train ticket.

HAYLEY: Are you actually serious?

OLIVER: Yup. Pack your posh frock, Cinders. Mr Wright is taking you to the ball.

HAYLEY: THIS HAD BETTER NOT BE A JOKE! Tell me this is real. A ball in London? OMG OMG OMG OMG... What kind of dress do I need? This is sooooooooooooooo exciting!!!!!!!

Why was he grinning? He could see her excited face in his mind's eye and it made him smile. Yes, Oliver Wright was smiling in public. No one here would know or care but his friends and family would understand how unusual that was. Thankfully, she didn't seem to care that she'd be there with *him*. She was the party queen, and with her on his arm, he might be able to bear it, assuming he could control the fire in his soul. He took a deep breath. *There. I've got this.* He would be master of his feelings.

His phone buzzed again.

HAYLEY: I am actually going to burst with excitement. Tell me now what kind of event it is... I want to look at dresses. Pleeeeeeeeeeeze!!!!!!

The smile grew on his face. Her reaction was exactly what he'd expected, but seeing it like that... He shook his head. At least he couldn't pick a more grateful recipient for this 'role'. He located the email from Nathan with the details, took a screenshot and forwarded it to her. He'd barely hit send when her reply pinged back.

HAYLEY: Bloody hell!!! I think I need resuscitation...

HAYLEY: This looks amazeballs... I need to find a dress. OMG!!

HAYLEY: Never thought I'd say this, but you are actually the nicest, bestest, most amazingest man ever!!

He huffed out a laugh. Unfortunately, he wasn't, and she knew it too, so he was happy to accept the false praise, knowing she was just thrilled she got to go to a fancy dinner in London, plus the Hair Show. Now all he had to do was get through the week. With his head and heart locked in a constant conflict, it would be no mean feat to do so unscathed. The oddest thing was perhaps that the raging fire which constantly accompanied thoughts of Hayley had settled, leaving something much gentler and pleasanter. Whether that was a good thing remained to be seen.

CHAPTER SEVEN

Hayley

November

Hayley squashed her clothes into her suitcase and sat on it to shut it. How was this actually happening? She'd gone from it being a jokey idea to it becoming the most exciting trip she'd had in ages.

'You're going where?' her mum said when Hayley called her to let her know.

'The Hair Show and a fancy dinner in London.'

'I'm in the wrong job. How come you get to do that?'

Hayley didn't like fibbing to anyone, but she didn't want to let on she was doing this with Oliver. In her head, she was just dressing up and going to a fancy roof top bar in London and he happened to be her date. Who was she to knock it? But other people wouldn't see it like that, she was sure. There would be tricky questions and her mum wouldn't shy away from asking them. No one in their right mind could deny Oliver was extremely handsome. He had that perfect combination of dark hair, just the right amount of tan and beautifully chiselled features. Not a bad bit of stuff to be seen with. Shame his face always had a scowl on it, but she was working on it and if he was grumpy, she always had enough cheer to go around.

'Oh, just a last-minute thing. I'll tell you all about it when I get back.'

'You take care,' her mum said, 'and message me loads. Let me know you're safe.'

'I will.'

Her mum liked to know her children were ok, even now they were grown. Hayley had always had a close relationship with her. Her parents had separated when she was younger and her dad had moved away. She hadn't ever been quite as close to him, but she still met up with him and his partner, Liz, whenever she could. But her dad wouldn't be bothered what trips she went on or who with, so there was no need to tell him. In fact, other than her mum, no one else knew she was going, except the girls at work. Hayley hadn't broadcast the fact that she would be travelling with Oliver and sharing a room with him. Her colleagues would have a field day with that information. Hayley, being a top-class speculator herself, knew the rumour mill would be spinning at a hundred miles an hour if people got wind of her travel arrangements. Innocent or not, who would see it like that? She almost didn't see it like that herself and the naughty part of her would love to throw caution to the wind and use this as a week to have hot sex with a smouldering guy whose body was second to none, but that most certainly wouldn't be happening. She needed to pack the idea away with the rest of the squashed luggage and keep things on the straight and narrow. Oliver was not to be used in such a way. How could she look him in the eye again if she did that? They still had to get through the wedding together and she didn't want to mess that up by making things awkward between them.

She pulled a face at her giant pink suitcase. Getting it on and off the train and around London would be interesting. This thing weighed a ton and there was nothing in it she could ditch. Going to London for a week when she'd be frequenting posh places needed careful packing and lots of outfits. With Oxford Street calling, no doubt she'd buy herself lots more while she was there and need an extra suitcase to come home with.

Toying with her phone, she had to forcefully remind herself not to mention this to Genevieve. So irritating when normally she told her everything, but Genevieve and Finlay didn't need to know what their chief bridesmaid and best man were doing. That would cause way too much chitter-chatter. Hayley didn't want to imagine how her brother would look at them at every pre-wedding event if he found out. Finlay wasn't the type to try to stop them from doing anything. He was a good big brother, and he'd never stand in the way of what she wanted, but that was the point. She didn't want Oliver. Not like that. Not for a relationship. He was far too grumpy and uptight for her. But Finlay would read all sorts into a trip like this and be annoyed with them both if he thought either had used the other. Simpler to keep schtum. She just hoped Oliver hadn't blabbed.

As the sleeper train didn't get into Glenbriar station until eleven o'clock in the evening, Hayley had left her packing until the late afternoon. If she packed too soon, she'd just sit around, desperate to leave. Previous experience had taught her she wasn't at all patient in that kind of situation. After her case was done, she had a quick dinner and did a clean around the flat, so when she came back everything would look nice. She'd snuck a bottle of wine into her case because if all else failed and she couldn't get to sleep, she could always drink herself into a stupor and hopefully pass out.

The station at Glenbriar had a small car park and an old Victorian ticket office and waiting room. These days, the ticket office wasn't staffed and tickets were either pre-booked or bought from a machine on the platform. The office was now used during the day as a bookshop, but at this time of night it was all closed up. She got out of her car and trundled her suitcase through the floodlit car park and onto the very small platform. Standing not far along was a figure dressed all in black. She recognised it at once as Oliver. His suitcase was less than half the size of hers and he had a small backpack she assumed contained his laptop. He also had a suit hanger looped onto the handle of his case. She approached him, unable to stop the smile from spreading across her face. His usual serious expression was firmly in place.

'Good evening,' she said brightly.

'Hi.' Oliver glanced at her suitcase. 'What have you got in there and how long do you plan to stay for?'

'There's barely enough in here to keep me going for the week, especially as I didn't expect to be going to fancy functions. I've had to pack a whole lot extra.'

'Oh, I see.' His tone was slow and sarky. 'Blame it all on me, why don't you?'

'Don't worry, I will,' she said.

'At least you made it before the train. I thought you'd changed your mind.'

'Why?' She checked the time on her phone. The train wasn't due for another ten minutes. 'It's not like I'm late.'

'Maybe not. I just like to be there in plenty of time.'

She restrained her eye roll. This was so Oliver. Uber punctual and organised when he wanted to be – he just didn't want to be organising anything for anyone else. 'You and I are going to get along so well.'

'I take it from your tone you mean you're never on time.'

'Exactamundo!'

Oliver didn't hold back the eye roll.

'I can't wait for this,' she said. 'I have the whole of tomorrow free because the Hair Show doesn't start until Wednesday. I've booked up for sessions on all three days. I might see if I can get tickets for the after-show party on Friday. You could come with me.'

'Why?'

'Because I'm going with you to your thing. It's called reciprocity.'

'Nice word, but I didn't think we were working this trip like that.'

'It's how life works, Oliver, and it's also known as manners.'

'Seriously? If you're going to be this annoying, I won't last five minutes, never mind a week.'

'Annoying? Moi? That's insulting.'

'I hope there's room for your case in the cabin. It's not that big, you know?'

'Well, we can stick it in your bed and you can sleep standing up then.'

'Oh, ha ha,' he said in a low drone.

'So, what's your timetable for the week? Apart from avoiding me?'

He raised an eyebrow, as though her thinking impressed him. 'Just business. A conference, some meetings, that kind of thing.'

'Do you get any time off?'

'There are some gaps, yes. Why? I won't be able to hang around the shops and carry your bags or anything like that.'

'Like I would want that. I just wondered because it sounds a bit dull.'

'It's work. It's not meant to be exciting.'

'I guess not.' She looked up at a rumbling sound. 'I think that's the train.' Bright lights came into view, getting slowly closer. The train screeched to a halt, and they waited until the doors opened.

'After you,' Oliver said.

As she climbed on the rather steep step, wrestling with her case, he took the handle and gave it an extra lift. Hayley was torn between being grateful or being narked at him for thinking she needed him to help her.

'Can I see your tickets, please?' A guard greeted them in the corridor.

Oliver pulled out his wallet, flipped it open, and handed over two tickets.

Hayley's stomach turned over as she watched him and she fiddled with the handle of her case. She hadn't bought a ticket or even considered she might need one. She'd assumed Oliver had paid for the cabin so there would be a free bed. So why did he have two tickets?

The guard pointed them down the corridor.

They shuffled down and Oliver opened the door, making his way in and holding it so Hayley could follow. The train had started moving already.

'Well, isn't this cosy?' Oliver said, as the door shut behind her. Now they were both in, only their luggage separated them, and even Hayley's enormous suitcase wasn't really a barrier. He smelled amazing. Aftershave? Cologne? Was he a closet fragrance enthusiast with a bathroom cabinet full of choice scents? Or did he have a go-to label? Whatever he'd chosen tonight was intoxicating. A mixture of musk and a woodsy fragrance that filled the compartment with a heady aroma presumably designed to attract women, then drive them insane with desire. Hats off to the manufacturers because it was doing its job perfectly.

Fuck!

Couple that scent with his stunning face and the hot bod she'd seen beneath the cycling gear and he was almost irresistible. But wait a second. *Stop thinking these things right now!* She wasn't going to use Oliver like that. He raised one of his thick, dark eyebrows and folded his arms. Something told her he knew exactly what she'd been contemplating, and it didn't amuse him one bit. So, even if she wanted to, he would not.

'I suppose it's quite cosy. Do you snore?' she asked.

'Not that I know of. Do you?'

'Probably, but no one's ever complained.'

'So far.'

She chuckled. 'Well, if anyone's going to, it'll be you.'

'Too right. Now, I hope you don't want to stay awake all night and chat because I don't and I really need to get some sleep.'

'I'll be good, I promise.' She took another look around. 'It'll be interesting getting dressed for bed in here.'

'I put on my sleep shorts under my jeans before I left, so I'm ok.' Oliver tossed the virtual ball back into her court.

'Well, smartie pants, you can wait outside while I get changed then, because I didn't.'

After a bit of shuffling around as Oliver got the cases under the bed, he took a bathroom break while Hayley got into her pjs. She was just removing her socks when Oliver knocked to say he was back. She kicked her clothes under the bed next to her case and opened the door. He came in already in a grey t-shirt, showing off his thick arm muscles.

'Turn around, will you?' he said. 'I'm not taking these off with you watching.'

She smirked and looked away as he unbuttoned his jeans.

'I thought you went to the bathroom to do that.'

'I'm not walking down the corridor in my shorts.'

A laugh was on the verge of bursting out, but she held it in, as she listened to him pulling off his jeans.

'Right,' he said.

'Safe for me to look?'

'I suppose so.'

He was folding his jeans, not meeting her eyes, as she turned around. Nice sturdy legs. Man, would he be hard to resist with that delectable bod?

'Who's going on top?' Hayley waggled her eyebrows and grinned.

He blinked slowly and shook his head. 'You decide.'

'I'm happy anywhere.'

'I bet you are. But fine, you go on top.'

'Ok.' She climbed up and snuggled under the cover, resisting the urge to peek over and nosy at Oliver. Her phone was on charge down below, so she couldn't look at it like she usually did before she went to sleep. The *kerthump* of the train as it rattled along was kind of soothing, but now and then it jolted and her eyes bumped open.

'Oliver,' she said after a few moments. 'Are you awake?'

'Uh-huh. Why?'

'Why did you have two tickets? I thought you just bought a ticket for the compartment. I didn't realise we needed one each.'

'Don't worry about it.'

'What do you mean? Did you buy me a ticket?'

'Yes.'

'Oh my god. Why didn't you tell me?' She leaned over and stared down at him. 'I should pay for it.'

'It really doesn't matter.' He pulled the sleep mask over his eyes and rolled onto his side. 'Just go to sleep. Night-night.'

'Night.' She lolled back on the thin mattress. 'And thanks.'

'Sleep well.'

For a long time, her eyes wouldn't close. She stared up at the semi-darkness. Every sleeper on the track and each little bump hammered into her consciousness. She wanted to get out of bed, grab her phone and google how much tickets cost on this thing because she had a feeling he'd paid through the nose for her. The thought didn't settle her. Why would he do that? He wasn't noted for his kindness or charity, but he hadn't even mentioned it. If she hadn't said anything, would he even have let on? What did it all mean? If anything.

Oliver's breathing changed. No snores, but it got a little louder, deeper, and more rhythmical. Almost hypnotic. She was close enough to imagine they were side by side and she rolled over, buried herself in the blanket, and closed her eyes. Letting her breathing sync with his, she focused on it, until she sank deep into the world of dreams.

CHAPTER EIGHT

Hayley

When Hayley woke, she opened her eyes and blinked. Had she actually been asleep? The train was quiet. Had it stopped? Maybe she was still in a dream. Or maybe she'd been awake for hours listening to Oliver's breathing. She focused on it again. It was still deep but quieter, like maybe he too was coming around or just dozing. The blind was drawn and the low-level light in the room that was always on made it hard to gauge what time it was. She shimmied to the edge of the bed and peered over the safety barrier. The sleep mask still covered Oliver's eyes; his thick dark hair sprawled across the pillow in what was a very endearing bedhead.

She needed her phone to check the time. Keeping as quiet as she could, she tossed back the cover, slithered down the ladder and tiptoed the few steps across the compartment to retrieve her phone. As she unplugged it, the cable dropped to the floor with a noise that seemed to crack through the still air like a whip. A split second later, the engine started again. She checked the time.

Three a.m. Was that all? She couldn't have been sleeping for more than a couple of hours.

'What are you doing?' Oliver asked, his voice husky and low. He'd propped himself up on his elbow and was holding the mask up.

'Just getting my phone. I wanted to know the time.'

'And what time is it?'

The train started moving again and Hayley braced herself, so she didn't topple over. 'Just after three.'

'Oh god,' he groaned.

'Sorry, I didn't mean to wake you.'

'It's fine. I never sleep well on this thing anyway. Maybe I should try sleeping tablets next time.'

'Yeah, it's a bit noisy and rattly. I didn't know it stopped anywhere this late.'

'It always stops and starts. If it didn't, we'd get there too fast. This journey was invented when trains were slower and it took all night. These days you can get to London in six to eight hours, so it's not quite the same.'

'I see.' Hayley yawned and climbed back into her bunk. She got back under the cover and couldn't stop herself from googling the cost of tickets.

'Bloody hell, Oliver,' she said.

'What?' His tone was on edge like she'd shocked him, and she realised she'd probably spoken a bit too loud for the time of night.

'I've just seen the price of tickets for this thing. I need to pay you back.'

'Is that all? Forget it. It wasn't actually that much more to add you, and the company paid for me.'

'My god, are you sure?'

'Very.'

She let out a sigh. 'Thank you.' What was he like? Where had this hidden nice guy come from? Had he always been there, hiding under layers of grumpiness? Or was this something new? Shoving her phone under her pillow, she closed her eyes again. She had a sleep mask too in the kit provided for them, but she didn't like wearing masks. They always irritated her and the one in the pack didn't look particularly comfy. Oliver seemed to have packed his own deluxe one.

Switching off wasn't easy, but she must have dozed because when she fully came to, Oliver was up and staring out the window.

'Have we arrived?' She yawned and stretched.

'We're nearly there, but don't rush.' He didn't look at her when he spoke. In fact, he never really looked at her. Maybe she was repulsive to him, especially in her nightwear. 'You get half an hour to leave. I'm going to the bathroom.' He had a toiletries bag with him and some clothes folded on top. Would he get dressed in those tiny loos to make sure he didn't have to do it in front of her? Well, it made sense, she supposed. She didn't really want to get dressed in front of him either. Not if the sight was so abhorrent to him. The easiest thing would be for her to put on her clothes while he was out. She shuffled out of bed, hauled out her giant case, shoved the clothes from the day before into a mesh laundry pouch and grabbed some clean items. She took a bathroom break and was still back before Oliver. Was he avoiding her? Or had he gone to the diner car for breakfast perhaps? By the time he returned, she was fully dressed and sitting on her top bunk, scrolling through her phone.

'What do you want to do for breakfast?' he said. 'Get something here or when we arrive?'

'Which is better?'

'I know a nice place near the station. It's much nicer than train food.'

'Let's do that then.'

'I brought you a coffee.' He handed her a paper cup with a lid on it but didn't meet her eye.

Hayley lifted the lid. 'Is it a—'

'Flat white.'

She frowned and sniffed at it. 'How did you know that?'

'What? Oh... I think you had one at Finlay's.'

When? She had no memory of that. How on earth had Oliver remembered, and why? So bizarre. She suppressed her questions and sipped her coffee. Not bad for train food. Still frowning at Oliver, she mentally teased out images of times he might have seen her drinking coffee or heard her ordering it. What had got into him? Not only had he bought her coffee, he'd invited her to breakfast. Well, maybe inviting was too strong, but he seemed to be including her in his plans. She'd assumed as soon as they arrived, he'd leave her to fend for herself and meet her at the hotel later, but hey, *don't knock it.* 'What will we do with the cases when we go for breakfast?'

He gave her a stern look, but was that the tiniest of smiles quirking at the corner of his lips? 'Should have thought about that before you packed the kitchen sink, the oven and the microwave, shouldn't you?'

'Ha ha, very funny,' She didn't scrimp on the sarcasm.

'We can take them to the hotel and leave them. They have a luggage store, even though we can't officially check in until three.' He checked his watch. 'We'll have time to drop them off before my first meeting at eleven.'

'And how did you get on with booking a twin room?'

'Very well, thankfully, or you'd have been the one sleeping standing up, or looking for a hostel for the night.'

'Always the charmer.'

He snorted what might have been a laugh as he sat back on his lower bunk.

Despite not having slept well, Hayley was so buzzed about being in London she felt wide awake and ready to conquer the world. By the time the train pulled into the station, she had her case out and was at the door ready. Oliver helped get it off the train and their eyes met as she went to say, 'I can do it myself.'

The words died on her lips, and something tugged in her chest, an almost desperate urge to lean up and kiss him.

Ok, not sensible or helpful.

'This way.' He blinked, breaking the eye contact, and led the way through the busy station. An early morning gloom hung over it as people strode past, staring forward with serious expressions. Hayley was a great people watcher and liked soaking up the buzz of city life, even if she had no desire to live it herself. She'd been to London several times before and knew this was nowhere near as busy as it would get later, but even as they made their way to the exit, more and more people were piling in as the rush hour was about to start.

Oliver edged out of the station exit and marched ahead while Hayley dragged her giant pink case along. *Why did I bring this beast?* Her wrist was aching. But how else could she ensure she looked her best for all the events? Shoes were the killer. They weighed so much.

Turning around a corner, Oliver headed up a side street, and Hayley hauled the beast along behind her.

'I hope there's room in here for that case,' Oliver muttered with one of his signature frowns, stopping at the door of a small café called Le Petit Four. In the window was an array of pastries, bread, and cakes. 'It's continental. I hope you don't mind that. I'm not really into fried breakfasts.'

'It looks great.' Her taste buds tingled at the array of croissants, brioche and pains au chocolat. She wasn't usually a big breakfast eater, but she'd make an exception for this. Some of the yummies were more like cakes than breakfast food and probably weren't great for the waistline, but so what? Life was short and she'd be doing a lot of walking over the next few days, which would make up for a few extra calories.

'In we go then.' Oliver opened the door and Hayley lugged her case into the fancy little café, decorated like a bistro with spindle-backed chairs and little round tables. She shoved the case into the corner near the window and took a seat. Oliver sat opposite, and Hayley experienced a tsunami of butterflies in her chest as he glanced over at her and fiddled with the collar of his shirt. She'd often seen him in a suit, but now she took the time to actually look, he was smoking hot in it. What the hell? This was Oliver. Grumpy Oliver. Admittedly hot Oliver. But not Oliver who caused her butterflies. That only happened with people you fancied… And ok, so, yes, she fancied Oliver – his hot bod anyway – but not in the butterfly kind of way. *Ignore it; it's just lack of sleep.*

She lifted a menu and read through the options, all in French, of course. Hayley's French couldn't even be classed as pigeon.

'Do you see anything you like?' Oliver asked.

'Oh, mercy buckets, trez bon.'

He raised an eyebrow. 'Is that meant to be funny? The servers here are all French, so don't insult them.'

'Have you ever watched *Friends*?' she asked.

'Not really.'

'Shame, because there's that episode with Joey speaking French that you'd just love.'

'I dread to think,' he muttered.

The server approached and smiled. 'Good morning, madame, monsieur. What can I get you both?'

Oliver ordered something in perfect French, and Hayley had no idea what he even said. She smiled at the server, and he beamed back at her expectantly.

'Avy non Francoise,' Hayley said. 'Sorry. So can I have a pain-au-chocolate and a flat white?'

'Of course, madam,' the server said. 'And I can help you with anything on the menu, if you would like me to translate.'

'Sure, can you please tell me what some of the specials are?'

He leaned over, pointing to the words, and explained. Hayley caught Oliver watching with his jaw clamped so tight he could use it as a vice.

'Merci.' She pointed to the menu. 'They sound delicious.'

'The puits d'amour, madam. Certainly.'

Hayley winked at Oliver as the server left the table. 'I avy le way with le Francais.'

'That's just rude.'

'Isn't. I'm trying my best with what I remember from two years in school. That l'amour thing sounds like love. Maybe it's an aphrodisiac.'

'Oh, for god's sake,' Oliver muttered, glancing out the window.

Hayley smirked. 'I suppose you speak French fluently.'

'Enough to get by in a café, but not fluently, no.' He took out his phone and opened it. 'Excuse me, I need to reply to some work messages.'

Hayley didn't mind. People-watching in here was something she could do all day, whether it was other customers or the passers-by. Everyone had a story and she listened in, trying to discover what it might be.

When the breakfast arrived, she ate quietly as Oliver carried on replying to his messages. The puits d'amour were delicious little pastry-like cakes filled with jam and sugary sprinkles on top. She'd never had anything like it and she gave a little moan at the sweet sensation. Oliver didn't look up, but his brow furrowed even deeper than usual. He was easy on the eye, even with a grumpy face, and this was like her own private show. Why was he so hot? Maybe the dazzling white shirt open at the neck to reveal his tanned skin or the way he seductively bit into pastries, then brushed crumbs from his lips. Possibly just the fact he was such a highflyer and seeing him at work was like watching competency porn.

When they were done, he footed the bill despite all Hayley's insistence that they should share it.

'No, it's on me.' He tapped his card.

She pulled an exasperated face at the server behind the till, who gave her a little smile.

'Let's get these bags to the hotel.' Oliver glared at her case again. 'You realise we need to get that on the tube?'

'Sure.' Other people did it. There were always people with cases on the tube. She just hoped she wouldn't be the one who ended in a heap at the bottom of an escalator with her case on top of her.

Oliver seemed to know where he was going, so she followed. First, they needed tickets from the machine, then it was escalator time. They got through the luggage barrier and headed for the downward stairs. Hayley's stomach lurched when she saw how long it was. Even getting her case on that would be some feat.

'Do you want to swap?' Oliver said.

'Swap what?'

'You take this case. I'll get yours down.'

'I... Well, ok.' She couldn't deny how much it was freaking her out. His smaller case was much easier to pull. Oliver stepped onto the elevator with hers like it weighed nothing. She followed with only a little wobble. Thank god he was in front of her. *He'll catch me if I stumble, won't he?* Because there was a nice Oliver in there. A strangely thoughtful one she'd caught glimpses of over the last twelve hours.

The tube was standing room only, and Oliver kept hold of the pink suitcase, even though it earned him one or two funny looks and the odd snigger. That wasn't exactly the open-minded attitude Hayley had been led to believe existed in London, though really, she couldn't help giggling herself. If they hadn't been moving at breakneck speed between every station or being tossed around in the carriages, she'd have taken a picture so she could refer back to it whenever a moment of sadness hit, because she knew the sight would always make her smile.

The Royal Saxon Hotel in Mayfair was a masterpiece of Georgian architecture, its cream-coloured façade adorned with intricate stonework and grand arched windows.

'Wow.' Hayley goggled at the imposing structure. She liked hotels and often saved up to stay in pleasant locations, but this was somewhere she wouldn't have chosen for herself. Not because there was anything wrong with it, it just looked a little too grand, maybe a bit stuffy for her. But now she was here, she liked the smart location and the grandeur.

'Yeah, it's a nice place.' Oliver hopped up the stairs, still with her case in tow. He spoke to the receptionist, who took their cases into a side room. 'Right.' Oliver turned to Hayley with what was clearly his business face. 'I've got a meeting to go to and I'm sure you have lots you want to do. We can meet for dinner later, if you like. Or I'll see you back here this evening if you prefer.'

'Dinner sounds great.' This really was surprising. Why was he being so attentive?

'Ok.' He adjusted his cuffs, not meeting her eyes. 'I'll message later and let you know where I am and we can fix a place to meet.'

'Great. See you then.'

'Yes…' His gaze linked with hers and for a weird moment, he seemed to sway, almost like he'd considered dipping in and giving her a goodbye kiss. But he wouldn't do *that*… Would he? No.

'See you.' He cleared his throat and raised his hand in what was presumably meant to be a wave, then marched through the foyer doors. Hayley watched him for a moment before following. She had a whole day to spend in London. The sun was out, and she was having dinner somewhere fancy later. Life was definitely good.

Chapter Nine

Oliver

Oliver headed straight back to the tube, making for the Docklands and Regalia's HQ. The firm was well known for being a forerunner in its approach to family law by hiring lawyers versed in both Scottish and English law. They worked on cross-border cases as well as international ones.

Being jostled from side to side made Oliver's breakfast churn in his stomach. He held his place in the packed compartment, close to the sliding doors. More and more people piled in until he was squashed against the glass barrier. Unable to move a muscle without knocking into someone, he was prevented from checking his phone. Frustration simmered inside him, along with disgust at the growing heat of too many bodies and the somewhat nauseating mix of smells. He screwed up his nose, needing a distraction, and not just from being squashed like a sardine: thoughts of Hayley were still far too prominent in his mind.

This was a hundred times worse than usual. Sure, he occasionally thought about her... Ok, sometimes a bit too much, but this was a whole new level. When she was so close, he couldn't switch off his mind or control his body reactions. Carnal instincts kicked in, making him want her so badly. The sleeper train ride had been nothing short of torturous. How he'd slept at all was a miracle while she pranced about in those skimpy PJs with her long hair bouncing around. That hair. Jeez, how badly did he want to touch that hair? And the perpetual smile on her face, those beautiful soft lips... How would they be to kiss? And her fragrance, a dreamy scent that seemed to come straight from a field of happy flowers. It did things to him. Changed him. Made him want to be someone else, doing things he never normally did.

Where was business Oliver when he needed him? He must have left him back in Glenbriar and brought along some strange Oliver in his place. One who was finding it utterly impossible to keep up the iron front when Hayley was around. Since when did Oliver Wright invite women to breakfast and dinner? Christ, he'd even pulled that ludicrous case for her. Not that anyone with a morsel of kindness would have left her trying to get it down the escalator on her own. She'd looked petrified. And here he was, ready to jump in like a knight in shining armour. She'd wormed her way under his skin with all her niceness and made him soft. Maybe there was nothing wrong with that. Nothing apart from the danger his true feelings would be uncovered. She didn't need to know how much she was on his mind and how she messed with his head. How he hardly dared look at her in case something betrayed him. She deserved someone oh so much better than him. Someone with the ability to love and care for her properly.

Someone who would laugh with her and make her happy. Not a sad, emotionally repressed guy like him.

A twinge in his gut reminded him of the meeting, and he steered his brain around a tricky bend to focus on that instead. If he got the job here, this would be his daily commute. Glancing around the tube at the mass of tired workers, he wasn't sure it was what he really wanted. Working in London carried some kudos and it would be a great experience, but lots would change. His best friend would be far away, his cycle rides wouldn't be as picturesque, and his working days would be very long.

After he got off the tube, he followed the satnav on his phone towards the towering office block, its glass front gleaming in the pale morning sun.

He stopped outside and put his laptop case down on a low wall that surrounded a neatly arranged collection of shrubs, forming an urban garden. Inside his case, he found his tie and slipped it around his neck. No way could he have worn it on the tube with the already cloying and choking sensation. Knotting it, he gazed up. Was this the place he wanted to be every day? Tie in place, he was ready to find out.

He lifted his bag and headed inside, straight to the reception desk.

'Nathan's expecting you,' the receptionist said. 'He'll be down shortly. Just take a seat.'

Oliver sat on one of the soft blue seats near the window that overlooked the little shrubbery he'd stopped at moments before. He'd barely touched the chair when he heard a familiar voice.

'Oliver!'

He got to his feet as Nathan threw out a hand, then shook his vigorously, almost taking his arm off in the process. 'How are you? I hope the journey wasn't too bad.'

'It was fine, thanks.'

'Great to see you. Come with me and I'll talk you through the different departments and where your office would be.'

Oliver frowned, but Nathan was still talking, and in a way that seemed like Oliver had already got the job.

'I still have to do an interview,' Oliver reminded him.

'Honestly, it's in the bag,' Nathan said. 'Your credentials are well known. There are two other applicants and I know both of them vaguely. Neither of them is a patch on you.'

Oliver adjusted his tie as they stepped off the escalator into a large, open-plan office. He stared out the floor to ceiling windows at the view over London. This place was really something compared to that tiny little room he had back in Glenbriar.

'Drinks after work tonight, if you want,' Nathan said.

It was almost part of the process and if he was newly out of university, he would have agreed straight away and been desperate to make a good impression. But he'd promised Hayley dinner.

'That's a kind offer,' he said. 'But I'm not travelling alone and I promised dinner to—'

'Ah, say no more.' Nathan smiled. 'I quite understand. Don't want to disappoint the ladies, eh?'

'Exactly so.'

'How about we lunch out instead?' Nathan suggested.

'Perfect.'

How quickly would his wages deplete on restaurants and bars if he moved down here? While the food in the warehouse style café Nathan chose was delicious, Oliver wasn't sure he needed this temptation on a daily basis. Both the Cosy Bean Café and the Drip Drop Coffee Shop in Glenbriar were bad enough. Popping into one or the other on a morning for a coffee or grabbing a baguette at lunch time was already a habit he'd got into. All that seemed very rustic compared to this city chic.

He messaged Hayley to find out where she was and what she was doing. Three dots bounced up and down for a long time as he chatted with Nathan before Hayley's answer came in. It was long and accompanied by photographs. She seemed to have done her own walking tour of London and was now having a flat white and a wrap in a café in Covent Garden.

'Is that your wife?' Nathan asked, craning his neck a little to see the pictures. 'I didn't know you were married.'

'I'm not. She's not my wife.'

'Ah.' Nathan sat back, interlocking his fingers, clearly waiting for Oliver to elaborate, but he didn't. Launching into a story about Hayley wasn't his style, and he had no idea what to say about her. Who was she really? A friend? His best friend's sister?

Someone he'd invited along so he didn't have to attend a formal dinner alone? Or someone he'd wanted to come along because he hated thinking how disappointed she'd be if she didn't get to the Hair Show, when it clearly meant so much to her? Oliver didn't want to share any of those answers with Nathan or leave an opening for more discussion.

'What about you?' he asked. 'Are you married?'

'Yes. I've been married a year now. It goes past quickly. Can hardly believe it's been that long already.'

'Yes, time certainly flies. Do you mind if I reply to this?'

'Of course not, go ahead.'

Oliver thumbed out a quick message.

OLIVER: Just having lunch. If we meet at the hotel later to check in, we could grab some dinner nearby after. Does that sound ok?

Was he pushing his luck with this? Playing a little game where he got to wine and dine her? She seemed to enjoy things like that in general, but did she really want to do any of it with him? Maybe she'd prefer to be left alone.

Her message pinged in almost immediately and Oliver caught Nathan smirking.

HAYLEY: Ooh, that means we're eating out in Mayfair. I better go count my pocket money.

OLIVER: Don't bother. It's on me. Meet at the hotel at five thirty. See you there.

He placed his phone down. Fuck it. He was doing this even if it was leading him onto risky ground.

Oliver left Nathan midway through the afternoon. He wasn't employed at Regalia yet, so leaving while everyone else was still working away at their desks didn't provoke any guilt. Nathan didn't seem to mind and said, 'I hope you have a good dinner. I'll see you at the interview tomorrow and the conference and dinner on Thursday.'

Yup. Whether or not he got the job, he would attend the dinner, but it would be much sweeter if he had the job in the bag.

As he travelled across London on the tube, a bizarre sensation of displacement crept over him, like he didn't really belong here... or anywhere. Like he was watching life as a spectator from another dimension and not really involved in any of it. He leaned on the pole and let out a sigh. What should he do? A twinge of discomfort stirred in his chest, and he rubbed at it, trying to push it away. He wasn't a stranger to this. It hit often, usually when he was conflicted and always when he thought about his mum. It had been such a long time since she'd left him, so far back he could hardly remember what she was really like. And yet the aching gap caused by her absence still lingered, sometimes in the background, other times fresh and painful. He'd lost so much. Memories had mingled with vague feelings that had, over time, become more like wishes. Wishes for someone to talk to, to guide him, to care for him and to love him. Was that shameful?

Maybe he should have sought those things from someone else by now. But how? Did anyone exist who could care that much for someone like him? He wasn't exactly loveable.

Finlay would help if Oliver asked him, but he didn't want to tell Finlay about this. Not yet. Maybe that was silly too, but the timing wasn't right. Maybe there would never be a right time. He closed his eyes, still leaning on the pole, hoping when he opened them, everything would be clearer.

Chapter Ten

Oliver

Hayley sat on a chaise under an arch in the foyer of the Royal Saxon Hotel, surrounded by shopping bags, looking like a model for a fashion company with her legs crossed in front of her, knee-high boots accentuating her calves. Her glossy hair tumbled over her shoulders in neatly formed coils. Oliver's body heat rose a notch. She was so incredibly beautiful. And obviously she'd worked some hairdresser magic because no one seeing her would know she'd stepped off the sleeper train nine hours ago and not walked out of the salon twenty minutes previously.

'You've been busy,' he said as she got to her feet.

A smile split her face and seemed to light the whole foyer with sparkles. Oliver loosened his tie, the heat reaching fever point.

'I've probably spent far too much,' she said. 'But I couldn't resist. And why should I? Life's too short and all that.'

'True.' His thoughts darted to his mum again. How often he'd heard his classmates as teenagers moaning about their fussing mums and thinking up ways to trick them so they could sneak out from under their ever-present gaze. *Wow, if only*. At least their mums were watching from the window and not heaven. He'd spent his teenage years wishing his mum was there to fuss over him and look out for him. Hayley and Finlay's mum, Lisa, was nice. She'd always been kind. Even now she gave him free coffees if she was working when he nipped into the Drip Drop Coffee Shop. She'd told him she did the same for Hayley and one time she had a flat white in progress as she was expecting her daughter at any second. Oliver had banked the fact, along with so many other little pieces of information about Hayley.

Growing up, he'd lived out of town on his dad's farm. If he wanted to see Finlay, he had to rely on lifts and that was always too much of an inconvenience for his dad and his stepmum. He was like the unwelcome guest at their party, and he'd learned not to ask for anything. Often, Lisa would give him lifts to clubs along with Finlay. Even Finlay's dad, who didn't live with them, would take the two of them out more often than Oliver's own dad. More and more, Oliver had learned to keep his own company in his room, and really, it was better that way. He wasn't a social butterfly. Never had been and never would be.

This week he'd made an exception. For the first time in what felt like forever, he'd be sharing a room with someone, going out with someone... Not being alone.

'Let's get checked in then.' He crossed the marble-floored foyer through two large pillars and approached the reception desk. This morning, he'd been so tired and overwhelmed by thoughts of what was coming he hadn't paid attention to the hotel. Its grandeur was ostentatious and kind of fake. Hayley looked around bright-eyed and smiley, appearing perfectly at home. If only he could muster the same easy energy... But the very fact she was with him made his shoulders tense. How could he relax in her presence with all the raw lust in his body? But then how would he feel if she weren't here? Like he usually did. Alone. Was that any easier? He wouldn't have to bother with fancy meals if he was alone. Not that he *had to* with her... But he wanted to. If she wasn't here, all he would do would be to stay in the room and immerse himself in work. He might not even have left the office yet. Such was his existence. Finlay often jibed him about being a workaholic and told him it wasn't healthy. Maybe he was right. He was trying to be more balanced and leave at five each evening, but sometimes he didn't see the point. His career was all he had that mattered.

Hayley gave him another huge smile as they reached the desk. Why did she always look so cheerful? Wasn't it exhausting?

'Oliver Wright,' he said to the receptionist, and she found him on the screen.

'You're in room nineteen,' she said, before talking them through the times for breakfast. 'We also ask guests not to play music in their rooms after ten p.m.' She handed him a keycard.

'We need two.'

'Of course.' She took out another card to authorise it. As soon as she passed it to Oliver, he gave it to Hayley. 'Your luggage has already been taken up.' The receptionist smiled at them both.

'Thank you,' Hayley said. 'I love your hair, by the way.'

Oliver frowned, glancing back at the receptionist. Maybe the style was a little unusual, kind of asymmetric, but he'd never have thought to comment. Yet here was Hayley chatting as if they were old friends. How did she do it?

He was at the bottom of the stairs when she caught up with him.

'Stairs or lift?' she said.

'It's only the first floor. I think we'll survive the stairs.'

'Good idea. It'll help me work off those extra calories.'

He raised an eyebrow. Like she needed to. She looked in great shape to him, but he couldn't imagine not finding her attractive, no matter what shape she was in. Because the whole package made her. Taking the stairs was a sensible move. *Imagine getting stuck in the lift with her?* His body jolted at the thought, and he marched down the corridor, trying to ease the tension in his limbs. He opened the door to the room and let her go in first.

She strolled in, gazing up at the high ceilings with elaborate cornice work, then at the plush beds. He often stayed in hotels, but this had a touch of class with the velvet bed runners, thick brocade curtains, and large ornate bedside lamps. It was definitely less clinical than the ones he usually stayed in. Being a twin room – as ordered – it had two beds, but both were almost large enough to be doubles.

'Well, this is rather nice.' Hayley twirled around as she looked at everything.

Oliver crossed to the window and stared out.

'Not a bad view either,' Hayley said.

He whipped his head – wait, she couldn't see through the window, could she? Was she looking at him? 'What? Oh... The street? It's a nice area.'

'Isn't it just?'

Oliver loosened his tie further and pushed open the door to the en suite. 'Nice bathroom too.'

Hayley appeared at his side to peek in. 'Wow, love the bath.' She grinned at the large claw-foot tub. 'This is all rather grand. I wouldn't mind a soak in that before we go anywhere.'

'You go ahead, though if you're planning on being long, maybe I should shower first, then I can get ready while you're soaking.'

'Sounds good to me.'

He kept his eyes anywhere but on her as he collected the fluffy white towel from the end of the bed. He didn't want to imagine her in that bath, surrounded by bubbles, hair all piled up, rosy skin... Christ. Of course he was going to imagine it. He couldn't think of anything else.

Washing off the London dirt was like a purge, but all he could think about was Hayley. If he could as easily wash her out of his hair, he would be fine. He scrubbed himself, then leaned one arm against the shower wall while the boiling water doused him, letting his imagination take over.

He emerged with a towel wrapped around his waist. Hayley sat on the bed closest to the window, propped on the pillow, scrolling her phone. She peered up, giving him a very obvious once over. His stomach clenched. Was she checking him out? Did she like what she saw? He wasn't ashamed of his body. He was in good shape after all his cycling and home gym sessions, but something about her eyes on him like that made him tingle, in a kind of uncomfortable way, but also like he was proud, maybe hopeful even. Not to mention the uncensored, raw desire pumping around his veins like rocket fuel.

'My turn.' She gathered some bits and pieces from her case. 'Ooh, it's steamy in here.' She opened the bathroom door. Not as steamy as it would be if they were in there together.

As soon as Oliver heard the bath running, he got dressed, paying close attention to his hair, which he always did anyway – he prided himself on being well-groomed – but for some reason it felt even more important right now. He ran his fingers through it several times, cocking his head to check it was in place. Sounds of splashing water distracted him. He tried to force images of Hayley lathering soap up her arm out of his mind.

'Just fuck off,' he muttered.

He was mid tying his shoelaces when she stepped out of the bathroom, already dressed in a long black jumpsuit with chiffon sleeves. Her chestnut hair was piled atop her head in a perfectly constructed 'messy' updo that enhanced her long neck. Jeez, how he'd love to unclip it and let it fall over her bare shoulders.

She hung her towel over the rail, then opened her case and took out a pair of nude heeled pumps. 'Are you ok?' she asked.

Why am I staring? 'Eh, yeah. Sure.' He adjusted the cuffs of his white shirt and tried to force his eyes elsewhere, but they were determined to follow Hayley as she slipped into her heels. 'You look... Nice.' The words came out so quietly he wasn't sure she'd even heard him.

She pulled a clutch bag from her case, smiling with a furrowed brow. 'Why, thank you.' Her eyes met his. 'You don't look too bad yourself. So, shall we go and wow the town?'

'Yes, let's.'

She lifted her black, belted coat and swung it on. Oliver did the same with his, then opened the door for her and they made their way into the corridor and down the stairs. Outside, the street was dark and slightly quieter than it had been earlier. But a short distance past the wide stone staircases and Georgian railings of the buildings, they turned onto a main road that was nose to tail with traffic, headlights beaming and blinking. People bustled up and down the street past a mix of beautiful old buildings and modern shops, bars, and restaurants, all lit up for the evening.

In one of the old buildings was a restaurant named the Silver Vine Brasserie. 'Shall we try this?' Oliver asked. 'It looks ok from out here.'

'Sure does.' Hayley strolled to the menu that was placed on a large, well-lit lectern outside. 'Looks amazing. I would eat anything on here.'

Oliver strode up the wide stone stairs to the large front doors and opened one side, holding it for Hayley to go through. A server greeted them and led them into the dining room. Enormous chandeliers hung from the ceiling, and plant screens and trailing vines shielded the tables. The server pointed to a table in the corner lit by candles and fairy lights. Oliver let out a low sigh. Did it have to be so obviously romantic? But he couldn't exactly refuse and make a fuss by telling a random stranger they weren't actually a couple. He took his seat on one side and Hayley took the other. As soon as they were settled, the server handed them large leather-bound menus with silver vines embossed on the front and asked if they wanted drinks. Oliver needed a clear head for the next day, so ordered a soda water. Hayley ordered a sparkling white. How apt, sparkling wine for a sparkling personality.

'This place is amazing,' Hayley said. 'I need some photos.' She took out her phone and held it up to the ceiling. 'Even the chandeliers are made from twisted silver vines.'

Oliver had a quick peek, then stared into the middle distance, becoming almost mesmerised by the candle on a nearby table. His mind drifted to the interview and 'what ifs'. What if he got the job? What if he didn't? So much would change. Even if he didn't get it, life wouldn't be the same. He wasn't sure he could go back to Glenbriar and go on as he always had.

'Are you ok?' Hayley's voice broke into his reverie.

He blinked the candlelight from his eyes and glanced at her. 'Fine.'

'Really? You seem far away. Are you worried about something?'

'No,' he said automatically, though she was right. How did she know? Had he let his guard slip too far?

'Are you tired? That was quite a journey, wasn't it? Or are you annoyed about me being here?'

'No, I invited you.'

'You did, but if you've changed your mind and don't want me bothering you, I'll keep out of your way. I don't want you to feel obliged to do this kind of thing.' She gestured around the room. 'I mean, I love it, but I don't *have* to be here.'

'It's not that.' Definitely not that. He wanted her here. Really, really wanted her even if it seemed inexplicable. 'I am tired after last night though, so maybe we shouldn't stay out too late... Or I certainly shouldn't. You can, of course, if you want to.' A strange pang suckered his chest like he was letting her down somehow. If she wanted to go out on her own, he should be with her to protect her. Not that she couldn't look after herself, and maybe she wouldn't want him tagging along, but it seemed wrong to have her wandering off into London on her own while he was asleep... Scratch that. Like he'd even sleep in that scenario. He'd be far too scared to close his eyes.

She was still smiling at him when he caught her eye again, but there was more in that look than happiness. Was she trying to x-ray him or solve a puzzle? 'I'm tired too, so I won't be going anywhere after this apart from bed.'

He nodded and some of the tension lifted from his shoulders. At least he wouldn't have to worry about her being out alone.

Neither of them ordered a starter, although they did look good, since both had eaten decent lunches and neither wanted to be out too late. Hayley chose the herb-roasted chicken for her main and Oliver the salmon.

It was delicious, if on the small side.

'I almost wish I'd ordered a starter.' He eyed over his empty plate.

Hayley smirked. 'Can you imagine if Finlay had seen that? He'd have eaten it in one go.'

Oliver nodded and gave her a brief quirk of his lips. Finlay was well known for having quite an appetite.

'I'm not really into desserts.' He dabbed the corner of his mouth with his napkin. 'I think they take away the taste of the savoury stuff and I'm not ready to let those flavours go yet.'

'I'll pass too.' Hayley stifled a yawn. 'I don't think I'd enjoy it properly. I'm too tired.'

They sipped their remaining drinks before Oliver got the bill.

Hayley chatted with the server who brought it in the same way she'd done to Oliver throughout the meal. She had that easy way of talking about anything and nothing and making it sound entertaining. But was it his imagination or did her eyes keep straying to him like she was watching him?

'Are you sure you're ok?' she said as they left the restaurant and made their way down the stairs onto the pavement, the street now lit by street lamps and headlights. 'You've been very quiet all evening.'

'It's just my way,' he said. And it was true. He didn't talk a lot or make conversation easily, but she was right because his mind *was* elsewhere.

'I don't think so,' she said. 'I know you can be quiet but where has all the Oliver banter gone?'

'Banter? I don't do banter.'

'You so do,' she said. 'At least in messages.'

He carried on walking and didn't respond. Would it be so bad to tell her the truth? Maybe having a confidante would ease the weight on his chest, but not her. She was a well-known gossip. Even she would admit it. He let out a sigh and something nudged him inside. A little voice saying *just tell her; she's kind. She can help.*

'Actually, there is something bothering me.'

'Oh dear,' she said. 'And is it something you want to talk about?'

'I'm not sure. It's definitely something I don't want spread around. If I do tell you, I need you to keep quiet about it for now.'

'I swear I won't tell a soul.'

'I've got an interview tomorrow. It's for a job here. In London – a really good job. But I'm conflicted about it. I guess it's normal to feel like that, but, well…'

'Ah, that explains it; I didn't realise you were thinking about changing jobs.'

'I wasn't really, but this opportunity came up and it seemed stupid not to go for it. Now I'm here I see a lot of positives, but there are cons too, and I don't know if one clearly outweighs the other.'

'It's a tough choice, and sadly, no one can make it for you.'

'I know that. At least it won't affect anyone else. I don't have a family to uproot.'

'Finlay will miss you.'

'He'll live, considering he was ready to eff off to Dubai for three years.'

'True. But don't you have a dad… I remember…' She stopped and Oliver knew she was thinking about his mum and the accident. Hayley was younger than him, but she would know about it, even if she'd been too young to register much about it at the time.

'My mum died, yes,' he finished her sentence as memories flooded back of his return to school, days after it had happened. People avoiding him and not knowing what to say to him or how to act around him. When he really needed friends, they'd all abandoned him, except Finlay. He'd stuck around, always easy-going and cheerful. Finlay wasn't one for deep chats, but he'd been good at keeping Oliver busy and distracted. They'd joined the cycling club and spent evenings and weekends training. Lisa had taken them there and back, sometimes with little Hayley in tow. Oliver wasn't sure he'd have kept going if it wasn't for their family.

'Yes,' Hayley said quietly.

'I do have a dad. And a stepmum and two half-sisters. None of them will mind whether I'm in Glenbriar or London though.' It wouldn't make any difference.

Hayley placed her hand gently on the arm of his coat, and he twitched involuntarily. His skin prickled with goosebumps. 'Finlay told me you weren't close. I'm really sorry they're horrible to you.'

He scoffed. 'They're not horrible,' he said. 'They're just not interested in me.' He was invisible and unimportant to them. 'It's easier just to get on with my own life.'

'I know, but still. It's a kick in the teeth. Your dad should have concentrated on you after your mum died.'

'He had his own life too. And he moved on.' He'd done that good and proper, not to mention quickly.

'He could have done that without abandoning you.'

'He didn't—'

'Emotionally I mean.'

How could he argue with her? She was spot on. 'It's all in the past now.'

'You must miss your mum,' she said. 'I can't imagine life without my mum. I love her so much and she's the rock in our lives.'

Oliver gave a brief nod. He'd like to shrug it off, saying he was fine now, and it was all in the past. But he would never forget. 'I miss what I'll never know and never had. Maybe it's a false ideal, but I'll never know that either.'

Hayley took hold of his arm, preventing him from walking. In the glow from the streetlamp, he saw tears glistening in her eyes. 'It must be so awful for you,' she said. 'Do you... Would you like a hug?' She gave a little shrug. 'I know you're not a huggy person, but sometimes they help.'

He kept his eyes on hers and his lip twitched reflexively. She really was kind. 'Ok.' The word came out soft and slightly hoarse.

She smiled, tilted her head a little, then moved closer. He held his breath as she wrapped her arms around his stiff chest, under his arms, bending her elbows, so her palms held his shoulders. Why was he as rigid as a plank? He didn't dare move. She leaned on his coat, almost nuzzling into it. Her hair brushed his cheek and the fresh shampoo scent wafted into his nostrils. Like he'd been supercharged, electricity fired through him. He stood still. What the hell should he do?

Relax.

With a somewhat ragged breath, he moved his heavy arms around her and held her. She tightened her hold on him and amazingly the pain in his chest subsided. Warmth filled some of the vacant chambers in his heart and his breathing levelled, as he inhaled the scent of her hair, allowing his cheek to rest on her luscious locks.

He had no memory of a hug like this ever before. His brain was totally off balance, hurtling around space. Because this wasn't just satisfying some of the ever-present lust. It was even more powerful than that and it made him feel… different. Different and good. Very, very good.

Inhaling slowly and deeply, he allowed it to last as long as he dared before pulling back. 'Thank you.'

'Any time,' she said brightly. 'And you've got this.'

As they strolled back to the hotel, a little bubble swelled in Oliver's chest. Some of the weight had gone from his shoulders. He wasn't so alone.

They got ready for bed one by one in the bathroom. Oliver kept his eyes shut when Hayley emerged. He didn't need any more distractions tonight.

'Goodnight,' she said.

'Night,' he replied. 'And thanks again.'

'I really didn't do anything,' she said, and he heard the rustle of her covers as she got into bed. 'But if it helped, then I'm glad. Sleep tight and tomorrow you can blaze a trail across London.'

He smiled into his pillow. 'I'll do my best.'

Nothing more he could do.

Chapter Eleven

Hayley

Hayley watched Oliver as he picked at his breakfast. Interviews were hideous. Everyone knew that. No doubt ones for the kind of job he was going for were particularly stressful. That's what happened when you were a highflyer like him. She'd been lucky to get a salon assistant job at Cutting Edge when she was still at college, and she'd been there ever since. Far from feeling stagnant though, it felt like home, and she had no desire to be anywhere else.

'Just think, come lunchtime, it'll be done.' She caught Oliver's eye.

'I know. It's always the build up that's worse.' He took a sip of his coffee.

If only she could do something proactive to help, but what? Another hug? How surprising had last night been? He agreed to a hug! And what a hug. She'd had to remind herself to keep things platonic, because being pressed up against Oliver like that was very hot. Everything about him set her insides on fire. That white shirt, for example, with the top buttons just undone enough to hint at a smattering of dark chest hair. Sleeping so close to him didn't help matters, but it really wasn't close enough, not to satisfy all the urges inside her.

'When will you find out if you've got the job or not?' She touched the corner of her lip, checking for toast crumbs.

'There are two other interviews and I think one of them is either tomorrow or Friday. I guess that means I won't find out until after that.'

'That's a long wait.'

'Yeah, it's not ideal.'

Hayley pulled out her phone and rechecked the route to Ex-CeL London. It was a thirty-minute tube ride, then a further ten-minute walk to get there, but she was confident she could do it without any mishaps.

'I have to leave quite soon,' she said.

'Of course. I hope you have a good day and I'm sorry if I've put a downer on your trip by telling you about the interview.'

'You haven't. It's better knowing than worrying about why you're so quiet and off your food.'

His lip quirked a little and Hayley watched him. Would he smile? Did he ever?

'Does your conference start after the interview?'

'No, it's not until tomorrow. I'm not doing anything after the interview.'

'Well, how about I let you know when I'm done at the show for the day, and we can meet for food again?'

'Sounds good to me,' he said, and there was something genuine in his expression. Hayley got up from the table and gave him a gentle nudge on the shoulder as she passed him.

'You're gonna ace it.' For a second, she considered giving him a kiss on the cheek, but better not. 'Best of luck and I'll see you later.'

'Thanks, and yes, see you.'

She glanced back as she left the breakfast room. He was still watching her. What had happened to him? Where was grumpy Oliver? He was actually ok. Still sullen and unsmiley but he wasn't as awful as she'd always thought. Shame she had to discover that just as he was thinking about moving to London. So brave of him. She'd never want to make a move like this. A momentary image burst into her mind, so quick she almost missed it, a teasing little picture of her and Oliver both living and working here... together. A laugh almost escaped her out loud as she crossed the foyer. That wouldn't be happening. She knew from Finlay that Oliver didn't do long-term relationships even if she'd wanted one with him... which she didn't. Of course she didn't. Where were these daft thoughts coming from?

A crisp autumn morning greeted her outside and leaves swirled around the pavements, rustling up the side of giant wheelie bins and around lampposts as Hayley strode towards the main road. Under her cosy black coat, she wore a short brick-orange skirt, knee-length boots and a cashmere cream polo neck. Her hair was styled in a cascading high ponytail with a slight sixties vibe. She'd wrapped a side section of hair around the base and added a small bouffant just for fun. A few strands fell around her face, and she shook them away with a little flick. Hopefully this look gave the right mix of casual and stylish. This hairdo would be in front of so many hairdressers today. She really hoped she'd got it right.

Travelling around London on her own made her slip into thoughts about what living here must be like. She had to remind herself that even if she moved here, she was unlikely to have a house in Mayfair and she'd probably have a long commute every day and a small apartment – even smaller than the tiny flat she already owned in Glenbriar.

Her mind returned to Oliver. Where would he live if he moved here? Would he have a spare room? Quite a fun thought... She could visit him and go to the theatre and the shops. If he didn't mind. She let out a sigh. Poor guy. He'd had a horrible time growing up. She remembered her mum talking to Finlay about it when they were kids, telling him to be nice and always to make sure Oliver wasn't on his own. Finlay had followed that directive, and probably would have been his friend anyway. But what a shame about the way Oliver's dad treated him. Oliver may say it didn't affect him now, but some hurts ran so deep they were ingrained in people. He was so obviously unhappy. He had been as long as Hayley had known him. Surely that harked back to him losing his mum. Had he lost the ability to be cheerful? To smile? To see love and light?

As she was jostled down the busy street, she rolled her eyes for the umpteenth time as someone cut across her. Nope. She wouldn't want this every day. The hustle and bustle in London could be fun, but not on a daily basis. No wonder Oliver was conflicted. She'd be the same. If she was offered a stylist job in a London salon, it would be hard to turn down such a huge opportunity, but there was so much more to consider. A job was just a job and while she loved what she did, it wasn't the be all and end all of her existence. What about Oliver? Was his career the most important thing in his life?

Iconic red buses rumbled by, and Hayley followed the directions on her phone to Bond Street tube station. She screwed up her nose at the grimy city aroma mixed with coffee and oily cooking smells from the many cafés.

When she reached the station, she hopped on the escalator, holding tightly to both the rail and her bag. Thankfully she didn't have to drag her huge case around with her; the thought of Oliver pulling it along made her smile again. She made her way through the labyrinth of tunnels and platforms. A cold gust as a train left whipped past her and she shivered. Making a quick check of the sign, she chose a platform and joined the throng of commuters. People watching became her thing again as she waited until the busy train whooshed in. She hurried on with all the others, standing close to the door and clinging to a pole as they hurtled into darkness.

For the first part of the journey, everything was underground, and all the stations looked the same. This was the monotonous part, and the bit Hayley was sure she'd tire of if she had to do this every day.

When she'd been here with Amber last year, it had been much nicer than being on her own. They'd chatted and gossiped non-stop for days and still didn't have enough time to tell each other everything.

Custom House Station was above ground and all glass fronts and shiny floors, not like the grubby stations in the heart of London. The way to ExCeL was a short walk through streets with warehouses and a backdrop of pylons. She didn't need the map anymore; she remembered this bit and enough people were heading the same way to make it obvious. If in doubt, follow the group with the most interesting hairstyles.

As she got closer to ExCeL, she fired off a text to Oliver, wishing him luck for the interview. An inexplicable pang of sadness washed over her, making her fan her face. *Get it together! What has got into me?* Maybe coming here alone wasn't what she really wanted. But it ran deeper than that, almost like she didn't want him to get the job. Not because he didn't deserve it, but because she didn't want him so far away. Seriously? Why would it matter? Normally, she had nothing to do with him. But he'd been different over the last couple of days, almost vulnerable, and her heart hurt for him.

ExCeL was a massive, contemporary complex that stretched endlessly along the waterfront. Its reflective glass façade sparkled in the morning sun, and hundreds of people gathered around it.

Hayley joined the stream of attendees and located her online ticket. The buzz of chat and laughter was infectious, and she struck up easy conversation with a group of three people in front of her. She discovered they were from a salon in Birmingham, and they chatted as the queue moved slowly, sharing salon stories and discussing the banners and billboards at the entrance, showcasing the event's sponsors and featured artists.

'I love their new collagen conditioner,' one stylist said.

'Me too,' Hayley agreed. She took some photos on her phone of the fashion-forward and somewhat wild hairstyles on the posters. Ok, so they were sometimes controversial, but they were still amazing and only a few stylists ever got to do anything that exciting during their careers.

Eventually, she got to the registration desk and collected her badge and welcome pack. The hum of voices around her sounded happy and enthusiastic. She caught snippets of conversations about hair products and styling techniques. If only Amber was here too. There was so much to chat about. She fired off some messages, telling her how much she missed her.

Blinking and taking a deep breath, Hayley entered the main exhibition hall. Booths and displays from top hairstyling brands and salons from around the world lined the floor, each showcasing their products and services. Loudspeakers announced what was coming up and music blared from somewhere nearby. Where to even start? Hayley raised her phone to take a quick selfie as a message from Oliver pinged in.

OLIVER: I'm sure it'll be fine. I hope you have a good day. And thank you for your understanding. You really are a very kind person.

She gave a little snort laugh at the message, then snapped the picture. High praise from him but at least he wasn't annoyed with her, which was progress. She sent the selfie in reply and to prove she'd made it.

Moving through the stands, she stopped frequently to examine products and take notes or pictures. Although she was here for work, she couldn't help checking out everything wedding related. Her phone was soon full of snaps of potential styles for Genevieve, and she'd collected several samples before stopping to watch a live demonstration of a new styling brush. The miked-up stylist talked and gesticulated as he worked. Bright lights illuminated the model, who had gone from a head of sleek straight hair to picture-perfect curls in seconds. It would be fun to have a go of that later if she got the chance.

The afternoon schedule looked just as entertaining with fashion shows and a live competition. *Must call Oliver before it starts and check how his interview went.*

Being surrounded by all this inspiration and creativity was overwhelming. Hayley took a moment to stand back and ordered herself a coffee. As she sipped her flat white, her thoughts drifted back to Oliver again. Why couldn't her mind stay focused on where it should be and not go wandering off where it didn't belong?

As soon as midday had passed, Hayley deliberated over calling Oliver. Should she do it straight away or give him time? Maybe he wasn't finished yet, but the suspense was killing her.

When she couldn't stand it any longer, she picked up the phone and called.

'Hello,' he said after a couple of rings.

'Hey. How'd it go?'

'I'm just out. It went ok as far as I know. I did my presentation to the best of my ability anyway, so at least I've given myself a shot.'

'Great. Well done. You can relax a bit now.'

He let out an audible sigh. 'Yes. I suppose so. What are you doing? It sounds noisy.'

Music blared over the loudspeaker and people were chattering everywhere. Hayley hadn't really tuned into it until he mentioned it. 'It is, isn't it? I'm going to watch some shows this afternoon and there's a competition.'

'Sounds... Interesting.'

She chuckled. 'It is for me. How about we meet around six tonight? That'll give me time to see everything and get back into the city centre.'

'Let's meet on the south side of Westminster Bridge. I'd like to walk by the Thames.'

'Sounds fab. I'll meet you there.'

'Great. Message when you get there.'

'I will. See you later.' She ended the call and smiled at the phone. Oliver was so much nicer in London than he ever had been back home, and it made her insides soar just thinking about it. How enjoyable did walking along the Thames with him sound?

As soon as the competition ended that afternoon, she made her way back to the station and hopped on a train. She was lucky to get a seat, and for a moment, she rested her feet and took time to relax. Her brain was still in overdrive from the show. When she'd gathered her thoughts, she messaged Oliver to tell him she was on her way.

OLIVER: I'm near the bridge already. Meet outside the station.

It didn't take long to get there, and she jostled her way through the crowd around Westminster, looking everywhere until her eyes were drawn to the tall figure of Oliver, standing near the entrance, checking his phone.

She marched up to him and tapped his shoulder. 'Hey.'

'Ah, there you are.' He pocketed his phone. 'How did you get on?'

'It was brilliant, but I missed having people about that I knew. I talked to some people, but it's not really the same. Shame Amber couldn't have come with me.'

'There isn't exactly room for her and I'm not sure I want to have three to a room, especially on the sleeper.'

Hayley giggled. 'Yeah, we couldn't have travelled like this if she'd come. You'd have been free.'

He gave her a rueful glance. 'Maybe I'm a little glad she couldn't come then.'

Hayley's insides did a backflip. 'Are you saying you're enjoying my company?'

'I suppose I am. Thank you for listening to me yesterday.'

'It wasn't a problem.'

'Well, it helped me. I'm not good at talking about stuff. It's easier to keep things to myself, but I'm glad I shared this time.'

She smiled at him and placed her hand on his arm. 'I didn't really do anything, but I'm happy it helped.'

His eyes lingered on her hand before straying to her face. 'I don't know whether to take the job or not, assuming I get it.'

'It's an opportunity, isn't it?' She moved her hand and turned to walk. 'And your career is important to you.'

'Yes. It is.'

They crossed the bridge to the south side, and Hayley took some photos of the palace of Westminster and Big Ben. How odd to be counselling Oliver to take the job when she kind of wanted him to stay. A lead weight sank in her tummy, along with the suspicion that as soon as they were back in Glenbriar, he'd go back to his cold self. Well, if that was the case, it wouldn't matter where he was.

They found a place selling street food near the London Eye and sat on a bench beside a park to eat as dusk fell and the city started to sparkle around them.

'I love the city lights at night,' Hayley said. 'And nosing in people's windows.'

'Isn't that a bit creepy?'

'I don't mean like a peeping Tom. I just like it when you walk past and get a quick look into other people's lives.'

'I'm not sure it's something I've ever really thought about.'

'I could sit here for hours and watch the world go by, wondering about the people and their lives.'

'Sounds like you should be the one contemplating moving here.'

'I can people watch anywhere. London is great, but I don't want to live here. I like Glenbriar and living near to my family and friends.'

'It's definitely not a move to take on lightly. I'm lucky, I suppose, that I don't have any ties.'

Hayley wasn't sure that was lucky at all. It sounded the exact opposite to her. 'Well, I do. And at some point, I want to get married, have kids and all that jazz. I wouldn't want to do that here. I want my kids growing up near the countryside like I did with fresh air and less traffic.'

Oliver glanced at her. 'You're really invested in the romantic ideal, aren't you?'

'If you mean do I want to be happy, then yes.'

'Do you need to be married with children to be happy?'

'No. I'm happy now, but being happy isn't static and doesn't mean you can't change. What made me happy at four isn't what made me happy at twelve and so on. Happiness isn't a destination. It's an ongoing journey, and it adapts to different stages in life. Right now, I'm happy being single.' Mostly, though she wasn't about to admit it wasn't as rosy as all that. 'But later I want to be happy with someone else.'

'Well, I hope it works out for you. In my experience, it doesn't. Happy endings are the stuff of myth.'

'Oh, Oliver.' She let out a sigh. He was hopeless sometimes. 'Happy endings don't mean once you've found your special person, you don't have to do anything for the rest of your life. You'll still have ups and downs, but you've always got someone to help fight your corner. Love is an action. It doesn't stop once you've found it. It's something you have to keep doing; it might not look the same all through your life but it's there, and it's worth it.'

'Is it? Why?'

'Because it's lonely without it.'

'And what if you lose it?'

'There's always a risk, but you can't go through life avoiding everything on the off chance of pain. What if you let years of happiness slip by because you've spent them worrying about something that might never happen?'

He gave a little shrug. 'Sometimes you have to protect your heart or the little you have isn't worth it.'

His hands were resting on his lap, his fingers twitching. Hayley placed her hand on top of them. 'I understand where you're coming from, and I get it, but take care. You agreed with me yesterday that life was short, so it's all about taking opportunities when they arise.'

'You're right again.' He nodded and stared into the distance.

Hayley followed his sightline and watched as the London Eye moved slowly around, all lit up against the inky black sky.

'It's getting a little cold,' he said. 'Should we walk for a bit?'

'Sure.' They deposited their litter in the bin and walked along the wide pavement at the side of the Thames. She'd never have wanted to do this on her own, but with Oliver beside her, she felt invincible. Holding back from taking his hand was a struggle because it seemed like the right thing to do. To her heart anyway, though her head knew better, and she thrust her hands into her pockets to keep them out of trouble as she took in the lit-up boats and buildings.

After a while, they turned and went back towards Big Ben. They crossed the bridge and carried on towards Trafalgar Square. They were getting close to Theatre land and Hayley wished she could go to a show, but she stifled a yawn. She was already running on empty from the lack of sleep on the train and all the excitement of the day.

'Do you want to head back?' Oliver asked.

'Not really, but I'm too tired to do much else.'

'How about we walk back instead of getting the tube? It'll feel like we've done something then.'

'Great idea.'

She kept close to him as they made their way through the heart of London. Businesspeople were still dashing about, tourists were snapping photos, bars and clubs were jumping and the buses and taxis were rolling up and down, occasionally honking horns. All of it was so London. So much to take in and enjoy... sparingly.

For what Oliver had said would be a half-hour walk, it seemed to go much quicker, and they were soon back at the Royal Saxon Hotel. Hayley checked the time on her phone.

'It's nine o'clock,' she said.

'Shall we go for a drink?' Oliver asked.

Like she'd turn down that offer!

The bar had the same olde-worlde chic as the rest of the hotel. Hayley and Oliver took a seat in the corner. She ordered a cocktail while he settled for a cold beer.

'Cheers.' Oliver raised his glass. 'Let's hope we have another successful day tomorrow.'

'Let's hope.' She clinked her glass on his before sipping the ruby red daiquiri. 'Ooh, this is lush.'

His lips quirked in that little half smirk of his. Would he ever smile properly? He still didn't seem to be in a talkative mood, so she filled the silence with chat about cocktails, people passing by, and pretty much anything she could think of.

By the time they got back to the room, she was yawning almost uncontrollably. 'I need to sleep.' She flapped her hand in front of her mouth.

'Me too.' Oliver opened the door.

After getting ready for bed in the bathroom, Hayley climbed under the covers and closed her eyes, still listening to the faint sound of the traffic on the main road.

'Night-night,' she said.

'Night,' Oliver replied.

Soon, she heard his breathing go heavy. The urge to jump out of bed and kiss him goodnight burned like blue fire inside her. She steadied herself, taking slow deliberate breaths, until she drifted off to sleep.

Chapter Twelve

Oliver

Oliver sat at a large table in the conference room at Regalia HQ and stifled a yawn. What had got into him? He'd slept well and wasn't tired, but the day was dragging. Why was everything so deadly dull? Things he would normally enjoy just weren't keeping his interest at all.

He checked his phone; how was Hayley getting on at day two of the hair show? He'd gone from not wanting her anywhere near his life to wondering what she was doing every second of the day. That couldn't be good. What would he do when he had to go back to being without her? It wasn't his business to worry about her. That was the last thing he wanted. The very reason he didn't do relationships. They brought this kind of panic with them, and he didn't want it.

Seriously? He searched around for a blunt object. *Maybe if I whack myself over the head with it, it'll stop me from being so sentimental and knock my good sense back into place.* He couldn't let himself fall into the trap. Relationships were not for him. He'd always found Hayley attractive. She made him feel good, so he wanted to be close to her. She was nice to him, and it gave him a boost. The idea she cared about him was comforting and warmed his soul. But this kind of thing didn't last.

Hayley thought working at love made relationships last, but that wasn't true. His mum had been a good, loving person, but his dad had never appreciated that when she was alive. Their wedding photos had sat on the mantelpiece, watching every evening as he came home and threw himself into a chair, waiting for his dinner to appear on the table. Sometimes Mum let out her frustration and cried after Dad left in the morning. Oliver could still hear the sobs in the caverns of his mind. Occasionally she'd shout, other times she was like a zombie. And then she was gone. Oliver's stepmother had come on the scene way too soon. Had she always been waiting? He never dared ask. She seemed to accept her lot as wife and mother, which suited his father. Was it true love? More like convenience and status on her side. She got a big house and loved rubbing shoulders with other farmers, landowners, and estate owners. As for his dad... pure luck. All he seemed to want from a relationship was a cook and a maid.

With no messages from Hayley or anyone, Oliver returned his attention to the speaker and tried to focus. He didn't remember a day going this slowly for a long time. At lunchtime he had a quick catch up with Nathan, but even that was a little strained because of the limbo of not knowing whether he had the job or not.

When he finally left, he couldn't relax as he had the meal that night. Hayley had messaged him with lots of emojis and gifs about how excited she was to be going to Nimbus 9, the rooftop bar. Christmas had come five weeks early by the sound of her hyper voice messages. And actually, it had because Christmas trees and decorations were everywhere. Annoying really how the obsession for everything glittery and over-indulgent took over the last quarter of every year. A pointless waste of money. Much like weddings.

By the time Oliver got back to the hotel, the rush hour was in full flow, and he was glad to step into the cool quiet of the foyer. He took the stairs two and a time, zapped open the door, and entered.

Hayley sat on the bed, wrapped in a fluffy hotel robe, painting her toenails. Oliver turned his gaze away. *Christ's sake*. He loosened his tie. Why did she always look so damn seductive?

'Hello,' she said. 'I left a bit earlier today because I wanted to make sure I was ready for tonight.'

'How long does it take?' he asked.

'Ages. I need to be perfect. You have no idea how many pictures I'm going to take.'

'Hmm. I could probably make a guess.'

'You can take some of me on the roof. Apparently, there's an eighteen-foot Christmas tree outside. I'll need a photo with that.'

'How will I get the whole thing in and you? You'll look tiny.'

'Just try.'

He sat down on the bed opposite her, resting his wrists on his knees and leaning on them. 'Does Finlay know you're here with me?'

'Nope.' She continued along her toes.

'And I assume you aren't planning on telling him why you're at the roof-top bar.'

'I don't really mind if he knows where I am. It's not like we're doing anything wrong, is it?'

'No, but I doubt he'll see it like that. I'm sure he'll be curious, at the very least.'

She let out a little laugh. 'You mean he'll jump to all the wrong conclusions?'

'He won't be the only one.' Oliver got to his feet, tugged off his suit jacket, and tossed it on the bed. He yanked off his tie, then undid his top button before he caught his reflection. But he didn't look at his face. His eyes were drawn to the reflection of Hayley on the bed behind. She'd stopped polishing her toenails, her hand suspended above her foot, her focus unwaveringly on him. He froze. What the hell? They were eyeing each other in a way that wasn't healthy given their current situation... her in nothing but a bathrobe and him dangerously close to removing his shirt. What was he thinking? It had seemed the natural thing to do, but not now. Now the only thing that seemed appropriate was removing his shirt, then the rest of his clothes, and joining her on the bed. Once he was there... Oh, the things he would do. Maybe his eyes were telling her exactly that because she gave a choked little cough, possibly a laugh, and went back to drying her nails with a little pink device like a mini torch. Oliver walked to the other end of the room, still unbuttoning his shirt and keeping his back to her. There were some things he wasn't sure he wanted her to see.

'Hey. Would you like to be my model?' she asked.

'Your what?' He glanced back at her.

'I got all these freebies today.' She jumped off the bed and lifted a large carrier bag. 'Including this rather fancy male grooming pouch with loads of cool products.' Holding up a faux leather bag, she beamed at him.

'And… er… What exactly do you want me to do?'

'Sit back and relax. I'll do the work.'

Her smile was so endearing. How could anyone ever say no to her? She must have had her parents wrapped around her little finger as a child. Flash that smile and she'd have every toy in the shop, every sweet from the packet… Now, she must have guys queuing up at her door, wanting to be the one to please her. How the hell was she single?

'Well… ok. What does it entail exactly? Are you going to cut my hair? Because I quite like it as it is.'

'Of course I won't cut it without asking you. I could trim the back and level the edges, if you like, but I won't change the style. And I'll give you a close shave using these rather nifty' – she popped off a lid and sniffed a bottle – 'and heavenly scented products. All made from natural ingredients.'

'You want to shave me?' He ran his hand around his jaw. There was some five o'clock shadow there, but holy fuck. He might die if she touched him. One flinch and she could cut his throat. But that wasn't really what was bothering him. *Help*.

'Only if you want me to.' That smile was back, and Christ, he was a weak man.

'Well, ok.'

'Fab.' She put the bottle back in the pouch and laid it on the dressing table. 'If you take off your shirt and sit here.' She pulled out the chair. 'It's not as good as the salon chairs, but we'll make it work.'

Take off my shirt...? Just like that. Man, was he screwed. He did as she said, discarding it on the bed. Her eyes raked him over as he approached and sat down. She flicked out a towel and covered him with it. The disturbance in the air and her closeness sent a shiver across his skin, though the room was warm.

She began combing his hair. He couldn't avoid seeing her in the mirror unless he closed his eyes, and that would look weird. Her soft floral scent was both erotic and calming. It was messing with him again. She put down the comb and smoothed up the back of his neck with one soft palm. *Jesus Christ*. This would be the death of him.

Pulling out a little razor from the leather pouch, she uncapped it.

'Do you know how to use one of them?' he asked, barely concealing his panic.

'Of course I do. Hang on. I need some water.' She rummaged in her case and pulled out a little spray bottle. What else did she have in there? Nipping into the bathroom, she ran the tap. When she returned, she spritzed the back of his neck, and droplets landed like a soft mist on his skin. Then she squirted a little foam from one of the miniature bottles from the pouch. It smelled deep and intense, a little spicy. Not bad at all.

'Ok, you have to sit really still.' She gently patted the foam onto the back of his neck.

'I'll try.' His back went rigid at the tickling sensation of the foam. Her hand landed on his shoulder, holding him fast. She leaned in, her soft breath skimming his neck as she scraped the razor across his skin. He clamped his jaw shut, trying to pause his brain and stop his thoughts developing, or travelling to any other part of his body; his anatomy needed no extra reminders on what it might like to do right now.

After a few swift strokes, she stopped.

'Is that it?' he asked.

'Not quite. Stay still.' A few more strokes. Hayley tilted her head and leaned right in, concentrating. 'There we are.' She cleaned off the foam with a damp flannel. How was she so well prepared?

'Now for the front.' Still standing behind him, she placed her palms on his cheeks and ran them down like she was feeling for the grain. He was in danger of losing consciousness now, because he didn't dare breathe. He watched her in the mirror. The eye contact was strong. His body was ready to respond to her touch in all number of inappropriate ways.

She smiled rather wickedly like she knew exactly what she was doing to him. 'Let's smoothen you up.' She sprayed more foam onto her palms, then gently patted it onto his cheeks. Every particle of his energy was being spent forcing himself not to be visibly affected by this.

With deft movements, she glided the razor along the curve of his jaw. So confident and precise. She seemed to know exactly where to move the blade without a second thought.

The soft scrape of the razor against his skin sent a shiver of pleasure down his spine. He half closed his eyes, allowing her to tilt his head back, exposing his neck. Gently, she worked along the underside of his chin.

'Gorgeous.' She wiped off the remaining foam.

Does she mean me?

'Let's put on a little moisturiser.' She applied it with gentle pressure, then stepped back.

Oliver blinked at his reflection, running his hand over the smooth skin. 'Good work.' He moved his head from side to side. She was a pro right enough.

'Not too scary, was it?'

'The jury's out.'

She giggled. 'Aftershave? Or would you prefer your usual brand?'

'May as well use that one and complete the experience.'

'Allow me.' She patted some onto her hands, then gently tapped his cheeks. They smarted momentarily, then the cool sensation spread over his face.

'Thanks.'

'Any time.' She smiled and their eyes met in the mirror. Nice promise, but she wouldn't be around the next time he needed a shave. Still running his fingertips over his jawline, he got to his feet. He pulled the towel from his shoulders and dropped it over the radiator. Hayley's gaze was like a targeted missile. He didn't have to look to know she was watching him.

He opened his case and took out a clean shirt. Back home, he could get away with wearing the same one he'd worn earlier, but London grime and dust made his skin itch and crawl.

'I'll just get dressed in here.' He took his clothes into the bathroom and splashed water on his chest and arms.

When he came out fully dressed in his evening suit, he froze. Hayley had put on a dark red sheath dress with a low-cut V-neck. She stood before the mirror, putting the finishing touches to a perfect up-do. As she turned to check it, Oliver was presented with the view of her bare back as the dress plunged low, with only a slender gold chain running across her shoulder blades between the straps. Could she be any hotter? Men everywhere dreamed of women like her on their arms for a function like this. How could he explain who she was without sounding like an idiot? Because any single man who wasn't interested in her *must* be an idiot.

'Is this dress ok?' She turned to face him. 'Or is it too short? I've got a longer one, just in case.'

Oliver raised his eyebrow, though he didn't really mean to. He seemed to have lost control of his anatomy. 'Looks great from where I'm standing.'

'Really?'

'Really.'

'I'll take that as a compliment,' she said.

'And so you should.' He checked the time on his phone. 'We should head down. The Uber will be here soon.'

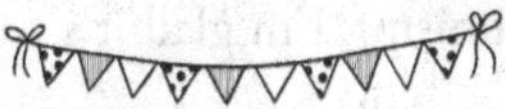

Hayley beamed at Oliver as they sat in the backseat of the Uber. She smoothed the skirt of her dress, her tanned knees jutting out beneath it, and Oliver forced himself to look away. This was what he'd spent most of his adult life trying to avoid or not to notice. Never since the day he'd come home from uni and gone to visit Finlay only to find his kid sister all grown up had a minute passed when he hadn't found her attractive. She'd gone from a girl he never paid any attention to, to a stunning young woman. Ten years on and she was just as gorgeous, if not more so. Now she was here, within his grasp. *Must not act rashly.*

Even thinking about it made him cringe. What exactly would he say or suggest? A hook-up for the next couple of nights? Not awkward at all – much. Inviting her here had been stupid enough. He hadn't thought it through. All he'd wanted was company for the function, but he hadn't planned what he would tell people. He leaned his forehead in his hand and moved closer to the cab window with a groan.

'Are you ok?' Hayley asked.

'Yeah. Absolutely fine. You?'

'Completely overexcited. I can't wait to see this place. I've heard about it, but I never expected to be going there anytime soon, especially when it'll be all decked out in its Christmas finery.'

Oliver gave her a little smile. It was hard not to imbibe some of her constant optimism. 'I'm glad it's to your liking. I can't guarantee the company will be very interesting. People like to talk shop at these events, and you'll probably find it deadly dull.'

'I don't think so. I like people and I usually find interesting things to chat about. It's part of my job, you know? Cutting hair is just one part of it. If I don't actively engage with clients, they won't come back.'

'Then you must be one of the best.'

She gave him a quizzical smile. 'Is that you being sarky?'

'No. I mean it.'

'Well, thanks. But after seeing some of the stylists at the show today, I'm definitely not one of the best.'

'I beg to differ.' He ran his hand over his jaw. 'You did a good job on me.'

'Did I now?'

With a resigned sigh, he said. 'You know what I mean. I've never even let the barber shave me before.'

'I'm honoured.'

'You should be.'

She gave a little smirk. 'Do you know most of the people who'll be here tonight?'

'Some of them, but not everyone.'

'Is there anyone going that you're close to? Friends? Colleagues? That kind of thing?'

'Just Nathan. He's someone I've known for a long time. We were at uni together and we kept in touch, though I wouldn't say we were close. We've supported each other, and he's been instrumental in getting me in a good position to get this job.'

'He sounds great. I can't wait to meet him.'

Oliver gazed out the window at the passing traffic and the city lights. Nathan was a good person. Oliver had helped him with tricky cases, and they'd traded useful info, but he was so much more gregarious than Oliver. Thankfully Nathan had a wife, otherwise Oliver's hackles would be up and his fists clenched. Nathan had an easy way with women and Hayley would doubtless be charmed... But why did that matter? *And why am I bothered?* He glanced back at Hayley and heat and energy surged through him, urging him to reach out and place a hand on her knee: *claim her, protect her, keep her.* But he couldn't.

The cab pulled up outside the bar. Oliver paid as Hayley got out and gaped up at the entrance, surrounded by sparkling fairy lights. Impressive stuff with the giant Christmas trees, all twinkling and gleaming, flanking the doors. By the time he reached her side, she had her phone out and was snapping pictures and selfies.

'This place is just wow.'

Oliver straightened his jacket, looked at the door, then back at Hayley and put out his elbow. She stared at it for a second, then with a broad smile, linked her arm into his. A sharp sense of satisfaction rose within him as he strode forward. With Hayley beside him like this, he was ready for world domination. He could shoot down all the awkwardness he usually felt when attending events like this by himself. He wouldn't have to scan the room for familiar faces or latch onto random groups and pretend he was part of their conversation.

They made their way through the first level and up the stairs. Perhaps Hayley's heels weren't the easiest to walk in and that was why she was holding his arm so tight; he didn't want to think it might be anything else. Definitely not the possibility that she might like him... As in *like* like him. More than she should. More than was sensible... For them both.

'Oliver,' a loud voice called from the top of the stairs and Oliver spotted Nathan leaning over from the gallery and waving. Oliver raised his hand in return.

'Evening,' he said as they reached Nathan.

'Glad you made it. Traffic was a nightmare as usual.' Nathan clapped Oliver's arm, then beamed at Hayley. 'And you must be—'

'Hayley,' Oliver said.

'Of course.' Nathan beamed at her. 'Oliver mentioned someone was with him but didn't say who. Please to meet you. I'm Nathan Shelby.'

Hayley shook his hand, returning his smile, then pulled a face at Oliver that clearly said, *you never even told him my name.*

'Nice to meet you, Nathan,' she said. 'I've heard all about you.'

'Indeed?' Nathan blinked dramatically and Oliver almost rolled his eyes at his utterly fake and over-the-top look of shock.

'Of course. After all the help you've given Oliver with the possible new job.'

Nathan swatted his hand in front of his face. 'It was nothing, really. Just gave him the heads up.'

'Where's Emma-Jane?' Oliver asked.

'Somewhere about,' Nathan said. 'She saw some people she knew and went off to chat. I was waiting for you. Have you heard anything new about the job yet?'

'Nothing.'

'That's annoying. I thought they would have been in touch by now.'

'They said it might be tomorrow.' As the words came out, Oliver suppressed a discomforting sensation in his stomach. Much as he wanted to know, all the dilemmas he'd been putting off thinking about would crash through the floodgates like a tidal wave as soon as he got that call. Decisions would have to be made no matter what the outcome.

'I just know you'll get it,' Nathan said.

'Me too,' Hayley added with a half-smile that didn't quite reach her eyes. How could she possibly know? She knew nothing about his career unless Finlay had told her. But Oliver wasn't sure Finlay knew either. Oliver had an impressive track record, but he didn't brag about it. The constant cycle of betterment got to him more than any celebration of his success. Once he'd achieved a giddy height, there was always that sense of not wanting to look down. How could he maintain this position? Or repeat the climb and perhaps go one better? A perpetual and exhausting wheel of hard work, self-doubt, and fear.

'And how do you feel about coming to live here?' Nathan asked Hayley.

'What do you mean?'

'Well, as we're all pretty certain Oliver will get the job, it stands to reason you'll be moving here.'

'We don't live together,' Oliver said.

'Oh...' Nathan huffed a little laugh, his cheeks reddening slightly. 'Sorry, I just assumed. I apologise.' His gaze shifted subtly between Oliver and Hayley, and Oliver was certain a question was coming, but Nathan took a sip of champagne and said nothing.

'Don't apologise,' Hayley said. 'An easy mistake to make.'

Oliver's focus darted to her.

'Too right,' Nathan said.

'Where do we get champagne?' Hayley asked.

'Oh...' Nathan looked around. 'There was a man walking around. Where is he?'

'I see someone. I'll go grab us some.' Hayley sashayed off through the crowd, like a movie star arriving for a film premiere.

'I am sorry,' Nathan said quietly. 'I hope I didn't put my big foot in it. Isn't she your girlfriend?'

'No.' Oliver shook his head.

'Who is she then?'

'Just... Someone I know.'

'Come on, Oliver. You didn't come to London with some random woman, did you? Is she just a casual hook-up you brought for a bit of—'

'No, nothing like that. She's a friend. An acquaintance.'

Nathan patted Oliver on the arm. 'You might be a good lawyer, but you're a strange man sometimes.'

'Why?'

'If you can't work it out for yourself, then it's really not my place to say.'

Chapter Thirteen

Hayley

Hayley snagged two drinks from a server carrying a tray. This place was the stuff of dreams. If Amber and the girls from work were here, it would be even better, or make that Genevieve, Felicity, Willow, Lilah, or any of her other friends. She turned to head back and caught sight of Oliver again. Being out with him wasn't that bad. He was good eye candy to start with. Who was she kidding? He was hotter than hell, and it was taking all of her energy not to notice or care. But how could she help it?

Shaving him earlier had been verging on foreplay. Such close touching. His soft, warm skin. Why had he agreed? She'd been so sure he'd say no. It had taken all her energy to keep her hand steady. London-Oliver was like a different man. He'd always been good-looking, but she'd discarded him as dating material because he was so gruff and unsociable. Plus, he'd always disliked her, hadn't he? That argument was wearing thin. Had she unkindly dismissed him without properly getting to know him? Not that it really mattered. He was London bound, and she was a Glenbriar girl through and through. Dating him would be impractical, at the very least. And probably not what he wanted. According to Finlay, Oliver was serially single and had no desire to change that. The opposite was true for Hayley. She wanted love with roses, champagne, and possibilities – a wedding, a house in the country, a family.

She returned to Oliver and Nathan. A pleasant-looking woman stood next to him. She had dark curly hair, glasses and a pretty black dress covered in red flowers that clung to her curves.

'This is Emma-Jane, my wife,' Nathan said as Hayley handed a drink to Oliver.

'Hi. I'm Hayley. Lovely to meet you. Are you a lawyer too?'

Emma-Jane nodded. 'For my sins, yes. Are you?'

'No. I'm a hairstylist.'

'Really? Oh wow. I'd love to have a talent like that. I can see from your hair you're good at it.'

'Thanks. I enjoy it. I'm here for the Hair Show this week. It just happened to coincide with Oliver being here, so I tagged along.'

'Oh.' Emma-Jane gave them a slightly puzzled look. 'So, you two aren't together?'

'No.' Hayley took a sip of her champagne, and the bubbles danced on her tongue.

'How do you know each other?'

'Oliver is my brother's friend.'

'Nice,' Emma-Jane said.

'I got the wrong end of the stick too,' Nathan said. 'I mean, I'm probably overstepping completely here, but you look like a couple.'

'Do we?' Hayley winked at Oliver, on the side Nathan and Emma-Jane couldn't see. 'Must be the way you look at me. Those long, loving glances.'

'What?' Oliver almost choked on his drink.

Hayley laughed, and the others did too.

'Forgive me for saying.' Nathan patted Oliver on the arm. 'But it looks to me like you're in trouble.'

'Maybe.' Oliver took a sip of champagne. 'But getting people out of tricky situations is my speciality. I think I can manage it for myself.'

Hayley gave Emma-Jane a brief grin, hopefully giving off unconcerned vibes. Why should she be bothered if Oliver wanted nothing from her? It was mutual, right? A little sting of rejection caught her where it hurt though, and her smile wasn't completely genuine.

They moved from the top of the stairs into the upper bar that led out onto the roof. Even on a cold November evening, it looked inviting, with a Christmas tree and fairy lights all around the balcony and the glowing patio heaters.

'Can we go outside?' Hayley said.

'Sure.' Oliver put his empty glass on the table. 'Do you want another drink? I'll get them, unless you want to spend the night knocking back the free stuff.'

'I'd love a cocktail,' Hayley said. They approached the bar and waited in the short queue. 'I spotted on their website that they make some amazing ones.'

'Ok. What do you fancy?'

She ran her eyes over him before she could stop herself. Why lie? She fancied him something chronic... Maybe she always had from a distance. Probably pure lust, because the urge to kiss him was suddenly strong. She burned to have his lips on hers and didn't want it to stop there. A harmless fling might be just the tonic. Except it wasn't like she could make him vanish from her life afterwards. They still had a wedding to get through, even if he was in London and she was in Glenbriar. This wasn't the time for a crazy fling. Or was it exactly that?

How bloody confusing.

'Hayley?' His low voice was questioning and made her bounce back into the bar. The soft jazz version of Christmas songs echoed in her ears like someone had fired up the volume.

'Oh, I'd love to try the gingerbread white Russian.'

Oliver watched her as he leaned on the bar. 'What are you thinking?' he asked quietly.

'What do you mean?'

'You looked like you were deep in thought about something.'

Should she tell him the truth? What would he make of it? 'I was.'

'And are you going to share?'

'What can I get you?' the bartender interrupted, and Oliver made the order before turning back to Hayley.

'Well?'

'Maybe.' She tapped her nail on the bar, not sure what to say.

He arched an eyebrow.

'Why do you want to know what I'm thinking?' she said.

'Curiosity, I suppose.'

'You're not normally curious about me. Normally you don't speak to me or even look at me.'

'Self-preservation,' he muttered, turning back to the bar.

Hayley moved closer and leaned on it beside him. 'What exactly do you mean by that?'

'Isn't it obvious?'

She froze, putting the comeback she had ready on ice because his response wasn't what she'd expected. 'Obvious? Isn't what obvious?'

'You're a very attractive woman,' Oliver told the bar, not making eye contact. 'You have been for a long time. But it never seemed right for me to notice.'

Hayley put her hand to her forehead. 'Oh my god.'

'Yup. Should probably have kept that to myself, but now you know.'

'I do,' she said. 'And would it surprise you to know I was thinking something similar about you?'

He glanced back at her. 'Are you serious?'

'Completely.'

'So, it's mutual?' He cast her a look and frowned. 'I don't know about you, but I'm finding it difficult to ignore it.'

'Me too.'

Two cocktails landed in front of him, and he lifted them, handing one to Hayley and wrapping his fingers around the other. 'Let's get some air.'

She walked towards the doors leading outside. Oliver was very close behind her and she sensed the heat. The delicious scent of the aftershave she'd clapped on his cheeks earlier wafted into her consciousness. The sensory overload was driving her crazy. *Please, please, let him keep talking! Do not clam up now.* Not when they were getting somewhere. Even if where they were going was a dangerous path, or at least not a sensible one.

As she reached the door, he leaned past her and pushed it open, holding it for her.

'Thank you.' Hayley went out into the chilly night air, put her glass on the thick rail surrounding the roof terrace, pushing a gap in the thick foliage and fairy lights decorating it. London lights sprawled around them, Westminster all lit up in the near distance and the bridges over the Thames still packed with buses. 'So, we've established the attraction between us is mutual.'

'We have.' Oliver stood beside her, cradling his cocktail.

'So, what happens now?' Hayley fiddled with the strap of her dress.

'Nothing.'

'Are you serious?'

'Yes.' He took a sip of the creamy cocktail, wiping some from his lips with his fingertips. Hayley tried not to stare or imagine herself licking it off. 'I mean, what can we actually do about it?'

He had a point. While she could imagine many things, they all had consequences that weren't quite so appealing. 'Maybe just one kiss,' she said. 'One kiss to acknowledge this exists and to nip it in the bud before it drives one or both of us crazy.'

Oliver looked back at her with a wry smile. 'You honestly think that'll work? You'll accept one kiss and leave it there.'

'Won't you?'

'If that's all you want, then yes.'

'And what do you want?'

He looked away again. 'I don't know.'

Hayley lifted her cocktail and sipped it. The beautifully sweet and spicy taste of gingerbread and cream tickled her tastebuds, and she took some more, letting its warmth seep into her. Out here was cold, and she wasn't dressed for it, but between the drink, the patio heaters and Oliver, she was coping. Her heart was working a little too fast, and she tried not to imagine Oliver pulling her closer and wrapping his arms around her. They'd shared a lovely hug the other day, but what she wanted now had carnal undertones, which she really needed to put a stop to. Perhaps Oliver was right to hold back.

'Ok,' he said.

'Ok? Ok, what?'

'One kiss.'

Hayley's heart hammered again. 'Right here? Right now?'

He glanced around, perhaps checking for Nathan or anyone else he recognised, but very few people had ventured outside. 'Yes.'

She gazed into his deep, dark eyes. His pupils were very wide. Her heart thudded against her chest like it was trying to get out. She leaned closer as he did the same until they were too close to stop unless someone burst through the doors screaming. But nothing happened to prevent it and with the soft jazzy version of 'Winter Wonderland' playing in the background, Hayley pressed her lips to his. The instant heat sent an electric shock zinging through her, but it was gentler than she'd expected. Soft and sweet, almost like an extension of the richly flavoured cocktail. His hand slipped around her cheek, and he deepened the kiss, just a little, but his tongue caught hers enough to make her pulse flicker. Her eyelids closed, and she abandoned herself to the dreamy scent of his aftershave and the lingering taste of the white Russian on his tongue. He pulled away first, their faces still close, his dark brown eyes boring into hers. She let out a shaky breath but didn't move away.

He slipped his arms around her waist and drew her close to him. For a second, she held her breath. Would he kiss her again? Gently, he embraced her, leaning his super smooth jaw on the side of her forehead. He inhaled deeply and shifted slightly, like he was nuzzling her hair. She let out a little moan. 'This is... nice,' she murmured.

'Indeed.' Slowly, his hands fell away, and he stepped back. 'Very nice indeed.' A smile grew on his face. Not huge, but enough. A little wistful and uncertain, but present. God, he'd been handsome before, but that smile multiplied it tenfold.

Hayley smiled back for a long moment. Eventually, he looked away with a sigh. She blinked and returned to her drink, suddenly a little shivery. The air still fizzed around them. Now they'd crossed that barrier, it would be too easy to keep going. They had a hotel room together. Why waste it? But that would be really silly, and she knew it.

'Let's go inside,' she said. 'It's getting cold out here.'

'Ok.' Oliver glanced at his phone as he moved closer. He didn't put his arm around her but was near enough to be a comforting presence. Really, it didn't come close to what she wanted. This was what they'd agreed on though, and she didn't have any excuses to do anything further. The attraction would just have to simmer on in the background, then fizzle out and die once they went back to normal. 'We should find our table,' he said.

Once inside, they found it and sat quietly for a while. Hayley sipped her cocktail, digesting what had happened, and assumed Oliver was doing the same. Other people joined them, and Hayley chatted with them in her usual way. Oliver occasionally chipped in if the topic was work related, but mostly he was silent... even more so than usual.

Apart from the kiss, it turned out to be a somewhat underwhelming night. The venue was amazing, but the company had been as uninteresting as Oliver had predicted. All the legal talk wasn't really Hayley's thing, though she might have enjoyed it more if her head was in a better place.

Oliver remained quiet in the Uber on the way back to the hotel and they got ready for bed separately with barely a word passing between them.

Despite knowing she was tired, sleep wouldn't come. Hayley's mind was too buzzed and she couldn't switch off. It kept coming back to the kiss, over and over again. She lay staring into the darkness, listening to Oliver breathing... so close, but so far. She wanted him next to her so they could hold each other. A laugh almost escaped her. Like he'd ever do that. He so obviously wasn't a cuddler... but then, there had been that moment after the kiss when he'd held her. It had been brief, but he'd initiated it and it had made him smile. Maybe he had a softer centre than she thought. He definitely had self-control. If she'd gone on dates with guys and had a kiss like that, the majority of them would have expected it to go further, especially if they were sharing a hotel room. But there was Oliver in the next bed. Just out of reach.

Friday morning arrived like a bus colliding with a wall. How had their last day in London come round so soon? Oliver was still quiet and Hayley packed up her case as he got ready in the bathroom.

I'm not ready for the return of grumpy Oliver yet, she thought. But he was here whether she liked it or not.

'We can put the luggage into the lockers at Euston Station this morning.' He tugged on his tie. 'Then we'll be hands free for the day.'

She caught him watching her in the mirror and raised her eyebrow at him.

'Unless you want to be lugging that case around the Hair Show.'

'No thanks,' she said.

They ate a quick breakfast. Hayley couldn't face much and was still full from the night before. Oliver appeared to be the same. They left the hotel together and checked their luggage into the lockers at Euston Station. Hayley hadn't been able to get tickets for the after-show party that evening, and it was maybe just as well. It would have been a rush to get there, then get the train after. And another party with Oliver was probably not a good idea, especially with him in this mood.

'Should we meet back here later?' she said. 'The train isn't until late and I'll be away from the show around five.'

'Let's meet somewhere for dinner.' Oliver checked the time on his phone. 'A farewell to London.'

'Ok.' She met his gaze. A farewell to an all-too-brief encounter more like. 'Message me if you think of somewhere good.' Should she kiss him goodbye? She sucked on her lower lip. No, that was over the top, so she gave a little wave and made her way to the underground for ExCeL.

The last day of the Hair Show was always good, and the demos were incredible, but Hayley couldn't stop yawning. Her thoughts were all over the place and she was too tired to concentrate. She'd barely slept a wink last night. Maybe she was disappointed in not getting to sleep with Oliver, but in the cold light of day, she was glad she hadn't. The awkwardness would be off the scale.

Midway through a show on bridal hair – the one she'd been most invested in all day – a text buzzed in. She guessed what it was before she opened it.

OLIVER: I got the job!

A sharp pain shot through her like a knife had caught her. Everything would change now. Just as things between them had moved on, they'd be even more like strangers than ever.

Why did I even have to come here?

She put her head in her hand and rubbed her forehead. If she'd just not bothered, none of this would have happened and she wouldn't have cared about Oliver getting a job in London. In fact, she'd have been thrilled to have him far away. Not so much now.

Why had everything got so complicated?

As soon as the demo was done, she got to her feet, shuffled along the row, and left. Maybe she should just leave altogether.

She wasn't exactly taking stuff in. But what else would she do? A café area was nearby, and she ordered a flat white, took it to a table and sat down before replying to his message with as much gushy cheer as she could. But inside, her heart was achy and energy gone. Nothing looked interesting anymore, and she wanted to be far away... Though she wasn't sure where.

CHAPTER FOURTEEN

Oliver

Nathan clapped Oliver on both arms. 'I knew you'd get it. When do you start?'

'I have to negotiate that,' Oliver said. 'I'm bang in the middle of some cases I'd like to finish, or at least get to a point where I can easily hand them over to someone else. I'm thinking new year at the earliest, but probably more realistically in February.'

'Sounds great.' Nathan gave him another look. 'You sure you can't persuade Hayley to come with you?'

'Why would I do that?'

'I just think you'd be great together.'

'Not going to happen,' Oliver said. 'We want very different things from life.'

'Ah, pity. But let me show you this.' Nathan led Oliver through the office building where, in a few months, he would spend most of his time. He'd need to source accommodation too. Nathan had already offered him a spare room until he found something, but Oliver liked his own company.

'I get an induction month first,' Oliver said. 'I'll probably need it. This is a whole new way of working for me.' A twinge tugged his insides alongside thoughts of long hours, lengthy commutes, and very little downtime. But thousands of people did it and loved it. Why not him? He was already a workaholic, according to Finlay, so this would suit him fine.

He and Nathan sat together through day two of the conference. By the end of the afternoon, Nathan had googled about twenty properties he thought would suit Oliver. No doubt they were all very nice, but Oliver wanted to choose for himself.

'Look forward to having you back in February.' Nathan shook Oliver's hand as they got ready to go their separate ways.

'Thanks for all your help with this,' Oliver said. And while he appreciated it, he had a niggling sense that, without Nathan's insistence, he wouldn't have this new job at all. He should be thankful for that, shouldn't he? Only something didn't sit right. Why did it feel like he'd been pushed in a direction he hadn't wanted to go in? Or if he did, he hadn't fully made up his mind yet. *Why are you just going with the flow?* Because it was the right thing to do? A sensible career progression. Not because he wanted to. His current job wasn't working out, but he wasn't convinced this new one would be any better. Something was still missing.

Chalk it up as an experience. He tried to channel that thought as he headed for the tube. Even if he stuck with it for a year or two, he might be in a better position to get a partnership or open his own practice. Technically, he could do that now, but something had always held him back.

As the tube trundled off, he messaged Hayley, suggesting they met at an Italian restaurant on Piccadilly. Her gushy message back was in a similar tone to the ones that afternoon. She sounded delighted he'd got the job. No doubt she couldn't wait to get rid of him.

Even now? Now she knew he was attracted to her? Their confession the previous night had changed things, but also complicated matters. When he'd thought it a one-sided attraction, he could deal with it, but her feelings in the mix made it so much harder.

And what about the kiss?

The question had been at the back of his mind all day. As he nipped up the steps at Piccadilly Station, he tried to push the analysis away and not think about it. They'd been silly to do it, but that wouldn't erase the memory of just how good it had been.

Hayley was waiting outside the restaurant, her gorgeous hair tumbling around her shoulders, her face all smiles as ever. Oliver suffered the usual gut-punch. More so this time, as he knew what it was like to kiss those lips. Oh god. He wanted to do it again so badly. His body ached at the idea of not being able to. He flexed his hand and tried to smile.

'Congratulations,' she said, and in a typical Hayley move, she launched herself into his arms and hugged him around the neck. He'd seen her do this kind of thing heaps of times with other people, but she wouldn't normally with him. He stood rigid for a moment, but why not accept it? With a little huff, he snaked his arms around her waist and held her close. His nose drew close to her hair, and he inhaled the beautiful scent. Last night, her hair had been piled up and out of reach when he'd held her, but now, with it trailing down her back, it was just there. He shifted his hand so it brushed over her smooth curls. No one else had hair as stunning as this. With a very light touch, he stroked it. The softness of it, along with Hayley's warm weight in his arms, had a deep effect on him. Blood raced to his groin.

Control, Oliver.

Having someone in his corner and so delighted for him was unusual. But pleasant... Very, very pleasant.

'Thank you,' he said quietly, aware he hadn't verbally responded to her.

She increased her grip on his neck, then placed a tiny kiss on his cheek, holding her lips there for a beat longer than necessary. 'I'm so happy for you.'

A jolt of energy pulsed through him, and he almost threw caution to the wind and kissed her again. But no. This would end here. He took a deep breath and pulled back. 'It'll be quite a change,' he said. Part of him wanted to tell her about the conflicting feelings he'd had on the tube, his uncertainty, and worries. But why bother her? No need to bring a downer on the meal. He pushed open the restaurant door and held it for her.

'This looks lovely.' She checked around.

'Yeah, I like Italian food and I'm planning on overeating and drinking a fair bit this evening.'

'To celebrate?' She gave him a funny look, like it surprised her.

'Kind of, but more to make sure I sleep on the train.'

'Oh yeah, good point.'

The food was so delicious Oliver had no problem filling up with olives, crunchy bruschetta, creamy mozzarella, juicy fat tomatoes, pasta, pizza and pretty much a little of everything available at the all-you-can-eat buffet. Hayley was the same. She giggled as she held up her plate. 'I need to send a photo of this to Finlay. He'll be so jealous.'

'Just don't tell him who you're with.'

'As if.' She put her plate on the table and pulled out her phone.

'I've ordered some wine too,' Oliver said. 'Hopefully that'll knock us out.'

'I've still got a bottle in my case. We can use that if we need it too.'

He sat down at the same time as the server appeared with the wine bottle and two glasses.

'Should I be surprised that you carry bottles of wine in your suitcase?'

Hayley smirked. 'For emergency use only.'

'No wonder that case was so heavy. What other emergencies were you prepared for?'

'Ah, you know, this and that. I've got a full hazmat suit in there too.'

He shook his head and poured some wine into her glass. 'You really are mad.'

'Thank you.' She took the glass from him. 'Speaking of which, are we going to behave on the train?'

Oliver poured his wine, then took a long, slow sip. 'Would you rather misbehave?'

'Probably.'

'In what way?'

'In an energetic way that might help us sleep.'

He snorted. 'I'm guessing you don't mean running up and down the carriages.'

'Er, no.'

'Ok. So, say we did, don't you think that would be problematic?'

'I know it would be.'

'You do?' He nodded. 'So, if we do anything, it has to have strict boundaries.'

'Such as?'

'It's a one off. It's not a precursor to anything else, like a relationship or even a friends-with-benefits arrangement. Nothing like that.'

'Makes sense.' She stared at her food. 'Oh, for heaven's sake, why are we even contemplating this? We're adults. We can control ourselves.'

'Yup.'

'And in a month or so, you'll be here, and I'll be in Glenbriar. Whatever this is between us will fizzle and die.'

He blinked at his food and took another mouthful of wine. She was right, but snuffing out the faint hope of a night of passion on the train left his insides roiling. Why had he chosen so much food? Why had he let her get to him? If he'd just kept his mouth shut yesterday and not mentioned the attraction, he could have kept everything safe and as it should be.

They boarded the train later that evening and silence descended on them. Hayley seemed abnormally quiet and subdued. Oliver decided not to mention it or even say anything. It was all for the best. They'd return to Glenbriar and go back to normal. That one kiss would sit there as something he wished he'd never let happen.

The food and the wine might have worked to get him to sleep if his head wasn't in such turmoil. What was happening in his life? Normally, it was so well ordered and predictable. It might not be full of joy, but it was steady and safe. Now, everything was topsy-turvy and unsettled. His mind was all over the place and tension had seized him, holding him like a vice. How could he escape and find something stable and familiar to cling to? Because there wasn't anything. He'd made a choice. Things would change and he had to deal with it. Just like he'd dealt with losing his mum as a child. He'd cope. Perhaps he wouldn't thrive, but he'd manage.

By the time they got to Glenbriar station just after six in the morning on Saturday, he'd barely slept a wink.

Hayley peered at him, bleary eyed. 'I'm going home and straight back to bed.' She stifled a yawn.

'I think I'll do the same.'

'Thanks for letting me tag along. It's been an awesome week.'

'It really has. And I apologise if I overstepped on Thursday night. Maybe I should have kept my thoughts to myself.'

A little smile grew on her face. 'I'm glad you didn't. I enjoyed it.'

He nodded but said nothing else. Sure, he'd enjoyed it too, but didn't want to say so. It would only lead to trouble and push him to places he was afraid to go. With a brief wave, he headed to his car, and she went to hers. He sat for a long moment in the driver's seat before finally heading home.

Sitting opposite his boss, Hugh Sterling, on Monday morning, Oliver kept his face impassive as he watched Hugh read over his letter of notice for the second time.

'Well, I'll be sorry to see you go,' Hugh said. 'Between you and me, you're by far the best lawyer here.'

'Thanks.'

'But I understand the need to spread your wings. This is too small a place for someone with your talents. I'm surprised you've stuck with us this long, if I'm honest. What about your current cases? I'm especially worried about the Camelle one.'

'I'll see that one through as far as I can. If we don't get a settlement after the next court date in January, I'll have to pass it to someone else, but I'm quietly confident we can win this time.'

'Alright, good.' Hugh steepled his fingers and gave Oliver a strained smile. 'I'm truly sorry to see you go. It'll leave a big gap here that'll take some filling. I was hopeful I could hang on to you until Denise retired and I could have offered you a partnership.'

Oliver frowned. Denise was Hugh's wife, and they'd run the practice together for ten years plus, but Denise was only around fifty. 'I didn't think she was close to retiring.'

'Age-wise, she's still got years left, but she's not enjoying it as much anymore. She's already looking to cut back her hours. She wants to get more involved in the community and run clubs and things. But we don't have a timeline or anything, so it's a bit pie in the sky. It's not like I can offer you anything concrete in the hope you'll change your mind. It could be another few years.'

'I see.' Oliver wasn't sure it would work anyway. The business was well-known as Sterling Family Legal. Would they change the name if he became a partner? Sterling and Wright Family Legal had a neat ring to it but was that what he wanted? He tried to think about it objectively, imagining he didn't have the London job. Did he really want to stay in Glenbriar even with a part-nership? None of the options neatly filled the hole in his chest. Something was always missing. Maybe the dream job didn't really exist. They all had pros and cons. Perhaps the change in itself was all he needed.

He'd messaged both Finlay and his dad before the meeting with Hugh to tell them about the job. His dad hadn't replied yet. No surprise there. He often took days to reply to messages, if he bothered at all. Even though Oliver could see he'd read it, he didn't expect anything.

But there was a message from Finlay.

FINLAY: Wow!!! Congratulations. But no way! How can you go live in London?

Oliver raised his eyebrow. Seriously?

OLIVER: Says the man who was planning on going to Dubai for three years!

FINLAY: Yeah, I know. A bit rich coming from me. But I was only going to Dubai to run away from the mess I'd made of things here. At least that's all cleared up now. I'll miss you! Who will I go cycling with?

OLIVER: Aidan?

FINLAY: It won't be the same. Still, I'm happy for you. I think you'll rock it in London. You've outgrown us. Just make sure you get a two-bedroom apartment, as I know Genevieve will want to visit. She loves London. So there'll be no keeping us from coming.

London prices were so ridiculous he wasn't sure he would find anything big enough, but he appreciated the good wishes. Oliver reread his messages. They gave him a weird sense of belonging. Someone here cared and would miss him.

What about Hayley? Would she come to London with Finlay? Probably not and maybe just as well. Why could he not stop thinking about Hayley? *Screw it.* It had always been hard not to, but now it was downright impossible. All day, she was never far from the top spot in his mind, pushing her way in like she had some claim on him.

When he left that afternoon, his eyes almost popped when he saw her waiting outside the office again. Had he summoned her just by thinking about her again?

'Hey.' She gave him a cheery wave.

'What's up?' he said. 'You don't work on a Monday, do you?'

'I've not been at work. I was in town having a coffee with my cousin, Willow. We've chatted all afternoon. I'm on my way home and I thought I'd hang about here and see if you came out.'

'Why?'

'Because I want to talk to you.'

'And have you forgotten about phones and messenger?'

She pulled a face. 'Obviously not, but I was passing anyway. It's nice to talk face-to-face, you know?'

'Is it?'

'Oh, for heaven's sake, Oliver! You need to lighten up a bit.' She did a quick scan around. 'Maybe fooling around with me wasn't a good plan, and you made a sensible choice, but why not get together with someone else?' She prodded him. 'It might stop you from being so uptight.'

'I'm not uptight and I don't need to be set up.' He narrowed his eyes.

She was smirking. 'Did I say I was going to set you up? Though I do know a lot of people.' She tossed her hair over her shoulder.

Oliver loosened his tie. *Her hair, Christ.* He mustn't dwell on it. And how dare she call him uptight? Had she hit too close to the mark? She couldn't know it had been a while since he'd been with anyone. But his private life was none of her business.

'I don't care if you know a lot of people. I don't need a setup.'

'Fair enough.' She gave him a thorough once over. 'But I know a lot of people who wouldn't mind. One in particular.'

Was she talking about herself? Or did she have a friend who'd been eyeing him up? That thought made him grind his teeth... whereas if it was her...

'Is this why you're here? To set me up?'

'No. I have other matters to discuss with you. I saw a flyer for this in the café. Look.' She pulled a folded piece of paper from her pocket.

Oliver read the headline: *Banquet and Ballroom Weekends at Thistle Lodge – cook your own banquet and learn to Scottish country dance like a pro.*

'Why are you showing me that? I don't want to cook my own banquet or go dancing. It sounds awful.'

'I meant for the sten.'

Oliver just held back from groaning audibly. Back for two days and she was going on about the sten already. London suddenly looked very appealing.

'I contacted the people running it,' she said, 'and they said we could go up for a taster session before we committed to anything.'

'You feel free to do that, but I am not ballroom dancing.'

She rolled her eyes. 'Ok, whatever.' She stuffed the piece of paper back into her bag. 'I guess I'll just book something and get on with it. You'll be in London, wrapped up in your own world anyway, so what does it matter? You're too big for us now, I suppose. All of this too provincial for you? And why should you care about your best friend's wedding? You've got Nathan now and lots of other city mates. Why don't you just fuck off to London already and forget about us?' She stalked off up the street.

Ouch. Oliver ground his teeth and forced a breath, but a pang of something else trickled through him. Would it really be so bad to help her or at least show a little enthusiasm for what she was doing? Of course he cared about Finlay's wedding... Though really, his actions hadn't shown that at all. He rubbed his forehead and sighed. He'd been a total arse about all of it.

His phone buzzed, and he pulled it out, half expecting to see Hayley's name again, but it was his dad. *Wow*. That was a speedy response for him.

DAD: Good to know. When do you leave? Does that mean you're not coming for Christmas? Need to know soon so we can sort everything out.

Oliver's teeth were in great danger of wearing away completely. Was that all his dad had to say? Not a word of congratulations or anything to suggest he was proud, even sad, to hear the news. Nothing. Just cold empty words. Even if his mum was still around, this could still be the norm – for Dad anyway. Surely his mum would never be so aloof and unconcerned. She'd always been so warm, so affectionate and giving. What must it have been like for her being constantly pulled down by a gruff and cold-hearted man like his dad? His mind leapt back to what he'd just done to Hayley. *Shit.*

He had no right to throw stones when he was just as bad himself.

CHAPTER FIFTEEN

Hayley

December

The tinkling opening of Mariah Carey's 'All I Want For Christmas' had started playing in the salon. Decorations gleamed on the window display and the naughty elf had moved from his place among the conditioner bottles to swinging from one of the lights. Hayley teased out Willow's extremely long blonde hair, half hearing bits of conversations over the drone of hairdryers. Everyone seemed to be chatting about how organised – or not – they were for Christmas.

Except Hayley.

She and her cousin were talking about the subject that she always seemed to be talking about. Weddings. Even at Christmas, she was the one who got the clients getting ready for a wedding, either their own or as a guest. And hen parties too. Part of her was flattered that so many came to her to have their hair done, but the constant wedding chat was taking its toll. A headache loomed. Not that she'd ever let it show, especially when Willow was so happy. Hayley would never rain on her parade. She loved Willow and was delighted for her. Willow deserved to be happy. She was so sweet and lovely. Her husband-to-be was a famous weather presenter and both he and Willow had made a name for themselves over the past year as a presenting duo on a TV show, *Destination Forecast*. It still made Hayley smile to think her wee cousin was on TV when she'd been such a little mouse as a child. How she'd come out of her shell.

'And you're sure you want this much off?' Hayley held up the section she'd marked off with bands. Willow could afford to have six or seven inches taken off and still have very long hair, but once the cut was made, there was no going back.

'Yes. It needs a proper tidy up. It's got completely unmanage-able.'

'Ok. As long as you're sure.' Hayley took out her scissors and trimmed the sections off. 'This will still give you plenty of length to play with. And it'll be easier for the stylists on *Destination Forecast*.'

'Yeah, one of them said it was far too long for the curls she wanted to put in it.'

'I can style it in curls today if you want. You'd suit some loose barrel curls.'

'Ok, sounds good. Do you think I should wear it loose for the wedding too? Most people go for updos but I don't know if I really suit them. Do they make me look really short?'

'Not at all. If I did one high on the back, it could give you the illusion of more height. But Willow, it doesn't matter what size you look, you'll be beautiful anyway. You always are.' And Marcus loved her, no matter what.

Willow smiled at her in the mirror. 'You've always been the best cousin.'

'One does one's best,' she said with a fake curtsey. 'Now, let's get this shampooed. I can neaten the edges properly when it's wet.' She led Willow to the back of the salon and got her seated at one of the sinks. Willow had cerebral palsy and sometimes found sitting at these sinks awkward, but with the footrest she was usually ok. 'Is this comfy enough?'

'It's fine just now,' Willow said.

'Just shout at me if you need to move.' Hayley shifted around behind and started the water.

'How are Finlay's wedding plans going?' Willow asked, as Hayley splashed water on her hair. 'Have you booked a sten yet?'

'Oh, don't get me started on that. I'm running out of time. I saw something that looked cool. It's a weekend in a big house where you get cooking lessons, and everyone cooks the evening meal. Plus, you get to do ballroom dancing and cocktail making. I thought it sounded really good.'

'It sounds like lots of fun. I'm sure Genevieve would love it. She's really into cooking, isn't she?'

'Yes, she is.'

'Why not book it then?'

'I think I will. The organisers said I could go up on Saturday night and have a sneak peek at what they do.'

'Sounds perfect.'

Hayley let out a sigh as she squeezed a blob of shampoo onto her hand and began massaging it through Willow's hair.

'What's wrong?' Willow asked.

'Nothing. It's just annoying because I was meant to organise this with Oliver. You know, Finlay's best man. But he's being so...' She let out an exasperated huff.

Willow grinned. 'I guess he's not as enthusiastic as you.'

'He's about as enthusiastic as a slug in a coma.'

'Oh dear.' Willow put her hand to her lips to stifle a laugh.

'Honestly. I thought we'd made some progress. I didn't tell you before, but I went to London with him a couple of weeks ago.'

'Did you? You said you'd been to London, and you showed me all the photos when we were at lunch last week, but I didn't know you were with him.'

'Well, I wasn't *with* with him. As in, we weren't *together* together.' Hayley started the water again, rinsing out the shampoo.

Willow frowned and Hayley knew she was making no sense, but it was impossible to describe what had happened in London... Particularly some of the things that had happened.

'What I mean is,' Hayley said. 'He was going anyway and had a spare bed in his hotel, so I went along too so I could go to the Hair Show. We just travelled together out of convenience.'

'Ah, ok.'

Hayley would like to say they'd shared food and transport costs, but they hadn't. Oliver had paid for everything when they were together. She was pretty certain it wasn't coming off his expenses either. This was exactly what caused the conundrum. Sometimes he was so generous, other times he was a complete grouch.

'Anyway.' She massaged the sweet-scented conditioner into Willow's scalp. 'He seemed much nicer in London than usual. We got on fine, but the minute we got back here, he started being grumpy and unconcerned again. And completely disinterested in the sten. Which I suppose I just have to accept, but it's so irritating.'

'Maybe he hates living here and wishes he could move to London,' Willow said. 'Maybe that's why he's happy there.'

'I think you're right.' And he'd get his wish soon.

'I'm not sure I get why Finlay is his best friend. They don't seem at all like each other.'

'They even each other out.' Was that actually true? Finlay had always stood by Oliver, but did Oliver really do much in return? Not that friendships had to work like that, but if it was always one-sided, what was the point?

'I'm glad Finlay's back to his old self again. He always looked so depressed when he was with Elise,' Willow said.

Hayley lifted the nozzle and washed off the excess conditioner. 'Yeah, that was not good. I'm cross with her for hurting so many people, but she's still my friend.'

'Do you ever see her?'

'Not that often anymore.' Hayley helped Willow sit up straight and wrapped a towel around her wet hair, before leading her back to her seat in front of the mirror. 'She's moved to Glasgow, but I keep in touch.'

It was hard to sever connections completely with someone who'd been a friend for so long. Hayley just wished Elise hadn't messed things up with both Finlay and Aidan, two people Hayley cared so much about. At least things had worked out for them both. She could only hope things would work out for Elise too.

She brushed out Willow's hair before neatening the edges, drying, and styling it with the wand. Willow beamed at the finished result, moving her head from side to side and admiring it.

'You're amazing,' she said to Hayley. 'I don't know how you do it.'

'I've had years of practise.'

As Willow got up, Hayley gave her a hug. 'Good to see you. We'll have another catch up soon.'

Colette, the salon assistant, took Willow to the desk to pay, as Hayley's next client had arrived.

'Hi, Nina. How are you today?' Hayley asked her.

'Great thanks. Well, kind of.'

'Oh. Is something wrong?' Hayley combed Nina's strawberry blonde hair. Nina had been her client for a year or two since moving to the town, and Hayley didn't know her that well, but she liked to hear about her client's lives and took a genuine interest in them. She always tried to remember as much as possible about everyone. Nina was married to a high school teacher who worked in the same school as Finlay, and Nina herself worked just up the street in a furniture upcycling store named Wood 'n' Chic.

'I'm pregnant,' Nina said half apologetically. 'We've just started telling people and weird smells have been making me sick, so I thought I better let you know in case I throw up all over the salon.'

Hayley chuckled. 'Oh gosh, congratulations! But should I get you a bucket? We've got the wee bowls we mix up the colour in, if you want one?'

'That might actually be a good idea. If it gets really bad, I'll leave. I don't want to put people off.'

'Don't worry.' Hayley went to fetch a plastic tub from the back, just in case. Her heart raced a bit. Nina must be about the same age as her or just a little older. Everyone of her age seemed to be getting married and having families while she was still single and didn't even have a casual date for the weekend, never mind anything else. Sometimes, she inwardly despaired at the state of her life.

As she brushed out Nina's hair, she watched for any change in her skin colour or expression, but her cheeks stayed rosy, and she smiled and chatted as normal. Her Christmas plans included visiting her brother, who used to be a professional footballer. Hayley had never heard of him, though she was sure both Finlay and her dad would know exactly who he was. Finlay was sport daft and her dad had *Mastermind*-level knowledge when it came to football teams and players.

'What team did he play for?' Hayley asked. 'So I can tell my dad.'

'Celtic,' she said. 'But not for a while. He was in a car crash and couldn't walk for a long time, let alone play. Then he quit and now he and his wife run a health retreat on the Isle of Mull.'

'Oh, wow.'

'Yeah, they've just had a wee boy a few months ago. They already have a wee girl, who's three, so they're thrilled. It's exciting to think this time next year I'll have a baby cousin for them.'

'Aw, that's lovely.' Hayley smiled as she always did, but bitterness settled in her heart, making it burn. She didn't like that sensation or want it. *I'm not like that.* And she certainly wouldn't direct it at Nina or anyone else. She was bitter with herself and her inability to find someone who wanted to do these things with her.

Her mind drifted back to Oliver and the kiss. Just one kiss. That was all it was. But what a kiss. Why couldn't she have had a kiss like that with a nice local guy who was happy to live up here forever, get married, have kids, grow old together, and have a happy life with her? Why did she have to have it with a grumpy guy who didn't do relationships, didn't want to stay up here and was moving to London in a month's time?

'Right. I'll get Colette to shampoo you and I'll do your cut and blow dry after.'

Nina went off with Colette, and Hayley took a moment to nip into the back room and grab a drink and a snack. She checked her phone and noticed a message from Oliver. She frowned as she opened it. What did he want? She wasn't sure she wanted to know because she didn't really want to talk to him. The grouch.

OLIVER: What do people wear to ballroom dancing? Please tell me it's not frilly shirts and trousers so tight my eyes will be watering and I won't be able to sit down... Because if you still want me to come with you to check out the sten venue on Saturday night, I will... As long as I don't have to wear the aforementioned costume.

OLIVER: P.S. Jumpsuits are a no too. As is any form of leotard or tights.

OLIVER: P.P.S. and leather.

OLIVER: P.P.P.S. and definitely no body glitter.

Hayley pouted and tried not to laugh. Was this his attempt at a peace offering? Did he think she was that easy to bring around? The laugh burst. Ok, screw it, she was that easy. Part of her wished she'd managed to stay mad at him for longer, but hey ho. She'd never been able to hold a grudge, especially when her mind was preoccupied with creating mental images of Oliver strapped into leave-nothing-to-the-imagination tights and a ruffled red shirt open down the middle to reveal his gorgeous, toned abs covered in a smattering of dark hair and a liberal dusting of gold glitter.

HAYLEY: I appreciate your change of heart and you are of course welcome to come with me... However, I must express my severe disappointment at your lack of enthusiasm re. the costumes. I think your lack of love for body glitter is frankly disturbing and also distresses me, as now I'll have to think of something different to get you for Christmas. I was so sure the Lush Shake 'n' Spritz sparkle was the perfect gift too... Dang it!

She sent it, wishing she could see if it brought a smile to his face or if he impassively dismissed it.

After she'd seen to Nina, she had two more clients, and it wasn't until she'd finished them she could check for a reply.

OLIVER: I'm tempted to wear it now just to see your reaction if I did.

She raised an eyebrow before replying.

HAYLEY: I'd rather see you in the tights.

OLIVER: Yeah? You've already seen me in my cycling shorts. I think you get the picture.

That was enough to bring colour to her cheeks, and she was glad she was safely in the backroom where no one could see her.

HAYLEY: Wear them then and I'll bring the sparkle!

OLIVER: You always do. See you on Saturday.

Her heart skipped a beat, and she reread the message. Was that a compliment or a sarky remark? With him, it was so hard to tell. He was so hot and cold she couldn't figure him out at all.

Chapter Sixteen

Oliver

Oliver pulled his coat on over his black shirt and black jeans. Thankfully most of his wardrobe consisted of dark clothing, so finding something that looked dressy and 'dancy' wasn't too difficult. This shirt was a good fit, and he'd deliberately left a couple too many buttons open. Not his normal style at all, but Hayley would appreciate it. At least he hoped she would. Not because he wanted her ogling him – well, maybe he did a little – but she'd enjoy the joke. Hopefully. Anything to cheer her up and show her he wasn't a total bastard. He had several amends to make, and this was just the start.

He grabbed his keys and headed into the dark driveway. His house was on the outskirts of Glenbriar, in one of the new estates that had popped up. The town was already quite a bit bigger than it had been when he was a boy. His father's farm, where he'd grown up, was to the south, less than a fifteen-minute drive away. As Oliver got into the car, he squirmed like a sharp needle had prodded him in the ribs reminding him of his failings. He hadn't visited his dad for ages. Fifteen minutes away, and he hadn't made the effort. What a shit son he was. He started the engine, letting out a long sigh. It wasn't like his father had made an effort to visit him either. Oliver had moved into this house just over a year ago and his dad had never been here.

He pulled out of the drive and into the cul-de-sac past the other houses, all with wreaths on the doors and large trees in the windows. Some had fairy lights on the fences or around the eaves and one or two had huge, garish lit-up reindeer. His was the only house that had nothing. What was the point of putting up a tree and decorations just for him? He flicked on the wipers to push off some sleety rain as his thoughts drifted to his mum. The hollow pang in his chest intensified. She'd have loved this place, loved the fact he could afford a big house in such a good part of town. Was she up there somewhere, watching? Maybe she'd be sad to see him living here all alone and, despite having three spare rooms, never having anyone to stay.

Hayley had given him directions to her flat – not that he need-ed them. She lived not far from his office, at the top of the main road and one street back. This street was full of higgledy-piggledy buildings, all built at different times and with random extensions that didn't match the fronts. Some of them had bizarre roof extensions that were like outsized dormer windows, and Hayley's flat was apparently in one of them. It must be tiny inside, but Oliver wouldn't get to find out, as Hayley was waiting on the street as he pulled up.

'Hi.' She jumped into the car, wearing a long coat, and as she leaned over to close the door, the side of the coat slipped, revealing a flash of something glittery. Oliver smirked as he eased the car forward. She really had brought the sparkle, as he knew she would.

'I should apologise,' he said.

'Oh yeah?' Hayley rubbed her gloved hands together.

'Yeah. I should have been more proactive.'

'Well, consider yourself on probation. We'll see based on how you get on tonight if I forgive you or not.'

Best he could hope for under the circumstances.

'Does this car have heated seats?' she said. 'I'm freezing.'

'It does.' He pressed a button on the console. 'It's chilly out there, isn't it?'

'I hope you're wearing something scorching hot to compensate.' She cast him a little smirk.

He rolled his eyes and chewed on his tongue. Thank god she didn't hold a grudge. He'd been expecting to grovel a lot more. 'I might be.'

'Ooh, such a tease. Do you know where you're going, by the way?'

'Thistle Lodge. It's in the satnav.'

'Have you been there before?'

'No. Have you?'

'I did a wedding up there a while ago. It was one of the stylists and we all went up and did the hair as a wedding present. It's an awesome place. Looks like a castle and it has so many rooms I got lost.'

'And are we gatecrashing someone's sten tonight?'

'Don't be ridiculous. As if. This is the first one they've run, and it's not a sten this time but an "experience". A mix of people are going so they won't all know each other. The woman on the phone said we could join in with the dancing if we wanted before the guests went for their meal, or she would just show me around.'

'So we didn't actually have to do any dancing?'

Hayley chuckled. 'I didn't want to spoil your fun.'

'You know, sometimes I really don't like you.'

'Interesting... Does that mean other times you do?'

He grunted in response because he wasn't going to answer. Experience in court told him not to give away anything that valuable.

'Was that a yes or a no?'

'It was an "I'm not answering that question".'

'Sometimes I really don't like you either.'

'Touché.'

'So...' She lounged back into the lovely warm seat, turning her head to face him. 'What made you change your mind about coming tonight?'

'This is worse than a cross-examination.'

'Well, you should be used to it then, so answer the question.'

'Seriously?'

'Yes.'

'I'm upholding my duty as best man.'

'Finally.'

'Indeed. I realise I've got some catching up to do, but let's face it, you wouldn't have liked it if I interfered too much. You're the one who's good at organising.'

'Stop trying to make your lack of action sound honourable.'

'Lack of action? I'm not sure exactly what kind of action you were looking for.'

'I could ask you the same question. I draw your attention to exhibit A... London.'

He shook his head with a wry smile. 'That is not what I meant. And I wasn't the only one. That was a mutual decision.' He let out a huff. 'We even managed to take the sensible road... Somehow.'

'True.'

Though he wasn't sure how. The fire in his soul still roared at the thought of pulling Hayley close. Would that happen tonight at this dance? The need to have her close to him was so overpowering, it was alarming. But he was the master of control.

The gates to Thistle Lodge were all lit up and an enormous Christmas tree marked the main entrance. Oliver parked beside the rows of other cars and he and Hayley made their way to the entrance. Their breath plumed in front of them in the cold air.

'I assume there's a bell or something we ring.' Hayley peered around the door. 'Or should we just go in? It's not a hotel so I don't know if there are staff at the front of house.'

'Try the door.'

She turned the doorknob and the heavy door opened onto a porch area with a large set of glass doors. An intercom was mounted on the side. Hayley pressed the button and they waited. Invisible energy was buzzing around them, pulling him towards her but stinging him if he got too close. The insatiable desire burned so strongly it was agony. How could he keep resisting? Did the attraction still exist for her?

A woman wearing a black shirt and trousers approached and opened the door.

'Hello,' she said. 'How can I help you?'

'I'm Hayley McBride. I've come to chat about the possibility of holding a sten party here. The person I spoke to was called Tiffany Barlow.'

'I'll get Tiffany for you if you wait here.' She disappeared through a door at the side of the large entrance hall.

Oliver scanned the luminous decorations and winter foliage draped everywhere. 'Who owns this place?'

'No idea. Someone who rents it out all year round for stuff like this.'

A dark-haired woman strode through the door in a bright red dress with matching lipstick and beamed at them.

'Hayley, hi. So pleased you could make it. I'm Tiffany.'

Hayley shook her hand. 'This is Oliver Wright.'

'Hi, Oliver.' Tiffany shook his hand too. 'So, this is Thistle Lodge. I think you said you'd been here before.'

'I have.'

'You'll be semi-familiar with the layout then, though it's quite a difficult place to try and remember everywhere.'

'It really is.'

Tiffany and Hayley between them had smiles so dazzling they were both brighter than the lights on the twenty-foot Christmas tree extending all the way up the middle of the grand staircase.

'We'd be delighted to hold your sten here as part of our Banquet and Ballroom experiences,' Tiffany said. 'Though I have to warn you, we don't have a lot of dates left in your timeframe. That's not me trying to be salesy or pushy, it's just a fact. If you follow me, I'll give you a quick run through of what we do and then I can take you into the ballroom where the class is happening. You can join in if you like and get a feel for things.'

Oliver clenched his fists, forcing back the torrent of desire bubbling inside him. There was someone nearby he'd very much like to get a feel of. Her long hair coiled down her back in perfect loose curls, and he itched to reach out and run his fingers through them. What was it about her hair? A weird fetish? Whatever it was, he couldn't stop looking at it as they headed down the corridor.

Tiffany led the way down a flight of stairs. 'Down here is where we have the kitchens. The cookery classes are all led by, and overseen by, a trained chef. During the tourist season, this house is let out to big parties, which is why we're organising these events throughout the winter months, but it means the kitchens are in tiptop shape, because the house parties usually bring caterers.' She pushed open swing doors, and they entered a Downtown-Abbey-worthy kitchen fitted with all mod cons but in period style. A woman in chef's overalls was checking one of the ovens. The warm aromas were overwhelming after the cold outside and the airy corridor. Oliver undid his coat buttons, remembering his half open shirt just in time. He kept his coat together, ensuring nothing was on show.

'Genevieve would love this,' Hayley said to Tiffany. 'She's the one we're organising the sten for. We're just the bridesmaid and best man.' She waggled her finger between herself and Oliver.

'Ah, I see. And does she enjoy cooking?'

'Absolutely. She has a cookware range on sale at Duchan Fayre and she's got a cooking channel on the socials, so yes.'

'Does she? Amazing.' Tiffany's eyes widened, and she laid her hand on her chest. 'Well, this will be perfect. Once the food is all cooking, we leave it to the chefs, and we have waiting staff to serve up the dishes the guests have made.'

'Who chooses the menus?' Oliver asked.

'It's entirely up to you. We have some examples you can work from or if there are particular dishes you want, then that's fine. You just let us know so we can source the ingredients. We like to source everything as locally as possible, though obviously that's easier with some things than others.'

They left the kitchen, and she led them back into the hall, then up the stairs.

'We have bedrooms for up to thirty-six guests.'

'That many?' Hayley goggled at her.

'Yes, it's a big house. Some of the rooms are larger than others. There are a couple of family-style rooms that take four and not all the rooms are en suite, but it would be up to you how you divide them up. We also have live-in accommodation for staff on the ground floor, so there's someone on call twenty-four seven if your party needs anything.'

'It all sounds brilliant,' Hayley said.

Oliver nodded and said nothing. She was obviously sold on it and, objectively, he knew Finlay and Genevieve would enjoy it too. If he could just muster some enthusiasm. All this seemed so excessive for just one night.

Life's too short.

The words played in his head. What was he saving his money for? Why not be extravagant now and then if it brought happiness?

'Now, let's get you into the dancing.' Tiffany beamed. 'We call it a class, but really it's just a chance to have some fun. You learn some of the dance steps, then we break to freshen up and have dinner, then after dinner, we have the dance and hopefully everyone wants to join in with some of the steps they've learned.'

She checked her watch. 'It's a quarter to six, so there's fifteen minutes left before they stop.'

Music played somewhere nearby as they went down another corridor and Tiffany pushed open a large wooden door. Inside was an old-fashioned ballroom with a wooden floor and thick oak panels. Couples were making their way around as a man called instructions.

Tiffany approached him and he stopped to listen to her. He smiled broadly and waved to Hayley and Oliver. 'Join in when you're ready,' he said. 'Don't worry about perfection. Remember, that goes for all of you. Feel the music and the beat. Dancing starts in the heart and the feet come later.'

'Just leave your jackets here.' Tiffany returned to them. 'I'll be here until the end of the session and once everyone's out we can discuss the booking if you want.'

'Sounds great.' Hayley pulled off her jacket to reveal a silvery pink dress, covered in sequins, all shimmering and floaty. She looked as stunning as ever. Oliver removed his coat too and before he'd considered where to put it, Tiffany had taken it. Hayley's eyes lingered on his open shirt, and she grinned, then she took his hand and led him to the floor. Why was his palm so hot? Hopefully, it wasn't sweaty and horrible. *Oh Christ.* Why the hell were all the couples in such a close clinch?

'Here we go,' Hayley said. 'Grab on...' She raised an eyebrow. 'Love the shirt, by the way. And these jeans are nice and tight. Glad you followed the memo.'

'Yeah.' Before he could second guess himself, he put his hands on her hips and tugged her close. Her eyes were on his as he pinned her to him, and she made no attempt to move or change her position. All she did was land her hands on his shoulders.

'Is it just me, or were our bodies made to fit each other?' she whispered in his ear, and it sounded sultry and provocative.

'That's the point of male and female anatomy.'

'Oh, shut up,' she said, possibly louder than she meant as she winced slightly through her laugh. 'Trust you to come out with something like that.'

He couldn't take his eyes from her: holding her this close was dangerous and exciting. 'Trust me, indeed.'

'Actually, I do.'

'Good.' He tugged her even closer. Now they weren't dancing; they were just two people in a room, rubbing against each other, wallowing in the touch, the friction, and that scent – the mingled softness of Hayley's light perfume, his spicy cologne, and that unmistakable aroma of desire. He gently tangled his fingers in her hair, keeping his palms on her back.

'I trust you to do what's right.' Her words landed like a cool breeze across his hot, bare neck.

'And what would that be?' he replied into her ear, letting the scent of her shampoo fill his lungs. It hit his senses, rocketing through him, straight to his groin. Her body tremored in his arms. If she was already this responsive...

He took a deep breath, trying not to get ahead of himself.

'Right now, everything I know is wrong feels right and every-thing right feels wrong,' she said.

'I know exactly what you mean.' He gently steered her around the floor, vaguely following the instructions, but mostly just using the moment to keep her pinned to him. 'The question is, are we willing to cross to the dark side?'

'I feel like I'm halfway there already.'

'Me too.'

'This is wonderful.' The instructor clapped his hands. 'Bravo to our newcomers. You really have the feel for the music.'

'I can definitely feel something,' Hayley muttered. 'Though I'm not sure it's music.'

'It's definitely not,' Oliver said, and she smirked.

'Such passion,' the instructor continued. 'It oozes from every pore. Great work.'

'If this is work, I'm in the wrong job,' Oliver murmured.

Pure lust had taken control. But was it just that? He wasn't a monk, and he'd had his share of hookups before, but that kind of lust wasn't this kind of lust. He wasn't just chasing a quick physical release. Ok, so that was part of it, but Hayley mattered too... Like really mattered. Everything he wanted hinged on her wanting it too – and really wanting it. Desiring it. Desiring him. He needed to know this was important to her. Which also meant admitting it was important to him. And it was, damn it. *She* was important to him. Long-term relationships weren't his thing, but what about in the short term? Maybe this was what he needed before he went to London. Something casual but more meaningful than a one-night stand with a stranger.

'Hayley.' Saying her name seemed to electrify her even more, and she came out of a sort of dreamy trance, her eyes snapping back to him.

'What?'

'I need to tell you something.'

'Go ahead.'

'I do like you sometimes. Most of the time really.'

'You've got a damn funny way of showing it.'

'I know, and it's because it's sensible to keep my distance. I can't stop myself being attracted to you, but look what happens when we're together.'

'We fit? Is that what you're saying?'

'I don't really know.'

She raised an eyebrow. 'I see two options. One, we do nothing. Two, we act. Get it out of our system.'

He huffed out a laugh and kept his eyes on her, keeping her close. 'I'm leaning heavily towards two right now.'

'Me too.'

'But those boundaries I mentioned before. They still stand. Because we don't have a future together. I know you want that. Not with me. But you deserve it with the right person. I won't string you along. It isn't fair.'

'I understand the rules and I'm willing to play.'

'Then let's get out of here,' he said.

'Seriously? Right now?'

'Can you wait any longer?' He raised his hand to her face, his fingers a little shaky, and gently brushed a strand of her hair to the side. He tucked it behind her ear, burning to lean in and kiss her.

'Not really. But I need to see Tiffany.'

'Let's find her and tell her this place and this experience are the best things ever and we'll book right away. If she needs a deposit, I'll pay it. Anything. Let's just get out.'

Had the desire to be alone with someone ever burned so strongly before? He was pretty sure it hadn't, and he needed to do something about it, and soon, before he spontaneously combusted.

CHAPTER SEVENTEEN

Hayley

Tiffany went through the booking system with Hayley. Why did it seem like it was taking forever?

Oliver stood by her side, his heat palpable. She wanted to jump his bones right here and now. The fire in her chest would reduce her to cinders any second if she didn't.

Keep it together!

She had to make a quick phone call to Finlay and Genevieve to check which of the two remaining dates were most suitable for them. They plumped for the one at the end of January, which was just before Oliver left for London.

She smiled at him as she okayed it with Tiffany. He wasn't getting off the hook with this. Just as he wasn't leaving her tonight without something. Her low-level craving had bounced to high-level need on the desire scale. She had to have him. Why shouldn't they have a bit of fun before he left? She understood the rules. The physical charge was so high it was a shock not to see sparks zipping around them. Where was the harm in it? She was allowed a bit of lust too. Even if she hankered after Mr Right, it didn't mean she couldn't enjoy a meaningless hookup with Mr Wright.

But you don't want it to be meaningless, the warning voice in her head reminded her. It could shut the fuck up because she was doing this.

Tiffany took all the details, and Oliver flashed his card to pay the deposit. He may be terrible at organising, but he was epic at paying for things. Quite the gentleman really. Hayley couldn't wait to find out if he was a gentleman in the bedroom. Her insides coiled at the thought of his hot body close to hers. She'd had her share of sexual encounters. Some had been better than others, but none were much to write home about. She was still waiting for that transcendent experience with someone. After her one kiss with Oliver, she had high hopes for this. But was that a good thing? What if it was so good she wanted more?

Who cares!

She'd made up her mind.

Tiffany let them out the front door and waved them off. Bitterly cold air bit at Hayley's neck and the moon lit the garden beyond. She saw the outline of a statue, possibly a lion, and the silhouettes of bare trees. She and Oliver didn't talk as they crunched across the gravel area to the car. Oliver reached the passenger door first and put his hand on it. Total gentleman. But why wasn't he opening it? It was so cold.

'Open the—'

He let go of the handle and put his hands on her waist again, like he'd done when they were dancing. 'I can't.' His voice was breathy.

'Can't what? Open the door?'

He pinned her against the car with his hips. 'Can't wait.'

She let out a giggle. 'Well, you'll have to. I'm not doing anything out here. In a car in December? Have you lost your mind?'

'Yes. I think I have.'

Wow. This was new. Wild and horny Oliver had arrived. If only she'd known she wielded such power before. She slid her gloved hands around his cheeks and pulled his face closer. 'One kiss, Oliver. We managed it before. Just one more now, then we wait until we get somewhere warmer.'

'My house.'

'Do you have a Christmas tree?'

'Does it matter?'

She raised an eyebrow.

'Is it a deal breaker?' He threaded his fingers into her hair and groaned. His hard body pressed against her and even through their layers of clothing, she felt how turned on he was.

'Maybe.'

'Then we'll have to make a detour into Perth and the twenty-four-hour Tesco, so I can buy one. Can you wait that long?'

'You complete Scrooge.' She clapped his cheeks, then let her arms glide around his neck. 'But I'll let you off.' Pressing her lips to his, she reacquainted herself with his mouth and it was a divine sensation, soft and warm. But this time he was hungry and deepened the kiss quickly, holding her so close she could hardly breathe. These bloody coats were annoyingly in the way.

'Hayley,' he said, though it was more of a groan, and it made her insides purr.

'Yes.'

'I've wanted to do this for a long time. I just didn't want to admit that I wanted to.'

She smiled and held his face again. 'You're funny. You don't mean to be, but you are.'

'I'm being serious.'

'I know.' Maybe she should try it too and think objectively about what they were doing, but she couldn't. She also didn't want to analyse how she'd felt about Oliver in the past because lingering not far from the forefront of her mind was the niggling thought that maybe she'd always wanted this too... Maybe she'd secretly hoped for a lot more. Again, she pushed that thought away.

Oliver let go of her with a suddenness that made her wobble. He tugged open the passenger door. 'Let's get home.'

She hopped in and pulled her wool coat around her. The car was icy, and the windscreen was frozen over. Oliver's car didn't need de-icer or elbow grease and a scraper, however. He flicked a few buttons and almost at once, the ice started to melt. Warmth seeped up Hayley's spine as the heated seats kicked into action.

Of course he had a flash car. It went with his smart suits and lawyer lifestyle. Soon he'd have a London pad to go with it.

'Where do you stay?' she asked him.

'On the Fairways Estate.'

Typical! One of the most expensive areas of the town. 'Oh fancy,' she said. 'I went for dinner at the golf club last year when they were still building it.'

'The last house was just completed this summer.'

'Aren't all the houses there enormous?'

'They're reasonably sized, yeah.'

'So... You live in an enormous house, by yourself?'

'Correct.'

'Do you have lots of people coming for sleepovers or something?'

'No.'

'Should I be honoured? Or don't you want me to actually sleepover?'

'I want you for everything.' His voice was hoarse. 'Please stay if you want to. I won't be in a hurry to get rid of you.'

She smiled to herself and suppressed a little thrill in her nervous system. *He wants me for everything!* Everything? What exactly did that mean? She didn't want to pin anything to that comment because it could just be lust talking.

Darkness closed in around them, and Hayley was very glad not to be driving. Other than the tunnel of light from the headlights, it was completely pitch black. Oliver had seemed quite a casual driver on the way there, but now he was leaning forward, and his knuckles were tight on the wheel. Was it stress from the dark... Or desperation to get home?

Eventually, the lights of Glenbriar twinkled into view and they coasted past the first houses in the village. Oliver indicated and turned up the hill to his left, past the road that led to Hayley's flat and on towards the golf course. Just before that was the entrance to the Fairways Estate.

'Is this definitely ok?' Oliver said.

'Very definitely.' Hayley couldn't imagine going home now. Her body and soul needed to make this connection.

Beautiful decorations twinkled from every house until they pulled into the one at the end of a small cul-de-sac. One side must back directly onto the golf course, though it was too dark to see. The streetlamp shone across a sweeping mono-blocked driveway and a large white house sat back from the road. It had a red brick trim and a large garage to the side. The roof from the floor above sloped right down to the garage doors that were magically opening. Hayley glanced at Oliver and saw he had a small remote in his hand.

'Oh my god. This house... It's gorgeous.' And huge. Why the hell did he need somewhere this big? This was a family home. A fleeting image crossed Hayley's mind. She was living here, pushing a stroller and walking a small child to school. That was what should be happening in a house like this, though it wouldn't be her. Or Oliver. He'd presumably be selling this place when he went to London.

'Yeah. I like it. I know it's too big for me, but I like the location. It's peaceful and even though it's on an estate, it feels private.'

'Will you sell it when you go to London?'

'I'll have to. The money I get for this place won't stretch to much down there. House prices in Glenbriar sometimes look like silly money, but they're nothing compared to London.'

She got out in the garage and rubbed her hands together. Part of it had been walled off.

'What's in there?'

'My home gym.'

Hayley couldn't hold back her laugh. Finlay had once told her Oliver didn't like the gym and preferred to work out at home. She'd imagined him lifting weights in his bedroom or possibly having a rowing machine stowed under the bed, but a home gym? *Wow!* He was something else.

He locked the car and opened a side door. 'Let's get inside. It's cold in here.'

They entered a utility area and Oliver took off his jacket.

'Shall I take yours too?'

'Sure.' Hayley handed it to him. In her floaty dress, she was suddenly cold and exposed. When Oliver opened the door into the kitchen, her jaw dropped. It was show-home perfection with crisp grey cabinets and polished oak worktops.

'It's warmer in here.' Oliver led her into a large living area with minimalistic soft furnishings all in neutral colours but with a rather surprising pop of purple on the cushions and the curtains. 'I'll just hang up your coat.'

Hayley sat on the large L-shaped sofa, trying to shake off an odd sense of something... Was it shyness? She'd half expected them not to make it into any of the downstairs rooms and to have started ripping off clothes the second they got out the car, but clearly Oliver had other plans.

'Would you like a drink?' he asked, returning a moment later. 'I'm not good at cocktails, but I have gin or prosecco.'

'Gin and tonic would be lovely.'

While he was making the drinks, Hayley sat rubbing her bare arms and looking around the room. A cream-coloured, free-standing woodburner was in the corner and she wished it was on as it was still a bit chilly. What had possessed Oliver to buy a house like this? He reappeared with two glasses and sat down beside her.

'Do you like gin too?' she asked.

'I do actually.'

'And you have prosecco? You must be expecting guests.'

'I keep it for Finlay and Genevieve. You know how much they like it and they're the only people who really visit me.' He took a sip of his drink, and Hayley did the same.

'I thought you were going to ravish me the minute we arrived.'

His lip quirked up. 'It was definitely a possibility.'

'What stopped you?'

'Manners.'

'I thought you'd maybe changed your mind.'

'No.' He raised his hand and cupped her cheek in his palm. 'I haven't and I won't, but I want to do this properly.' He put his glass on the coffee table, leaned over and kissed her slowly on the cheek, his fingers lacing into her hair.

Hayley sighed and closed her eyes.

A phone vibrated somewhere.

'Bloody thing,' he muttered, shifting, and pulling it out of his back pocket, then placing it next to his glass on the table. 'It's been doing that all the way back.'

'Why don't you check it?'

'Because I don't care who it is. Nothing is going to spoil this.' He traced a fingertip around her earlobe and seemed to study her for a moment. She might have stopped breathing. His look held so much reverence, his wide, dark pupils boring into her. 'You really are beautiful. You bring the sparkle to everyone.'

'Even you?'

'Even me. I didn't think I wanted it, but I do. I need it.' He smiled. It started as an Oliver lip quirk but spread until it was wider than she'd ever seen before.

'You're smiling,' she said, and it made her smile too.

'Your fault,' he said. 'I'm always smiling on the inside when I see you.'

'I don't believe you. You look far too grumpy for that. But I'll let you off because I like it when you smile on the outside.' She abandoned her glass and moved closer. He took her face in his hands, ran his fingers into her hair and kissed her gently but firmly, even a little desperately.

Her hands found his shirt buttons, and she tried to concentrate, but the force of his mouth was overwhelming and so hot. Sparks were crackling through her, making her lose her mind and her sense of self. She groaned and poured all her energy into kissing him back. Fierce and wanton. His fingers were clamped into her hair. She could hardly breathe.

His phone buzzed again and this time it was constant, like someone was calling.

'Seriously,' he growled, pulling away. 'That is getting switched off.'

'See who it is first, just in case.'

He looked like he wasn't going to bother, then he frowned at the screen.

'Who's Carla?' Hayley peered at it too, and for a split second, an icy hand gripped her chest. She knew the name from somewhere. Where? A woman calling Oliver at this moment... A shiver ran through her.

'She's my stepmother.'

The icy hand let go and Hayley breathed again. Of course, that was why she recognised the name, though she hadn't heard much about her for a very long time. 'Why is she phoning you?'

'No idea. I don't think she's ever called me before.' He swiped up the screen, and Hayley saw several notifications. Most of them seemed to be from Carla too. Oliver opened a message thread and Hayley saw the first message clear as day.

Neil's been in an accident. He's gone in the air ambulance. Not looking good. You'll want to get to Ninewells soon if you want a chance to say goodbye.

'Neil...' Hayley stared at Oliver. 'Your dad.'

Oliver nodded.

'Ninewells... That's in Dundee.' She screwed up her face. 'You can't get there quickly. It'll be an hour at least and... When was that message sent?'

'An hour ago.'

'What if he's already...' She couldn't finish the sentence. Oliver's face had gone ashen. Was that why Carla was phoning? To tell him his dad had died?

He closed his eyes and dropped his head into his hand. 'I don't think I want to know. If he's gone then... Oh god. How can it have happened to him too? I've been a terrible son. My mum would never have wanted it to be like this.'

Hayley put her hand on his arm. Tears welled at the back of her throat, but she forced them back. Nothing she said could make this better, but she could be here. 'Hey.' She moved onto her knees and pulled him into her, letting his head rest on her chest. She stroked his face and was shocked to find the skin around his eyes damp. Her heart split clean in two. She leaned in and kissed his forehead. 'I'm here,' she said. 'For as long as you need me.'

CHAPTER EIGHTEEN

Oliver

Dad was gone.

That was the logical conclusion. But Oliver couldn't bear to hear it. It was so much easier to pause life and just exist in this moment. Of course that was wrong. But everything about the situation was wrong. The magnitude of it was too huge to comprehend. Only Hayley's arms around him gave him any relief. Her strength was his. She was holding him up until the moment he was ready to face the truth. He didn't remember anyone doing this after he lost his mum. Just silent tears in an empty room. Unheard wishes and a heart so shattered he'd never found all the pieces to put it back together.

'It's ok,' she said quietly. 'You'll get through this.' Her soft hair tickled his cheek and he leaned into it. Her beautiful hair, now stained with his pathetic tears.

'Yeah. I know.' He made to pull away, but her hold on him was so comforting, it was easier not to. And really, what place could be better than this? Their relationship had changed so much recently. But what he'd attributed to lust didn't seem to fit this situation. This definitely wasn't lust. And yet it seemed just as significant and powerful, maybe even more so. This was new; something he hadn't felt before or, if he had, not for a long time.

'Oliver.' Hayley's voice was hushed, almost a whisper, landing close to his ear like a warm breeze. She gently smoothed his hair with her fingertips. 'Maybe you should call Carla.'

Her words broke the spell, and he shifted, pulling away from her. Why was he being like this? He brushed his hand under his eyes. Was he crying? Since when had he let emotion get to him like this? It wasn't like he was exactly close to his dad. But his dad wasn't the reason he was feeling like this. Indirectly yes. But this was bigger. He'd failed his mum. She'd never have wanted her family to be broken like this. Even if she and her husband had never had the best marriage, she wouldn't have wanted this.

'I'm not sure I'm ready to talk to her yet,' he said, surprised at how hoarse his voice was.

'But you don't know for sure what's happened. What if he's not...' Hayley stroked his arm.

'Either way, there's nothing I can do from here.'

'If he's alive, you can go and see him.'

But he's not. His heart told him he was already too late. No last goodbyes. Same as with Mum. She'd gone out one evening and never came home. Sometimes, even now, he imagined the door opening and her walking in, saying she'd just got lost. Stupid. He knew that, but he couldn't help it. 'He wouldn't have wanted that anyway. I just get in the way.'

Hayley looked like she was grinding her teeth, perhaps irritated by his bullishness, but he didn't want to hear the cold truth. Memories swooped around like evil spectres, reminding him of the horrible moment he'd heard of his mum's death. How could he face that again? Denial was so much easier.

'Here.' Hayley leaned forward and lifted his phone from the coffee table.

'What are you doing?'

She pressed the button on the side to wake it and the password screen appeared. Behind it was a notification, and Oliver turned away in case his face automatically opened the screen.

'I can see the start of the message without opening it,' she said. 'Your dad is stable. That means he's alive... Oliver?' She put her hand on his knee, but he couldn't look at her. His mind was racing all over the place and his heart was on a rollercoaster, unable to settle on an emotion.

'Oh god,' he said. 'I don't know what to do.'

'Phone Carla or just go straight to Dundee. So what if you're in the way? He's your dad too. My dad has a partner who has other children. I don't see him very often these days and he spends more time with his partner's kids than me, but so what? He's still my dad. He's still there if I need him or want to chat. I get how it can feel strange, but families are. I meet so many people in the salon and, honestly, no one has a "normal" family. Everyone has someone who has messed up something somewhere. Your dad's alive and I'm sure he'll want to see you.'

'You'd think, wouldn't you? But my dad isn't like that.'

'Maybe not on the surface. But remember what you just told me about smiling on the inside? Maybe he's like that.'

Oliver was sure he wasn't, but didn't want to argue the point further.

'How about I come with you?' Hayley said.

'Why?'

'For moral support. It might make them behave with more manners around you if I'm there.'

He let out a dry laugh, and it broke some of the tension gripping his body. 'Maybe. But do you really want to go all the way to Dundee for that?'

She tilted her head and gave him a sad little smile. 'I want to help you and if that means going to Dundee, then let's go.'

'You want to help me?' He raised an eyebrow.

'Yes, because strange as it may seem, I actually care about you.' She gazed into his eyes and the rush of heat surged back. *Pull her close and keep her here. With me.* But the time for that was lost. He could have her company however, if he just agreed.

Let her come. Let her help. You don't have to do everything on your own.

'Thank you. And yes, please come with me.' He got to his feet.

'I will.' She patted his back, and he tried not to let the touch affect him. He collected their coats and handed hers over.

They got into his car, and he pulled out into the night.

'You'll have to fill me in on your family, so I know who's who. Finlay might have told me, but I don't remember, sorry.'

'It's fine. I don't see very much of them, and Finlay won't have seen them for years. Carla is my dad's wife. They have two daughters. Ava is twenty-two and Sofia is twenty. That's it really.'

'Ok. That doesn't seem too complicated.'

'And yet, it is.'

'Like I said, all families are.' Hayley brushed something from her leg. 'My family is totally messed up on paper and sometimes the politics are tricky, but you know what? We just get on with it. My dad has had quite a few partners since my mum and every time he does, we have to get used to them and their families. It's always awkward after a breakup.' She gave a little shrug.

'My parents didn't exactly breakup. That's not the issue I have. After my mother died, my father basically abandoned me and once he met Carla, his life with her became the all-important thing. Their family life together was what mattered, and I was just an extra. They couldn't have made it more obvious I wasn't wanted. I'm old enough to not let it bother me now, but it was tough growing up like that.' The words rolled out uncensored when he didn't normally talk about any of it.

'I can see why it would bother you and it sounds horrible, but I'm sure deep down your dad cares about you. I expect after your mum died, he was lost. It's not an excuse, but I can imagine he found it really hard.'

'Of course he did, because he had no idea how to live on his own. She was like his servant, and once she was gone, he was clueless. He'd never even cooked a meal.' His voice rose, but he didn't care.

'Oh, Oliver.'

'Yup. That's what we're talking about.'

The roads were reasonably quiet, and they made good time on the A90. Hayley chattered most of the way, and Oliver listened. Whether she spoke words of wisdom or was just filling silences, it didn't matter. The sound of her voice was soothing, plus it distracted him from thoughts of the impending meet up with his stepmum and half-sisters. As they circled the car park at Ninewells Hospital, searching for a space, Oliver wasn't able to shake off the squirming sensation in his gut. Any moment now, he would be face to face with three people he usually tried to avoid. And then there was his father. What state might he be in?

He locked up the car and took his phone from his pocket. Carla didn't even know he was coming. He hadn't replied to her message or returned her call, which would cement him as a terrible human in her eyes. Her message was still the last one open, and he fired off a reply.

OLIVER: I'm at Ninewells. Where are you?

'She probably won't reply.' He thrust his phone back into his pocket. 'She'll be too mad at me.'

Hayley patted his arm. 'Maybe, but she might be relieved that she doesn't have to deal with this alone.'

'She's not alone. She has two daughters.' Two daughters she always made a point of showing off and letting everyone know what great company they were. How she'd taken them to theatre shows, the ballet and on extravagant holidays since they were little. Oliver wasn't particularly interested in any of those things, but there had been no equivalent activities for him and that was where it grated.

'But they're still young and they won't know what to do either.'

The sterile scent of the hospital turned Oliver's stomach. Hospitals equalled bad news and almost certain death in his mind, even though he knew that was silly. He hadn't set foot in one since Carla had given birth to Sofia twenty years ago. His thirteen-year-old self hadn't liked it then either. He recalled that time too, standing near the door watching others cooing over the newborn and offering their congratulations to Carla.

He approached the reception desk and explained his reason for being there. His lawyer brain kicked in and spouted the details with surprising clarity.

The receptionist clicked at the screen, then gave him the ward number.

'This place is a maze,' Hayley said. 'I'm glad I don't work here. I'd never find my way around.'

'I'm glad I don't work here full stop,' Oliver said. 'I can't imagine anywhere worse.'

They made their way down a wide corridor, following the signs over doors. The squirming sensation in his gut was getting worse the closer they got. Seeing his dad in whatever state he was in would be dreadful, but facing Carla and his sisters was making it even worse. If it was just him and his dad, he could handle it, but Carla didn't hide her dislike for him at the best of times.

'This is it.' Hayley stopped outside a ward.

He peered in the small window on the door. 'I see them in there.'

Hayley leaned in to look too.

'Stand back.' He took her arm and tugged her. 'Don't make it so obvious.'

'Sorry.' She grinned. 'I can't help myself being nosey.'

'I noticed.'

'Are we going in then?'

'I suppose so.' He'd been so relieved to have Hayley keeping him company, he hadn't stopped to think what it might look like having her here. Would they assume she was his girlfriend? Did it matter? It wasn't like their opinions were that important to him. They might not even care enough to ask.

He pushed open the door before his thoughts got the better of him.

Carla's gaze flicked to him the second he stepped inside. Her eyes were red-rimmed and her haggard figure slumped on a chair replaced her usual poise.

'Hi.' Oliver approached the bed where a curtain was partly drawn, obscuring the view of his father.

'Hello,' Carla said stiffly. 'I didn't know you were coming.'

He glanced from her to his sisters, who were both on phones. Slowly he turned to the bed. His father lay still and asleep, strapped in bandages and wired to machines. Oliver's jaw clenched. Sure, he was glad his father had survived, but why couldn't his mum have lived too? Why couldn't she have been saved by doctors and machines? A soft touch on his arm reminded him Hayley was there too. Carla was looking at her, but Oliver didn't introduce them to each other.

'How is he?' he asked.

'He's stable, but the doctors want to check for possible internal injuries. They're running more tests.'

'Is he still out from an anaesthetic or is he concussed?'

'He's still tired from the anaesthetic. They want him to rest. All the obvious injuries have been treated. They had to operate on his shoulder. It should be ok but it could take years for him to be able to lift it properly.'

'I'll grab a couple more seats.' Hayley scanned around, then headed back to the door where there was a small stack of chairs.

'Who's that?' Ava pointed at Hayley with a nod of her head.

'Hayley,' Oliver said. 'She's a friend.'

Hayley returned with two chairs and plonked one down for Oliver, then sat herself on the other, in between Oliver and Carla.

'I'm Hayley.' She smiled around.

Carla nodded. 'Carla. These are my daughters, Ava and Sofia.'

Hayley gave them a little wave. 'This really is a nightmare before Christmas, isn't it?'

'It certainly is,' Carla said.

'Did they give you any idea about how long he'll be in for?'

'Not really. It depends on how the injuries have affected his brain.'

'Well, if you need anything, I'll give you my number. I know how busy it is at this time of year. I'd be happy to get your shopping or wrap presents or anything that would help. Just let me know.'

Carla's face said exactly what Oliver was thinking. Her jaw looked ready to hit the floor. Why was a perfect stranger being so nice to her? The thought was etched across her forehead along with, *who does she think she is?* Oliver's initial surprise at Hayley's words was slowly replaced with an internal smirk. Kindness cost nothing. Hayley was probably working on the assumption that Carla wouldn't want help from her anyway, but the fact she'd offered put her right up there as a kind-hearted soul and meant any mean-spirited remarks from Carla would appear even worse.

Oliver caught Hayley's eye and his lips twitched. She was such a kind person. Just like her brother. Finlay had stood with Oliver at school when he'd needed someone, and now Hayley was here for this.

'I, er, thank you,' Carla said after a moment. 'I suppose we won't know for sure until the tests are done.'

'Of course,' Hayley said. She smiled at Ava, who was gawping at her in the same way Carla had done when she first spoke. 'This must be so hard for you.'

'What?' Ava blinked like there might be some doubt as to who Hayley was addressing.

'Seeing your dad like this. Did you have trouble getting here?'

'No,' Ava said. 'We came with Mum.'

'That was lucky you were able to travel together. So... do you live at home or are you at uni?'

'I just finished uni in September. I did business studies, but I'm still working in a shop. There aren't really any jobs in the area I want to work in.'

'That's a shame,' Hayley said. 'What area is that?'

Ava gave a little shrug. 'I dunno.'

Oliver looked away, not sure if it made him want to laugh or roll his eyes. Neither was very kind, but it cemented his opinion of his half-sisters and how flaky they were. How typical of Ava to claim there were no jobs in the sector she wanted but not actually know what that sector was. He was quite surprised she'd finished her course at all.

'I completely understand,' Hayley said. 'It's so difficult to know exactly what to do or where to go with your career. Are you at uni too?' She moved her attention to Sofia.

'I'm at art college doing a design course, but we're finished for the Christmas holidays.'

'Oh wow, design. That sounds exciting.'

'It's ok.' Sofia's shoulder twitched a little.

'What kind of design?' Hayley said.

'Just like general design.'

'Does that include fashion and interior design?'

'A bit.'

'Definitely sounds enjoyable.'

Sofia looked like she might contradict her but didn't. Oliver fidgeted and rubbed his fingertips together, wondering if any of them would return Hayley's interest and ask her what she did, but that turned out to be a no. When Hayley stopped talking, they fell into silence, watching Neil or the clock.

After what seemed like hours but probably wasn't, some medical staff came along and wheeled the bed away, ready to run the tests. Sofia and Ava leaned on each other and closed their eyes. Carla had her head resting on the wall behind her seat and did the same.

Oliver glanced at Hayley and she stifled a yawn. Without speaking, they came to an agreement to emulate Sofia and Ava. Oliver rested his head on top of Hayley's and closed his eyes. She kicked off her heels and curled her stocking soles up on the seat behind her. They were still dressed for dancing under their coats. The surreal night wasn't over yet. This wasn't what he'd planned, but despite all the uncertainty surrounding his dad, something about this moment was beautiful. The sweet fragrance of Hayley's shampoo filled his senses and her warmth seeped inside him, saturating him with deep contentment and a weird sense that everything would be ok… even if it wasn't.

Chapter Nineteen

Hayley

What was that strange noise? Where was she? So many things were pounding around Hayley's befuddled head it was like being hungover. Was she? No. She hadn't drunk anything, but she had kissed Oliver. Like really kissed him. And what a kiss... But wait... That had stopped. More unfamiliar noises broke into her consciousness. Something warm was on her back and her cheek was pressed against a very firm pillow. Pillow?

She opened her eyes slowly. Ok, not a pillow. She was leaning on Oliver's chest. His hand was on her back, and she was curled into him. Shit. Had she drooled all over him? Blinking, she shifted into a comfier position and ran her finger under the corner of her lip just in case. He briefly glanced at her, keeping his arm around her, but she was aware his attention was elsewhere.

The hospital. Of course. They were still here. Under her coat, her sparkly dress had twisted at a funny angle and was not at all comfy. She sat up properly, moving out of Oliver's hold and trying to straighten herself out. What was happening? He let her go, but his hand came to rest on hers as she settled it on her lap. She linked her fingers with his, her heart filling with a desperate wish to make everything ok for him. Medical staff had repositioned his father's bed and were standing around either adjusting the machines or making notes.

'So, it's mostly good news,' a doctor said. 'The internal damage is just bruising. Some of it around his shoulder, neck and back will mean he needs to fully rest. He won't be able to work for some time.'

Hayley caught the expression on Carla's face; her wide eyes and turned down lips looked fearful. Oliver's dad was a farmer, and Hayley was pretty sure Carla couldn't do that job single-handed. Oliver wouldn't be much help. If he had farming skills, he'd kept them exceptionally well hidden, and in the unlikely scenario that he did, he had a full-time job anyway; he couldn't exactly give it up to go and work on his dad's farm. And he wouldn't want to. She knew him well enough for that to be quite clear.

'Hey.' She leaned over, still with one hand in Oliver's, and put her other hand on Carla's arm. 'I'm sure there'll be something we can do to help. I'm not a farmer, but there must be someone who knows what to do.'

Carla covered her mouth. 'I don't know where to start.'

'It'll be ok.' Hayley let go of Oliver and put her arm around Carla's shoulder. 'Oliver could find out about who can help.' She glanced over at him.

'What?'

'You could investigate what support Carla can get in this situation.'

'Oh... Yes.'

'Thank you.' Carla nodded and gave Hayley a weak smile.

Oliver was frowning, which was a fairly common expression for him, but Hayley could read his mind like an open book. He was wondering why she was being nice to Carla. Maybe it wasn't her place to interfere, but the woman seemed so desolate and lost. She hated seeing people hurting.

'Let me get your number.' Hayley took out her phone. 'Then you can message me if you need to. Once your husband wakes up, he'll be able to help too. He'll know people who can help.'

'Dad knows everyone,' Oliver said. 'And he's helped out lots of other farmers when they needed it. I'm sure someone will be willing to return the favour.'

'That's true.' Ava flicked her hair over her shoulder. 'He's always ploughing for Ian down the road, and he helped Gordon with the harvest just a couple of months ago.'

'Yes,' Carla said. 'Hopefully we can work something out.'

'You will.' Hayley released her and got to her feet. 'Does anyone want a coffee or anything? I'm going to get one.' Everyone except Oliver declined. He looked like he needed something to keep him going. Hayley slipped her shoes on and left the room. What would they talk about now she was gone? Would any of them speak at all?

The café had a short queue, and she wasn't away for long, but when she got back, Neil was awake. She slipped in beside Oliver and handed him his coffee, catching the end of a conversation that seemed to be proving him right.

'Yeah, yeah,' Neil said. 'I know friends and neighbours who'll help out and lend us farmhands to feed cattle when necessary.' He gave Oliver a funny look. 'I didn't expect you to be here. Does this mean we'll see you at Christmas? Or have we used up our quota?'

Hayley sat down with a sigh.

Neil frowned at her like he was about to say something, but returned his focus to Oliver almost immediately as Oliver shrugged a noncommittal response.

Hayley sipped her coffee. So much repair work was needed here.

An awkward silence ensued. Hayley usually covered gaps like this; it was a skill she'd picked up after her parents split when she'd been the peacekeeper. Since working at the hairdresser, she'd perfected it for dealing with tricky clients, but she found herself lost for words. No wonder Oliver didn't want to spend Christmas with them. That would be a special kind of torture.

'I don't know you, do I?' Neil turned his gaze to her.

'Hayley,' she said. 'Finlay's sister, you know, Oliver's friend.'

'Ah, right.' He gave her a quizzical look, then turned to Oliver like he expected more information.

'I'm glad you got through this,' she went on. 'Only sorry to meet you under such difficult circumstances.'

'We should go.' Oliver checked his phone. 'Unless you want to stay.'

'I don't mind,' she said, though she didn't really want to hang about.

Oliver got to his feet. 'Well, I'm glad you're ok. And if you want me to investigate anything regarding work cover, let me know.'

Neil opened his mouth and Hayley was certain it was to scoff or make a snippy comment, but Carla spoke first. 'Thank you. We will. And Hayley, it's been very nice to meet you.'

As Hayley and Oliver made their way out, she heard Neil say, 'Who is she anyway, and why was she dressed like that?'

Oliver let out an audible sigh as they left the ward. 'I'm so sorry.'

'Don't be. At least it turned out ok... Kind of.'

'I can't thank you enough.'

'You don't need to thank me at all.' Though she wished she dared ask him if this was the end to what they'd started yesterday. This wasn't a good moment to bring up the subject. 'These heels are killing me,' she said. 'And I need to change out of this dress.'

'Yeah. I appreciate what you did in there.'

'Anytime, but let's hope there isn't another time like that.'

Their conversation was muted and vague as Oliver drove home, partially from a lack of sleep, but also because she wasn't sure what to say under the circumstances.

When he dropped her off at her flat, he gave her a wistful look. 'Thanks again.'

'If you need me to visit again with you, give me a call,' she said as she got out of the car.

He linked eyes with her. 'I can't thank you enough.'

'Don't. Just let me know if you need anything. And call Finlay. He'll want to know too.'

'I will.'

That wasn't how she'd planned to spend the weekend. Her days were so eaten into with the Christmas prep that she had no idea when she'd fit anything else in, but if Oliver called, she'd try.

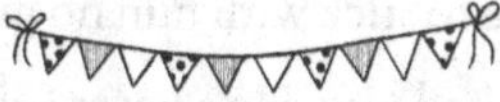

The following weekend, she had an early Christmas dinner with her dad. Finlay and Genevieve travelled to Dundee with her. She always loved seeing her dad, even if his new partner, Liz, was a bit overbearing. Dressed in a saucy Mrs Claus outfit, she had Finlay rolling his eyes within seconds.

'Her dress sense is mental,' he said. But it went well with her equally tacky taste in Christmas decorations. She looked like she'd been to a home store and bought something of everything.

Tinsel tat was everywhere, along with flashing lights and annoying singing Santas and Grinches on every shelf.

Hayley had got used to her over time and while none of this was to her taste, she'd learned to laugh it off. Genevieve was probably inwardly horrified. Her parents put on the ultimate tasteful Christmas. But she was grinning too.

'That was bad about Oliver's dad, wasn't it?' Finlay said, as they sat in the living room. Dad was at his built-in bar, pouring drinks, wearing his Santa hat.

'Yeah. It was.'

Finlay shook his head and sighed. 'I'm so fecking glad you were with him. He'd have gone off the rails otherwise.'

Heat burned in Hayley's neck. Oliver had told Finlay she was there? On what pretence?

'Honestly, I remember when his mum died. We were only eleven. Mum told me to stick with him no matter what and I did, but jeez, he was in a bad way. He's never fully recovered. I think it's like some kind of PTSD.'

'So horrible.'

Finlay put his arm around her. 'Thanks for helping him. I know he's been a dick to you at times, but he must be coming around a bit. Weren't you visiting the sten location together when he got the call?'

'Yeah. At least that's all booked up.'

'It sounds amazing,' Genevieve said.

'Ah, yes, the sten.' Dad came over with drinks. 'Liz and I are looking forward to it.'

Finlay exchanged a glance with Hayley and they both tried not to laugh. Dad loved parties, but sometimes he was wild.

This was just the first half of her family Christmas.

Christmas proper was spent with her mum. She'd texted Oliver loads to check he was ok, and he seemed to be, though he didn't seem to want to see her. Well, she had to take that on the chin. Being with her mum was always fun enough to forget her worries. Finlay and Genevieve came over for Christmas day and Genevieve's parents also dropped by.

Hayley messaged Oliver as they sat around the living room, opening presents.

HAYLEY: Merry Christmas! Hope you're having a good one.

She saw the bouncing dots almost straight away.

OLIVER: Thanks. Merry Christmas to you too.

Well, that reply told her nothing. Was he alone? Had he decided to go to his family? When she'd asked about his dad previously, he said he was out of hospital and doing ok, but that was it.

What had she expected? She could ask Finlay, but she didn't want to sound over-curious, and he'd probably tell her anyway if something really bad had happened. So no news was good news, right?

To add to all the Christmas mayhem, her friend Felicity was getting married on the twenty-ninth of December. Hayley headed to her house to do her bridal hair before the wedding. It was bright and frosty, perfect conditions for beautiful winter wedding photos.

'You look stunning,' Hayley told Felicity as she stroked her hair into an elegant chignon, leaving only a delicate, coiled strand free. Her chief bridesmaid was Briony, the owner of the Loch View Hotel, and Hayley did her hair next. Briony kept her hair shoulder length and wasn't keen on wearing it up, so she fixed it to the side with a sparkly flower clip.

Next, she worked on Felicity's other bridesmaids, her two younger sisters. Both of them were equally pretty as their big sister and also had beautiful long blonde hair. When they were all done, Hayley packed up her stuff, changed into a long pink dress, fur coat and fascinator, and headed for the beautiful Glenbriar Church. The path to it was covered in ice crystals, not enough to be treacherous, but enough to make it sparkle like it was encrusted with glitter. Hayley smiled. How perfect was this? The wedding photos would be so gorgeous, with the pretty old stone church building and the River Briar in the background.

She made her way inside and shuffled into a pew next to a familiar face.

'Hello,' she said to Zach Somerton, Briony's husband.

He nodded at her. 'Hi.'

'And how's little Leia?' Hayley smiled at the cute little toddler on his lap and tickled her under the chin. She had the sweetest little grin and masses of beautiful curls, not unlike her dad, though

Zach's hair was almost black, and Leia's was much lighter, like her mum's.

'She's good,' Zach said in his low American accent. 'She's dressed as a bridesmaid, but she's keeping me company for the service. It's easier this way.'

'She looks so adorable in that dress.' It was all frills and lace with a little fur bolero.

'Yeah.' Zach kissed her head, and an emptiness struck deep inside Hayley, an ache she longed to be filled. Would it ever be her? Would she ever find someone to be with and to have children with? Someone who would be a doting dad, like Zach. Someone like Gavin, Felicity's husband-to-be, who stood at the front dressed in a kilt and sash, looking confident and dapper, only betraying a few nerves as he adjusted his cufflinks once too often while chatting to his best man.

Where's the one for me? And why did her mind race back to Oliver every time she thought about this kind of thing? Even if Oliver was 'the one', he wanted different things. He didn't want to marry, have kids or stay in Glenbriar, but she did. She wanted a life here with everything familiar. Getting married and having kids was a life goal she didn't want to give up. The simple answer was to forget Oliver and get on with living her life, but forgetting Oliver wasn't as easy as all that.

The soft background music changed, and people shuffled in their seats as the minister made his way to the front. Hayley watched him shake hands with Gavin before the bridal march started and everyone stood up. Felicity's surname was Swan, and really it suited her so much. She glided down the aisle almost like she was on water. Her fishtail dress fanned into a train at the back that rustled along behind her.

'Mumma,' Leia called as Briony passed. She turned and waved to her daughter.

Zach lifted Leia up high and whispered in her ear, 'Wave to Mommy.'

By the time Felicity reached the front and Gavin took her hands in his, Hayley's eyes were bursting with tears. Weddings always did this to her, but this was worse than normal.

When the ceremony was over, she hung around outside with the other guests, throwing confetti and chatting with Fee McKenzie, a colleague of Felicity's and a hair client of Hayley's.

'What a stunning ceremony.' Fee rested her hands on her young daughter's shoulders. 'Felicity is just beautiful.'

'She really is,' Hayley agreed.

'And Rosie just loved her dress, didn't you, darling?'

Little Rosie nodded and twirled her hair around her finger. She must be about eight or nine and Hayley remembered being that age, looking at brides and loving the dresses. She'd even bought bridal magazines as a teenager. She gave herself a mental shake. Seriously she needed to stop thinking like this.

Normally, she was all in for celebrations and events, especially the dancing, but her heart just wasn't in it. Finding people to talk to and dance with wasn't a problem. The fact none of them were Oliver was. *Why the hell can I not stop thinking about him?*

She pulled her phone from her little bag while people at her table chatted and others danced to 'The Macarena'. She had loads of messages, but none from him. Not that she expected any. Still... She fired off a message.

*HAYLEY: Hi. How are you? Hope your dad's ok. What did you do for Christmas? Finlay and Genevieve are totally looking forward to the sten. What about you? Maybe we could dance again *wink emoji*. I'm at a wedding and nobody has moves quite as good as us *more wink emojis*.*

She smirked as she sent it. Maybe if she hadn't had quite so much prosecco, she wouldn't have.

'Hey, Hayley,' a man's voice said.

She checked up to see a tall, swarthy guy with a crooked grin looking down at her. Brann, a local builder and friend of Finlay's from the tug-of-war team. He was handsome in a rough-around-the-edges way and he had a bit of a reputation for making the ladies in the town swoon – her mother for one, even though he was way too young for her. Though, come to think on it, she wasn't sure what age he was, but he was smiling right at her.

'You ok?' He sat down opposite her.

'Fine.' She aimed for her most casual smile and took a sip of her drink.

'Yeah?' He cocked his head like he didn't really believe her. 'You look a bit lonely sat over here all by yourself. You're normally in the thick of things, giving it your all on the dance floor.' He put out his arms and did a silly wiggle.

She laughed. 'Yeah. I should be, shouldn't I?'

'Only if you want to. Are you here on your own?' He scanned around like he was expecting a partner to materialise out of the woodwork.

'Yup, just me on my ownsome.'

'Me too. Fancy a dance with a sad old lonely guy?'

She held her hand to her mouth, barely hiding her giggle. 'You really know how to sell yourself, don't you?'

He held up his hands. 'What you see is what you get.'

'I'm sure you're not that old, but yeah, I'd like a dance.'

'Well, let's just say the next big birthday has a four in it and it's fast approaching.'

'That's not old.' Hayley got to her feet and Brann followed.

'How's Finlay?' he asked.

'Getting ready for his own big day.'

'Ah yes. I got an invitation to the sten. Sounds like quite a do.'

'I hope so. It took long enough to arrange and to find something we thought everyone would like. Are you coming to it?'

'Sure, sounds like a laugh, though I hope there are better chefs there than me. I'm not sure people will want to eat what I cook.' He led her to the floor.

'Same. I hope the cooking is very step-by-step and completely foolproof.'

Abba's 'Dancing Queen' came on and Brann smirked at Hayley. She burst out laughing.

'Ok, this dance will be mad.'

Brann took her hands, and they did their own thing, which actually wasn't too bad. Oliver wouldn't have managed this level of wild… And there she went again, thinking about him. Where the dance with him had been hot, this was just crazy, but a lot of fun. Brann twirled her and they jived, laughing the whole time.

'That's cheered you up.' He smiled as the song came to a close. 'You looked a bit sad sitting there.'

She fanned her face. 'Yeah, thanks. That was fun.'

'You missing somebody, by any chance?'

'Is it that obvious?'

His lip quirked at one corner. 'Kind of. You just looked how I felt. The way you were texting. I dunno. I thought maybe there was someone you wished was here. It's not easy being on your own at things like this.'

His lopsided grin held a touch of melancholy, but at the same time it was obvious why women swooned over him. He wasn't just a looker; he was thoughtful too.

'Well, thanks for saving me.'

'You don't look like you need saving, just someone who might like to talk about random shit with another person all on their lonesome…'

'Sounds like the ideal plan.'

He grinned again. 'So, how do you know the bride and groom?'

'I'm Felicity's hairdresser. How about you?' she fired back as they sat back down.

'I'm their builder.'

'What are you building for them?'

'A house.'

'Oh yeah. I forgot they're building their own house. Or I should say you're building it for them. Is it amazing?'

'I hope it is when it's finished.' He pulled a face. 'The plans are ambitious and this is my first really big project. My business has expanded and I'm doing it with family now. So, it's a bit of a test. Nerve-wracking too, because I want it all to be perfect for them.'

'I'm sure it'll be great. You've got a lot of experience and I've only ever heard good stuff about you.' Though she wouldn't repeat half of it to his face... Like the stories of bored housewives hiring him to fix minor issues just so they could ogle the man at work.

'That's a relief anyway.' He laughed. 'Shall we get another drink?'

'Why not?' She picked up her bag and went to the bar with him. As they waited for drinks, she pulled out her phone and checked her messages. Her heart skipped a beat as she saw Oliver's name on the screen.

'Good result?' Brann said as she glanced at him.

'Let's see.' She opened the message and read.

OLIVER: Hey. Sorry, I didn't reply properly to your other messages. Christmas isn't exactly my favourite time of year. I went to Dad's, and he's doing ok. Frustrated more than anything that he can't really do much. To say I'm looking forward to the sten would be over-exaggerating, however, that said, I am looking forward to seeing you again. Maybe I'm crazy, but I miss you. Enjoy the wedding.

She stared at the screen.

'Well?' Brann handed her a drink.

'He misses me.'

'Result.' Brann clinked his glass on hers.

It was beyond unexpected. But where did it leave her?

Chapter Twenty

Oliver

January

Oliver zipped up his overnight bag and adjusted his shirt collar in the long mirror in his bedroom. Between packing up his life and arranging his caseload so he could leave work without feeling guilty, he hadn't had a spare moment for anything over the festive period. Christmas Day had been the usual strained affair, though he'd sensed an unusual softening in Carla. He put that solely down to Hayley.

Today was the first day he would see her since the hospital trip and it would be back at Thistle Lodge... Perhaps a repeat of their dance was on the cards. Oliver took a deep breath. Restarting something with Hayley was a thought never far from the front of his mind, but doing anything with so many people there – especially Finlay – didn't seem sensible. Not that any of it was sensible. More like an addiction. He just wanted to see her, breathe the same air and exist in the same space as her, even if it was only for a short period. And it would be exactly that because his days here were numbered.

How often had he thought about contacting her and asking her to come over in the last few weeks? But he couldn't. Using her like that was unfair. She'd probably be mad at him and with good reason. He'd been deliberately uncommunicative. He needed to retrain himself to not be dependent on her. Those few times he'd been with her had been so wonderful he'd wanted more and more. He couldn't swear nothing would happen this weekend – she always had that effect on him – but if it did, he could legitimately walk away because in just a few weeks, his life would be in London, not here.

The cold winter air bit into his skin as he stepped out of the house and locked up. Soon he'd be locking this door for the last time. He hadn't put it on the market yet. His job came with an induction period and while he was certain it would all go fine, it seemed safer to keep the house for another month, just in case. Glenbriar was a popular place to live, and properties were sought after, so he had no doubt he'd sell it quickly when the time came.

A blanket of frost covered the town, and the surrounding hills wore crowns of snow. So beautiful. Sometimes he didn't appreciate the beauty on his doorstep.

He slid into his car and set off through the town. Maybe he should have offered to give Hayley a lift, but that was pushing it. She'd be with her family, and he needed to limit contact with her, not increase it.

The pale winter sun cast long shadows over the fields, and the frost-kissed landscape glittered. Wintery trees stood like sentinels.

Thistle Lodge was like something from a fairy tale with this wintery backdrop. Other cars were parked around it, and Oliver drew into an empty space. The silence was almost unnerving as he opened the boot and took out his overnight bag. A squirming sensation lingered in his gut. He hated things like this with so many people, lots of them strangers, doing something he had little interest in and being alone. Normally he didn't mind being alone, but being alone at something like this was like being exposed in the cold – a horrible naked feeling.

As he reached the hefty front doors, he took a deep breath. This was it. No going back now.

He made his way inside to the foyer full of olde-worlde charm and grandeur, with its tartan carpets and stag heads on the walls.

'Hello.' Tiffany Barlow stepped forward with a broad smile. 'Can I take your name, please?'

'Oliver Wright.'

'Of course. I remember you. You're the best man.'

'Yes.'

'Lovely. Now, let me check you off on the list.' She glanced down a clipboard and made a tick. 'I can direct you to your room and give you a brief rundown of activities, though I expect you remember from when you were here to visit.'

'Yes.'

'Fabulous. Did you have a pleasant journey? The roads seem ok despite the snow all around.'

'It was fine, thanks.' Oliver scanned the foyer, adorned with antique furniture and the grand staircase that led to the upper floors. People were milling around, chatting and laughing.

'Lovely. So, your room is on the first floor. It's called the Red Deer Room, and it's to your left as you reach the top of the stairs. If you want to drop your luggage off there and take some time to settle in, then that's fab. Everyone is getting together at eleven for drinks in the drawing room before a light lunch, followed by the cooking class.'

'Thank you.' He headed for the stairs and as he did so, heard his name being shouted.

'Over here, Oliver!' Finlay was waving from close to a heavy panelled door. Beside him was Genevieve, laughing with Hayley. Oliver's heart missed a few beats. Hayley looked incredible. Her long hair was looped up high in a fancy ponytail and she was dressed in tight grey jeans and a sparkly black off-the-shoulder sweater with suede heeled boots. She'd nailed smart-casual. And gorgeous, sexy bridesmaid-to-be too. Her eyes met his, and she gave a little wave. His stomach flip-flopped.

Blinking, he held up his bag to Finlay, then pointed up the stairs. Finlay raised his glass to indicate he understood, and Oliver headed up.

How hard was this going to be? Did his face betray him? He needed to master himself and make sure his impassive, in-court face was the only one that showed up. He opened the door to the Red Deer Room and stared. A four-poster bed. Bloody hell. Was this the universe telling him to make good use of this? The Red Deer Room sounded like a place stags came to rut, and a horny beast was rampaging through his system right now. *Fuck's sake.* Ten seconds looking at Hayley and this was what happened.

But she probably had her own room with a similar bed and maybe she didn't want to share with him. Their almost-night seemed a long time ago. Maybe the moment had passed with it.

He dumped his bag on the luggage stand and raked his fingers through his hair. How long could he reasonably stay up here before Finlay sent a search party? And what if that search party was his little sister? Better just to face it. He adjusted his cuffs, rolled his neck, and left the room. Downstairs, the group had moved into the drawing room. A conversational hum filled the space, accompanied by the clinking of glasses and the soft melody of a piano in the background.

He spotted Hayley before anyone else. His eyes zoned in on her like a targeted missile. She was still with Finlay, so he could approach her without needing an excuse.

'Hi.' He moved in beside her to the group chatting with Finlay and Genevieve.

'Hey stranger. You made it.'

'How could I miss it? You know I've been looking forward to it for so long.'

She smirked. 'Yes, I do. And I'm glad I've caught you so soon. You realise as the best man and chief bridesmaid we have to dance together… It's not optional. It's a legal requirement. As a lawyer, I'm sure you'll know that.'

'Yes. I see.' He nodded slowly. 'But I think you've understated the importance of that dance.'

'Have I?' She pulled her head back and frowned.

'It's not just a legal requirement. It's an essential for life.'

Her eyes widened and a grin spread across her face. 'Actually, you are right.'

'I always am.'

'Seriously? And you're big-headed.'

'No. I actually am always Wright. Oliver Wright.'

'Oh puh-lease.' She let out a long, fake groan. 'I suppose you want me to call you Mr Wright?'

'If you must, or you could make it Mr Always Wright.'

'"Mr right pain in the arse", more like.'

He looked away and caught Finlay's eye. That wiped the smile from Oliver's face. Finlay shifted from Genevieve and the people he was talking to and moved in beside the two of them.

'I hope you two aren't going to argue all weekend.' He draped his arm around Oliver's shoulder.

'Us?' Hayley put her hand on her chest and pulled an outraged expression. 'Why would we do that? We're best buddies.' She linked her arm through Oliver's and beamed. 'Aren't we… Always?'

Her tone let him know she was using the word *Always* as a nickname, not just as part of her sentence.

'Of course.'

Finlay raised an eyebrow and slapped Oliver on the back. 'Ok, nice try. I completely don't buy it, but if you can keep up the pretence this weekend, I'd appreciate it. Sorting out a fight between my wee sis and my bestie is not how I see this weekend playing out.'

'We'll be good.' Hayley turned to Oliver, batting her lashes. 'Won't we?'

'Are we ever anything else?'

'Well, you are,' she said, and Finlay folded his arms. 'But this weekend, we'll behave like the best of friends, lovers even.'

'What?' Oliver and Finlay said together.

Hayley laughed. 'You two are so easy to wind up.'

Finlay rolled his eyes. 'Do whatever you want, as long as it isn't fighting, because I love you both too much for that.' He stepped towards Hayley and pulled her in for a hug. Holding out his left arm, he said, 'Group hug?'

Oliver moved forward slightly and let Finlay pull him into an embrace, but only for a second. Finlay winked at him as he released Hayley. 'If either of you can keep Dad off the booze, then I'll be forever grateful.'

'No chance,' Hayley said. 'I think he and Liz were drunk before they got here.'

'Yeah.' Finlay rolled his eyes as he returned to Genevieve. Hayley glanced at Oliver, her wicked smile still in place. 'I'd call that a win... We have his blessing.'

'For what?'

'Didn't you hear what he said? He doesn't mind if we're friends... or lovers.' She waggled her eyebrows.

'Is that what you're planning?'

'I'd be lying if I said it hadn't crossed my mind.'

'Me too,' Oliver whispered. 'In fact, I can hardly think about anything else.'

'Good. Then let's keep up this little "act" for everyone's benefit, shall we?'

'Yes. Especially our own.'

Oliver put on an apron in the kitchen at Thistle Lodge and pulled a face. *Me in an apron?* Whatever next. He took his place next to Hayley. She grinned and eyed him up and down. 'Very tasty.'

'Shut up,' he muttered.

She lifted a spatula from the countertop and slapped it against her palm. 'Ready to whip up a storm, Mr Wright?'

'As I'll ever be.'

The head chef spoke, and Hayley stopped talking.

'Isn't this just a way of getting cheap labour?' Oliver whispered as the chef explained the format. 'I mean, come the end of the day, we're paying these people but essentially cooking our own dinner.'

'Shh!' Hayley slapped him playfully on the backside with the spatula and he jumped.

'What the—'

Hayley burst out laughing.

The head chef cleared her throat and continued. 'So, we want teamwork and creativity.'

'How much creativity?' Oliver muttered. 'This stuff has got to be edible.'

'I expect they have a supply of frozen stuff they can heat up just in case.' She glanced over at Genevieve and grinned. 'She'll be in her element here. This is the type of kitchen she works in at Duchan Fayre. Have you ever been up to see her doing a demo?'

'No.'

'She's really good. And her cookware range is stunning. She's so talented.'

'So are you.'

Hayley gave him a little frown as she lifted a large knife and some carrots. 'Thanks.'

'Why do you need a meat cleaver? If you're thinking about giving me another close shave with that, you can forget it.'

'Oh, ha ha.' She raised an eyebrow at it. 'This is just a knife.'

'You're going to use that for vegetables?'

'What would you use, master chef?'

'Maybe this?' He pulled a shorter, slimmer knife from the block.

'Whatever. Hand it over then.' She screwed up her face. 'Are we meant to peel these first?'

'Probably. Here, I'll do that and you can chop.'

'Nice teamwork, Mr Always Wright.'

'Thanks, Miss McBridesmaid.'

'So not funny.'

'Touched a nerve, did I?'

'Actually yes. I've been a bridesmaid way too often.'

He shook his head as he peeled the first carrot.

As they worked through the recipe, laughter and chatter echoed around the kitchen. Finlay was doing an impression of Genevieve on one of her social media reels. 'And once you've done that, go right ahead and try adding some avocados. Everyone knows they're my all-time favourite.'

'Shut up, cheeky.' She smacked him with a dishcloth.

'Accurate though,' Oliver said aside to Hayley. 'Doesn't she have a thing about avocados?'

'I think she mentions them once or twice. Oops.' Her attempt at casually brushing the chopped veg off the chopping board and into the pan had gone tits up and cubed carrots, potatoes and celery had rolled off everywhere. 'That's not as easy as it looks.'

'Seriously? Would you look at this?' Oliver scooped up some of the stray vegetables. 'This is worse than a home ec class at school.'

'Look at those show-offs.' Hayley pointed across the room to her cousin, Aidan, and his red-haired fiancée. 'Lilah's a great cook. I bet whatever they make is excellent.'

'And you don't think everyone will love our soup?'

'Possibly.' Hayley checked the recipe. 'Ok, we need spice.'

'We sure do.' Oliver lifted the portable rack and set it between them.

'Um... Do you mean—'

A loud clatter made everyone turn around. At the far side of the room, a couple collapsed laughing and bent over to pick something up.

'Ok.' Oliver frowned in their direction. 'Whatever they're making, I don't want to try.'

'That's Brann.' Hayley smiled across at him. 'He's funny... and sweet.'

Oliver raised an eyebrow. 'Oh yeah?' A burning sensation in his chest made him want to kill Brann, and he balled his fists.

'Can you deny he's handsome?'

'Um... He's not exactly my type. Do you have a thing for him?'

'No.' Hayley smirked. 'He's a nice guy, but, well, just no.'

'Looks like you're out of luck.' He nudged his head in the direction of the woman beside him.

A frown crossed her brow, and Oliver eyed her. Was she actually interested in Brann? His insides simmered. But he couldn't expect her to stay single forever.

'That's our friend, Chloe. They're not together, are they?' she said, and it sounded like she was musing aloud, more than actually asking.

Oliver gave a little shrug. 'How should I know?'

'Aw look.' Hayley had turned her attention to another couple close by. 'That's my wee cousin, Willow. She's engaged to Marcus Bowman. Have you seen them on TV presenting *Destination Forecast*?'

'Destination what? I've never heard of it.'

'Where have you been?'

'In hiding, it would appear.'

'I actually believe it.' She gave him a prod. 'But don't worry, I'll keep you up to date.'

'Great.' His eyes met hers and she smiled at him. His heart flooded with heat. Why did this feel so easy? And almost... fun. He hardly dared even think it, but he was actually having fun in an unfamiliar place, surrounded by unfamiliar people. With Hayley beside him though, everything was ok – almost. He wished Brann would disappear, but now Hayley had stopped talking about him, she didn't even look his way and he didn't look hers. Maybe Oliver had nothing to worry about. For now, at least.

'This looks good.' A hand landed on his shoulder, and he turned to see Hayley and Finlay's mum.

'Hi Lisa,' he said.

'I'm at the table with Geoff and Hilary, Genevieve's parents,' she said. 'I feel a bit like a gooseberry. Everyone seems to have partners except me, so I'll annoy you instead.'

'Aw.' Hayley hugged her. 'Stick with us. You're a good cook. You can save our soup.'

Lisa peered at it. 'Looks ok as it is.' Her eyes wandered to another table where Hayley's dad and Liz were laughing with some other people.

'Who are the people with your dad?' Oliver asked Hayley.

'Liz's kids.'

'I don't want to sound bitter,' Lisa said, 'but is her dress not a bit inappropriate?'

'It's very short,' Oliver agreed.

'That's just her way, Mum.' Hayley waved her hand absently. 'She likes to be seen.'

They spent another forty minutes perfecting their dishes and when everything was ready and the baked dishes were in the oven, they left the kitchen. In the foyer, they were presented with more champagne before heading for the ballroom dance class. Lisa was back chatting with Genevieve's parents and Oliver was alone with Hayley again.

'Still going to dance with me?' She grinned at him.

'Unless you'd prefer Brann.'

She let out a little chuckle. 'I like Brann and I think he's nice, but I don't fancy him.'

'Does that mean you—'

'Obviously.' She raised an eyebrow. 'I would have thought you'd have worked that out by now.'

'Good.' He leaned closer. 'Because the feeling's still mutual.'

She gave him a wink and headed into the ballroom.

A soft melody played in the background. Oliver stuck close to Hayley. Finlay may joke about them pretending to be friends for the weekend, but Oliver wasn't planning on letting her out of his sight. He couldn't get through any of this without her. He eyed the dancefloor and drew in a breath. The last time he'd been in here with her... Well... Maybe this time the night wouldn't end with just a kiss.

'Alright, lovely people,' the dance instructor said. 'We have a wonderful mix today of couples, families, and friends. When we dance. You do you. Ok? There are no expectations. If you want your dance to be fun, make it fun. If you want it to be energetic, make it energetic. Same goes for entertaining, sensual, passionate. You make it what suits you and your partner. If you wish to change partners for different dances, that's ok too. This isn't *Strictly*. No need to panic.' He smiled and caught Oliver's eye. Did he look like he was panicking? Probably. 'Ah, I remember you two.' He pointed at Hayley and Oliver. 'You came for a visit and your dancing was hot. Such passion.'

For Christ's sake. Oliver's cheeks were certainly hot. Why was everyone staring at him and, worst of all, Finlay?

'Interesting.' Finlay sauntered over, looking between the two of them. 'Got something you want to tell me?'

'Don't be stupid.' Hayley flicked him. 'Obviously, we were hot dancers. I mean, just look at us.'

Finlay rolled his eyes and Oliver let out his breath. *God, she's good.*

'I hope Mum's ok,' Hayley said. 'I think she's a bit lonely.'

'Is she?' Finlay smirked. 'You seen who's dancing with her?'

They looked around to see Brann leading her to the floor and Lisa fanning her neck.

'He's so nice,' Hayley said.

'This is why all the housewives fancy him.'

'Sounds a bit sexist to me,' Oliver muttered.

'I'm sure the househusbands love him too.' Finlay patted his arm and smirked.

Oliver gave him the look he reserved for Finlay's bad jokes.

Several of the Scottish country dances involved sets, some needed threes instead of twos, and only a few were close waltzes, which was probably just as well.

'This reminds me of school,' Finlay said, as they lined up for a waltz. 'I have to teach this every November to high school students for St Andrews Day ceilidhs. Can you imagine a more painful form of torture?'

'I can,' Hayley said as he moved off. She had her hand clamped to Oliver's shoulder while he held her waist.

'What's that?'

'Not being allowed to have my wicked way with you.'

He leaned in so his lips were at her ear. 'Later. You can be as wicked as you like.'

'Fantastic. Do you have a four-poster bed?'

'I do.'

'Me too. How will we choose?'

'Maybe we could test them both.'

She chuckled. 'You're on.'

He led her around in a twirl.

'My-my, Mr Wright, if I didn't know better, I'd say you were enjoying yourself.'

He focused on the soft heat of her skin, and a shiver coursed through him. The dance instructor continued to call the moves.

'I am enjoying myself,' Oliver said. 'Your company anyway.'

'Me too.'

Her body moved with grace, her hand resting on his shoulder while his stayed clamped on her waist. The closeness was electrifying.

The instructor's voice faded into the background, leaving only the soft hum of the music. Hayley's gaze locked with Oliver's, and for a moment, the world around him paused.

'Later,' he whispered again, partly as a reminder to himself. The warmth of Hayley's breath brushed against his cheek, and the subtle scent of her perfume heightened his senses.

'Ok,' she said. 'Though my patience is low.'

'Mine too.'

Her eyes sparkled with mischief. 'See, Mr Wright, dancing isn't so bad, is it?'

'Nope. And neither are you.' He gently stroked a strand of her glorious hair from her face and for a split second considered kissing her. But in his peripheral vision, he was aware of other people. One of them could be Finlay, or her mum, or dad, or Genevieve, and kissing her like that, here, wasn't appropriate, no matter how much he wanted to.

CHAPTER TWENTY-ONE

Hayley

'This is so great.' Genevieve took Hayley by the hand at the end of the dance class. 'Thank you so much for organising it all.' She hugged her. 'I've not properly seen you for ages. Wedding mania has taken over. We have to do something soon. Just the two of us.'

'Of course we can.' She patted Genevieve's back. 'I just hope this is what you wanted.'

'Oh, more than.' She pulled back. 'This place is so beautiful, and everything has been so much fun. I'm glad we've got time to rest before dinner though. It's been so full on.'

'Totally.' Hayley was pretty certain Genevieve and Finlay wouldn't be resting the whole time, but she didn't want to imagine what her brother was getting up to in his bedroom. She'd much rather imagine what she might be getting up to with Oliver later.

Once Finlay and Genevieve had gone off up the stairs, Hayley hovered about, waiting for Oliver to catch up.

'Hey,' she said. 'My room has the most amazing views. Fancy having a look?'

'Is that code?'

She waggled her eyebrows. 'You betcha.'

'Then give me five. Which room is it?'

'The Snowy Owl Suite.'

'The room names are so weird,' he said. 'But I'll be there.'

Hayley refrained from clapping her hands together.

'Hey.' Someone tapped her on the shoulder, just as Oliver headed upstairs and she spun around.

'Willow.' Hayley beamed. 'Did you enjoy the dancing?'

'Yeah, it was good. I'm so knackered now.'

'You should be carrying her up,' Hayley said to Marcus.

'I offered.'

Willow giggled. 'I wouldn't mind, but not with everyone watching.'

'Feel free to carry *me*,' Hayley said.

Marcus laughed. 'This is a great place. How did you find it?'

'Fluke.' She gave a little shrug.

'I agree, it's fantastic.' Her cousin, Aidan, moved in beside her on the stairs with Lilah, keeping to one side to let others pass. Why did everyone suddenly want to talk? She didn't want to be rude, but she really wanted to get to Oliver. They kept talking though and Hayley smiled, nodded, and tried to inch up the stairs. More than ten minutes passed before she finally got away. Dammit. Oliver wasn't at her door. Well, she wasn't really surprised. It would have been pretty silly to hang about outside, but where was he? He probably thought she'd changed her mind and gone off in a huff.

With a sigh, she shoved open the door. She'd have to message him. But before she could get near her phone, arms wrapped around her and pulled her inside.

'I thought you'd never get here.' Oliver took her face in his hands and kissed her. And, oh god, what a kiss. 'I need this. I need *you*.' His words were husky and punctured by deep breathing.

'Then don't bloody stop.' Hayley dragged her sweater off, revealing her lacy black bra.

'Oh fuck,' Oliver muttered. 'You are so perfect and beautiful. I...'

'Shh. Just kiss me.'

The touch of his warm palms circling her back and the soft groans coming from his lips ignited fireworks inside her. She relaxed into him, needing him ever closer, and gasping as he kissed her harder. His fingers wove into her hair and he nuzzled it.

'You're just too good and your hair... It's just stunning.' He stepped back and untucked his shirt. Without unbuttoning it properly, he heaved it up over his head and tossed it away. His eyes darkened and Hayley's heart leapt several beats. His upper body was glorious, sculpted, and honed to perfection.

'Come back,' she said, and he moved closer, placing his hands on her waist. She threaded her fingers into his hair, and he slipped his hands under her bottom, lifting her body onto his. She went with it, wrapping her legs around him. He turned her around and held her against the wall. The heat of his bare skin against hers was electrifying. Their tongues played and Hayley's insides ached for more, so much more.

She gripped his bare back, moaning as he kissed down her neck, then found her mouth again. Her heart raced. This was so hot, so passionate and intimate. Her trust in Oliver was implicit. She wouldn't normally want someone lifting her like this, but she knew he wouldn't drop her. His muscly arms were too strong for that.

He carried her, and she held on, looking him in the eye and he gazed back. The intensity was overwhelming. He lowered her to the bed, and she relaxed into the soft bedding. She didn't want to let go of his beautiful body, so she kept her arms around his neck.

'I'm not going anywhere.' He gave her a little smile. 'I just want to take off my jeans. You can release me.'

She laughed and let go. 'A girl can't be too careful.'

Oliver eased off his jeans and Hayley lay back with a contented sigh and unfastened her own.

'I'll do that.' He returned to her and pulled them over her hips. She raised her legs and gasped as he took her knickers too. 'All's fair,' he said.

'In what? Love and war? So which one's this?'

'I'll let you decide that.' He lowered his body over hers and kissed her on the lips. He took it steady and slow, making his way over her collarbone and further down towards her stomach, before stopping to meet her eyes. She took in a sharp breath as his mouth connected softly with the inside of her thigh. *Control, Hayley, control.* But Christ, it was too late for that. He paused for a moment to take off his boxer briefs and used the moment to gaze down at her face. She held her breath. What a look. What did it mean? Did he look at all the girls like that, or was she just very, very lucky? Something deep inside her stirred, making her want to both laugh and cry.

'Are you ok?' he whispered.

'Very... Yes. You?'

'Never better.' He lowered his face and kissed her cheek. 'And you're sure you want to do this.'

'Sure.' She ran her fingers through his thick hair and waited for his mouth to return to hers.

'Ok then.' He kissed her cheek again, then her earlobe, then her neck, winding her hair around his hand and twisting it gently. He held it like it was a lifeline, then brought it to his lips, kissed it and dropped it so it landed in a thick coil over her breast. 'One sec,' he muttered and leaned over to the floor, lifting his jeans and fishing in the pockets.

'I assume that's why you went back to your room.'

'Better safe than sorry.' He smiled as he ripped a condom wrapper open.

Hayley rested her head back and flicked her hair out, so it spread across the white sheets. Oliver's expression was sexy as hell. When he looked back at her, his eyes were full of desire.

'Come here,' Hayley said, and he leaned over her. She brushed her lips over his, pulling him closer. The heat of his body on hers was like a furnace. She gasped as his kisses intensified. He popped her bra and slipped it off, then found her breasts with his warm hands. They pushed up to meet his palms, and he soothed them and caressed them. His mouth was on her neck, her nipples, her tummy, lower and lower, until she barely remembered her own name. Being kissed down there was not normal on dates, and this was so good. Oliver's groans were like music to her ears. His enjoyment pushed her over the edge and she climaxed on his lips more powerfully than she'd ever done before.

'Oh god,' she moaned as she caught her breath.

'I'm not sure I can hold on much longer.' He lowered his forehead to hers.

'Then don't. I want you.'

'Are you sure?'

'Hell yes. Let's make the magic happen again. That was just the starter, right?'

He smiled, and she melted, tracing the curve of his lips.

'You should smile more often. It suits you.'

'I'm not normally this happy.' He lifted her hips onto his and she relaxed for him. Gently, he nudged into her, groaning, and closing his eyes. 'Oh Christ. Oh god.' He seemed to have lost the power of speech as he leaned over her, bracing himself on the headboard.

She glided her palms over his shoulders, then down towards his tight bum. That seemed to jolt him into action, and he thrust slowly but deep. Her turn to moan. This was off-the-scale good. His thrusts intensified, and she dragged him in for a kiss.

'Kiss me. More.' She needed his lips, his kisses, all of him.

He broke away, panting, and his eyes caught hers and didn't leave. 'Hayley, oh god, Hayley,' he whispered her name repeatedly, moving faster and more urgently.

Hayley dug her nails into his back. The bedroom burst into bright lights around her and she held on for dear life.

'Hayley, oh god, Hayley. I love you, god, Hayley.' Oliver's words came out barely more than a breath as he jolted inside her. Hayley, so saturated with dopamine, wasn't in a fit state to process them immediately. They just fit the moment so well.

As Oliver lay on top of her, his back rising and falling under her hands, she slowly floated back down to earth. The warmth and softness of the bedding cocooned her. The slight roughness of his cheek against hers reminded her of the time she'd shaved him. And the wonderful weight of his body on hers covered her like a soothing blanket. She closed her eyes and smiled. But a slight frown crept in. Had he said... Love? Surely not? He wouldn't have. If he had, it was just the heat of the moment, right? But that had to be a big slip from Mr Wright! It would be a shock if he'd said it to anyone before, ever. But she still wasn't entirely sure that was what he'd said. Maybe it was a case of *hear what you want to hear*. And that had been a pretty seriously charged encounter. Talk about intense. But soooo satisfying. She let out another moan.

'Sorry,' he said quietly. 'Am I squashing you?'

'No. I like you just where you are.'

He shifted, withdrawing from her but not letting go.

'I didn't have you down as a cuddler,' she said.

'I'm not, but I'm indulging you as I kind of figured you were.' His arms pulled closer, holding her tighter.

This is the best feeling ever... almost.

'Oh, I'm a cuddler, alright. And look, if you just put your hand there.' She moved his hand to her hip, nudged him gently, then rolled, so they were facing each other. 'And I put this one over you, then, tada. We're cuddling and it's really not too bad, is it?'

'Not bad at all.' He intensified his grip and moved his other hand to her cheek to stroke it, then placed a long lingering kiss on her lips. 'Nothing about you is bad. That was the best.'

She smiled. 'It was, wasn't it?'

'Easily.'

'Can we do it again?'

'After dinner,' he said. 'We haven't got that much time.'

'Your room next.'

'Ok.' He continued stroking her face until her eyes closed. She could quite happily fall into a drowsy sleep, but they had a meal and a dance to get through and she had to get ready.

'Oh no.' Her eyes pinged open, and she sat up. 'I need to get dressed for the party. I don't want a just-tumbled-out-of-bed look.'

Oliver smiled. 'No worries. I'll go and you can get ready.'

'Make sure no one sees you.'

'I'll put my clothes on before I leave, then it won't matter if anyone sees me. We can just say I was talking to you.'

'Ok.' She got up and grabbed a blanket from the bottom of the bed to put around herself. It was cold now Oliver had left her.

He took his clothes into the en suite and emerged a few minutes later, looking almost normal. Only she would see the slight telltale flush on his cheeks.

'See you later.' He glanced at the door, back at her, then came over and gave her a brief peck on the cheek.

When the door shut, Hayley turned to the mirror, stared at her reflection, and touched her cheek. *Oh my god.* Who would have thought Oliver could be so sweet? She'd fancied a hot physical encounter, but she'd not dreamed it would be that intense and... loving? It had been. Or was she just crazy and imagining things because she wanted to? Who wouldn't want to be the woman to crack the iceman? Oliver wasn't demonstrative and always claimed to hate relationships and even the thought of them, yet here he was behaving like a man in love.

'Oh fuck it, I'm deluded,' she muttered, grabbing her clothes. 'How was that any different from anything else?' But it was. Even if she couldn't pinpoint what was different, she knew it.

The dining room at Thistle Lodge was decorated with winter flower displays and the dishes they'd prepared earlier all featured on the set menus. Hayley raised her eyebrow at the list. Would anyone pick the winter vegetable soup? If they did, would it taste ok, or had the chef perhaps made a new batch just in case?

Hayley sat next to her mum, who appeared a lot happier than before as she was beside her sister, Lorna – Willow's mum – and engrossed in chat with her. Thank goodness, because Hayley's brain couldn't focus on any of it. Her spirit was still upstairs, cuddling with Oliver.

Once everyone was settled and the air was alive with clinking glasses and the murmur of laughter, Oliver got to his feet and pinged a glass. Hayley gaped at him. She'd never imagined him doing anything so showy or drawing attention to himself like that, but she supposed he spoke in court, and this probably wasn't any worse. Sitting back, she watched with a little smile as he called for order. Dressed in his kilt suit, he looked edible. Slowly the noise died down and he replaced the spoon and the empty glass.

'Please forgive my interruption,' he said. Hayley raked her eyes over him. Less than an hour ago, that hot bod had been in bed with her. *Just my guilty little secret.* 'Now, this is just the sten and not the actual wedding, so I'll save my proper speech until then,' he continued. 'However, I can't let this moment slip by without saying a few words. Of course, I'd like to toast the bride and groom, but before we do that, I'd like you all to know that this event was made possible by Finlay's lovely little sister, Hayley. Most of you know her and know how feisty she is when she gets the bit between her teeth.' He cast her a look, and she wondered what he was going to say. She hadn't been the only feisty one this afternoon. 'Ever since Genevieve and Finlay asked us to be best man and chief bridesmaid, Hayley has bullied me mercilessly into making sure we did something special for this event. Now, I'm sorry to say, I've done next to nothing compared to her, but in fairness, I simply bowed to her superior organisation skills as I'm sure most of you would have.' He glanced up and smiled as a few people tittered in agreement. 'So, please, join me in a heartfelt thank you to Hayley for bringing this event about.'

Heat rushed into her cheeks as people applauded and cheered. She had *not* expected this.

'Thank you.' She held up her hands, smiling, and the clapping died down.

'And now,' Oliver said, 'to Genevieve and Finlay. I'm sure you'll all agree there couldn't be a couple more made for each other. Everyone in this room knows their story and if that's not one for the grandkids, I don't know what is. I'm possibly the most sceptical person in the room, and at first, I didn't believe the engagement would last, but I'd like to publicly eat my words. I'm sorry I ever doubted. Genevieve and Finlay.' He picked up his glass. 'I raise a toast to you and wish you a long and happy marriage.'

Everyone murmured the toast, and someone whistled.

Finlay laughed. 'Coming from a divorce lawyer, I won't take it lightly.'

Oliver resumed his seat and waiters started moving around.

'He is adorable,' her mum said. 'He's come through so much. Such a brave man.'

On Hayley's other side was Genevieve, then came Finlay and then Oliver. Probably best that she wasn't next to him. Her control was at an all-time low and that was saying something because she wasn't usually one for holding back.

'That was quite a speech.' Genevieve leaned towards Hayley, away from Finlay. 'He gave us a bit of the courtroom presence there, which is funny because I've hardly even heard him speak before. He's so quiet.'

'Yeah. He is.'

'And it was nice that he thanked you.' She squeezed Hayley's knee. 'Good too, because Finlay was really worried he'd be horrible to you.'

'Why?'

'Because the two of you don't get on, do you?'

'Oh well.'

Genevieve smiled. 'I appreciate you putting the war aside for us.'

Hayley took a sip of her drink. Oliver had told her she could choose between love and war and she definitely hadn't picked war. 'No problem,' she said. 'Did your brother not come today?' Hayley turned around. She'd spotted Genevieve's sister earlier but hadn't seen Rafe.

'No, he's really busy. He's promised to come to the wedding though. Why?' She looked intrigued. 'Because he is a very eligible single man, if you're interested.'

'No, of course I'm not.' Even though Hayley knew Rafe Harrington was very well-respected and rich. Perfect marriage material really, but he had a fault. He wasn't Oliver.

'Shame. That would have been funny if I'd married your brother and you'd married mine.'

'I don't think that would ever happen. I like my quiet life here and he lives in Edinburgh, doesn't he?'

'Glasgow. But I'm with you. Glenbriar is my happy place.'

'Me too.' She swallowed a gulp of champagne. Shame Oliver wouldn't say the same. His departure to London was going to hit like a tonne weight. Worse than ever now. How could she part with him? She'd been happy to have a fling with him. Jeez, she'd invited it. But how much bigger had it got already? She wanted to see him again later. And what then? Oh god, how messy.

Her ears tuned into the conversation between Finlay and Oliver. Finlay's voice carried. 'I'll miss having you around. Who am I going to share my cycling adventures with?'

'The same people I would have done if you'd gone to Dubai.'

'Never going to forgive me for that, are you?'

'Nope.' Oliver fake punched him. 'Just think, you can visit me in London. We can explore the urban cycle routes together.'

'Oh god, yeah. You won't be able to keep me away. Gen's already desperate to go.'

'Oh my god, yes,' Genevieve said. 'I'm definitely coming. You two can go cycling and I'll...' She sneaked a peek at Hayley and grinned. 'I'll take Hayley and we can go shopping.'

Hayley laughed, but her insides squirmed. If she went to London to see Oliver, shopping would be way down her list. She glanced at her food. But it wasn't like she could just dot up and down to see Oliver anyway. Why would she do that? She wasn't going to be some hanger on who waited six months just to have sex with a guy she thought was hot. That wasn't what she wanted. She wanted so much more. Each second with Oliver gave her nothing but false hope. If only she could stop caring and go back to disliking him, it would be so much easier.

CHAPTER TWENTY-TWO

Oliver

Oliver stood near the edge of the dance floor, a glass of champagne in hand, watching the dancing. Some of the men wore kilts and jackets like him, but a few had on jeans and shirts. Then there was Brann. He was in a tight t-shirt, showing off his biceps in all their glory. Was there any need? Oliver knocked back his champagne. Brann had better keep away from Hayley. A group of women were around him chatting, and he seemed to be lapping it up.

'Hey.' Finlay clapped him on the shoulder. 'You ok?'

'Yeah. Just watching Brann and his harem.'

Finlay chuckled. 'Yup. He's got them eating out his hand. I only recently found out he has a daughter in one of my classes. He wanted to bring her as his plus one. Can you imagine? No way did I want one of my pupils here.'

Oliver snorted into his drink. 'Yeah, that would not have been good.'

'Great place though,' Finlay said. 'You guys did good finding this.'

'It was Hayley.' Oliver swigged the rest of his champagne.

'Did someone say my name?' Hayley appeared at his side from nowhere, it seemed.

'Me.' Oliver briefly raised his free hand.

'Singing your praises as usual.' Finlay smirked. 'Which reminds me, when are we going to see this hot dancing?'

'Whenever Mr Wright is ready,' Hayley said.

Oliver looked at Finlay and pulled a face.

'Mr Wright?' Finlay shook his head. 'There's mileage in there I've been missing for years.'

'Quite surprising, really,' Oliver said. 'You dwell on that for a bit while we dance.' He put his glass on a nearby table and held out his arm. Hayley took it with a smile.

'Love you guys,' Finlay said. 'You're the best.'

'He thinks we're doing this just for him, bless.' Hayley beamed as they reached the dance floor and Oliver slipped his hand around her waist.

'Fine by me,' he said. 'Probably best he doesn't know the truth.'

The music was faster than Oliver would have liked. He wasn't much of a dancer, but Hayley had a knack for it even in her gravity defying heels. Her stunning dress clung to her elegant figure, and Oliver forced himself to breathe slowly. Memories of their afternoon together nudged his brain, and he barely contained the desire to take her in his arms and drag her back upstairs. *Hayley addict.* That was him. He couldn't get enough of her. Crazy,

crazy, crazy. On so many levels. She tossed her head, so her hair tumbled over her back.

'It's so hot in here.'

'You're not kidding,' he muttered.

Remember, nothing can happen. You're going to London. A little voice scratched at the inside of his brain. He didn't want anything to happen anyway! *Because you don't believe in lasting love, do you?*

Love? Where had that thought even come from? Love? He didn't love Hayley. *Yes, you do. You do and you know it. You told her you did.* Bloody hell, he had. But he'd said it so quietly and at such a heated moment she thankfully hadn't noticed. Lust had driven him to say it. Lust was to blame.

'I need to thank you.' Her eyes met his, and he was momentarily lost in her liquid brown irises.

He raised an eyebrow. 'For what?'

'For the speech. I didn't expect that.'

'You deserved it. Credit where credit's due. You've put a lot of effort into this. And with pretty much no help from me.'

'Well, I appreciate what you said, especially after all my bullying.'

'Which I deserved. I've been a total arse.' He glanced away.

'You made up for it this afternoon.'

'Did I?'

'Totally. That was pretty special, wasn't it?'

'Yeah. It was.' He raised his hand to her face and brushed a strand of hair behind her ear. 'More later. If you want.' Even as the words left his lips, he cursed inside. How stupid was he, encouraging this? He should be stamping on it. But he couldn't. His desire was too powerful.

'Of course I do.' She ran her hand along the shoulder of his jacket, flicking off a tiny piece of fluff as she did so.

He spun her around and pulled her closer. She let out a squeal and a giggle. 'I want you so badly it hurts,' he murmured. 'And I mean really hurts, like everywhere.'

'Me too. But we need to be patient. Too many people are watching here... Or could be watching.'

'Yeah. I know. But Finlay wanted us to be nice to each other and I really don't think I can be much nicer than this.'

'You're very nice indeed, but I also like it when you're naughty.'

'You're the naughty one.'

'Well, we can be naughty together then.'

The whole day had been so much better than he'd anticipated, and he wouldn't let anything ruin these last few hours together. If true love didn't last, what was he worried about? This weekend could be a happy memory to take to London with him. No regrets.

After a few dances, they sat at a table with Genevieve and Finlay, and some other guests, including Hayley and Finlay's dad Sam, and Liz, his partner. Sam was possibly a closet comedian.

He certainly had several funny stories to tell, and it was clear where both Hayley and Finlay got their laid-back personalities from.

Oliver was glad not to have to talk. Listening to the conversation was so much easier and no one would notice if his eyes strayed once too often to Hayley. Except her. She caught his eye more than once and flicked him a cheeky smile.

Eventually, people drifted up to bed. Oliver couldn't wait for either Finlay or Genevieve to say they were heading up. Once they went, he wouldn't feel bad about following. Midnight had come and gone before they moved.

'Night and thanks again,' Finlay said as they reached the top of the stairs. 'You two are the best.'

'It's been brilliant,' Genevieve said.

Finlay hugged Hayley, then she and Genevieve embraced. Finlay eyed Oliver for a moment and Oliver quirked a little grin. Everyone knew he wasn't a hugger, but Finlay looked on the verge of embracing him. And why the hell not? This was his best mate, after all.

Like he'd read his change of heart, Finlay opened his arms and gave Oliver a man-hug, including a substantial wallop to the back. Oliver returned it.

'Thanks, mate.' Finlay pulled back, grinning. 'I know it's not exactly your thing, but I appreciate you going the extra mile for us.'

'I hardly did anything.'

'You're here,' Finlay said quietly. 'And I know that can't have been easy.'

'No worries. You'd have done the same for me. You have done, many times. I should be the one thanking you.'

'Bugger off.' Finlay burst out laughing and clapped Oliver's back again. 'Since when did you get so sappy?'

'Since now. Because I've never really thanked you for sticking by me, even when...' He shrugged.

'That's what friends are for.'

Oliver nodded. It certainly was. And he was lucky to have found one of the best.

Genevieve sidled over and gave him a brief hug too. Hayley had moved away and was hugging her mum a little way off. She caught Oliver's eye over her mum's shoulder and winked.

He headed to his room, firing off a quick message to Hayley.

OLIVER: *See you soon.*

Leaving the bathroom door open, in case she came by, he gave himself a quick wash, brushed his teeth and got into his pyjamas. His phone was on the end of the bed and he lifted it checking for a reply. Nothing. He sat down with a sigh. What if she'd changed her mind?

Why am I so desperate?

A sharp knock on the door made him jump. He got to his feet and opened it. Hayley almost fell in.

'You're here.'

'Of course I am. Just had to pick up a few things.'

'What is all that?' he asked. She had her arms full of what looked like clothes and toiletries.

'Stuff. In case I end up staying here all night. Not that I'm making assumptions, but I'd like to be prepared just in case.' The words tumbled out at a hundred miles an hour.

Oliver took her face in his hands and kissed her. 'Stay all night. Please.'

Stay forever...

Really? Did he want that?

She smiled and her beautiful lips shimmered in the soft light. 'Ok.'

He scooped her up, and she squealed. 'Let's make this a night to remember.'

'Yes, please.'

He set her down gently on the bed and lay down beside her. 'You...' He kissed her. 'Are just beautiful.' He carried on the kiss, finding her tongue with his and indulging in long, lingering kisses. This was going to be slow and oh so enjoyable.

Hayley nestled in the crook of Oliver's arm with her eyes closed, her long hair splayed across his chest. Oliver ran his hand over her locks, coiling a strand around his finger, then leaning his forehead on hers. Moments like this wouldn't come often in his life, so he had to cherish this. Maybe love didn't last, but what if it existed for a short time in his life? Like this moment.

'Morning, Mr Wright,' Hayley murmured without opening her eyes. She trailed a finger down his chest. 'How are you?'

'Very well. You?'

'Never better.' She opened her eyes and smiled. 'What time is it?'

'Early yet.' He pressed a soft kiss to her brow.

Thistle lodge was theirs right up until midday, so there was no rush to leave. They had a little more time before they had to get up.

'I've got some games for this morning,' she said.

'I assume you mean for the party and not for you and me.'

'Ha ha, yes.' She peered up at him. 'Though you and me could play some of our own before they start.'

'I like the sound of that a lot more.' He pulled the covers over them and kissed her. *Got to kiss her like there's no tomorrow, because there isn't.*

Party games weren't his thing. He sat sipping coffee, watching Hayley sort everyone out, recalling the kind of games he'd played with her just a few hours before. His brain jumped from wishing he could get the hell out of here as soon as possible to not wanting these last couple of hours with Hayley ever to end.

He couldn't just sit here like a plank, not when he'd done very little to help her in the run up.

'I'll be quiz master.' He raised his hand when Hayley announced her own version of a 'Mr & Mrs' game. As he read the questions, he watched Hayley working the room. What a way with people she had. Something strange rose inside him, like he was proud, though he had no reason to be. His mind flew back to London when everyone had assumed they were together. How natural it had been, like it could be real if he wanted it. Only it couldn't. She'd told him unequivocally her life was here, and she didn't want to move. So even if in the unlikely event he decided he wanted to give a relationship a go, it couldn't be with her. This situation would never present itself ever again. Who else would ever be like Hayley? He didn't want anyone to be like her because he didn't want anyone else.

Almost before he knew it, the time came for them all to leave. Oliver went to say goodbye to Finlay and Genevieve first. Hayley was next to Genevieve. Oliver hesitated for a split second, then dipped in and kissed her on the cheek. 'Well done, for a great weekend.'

'Thanks.'

'Will you two be able to keep liking each other up until the wedding?' Finlay asked.

Oliver quirked a little grin at Hayley. She smirked back at him. 'We can give that a go,' he said.

'Don't push it.' Hayley poked him and tipped him a little wink.

Finlay laughed. 'You guys are great.' He clapped Oliver on the shoulder. That was his cue to leave. No need for anything else, but as soon as he was out the door, he missed Hayley. He wanted to know when he'd see her again. In a week, he'd be in London, and all this would be in the past. Unless he could wangle a way to see her in between.

He still had to say goodbye to his dad, Carla, and his sisters before leaving for London. Maybe Hayley would come with him for that. Selfishly he wanted to see her, but having her there would also ease the pressure considerably. His family liked her, and she was good with people. Before he set off from Thistle Lodge, he messaged her.

OLIVER: Don't suppose you would come with me when I go to my dad's to say bye before London. Could do with a friend, and I'd like to see you.

By the time he got home, she'd replied with a yes. Facing his last week at work was easier knowing he had a cast iron reason to see her again.

The days flew by, and Oliver worked his arse off to get every-thing in order before he left, not stopping to breathe, holding on to the thought of seeing Hayley again.

When the time finally came, he barely resisted the urge to drag her into his arms and hold her there. Instead, he gave her a brief peck on the cheek.

'Thanks so much for doing this.'

'No problem.' She jumped into his car, and he pulled off towards his dad's farm. 'Have you had your last day at work?'

'I finished on Friday.' He kept his eyes firmly on the road. Hayley was distractingly beautiful. Dressed down in her casual attire of grey jeans and a thick ribbed cream sweater, she looked a million dollars.

'Was it emotional?'

'Not really.' He didn't need to look to see her eye roll; he sensed it. 'They gave me a pot plant for my new house in London, but I don't have a new house yet. I'm renting a short-term apartment while I work my induction period, so the plant will probably die off.'

Hayley put her head in her hand and gave a wry chuckle. 'You are a funny guy. I'll go round and water your plant, if you like.'

'I'm not sure it's worth it.'

She smiled at him then gently ran her hand over his thigh, almost putting him off the road. 'Won't you miss your job? I know I would miss mine. The girls I work with are so lovely.'

He gave a little shrug. 'I thought it had grown stale, but maybe it was just so familiar I didn't find it challenging. I can't deny I'm happy to get away at this point. You should have seen the case that came in last week. A woman who cited her reason for divorce as, after spending twenty years systematically getting rid of all the tinsel her husband had accumulated, when he came home with a bag of brand-new tinsel, that was the last straw.'

Hayley laughed. 'Oh my god, that's hilarious. And you don't think you'll get tinsel-hating wives in London?'

'No doubt, but sometimes it's just...' How could he explain when he wasn't sure himself? 'It's like something is missing. The job feels kind of flat.'

'Sounds like you need a change of direction. Can't you go into another branch of law?'

'I could, but this is where my experience lies, so going else-where wouldn't be that easy. Regalia are great for working across the whole of Britain and internationally, so I'll get a broader experience.'

'Guess so. Just make sure you avoid the tinsel-phobes.'

'You couldn't make it up sometimes.'

His father's farm, Tullybrae, was a short drive south of Glen-briar. Oliver pulled onto the farm track, passing two large barns and continuing until he reached the traditional old stone farm-house. Chickens roamed around the yard at the side door and Oliver parked beside his dad's Landrover.

'Cute house,' Hayley said.

'It's falling apart, and it's a total mess inside.' Oliver popped his seatbelt. 'And watch the chicken shit when you get out. It's everywhere.'

'Not exactly a glowing review.'

'Just an honest one. I was never going to follow in my father's footsteps. Farming isn't my thing at all.' He got out, heeding his own advice and taking care of where he put his feet as he made his way to the front door. His knock echoed round and a few chickens stopped pecking to see what the disturbance was.

Carla opened the door and peered out. 'Oh, it's you. Hello. And Hayley. I didn't know you were coming.'

'Just tagging along. How's Neil?'

'Getting better, though not able to walk as well as he'd like and still not working.'

'Did you find someone to cover for him?'

'We've got an arrangement going with some nearby farmers. It's not ideal, but it's the best we can do.'

Oliver let her talk and lead the way. He followed as Carla headed through the kitchen into the hallway towards the living room. The house still held vestiges of what had once been Oliver's home. At the sight of the old stairs, a pain struck him square in the chest. When he was little, his mum had hung his Christmas stocking there with him. Why did it make him want to cry? Not just cry, but have her there to comfort him, just like she would have done when he was tiny and had hurt himself. Those memories were too old to know if they were real or if he was simply imagining what he hoped his young life was like. He knew it had been happy. He knew his mum had loved him. If she hadn't, it wouldn't have hurt so badly to lose her.

Hayley turned and smiled at him. 'Hey,' she said. 'Are you ok?'

'What?' Oliver focused on her face, those beautiful dark eyes, her long glossy hair, and blinked away the memories.

'Come here.' Hayley moved closer and slipped an arm around his back. With a sigh, he put his around her and placed his hand on her shoulder. 'Everything's fine,' she said, gently.

His father was sitting close to the woodburner, laughing at something on the television.

'Neil. Oliver's here,' Carla said. 'With Hayley.'

Neil fumbled for the remote and turned off the TV. 'Ah... What's this visit for? Are you finally going to tell us you're settling down? Is this the unlucky lady?'

'No.' Oliver removed his hand from Hayley's shoulder and stepped away from her.

'Any woman who got to settle down with Oliver wouldn't be unlucky,' Hayley said with a smile. 'He's quite a catch, don't you know?'

'Is he now?' Neil grinned at Hayley as though she'd been flirting with him.

'He certainly is.'

'Then why aren't you taking him off my hands?'

Hayley eyed Neil, then turned to Oliver with an appraising look. Her expression was still playful, but something in her eyes told Oliver she wasn't enjoying this as much as she was making out. 'I'll leave him for the fancy London girls.'

'Pah,' Neil said. 'Are you still going to London?'

'Yes. That's why I'm here. I'm leaving tomorrow. I've come to say goodbye.'

'Oh, right.' Neil pulled his lips down in an expression of mild surprise. 'Well, I'm sure we'll see you as much as we ever did, whether you're in London or here. It's not like you've ever been a frequent visitor.'

Oliver's jaw set and he controlled his breathing. No point in getting angry or trying to argue with his dad. Neil would never see it. He blamed Oliver for being distant but wouldn't understand how shut out Oliver had felt ever since his mum had died.

'Ava and Sofia are very excited to have a brother in London,' Carla said. 'They hope you've got a two-bedroom house so they can come and visit.'

He bit his tongue. They wanted to visit him in London? Clearly it was London they wanted to see and not him, as they'd never visited him in his Glenbriar house. Also, he wasn't sure Carla had ever referred to him as their brother before.

'I haven't got a house yet, so I'm not sure what size it'll be.'

'There's a long list of people wanting to visit him already,' Hayley said.

'Are you top of the list?' Neil asked.

She glanced at Oliver. 'Probably not.'

He locked his gaze with hers, hoping to impart his reply. *Yes, you are.* Because he couldn't say it out loud.

'I just want to say goodbye,' Oliver said. 'And... Well, that's all.'

'I can't get up.' Neil nodded at his leg. 'But we can shake hands.' He thrust his out and Oliver shook. That was about as demonstrative as his dad ever got with him. Oliver turned to Carla and went to shake her hand too, but she took him by surprise and gave him a quick hug and a peck on the cheek.

'Safe travels,' she said.

They returned to the car and Oliver sat quietly for a few seconds as Hayley strapped herself in. 'Was that all really weird?' he said. 'Or are all families like that?'

Hayley gave a little shrug. 'All families are different. My mum was beside herself when she thought Finlay was leaving for Dubai, but my dad was totally ok with it. Your dad seems more like that.'

'I don't think he'd have cared if I left and didn't bother to say goodbye.'

'But you did, Oliver. That's what's important. He might accuse you of never visiting or whatever, but he's wrong. He sees what he wants to see because it makes him feel better. You keep going back. Maybe not frequently, but you do it. You said he'd never been to visit you?'

'He hasn't.'

'Exactly. So he's the one in the wrong, but it's easier for him to blame you. And if your sisters want to come to London, let them. Show them and your dad that you're not the problem. Even if they only come for free accommodation at first, then so what?

They'll remember you let them stay and as they grow up, they'll realise what that means.'

'What does it mean?'

'That you're a good person.'

'Am I?'

'Yes, Oliver.'

He turned his head to face her. 'You really are top of my list to come visit me in London. In fact, you're top of my list for everything.' He leaned forward and placed his lips against hers. The soothing warmth instantly carried him away. A voice inside his head spoke, and it sounded like his mum... or what he thought he remembered her sounding like.

Don't let her go. What's more important than love?

But he couldn't love Hayley. He didn't believe in love... love that lasted. As he kissed her, his resolve faded further. Was he really doing the right thing?

Chapter Twenty-Three

Hayley

February

The Ever After Boutique was a shop Hayley passed every day on her way to work, the sort of place she'd happily stand and stare in the window of for ages, until someone shoved her out the way and told her to stop being so silly.

Normally she had no reason to set foot in here, but with Genevieve's wedding fast approaching, she had the best excuse ever. As chief bridesmaid, she had to go along to dress fittings, just for support.

Soft light glinted on the racks of pristine gowns, making the sequins on the fairy tale dresses twinkle. Hayley wanted to rifle through the dresses and look at them all. *Just as well I'm not getting married. How could I ever choose just one?*

'Look at that.' Her eyes widened as she took in the intricate lace details of a gown on a pedestal in the middle. 'That is just wow.'

'It's stunning,' Genevieve agreed. 'I think we've found a dress for you too.'

'If you find the groom that goes with it, let me know.'

Genevieve smirked. 'Not Oliver then?'

'Pardon?' Hayley gaped at her. No one knew about that, did they? Had he blabbed to Finlay? Surely not. He'd seemed as keen as her not to let their little fling become common knowledge.

'Just kidding.' Genevieve chuckled. 'I just thought it would be funny. You were doing such a good job getting along at the sten. I kind of hoped it was for real.'

'You know he's moved to London, don't you?' She brushed her fingers across her red and white spotted top, rubbing her sternum, trying to ease the ache that appeared there every time she thought about him being so far away.

'Yes, I do.' Genevieve moved across the plush carpet to the sales desk, where a woman waited, smiling at them.

'Hello,' she said. 'I have your dress ready if you want to step through to the fitting room.'

Genevieve looked ready to burst with excitement; it was infectious, and Hayley grinned too.

'You're going to look absolutely stunning,' she said.

Genevieve beamed. 'I can't believe it's happening. It's getting so real.'

They stepped into the changing area, and both Hayley and the assistant helped Genevieve into the gown. Genevieve stared at herself in the long, elegant mirror. Time seemed to pause as Hayley watched her friend's beautiful reflection.

'Oh wow,' she sighed, her voice catching with emotion, and she flapped her hand in front of her face. 'You're so beautiful.'

Genevieve twirled, her eyes meeting Hayley's. 'Do you really think so?'

Hayley nodded, her hand over her heart. 'Of course. Finlay is the luckiest guy in the world.'

Tears welled in Genevieve's eyes, and she leaned over to hug Hayley. 'I'm lucky too,' Genevieve said. 'I've got a great guy and I'm getting an awesome sister-in-law too.'

'Who'd have thought that? We've gone from friends to sisters.'

'It's just the best.'

Hayley released her, and the assistant checked the dress fitted in all the correct places. Once she was sure everything was perfect, Genevieve dressed in her own clothes again.

'Let's grab lunch,' Hayley said, and they made their way across the street to the Drip Drop Coffee Shop. Lisa was working and bustled over to see them.

'Hey, favourite girls.' She gave them both a brief hug. 'Drinks on the house for you, and what shall we get you to eat? Lunch menu or just cakes?'

'Hi Mum,' Hayley said. 'We'll have lunch, please.'

'Thanks, Lisa,' Genevieve added. 'I need to stay away from cakes until the wedding,'

'Aw, you'll be the most beautiful bride. My boy is so lucky.' Lisa gave Genevieve a pat on the shoulder. 'Let me grab a couple of menus for you, then I'll fix you some coffees.' She bustled off to a little dresser next to the counter.

'Finlay had a phone call from Oliver yesterday,' Genevieve said.

'Oh really?'

'I don't think he's enjoying London that much so far.'

'No?'

Lisa returned with the menus and handed them over. 'Is that you saying Oliver isn't happy in London?'

'Well, you know what Oliver's like,' Genevieve said. 'He doesn't exactly give much away, but Finlay thought he sounded a bit down. Homesick even.'

'It's bound to be a big change.' Lisa let out a sigh. 'And the poor lad's been through so much already. But listen to me gossiping. What can I get you to drink, the usuals?'

They both agreed, and Lisa hurried off behind the counter.

'Did you go to London with Oliver before Christmas?' Genevieve asked.

Hayley pressed her lips together. She hadn't actively told Genevieve about London, though she hadn't promised to keep it a secret either. Oliver must have blabbed.

'We shared accommodation when he was at a legal conference, and I was at the hair show.' She spotted Genevieve's wide eyes and semi open mouth. 'In separate beds, so don't get any funny ideas.'

Because those funny ideas didn't start until after that. In London, they'd behaved themselves… almost. Her chest ached so hard at the memories. That had been such a great week. No matter how much she wanted to tell herself she was just lusting over Oliver when she thought back to that trip, there was more to it. She enjoyed his company, and they got on well. When they were out together, they complemented each other and had fun.

'I can't help being suspicious,' Genevieve said with a little smirk. 'I mean, you went to London for a week, and you didn't tell me. That seems strange in itself.'

'I didn't tell you because I knew you would get suspicious.'

'You know Finlay wouldn't mind if the two of you dated; he's not the kind of brother who would object to something like that.'

'Yes, but I'm not dating Oliver, am I? He's moved to London and I'm staying here. So even if I did like him like that, it's not like we can get together, is it?'

'So, are you saying that you like him?'

'I don't dislike him as much as I used to, but that doesn't mean I automatically want to marry him and have his babies.' Though secretly that was exactly what she did want.

'I thought he was weird when I first met him,' Genevieve said. 'But he's grown on me. He's just a quiet guy. I think you'd be good for him.'

'Not going to happen.' The words sunk like a lead brick to the bottom of Hayley's stomach because she recognised the truth in them. 'He doesn't do relationships.'

'That's what he says just now, but people change.'

'Stop it,' Hayley said. 'If you have to set me up with someone, please try and make it someone who actually lives here.'

Genevieve grinned and patted her on the hand. 'Sorry.'

Dwelling on Oliver wasn't doing her any good. Not that there was much competition around here. She'd probably dated all the single guys in the town at some point. It felt like it anyway but she never fully clicked with any of them.

'Here you go.' Her mum laid a tray on the table and lifted their drinks from it. 'What are the two of you chatting about?'

'Men,' Hayley said. 'And the lack of single ones in this town.'

'What about Brann Duthie?' her mum said. 'The builder. I love him. We had a very nice dance at the sten.' Her eyes went dreamy. 'I think he took pity on me because I was feeling a bit lonely.'

'He did that with me at Felicity's wedding,' Hayley said. 'He is sweet. You should date him.'

'Me?' Lisa laughed. 'He's not really my type. Well, he is very rugged and a lovely guy, so I can see why people like him, but he's way too young.'

'Stuff like that happens,' Genevieve said.

Lisa grinned. 'I'm not sure I want it to. I like my own company too much these days. But I don't see why you won't consider him?' She stroked the top of Hayley's head, smoothing her hair down.

'I like him.' Hayley tapped the edge of the table. 'But I don't feel a spark, you know?'

'Yeah.' Her mum put her arm around her shoulder, dipped in, and kissed her forehead. 'You'll find someone soon, my love. I just know it.'

'Me too,' Genevieve said.

'Why is it that you can be attracted to some people but not others?' Hayley mused. 'What are the magic ingredients that make people compatible?'

Genevieve pulled a face. 'That's a big question, isn't it?'

'Sure is.' Lisa nodded. 'It can be so many things. Some people like to have things in common with their partners, others like their opposites. Some people like hot bods, some like a dad bod.'

Genevieve and Hayley laughed.

'Love you, Mum,' Hayley said. 'You just say it like it is.'

'I guess you just need to find someone who ticks all your boxes... Or at least the majority of them,' Genevieve said.

'It's funny how some people give you that instant spark, isn't it?' Hayley played with her fingernails. Her French polish needed redoing; her thumbnail was a little chipped.

'Yeah, but I guess that could happen with someone who isn't your ideal life partner. It's just good luck if the two happen to coincide.'

'True.'

'I better go,' Lisa said as some other customers came in.

'I had a call from Elise.' Hayley took a sip of coffee. 'I forgot to say.' Thoughts of Oliver had pushed the chat with Finlay's ex-girlfriend from her mind. Both Hayley and Genevieve had been friends with her, but after Elise messed about with both Finlay and Aidan, Hayley hadn't made much of an effort to stay in touch. Finding the right words was always difficult.

'She seems to be doing ok,' Hayley said.

'Well, I'm glad she dumped Finlay.' Genevieve swirled the coffee in her mug around. 'It left the door open for me, but what she did wasn't very nice.'

'Yeah, she was really silly.'

'I just hope it works out for her. She doesn't want to come to the wedding. I get that. I'll maybe meet up with her after.'

The subject kept them going until their soup and sandwiches arrived. 'Here you go,' Lisa said.

Genevieve placed her spoon in the bowl, then looked at Hayley. 'Wouldn't you consider moving to London?'

'Why are you asking me that?' The heat rose in her face and her mum turned back with a frown.

'No reason.' Genevieve took a mouthful of soup, unable to hide her smile, and Hayley narrowed her eyes.

'I don't want to move away from here. I like it and I'm happy here.'

'Yup. I feel the same. My brother and sister totally don't get it. They love city life and think I'm a strange little home bird.'

'Nothing wrong with that,' Lisa said. 'This is a great wee town.'

'I had no qualifications and wasn't much good at anything,' Genevieve said. 'So it made sense for me to stay here, but you're a really good stylist. You'd get a great job if you went to London.' She looked at Hayley, then glanced at Lisa.

'She has a point,' Lisa said. 'Though that's nonsense saying you're not good at anything. You're a brilliant cook and a social media superstar.'

'You are,' Hayley agreed. 'And it's kind of you to say I'm a good stylist, but that lifestyle isn't me. Working in the salon is exactly what I want. Everyone there is like part of my family. We enjoy it and we have good relationships with our clients. I don't care if my wage isn't as big as it would be in a bigger city and I don't see myself in a big salon. This is where I belong.'

'Yeah. I know.' Genevieve stirred her soup. 'I was just thinking about you and Ol—'

'Don't say it.' Hayley held up her hand.

'Oliver?' Lisa raised an eyebrow.

'Seriously?' Hayley put her spoon down. 'It's not happening, ok?' Genevieve seemed more determined to bring about the impossible situation than Hayley herself... And Genevieve didn't know the half of it. Hayley was barely holding herself together. Why did it feel like a breakup when they'd never been together? Not officially – just casually. Though at the time, it hadn't felt casual. Not unless casual had got very intense. Now she had to get used to the idea that Oliver was hundreds of miles away and she wouldn't see him until April, when Genevieve and Finlay tied the knot.

'Oh dear.' Her mum patted her shoulder. 'He's a long way away, but remember, you don't have to cut him from your life entirely. You're still best man and chief bridesmaid.'

That was true, and it made Hayley think.

As soon as she and Genevieve went their separate ways, Hayley pulled out her phone and typed a message. It filled the gap he'd left in her heart momentarily as she put down the words for his eyes only.

HAYLEY: Hi Mr Wright. How are you getting on? I was at lunch with Genevieve today and she was asking me about our trip to London. Did you tell Finlay about it? Also, what's this I hear about London not living up to expectations? Is everything ok? Speak soon x

Ah hell, there went the kiss. Oh well, she'd had one or two of them with him the past few months and they were all rather memorable, so maybe they could start having a text kiss every now and then, though it wouldn't get anywhere close to the real thing.

The following morning came and Oliver still hadn't replied. He hadn't even seen the message. Was he that busy? He'd antici-pated long hours. Hayley didn't envy that lifestyle one bit. She worked late in the salon on Wednesdays and Thursdays, condensing her hours, so she was off Sunday, Monday, and Tuesday. But two long days each week were enough.

'How's everyone today?' she asked Amber, Colette and Nikki, who were all on shift with her.

'All fine.' Amber checked the others were in agreement.

'I've got that man from the road department coming in for his cut today,' Nikki said. 'He talks about some strange stuff. I wish he'd just go to a barber.'

Hayley chuckled. 'I think he likes you.'

'Oh shut it.'

The bell rang over the door announcing the first client, and Hayley went to greet a woman with long blue hair. 'Morning, Cha,' she said. 'How are you?'

'Good thanks.'

'Let me take your jacket and you can have a seat here.'

Cha took off an impressive denim jacket, adorned with gold buttons and chains. Her hands glinted with thick rings, and she ran her fingers through her luscious locks. She was one of Hayley's most adventurous clients and liked to keep her hair blue. Amazing how well it suited her.

'So, what are we doing today?' Hayley asked after hanging up Cha's jacket. Colette had already fitted her with a black gown.

'Just the roots and a bit of tidying.'

'It keeps the colour so well.' Hayley took a comb through it. 'And it really suits you.'

Cha smiled. 'I hope so. I keep worrying I'm getting too old for this colour.'

'No way. What age are you?'

'Thirty-four.'

'That's not old. My brother's nearly thirty-four.' So was Oliver.

'Yeah, but does he have blue hair?'

'No.' Hayley laughed. 'I can't imagine that.'

'Exactly.'

'Well, if you ever want to change it, just let me know. I can take it back to a more natural colour and maybe just leave the blue as highlights. It's up to you.'

'Leave the blue just now. I'm so used to it. My sister-in-law, Nina, is pregnant, which means I'm going to be an aunty. I quite like the idea of being the cool aunt with the blue hair.'

'I know Nina. She comes in here too. And you'll definitely be a cool aunty.'

'My friend's kids all like it too. Wouldn't want to disappoint them.'

Hayley mixed up the dye and returned to Cha. Cha had told her before that she and her husband weren't bothered about having kids. They hadn't ruled it out, but it wasn't something they were dead set on. Hearing her talking fondly about her friends' children and her future nieces and nephews made Hayley wonder if she could be like that. What if she didn't find someone to have kids with? Would she be happy being an aunty to Finlay and

Genevieve's kids? Or to Aidan and Lilah or Marcus and Willow's children? They'd all have them at some point, she was sure. What about Felicity and Gavin? All these friends and relatives of hers would have children around the same time. They'd be pushing buggies together and being mums at the school gates with kids in the same class.

And I'll be left behind. Maybe occasionally picking up a niece or nephew if she was lucky, but it wasn't what she wanted. She'd be happy to be an aunty or an honorary aunt, but she wanted her own family.

Cha's hair took up most of the morning and when Hayley went into the backroom for a quick break, she checked her phone. A message from Oliver had finally arrived.

OLIVER: Sorry for late reply. I'm so busy. It's a bit of a nightmare really. I'm not getting finished until after eleven most nights, and my commute is pretty hellish. It's a nice apartment in Ruislip but the commute all in takes an hour. I barely have time to sleep before I'm up again. So, yeah, it's not exactly living up to expectations. I never thought I'd miss Glenbriar as much as I do.

I told Finlay about us going to London… Well, I didn't mean to. I forgot he didn't know and I said something about it, then I had to explain. Hope I haven't caused any problems.

Hope you're doing ok. x

She let out a sigh just as another message came in.

OLIVER: It's not just Glenbriar I miss… Certain people too.

OLIVER: I mean you x

OLIVER: I'll see you at the wedding. It's only six weeks away. Not too long now.

Hayley sucked on her lip, holding back an unexpected pang of sadness. Six weeks without Oliver was like a lifetime. And he missed her. She missed him too. A lot. An awful lot.

CHAPTER TWENTY-FOUR

Oliver

April

A brisk spring breeze touched Oliver's face as he stepped out of his car. Daffodils danced on the neatly mowed lawns on the Fairways Estate. Glenbriar hadn't changed much during his three-month absence in London, but he had. Previously, coming home to this house had never felt either good or bad, just something that happened every day. Seeing it now, though, gave him a tickling sensation in his gut. Not a nasty feeling, but not a completely positive one either. Something was missing. How often had that been the case in his life, no matter where he was or what he was doing?

He strolled up the path to his front door, glancing around. His apartment in Ruislip was pleasant enough and reasonably peaceful compared to the constant hum of the city, but it couldn't compare to this. Granted, the twittering birds and low buzz of a lawnmower were similar to the suburbs, but everything was more open and free. The distant clunk of someone teeing off on the golf course was so familiar. Oliver recalled coming back from work on summer evenings and sitting with the French doors open, reading or eating his dinner with that sound in the background.

Inserting the key into the lock, he pushed open the door. The house was cool as he'd set the heating to auto and it only came on low to stop the freezing, but once he put the burner on, it would quickly warm up. His furniture looked so comfy and familiar. It would be nice to sleep in his own bed again. Finlay had obviously been around and mown the lawn ready for his arrival and someone had put a vase of flowers on the dining room table. That definitely wasn't Finlay – probably Genevieve, though he wouldn't rule out Hayley. She didn't have a key, but she could have borrowed the spare from her brother.

He moved to the window, drinking in the view of rolling hills. His body was tense, like it had been chained for weeks and he wanted to unshackle himself and run free in the countryside. Raising his arms above his head, he linked his hands together and stretched high. The day had made him travel weary, but restless energy still bounded around his veins. Tomorrow he'd dust off the bike and go cycling.

He fired off a quick message to the wedding group chat to let everyone know he'd arrived, making it quite clear he was knackered just in case they decided to all call around. Both Finlay and Hayley were so affectionate and caring he could imagine them racing around to check he was ok. All he wanted was to prevent them from worrying. They could relax. He was here and wasn't going to miss the wedding. Despite his boss thinking it was excessive, Oliver had taken a full week off. He owed that and more to Finlay. With the wedding on Saturday, two days away, he'd make it to the rehearsal and be at home so Finlay could stay over the night before the wedding and keep alive the tradition of not seeing the bride before the wedding.

The house took a while to heat up and Oliver overrode the thermostat to make sure the radiators in his bedroom and the en suite were warm. He didn't mind a cold pillow, but he hated cold air after a shower and when getting ready for bed. His father's farmhouse had been like that when he was growing up. Some mornings he could hardly bear getting out from under his covers. He shivered at the memory.

He only had his small case with him, as he'd left a lot of clothes here. He took out his kilt from the wardrobe and hung it on the door to make sure it was aired. If it was a dry day tomorrow, he might even put it outside for a bit. His mum always said even if you could get the washing outside for a short while, it helped and made it smell better. He recalled finding socks and pairing them up at the kitchen table as she chatted to him. She may have been gone, but he still followed her advice when he could – the bits he remembered anyway. What would she make of the current state of his life? Would she be happy about his decision to go to London?

The induction period was up and the pressure was on to sell this house and look for somewhere more permanent. Now he was back, the uncertainty that had plagued him since he started in London doubled. He still wasn't sure he'd made the right decision, but coming back here didn't seem right either.

One thing that felt right was his bed. Compared to the somewhat lumpy thing in Ruislip, it was deluxe. He didn't bother with an alarm and it was luxurious to fall under the duvet at nine thirty and not have to worry about when he was getting up the next day.

He woke from the best sleep in a long time to the sound of birds going crazy outside his bedroom window. Pulling back the curtain, he gazed out on a beautiful day.

His shower, so spacious compared to what he'd been using over the last few months, was a joy and he spent way longer than necessary under the tropical rainstorm jet. How he'd missed this. Finlay and Genevieve were expecting him at the church later to help with their flower displays and orders of service, but that wasn't until the afternoon, so no point in getting properly dressed yet. He pulled on a pair of sweatpants and a t-shirt and smirked in the mirror. This was so not like him. He hardly ever had days like this. In fact, he only remembered wearing these trousers as pyjama bottoms one night when he'd felt cold. Other than that, they'd never been on.

Downstairs, he set the kettle boiling and checked his phone. Lots of messages had been added to the wedding chat. He scrolled down, checking he hadn't missed anything important. Mostly, it was everyone expressing delight at him being back and confirming arrangements for that afternoon.

He fired off a quick reply, saying he'd see them later before making himself a coffee and settling at the breakfast bar. He'd taken one sip when there was a knock at the door. *Who the...?* He placed his cup down, frowning. Hopefully just a delivery, though they must have got the wrong house. He wasn't dressed for receiving visitors. He opened the door. *Oh god...* He definitely wasn't dressed for receiving her.

'Hayley... What are you—'

Before he could finish, she pounced on him. Her arms were around his neck, her lips on his and her glorious body pressed against his. These sweatpants were such thin material, they were almost pointless. He kicked the door shut and joined in, kissing her, reacquainting himself with her. Oh Christ, just how good did this feel? And happy. Being happy was so unusual for him. Warm liquid was filling all the cold empty spaces inside him.

'Hello...' he said somewhat hoarsely, as she pulled away with a grin.

'Hi.' With her trademark smile in place, she patted his cheeks. 'I needed that. I missed you so much.'

'Me too.' He put his hands over hers and held them to his face. 'But I didn't expect you here. I thought we were done with our little fling.'

'I've reopened it,' she said. 'Why not? Unless you've got yourself a girlfriend in London.' She slipped her fingers free and ran them along his shoulders.

He shook his head. 'Definitely not.'

'Good. Well, naturally, I still don't have a boyfriend, so we're free to keep this going if you want to.'

'If we carry on with anything this week, we have to be careful. Finlay is staying here with me tomorrow night and there can be no sign that you've been here.'

She held out her hands and waggled her fingers. 'I have nothing with me to leave any signs... Unless you want to take pictures or something.'

'Er... I don't think so. Coffee?'

'That'll do, for starters.'

'You've already had starters.'

'So I have. Well, coffee will do as a palate cleanser because I don't want it to be the main course.'

'One flat white coming up.' Oliver smirked as he opened a pod for the coffee machine. 'Am I to understand you're only here for my body?'

'I can't deny it's a very nice body, but... Well, it's not the only thing I like about you.'

'Really?'

'Who wouldn't like a guy who remembers how I take my coffee?' She folded her arms. 'How do you know that, by the way?

Because I'm pretty sure I never had one at Finlay's or whatever you said before.'

'Your mum once told me when I was in the coffee shop.'

'Did she now? Meddling mother.'

He lifted her mug, handed it to her, and sat opposite her at the kitchen island. 'Listen...' How could he word this? 'I like you, Hayley, you know I do... And, well, it might surprise you to know I always did. You're a special person and I appreciate what you've done for me.' Though he didn't always like what she did *to* him without meaning to. 'I like being around you and how you make me feel.'

'But...'

'No buts, because feelings are just feelings. Just because they exist doesn't mean we have to act on them in a particular way.'

'You're such a lawyer.' She sipped her coffee. 'But I'm not sure I know what you're on about.'

'I mean, once this week is up, we go back to how we were.'

She gave a little shrug. 'Was there ever the chance of anything else?'

'Not really.'

'Well then.' She was smiling, but it didn't fully reach her eyes.

'That doesn't mean we can't enjoy this time together.' He finished his coffee. 'Why don't you come upstairs with me and let me show you how I feel?'

'And is this your turn to like me just for my body?'

He raised an eyebrow. 'I think it's safe to say we're as bad as each other in that respect, but I'm happy to go for a walk with you, sit and chat, watch a film, anything.'

A smile grew on her face. 'Let's save them for later. I'm way too curious to know how you feel. Up we go and you can show me.'

This was his chance. They'd done it before and it had been special, but now was the chance to make it the best. He took her hand in his and their eyes met. Fire raged through his blood. *Remember what you said in the heat of the moment last time?* Like he'd forget. Was that a case of his true feelings escaping? He couldn't let that happen again. Those little words were dangerous. They betrayed him and let her know his uncertainty. No one needed to know that. Long term relationships were not for him. But Hayley tested his resolve so strongly. She could break it any day now, and where would that leave him? What if he gave in? For a fleeting moment, he tried to imagine it, but his mind shut down.

He put his hands around her waist, pulled her hips close to his, dipped in, and kissed her. This was all that mattered. Kissing her and loving her like this. Emotional attachments weren't necessary. Somewhere in the back of his mind, thoughts still attempted to grab his attention. Scenarios that featured Hayley getting bored with his long hours or annoyed at having to move to London. They'd split up for sure. This was why he couldn't risk it. And that wasn't even the worst eventuality. What if she had an accident and was stolen from him?

'Oh god.' He pushed the thought away and pulled her close, pinning her against him. She was too precious to lose in that way.

'Are you ok?' she asked, and he lessened his grip.

'I just need you,' he breathed. Pulling back, he crossed his arms over his chest and ripped off his t-shirt. Hayley's appraising smile fired him up even more. He slid the neckline of her floaty top to one side and kissed her neck, running his hand over her breasts and capturing a nipple through the fabric. She let out a moan.

Fuck. I love her so much.

He could kid himself it was all physical, but was it? How could he ever feel this way with anyone ever again? In that case, did it mean everlasting love was real? This was the wrong time for deep thoughts.

Their clothes slowly came off as they made their way up the stairs, his sweatpants ending up draped over the banister. As they got to his bedroom, it struck him that no one had ever been in here with him. Any hookups he'd had were always in the woman's home. Even that seemed significant. He didn't want anyone else in his bed.

He kicked open the half-closed door with his foot, his lips still locked with Hayley's. Their arms snaked around each other, his hands moving across her smooth skin, stroking her glorious hair. Her fingers skimmed the planes of his back, tracing his shoulder blades, his obliques, and downward until she gripped his bum.

So much for wanting to take his time. This wouldn't last long at this rate. *Breathe. Control.*

'Lie down,' she said.

'What?'

'On the bed. I want to be on top.'

'Just like that?'

She nodded and grinned. 'I can't wait.'

He kissed her deeply. 'I'm so glad you said that.'

He fumbled to find a condom in his travel bag, then sat. The bed was soft beneath him and he lounged back, resting on the pillows as she straddled him. Her eyes bored into his as she lowered herself onto him. She tossed her hair like a goddess, her rosy breasts bouncing as she did so. Oliver clamped his hands to her hips and buried himself in her. Back in the most exquisite place in the world. She pinned him to the bed as their hips moved in sync, sitting up and rocking, then throwing herself forward so he could hold her, touch her, kiss her, love her. Their eyes met as she sat up again, rocking fast. He couldn't pull his gaze from her, but was he betraying himself? Eyes were the gateway to the soul, and she was so good at reading people. What was she seeing now? He slipped his fingers between them, touching her until her smile was huge and she was moaning wildly. Her long hair looped over one shoulder and fell carelessly across her swollen, rosy breasts. She was so beautiful, so joyful, so everything.

'Hayley, oh god.' He closed his eyes. If he didn't, something was going to happen. He couldn't be sure he wouldn't blurt out exactly how he felt.

'Look at me,' she said and as he opened his eyes, her lips were on his. She had her hands on his cheeks and she kissed him roughly, but it was hot. He moved his hands over her back, savouring the deep, most intimate connection.

I love you.

He gritted his teeth. *Must not speak. Not now.*

'Oh my god,' she cried, slumping into him and shaking. He held her tight as she came undone in his arms.

'It's ok,' he whispered, gently kissing her. And for this moment at least, it was.

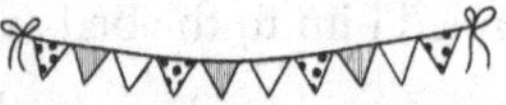

Later that day, Oliver and Hayley walked to the church from his house. The grand plan was that they'd return after and spend more time together. If they turned up together, no one needed to know they hadn't come from their respective houses and just happened to meet on the way.

'I can see why they called you for flower displays,' Hayley said as Oliver opened the creaky iron gate to the churchyard. 'I mean, you clearly have a flair for floral if that jug on your dining table is anything to go by.'

'That wasn't me.' He frowned at her, holding the gate open. 'I half suspected you.'

'Thanks, and not guilty.' She held up her hands. 'You must have another admirer who comes in and leaves you flowers.'

The gate shut with a clang.

'Genevieve I imagine... Though she's not an admirer.'

Hayley laughed. 'Just as well. That would really complicate things.' She gazed up at the trees that were coming into leaf all around them. 'Why do birds go mad in spring? What a racket.'

'Mating season, I guess.'

'You got that right.' She winked.

'Funny.' He glanced away. So many memories bounced into his mind when their eyes met. The conflicting thoughts were unbearable.

Genevieve was at the heavy studded oak doors talking to an older woman with short dark hair holding a large floral wreath.

'Best behaviour.' Hayley nudged Oliver as they strode up the hill towards them. 'Hello!' she called before he could reply.

Genevieve turned around and waved. Oliver let Hayley lead as ever and she was soon in full flow chatting about flower arrangements with Genevieve and the florist like they were her most favourite thing in all the world.

'This is Nancy.' Genevieve smiled at Oliver like she'd only just noticed him.

'Pleased to meet you.' He shook hands with the florist.

'You're the best man, aren't you?' Nancy adjusted her thick-rimmed glasses. She looked to be in her late fifties and had a kindly face.

'I am. Is Finlay inside?'

'Yes,' Genevieve said.

Oliver went through the main door and into a stone-floored vestibule that was lined with dark oak shelves filled with hymn books and bibles. This was where his mum's funeral had been. He remembered those shelves, but weirdly he'd never put two and two together and realised it was this church. How often he'd passed it on the way to and from the office. Such a pretty little place. Peaceful and beautiful. When he'd set foot in here before, his mind had been in such turmoil it hadn't registered where he was. His heart tremored a little as he stepped into the main area as if he was about to see her coffin at the front, but all he saw was Finlay with his hands in his pockets, looking up at the stained-glass windows.

'Hey,' Oliver said.

'Oh my god.' Finlay turned around, then winced. 'Will I get struck by a lightning bolt for blasphemy if I say that in the church?'

'I doubt it. Are you ok?'

'I am.' Finlay marched up to him and muttered, 'But all the wedding prep is driving me a bit crackers.'

Oliver clapped his shoulder. 'It's never too late to call it a day. It'll save me having to put you in touch with a divorce lawyer some time down the line.'

'Oh shut up.' Finlay shook his head. 'I still want to get married. I could just do with the organising bit being over.'

'It will be soon and I'm sure it'll all be fine.'

'Yeah. I know. It's funny how it seems to have taken ages to arrange, but at the same time feels like it's happened so fast I'm not ready at all.'

'Is that last-minute jitters?' Oliver asked.

'I don't know. It's more like a desperation for everything to be perfect.'

'It will be.'

'Thanks, man.' Finlay looked around. 'I hope this weather holds too. Genevieve has bought tons of umbrellas, just in case.'

'The forecast is good.'

'You checked?'

'I did. Didn't you?'

Finlay shook his head. 'I didn't dare.'

'Aha, best man duty done. It's all good, even that Rocky Rain-man says so.'

'You realise that's my cousin, Willow, behind that, don't you?'

'Yeah, and the forecasts are usually accurate, so I'm going with it.' Oliver let out a sigh and leaned his head slightly to check Hayley and the others were still outside. He couldn't see them, but their voices were chattering not far off.

'What's up?' Finlay said.

'Nothing. Why?'

'You looked like you wanted to say something without anyone hearing you.'

Finlay was an annoyingly perceptive friend sometimes. That was what came from knowing someone for a long time.

'I kind of do, but it's difficult.'

'Is it about Genevieve and me?'

'No. Not at all. I don't want anything to spoil your big day.'

'What then?'

'I've met someone.'

'Oh my god, that's great.' Finlay clapped his upper arm.

'It really isn't.'

'Why not?'

'Because her life isn't compatible with mine.'

'Why? Is this someone you met in London?'

'No. It's someone I met here before I went to London. But my life is there now, and hers is here.'

'You kept that quiet,' Finlay said. 'Who is she?'

'I'm not telling you that. I just needed to offload.'

'Well, isn't there some way you can see each other? Long distance maybe? It's never ideal but some people make it work.'

'I don't know. It's difficult. You know my feelings about relationships.'

'I do, even if they're bullshit.' He cringed again. 'Please, God, don't wreck my wedding. I didn't mean to swear.'

Oliver smirked. 'I'm just so confused.'

Finlay put his arm around Oliver's shoulders. 'How is London?'

Oliver let out a groan. 'Not really what I hoped for.'

'In what way?'

'Something's missing. Something always is. No matter what I do. Nothing's ever quite right.'

Finlay nodded his head from side to side as if weighing something up. 'What about when you're with this woman? Does that feel right?'

Oliver tilted his head and frowned. 'Well... I... Yes. I suppose it does.'

'Well then. Maybe that's what's missing. Maybe nothing will ever be right because you're not happy on your own. You always say you don't believe in lasting love, but why do you believe in a lasting career? Even when that career treats you like shit, you're willing to keep working at it, but when you meet a woman you like, instead of working on a relationship and trying to make it last, you're willing to sacrifice it. Jobs can be changed, Oliver. Girlfriends can too but remember with a person it's much more likely to hurt than with a job.' Finlay tightened his grip on Oliver's shoulder and gave him a gentle shake.

Oliver rubbed his forehead and looked away. Finlay had a point. A really good point. But what did it all mean?

Chapter Twenty-Five

Hayley

Hayley stood on tiptoes on the end of a bench, trying to attach a garland of flowers to the outside edge of the church door.

'Be careful,' Genevieve said. 'We should get Finlay to do that. He's taller. Actually, let's get Oliver just in case Finlay falls. I don't want him injured for the wedding.'

'But Oliver and I are expendable, are we?' Hayley pouted, pretending to be miffed.

'Actually no. Maybe we shouldn't do this.'

'Don't be daft. It'll be fine, but I'll get Oliver because I can't reach the top.' She hopped down off the bench and headed inside.

'Tell Finlay to come out here too. What's he doing in there anyway?'

Probably skiving. Hayley snuck into the cold, stone-floored vestibule. She knew flower arrangements weren't something that would ever interest her brother. He and Oliver were probably discussing cycling or something equally irrelevant.

Sure enough, she heard his voice as soon as she got inside.

'Why won't you tell me who she is? Do I know her?'

Hayley froze. This didn't sound like something she should burst in on or even listen to, but curiosity kept her rooted to the spot. She had to hear this. What woman? Had Oliver confessed what they'd been up to? Or was there another woman on the go? Hayley's heart flickered.

'I'm not giving you any details,' Oliver said. 'I don't want any intrigue or speculation. I just wanted to get it off my chest.'

'Well, I've given you my tuppence worth.'

'Yeah, and thank you. I appreciate it. It's just that my career has always been my priority.'

'I get that, and it's your choice. If you want that to be your life, then fine. But it seems to me you're doubting yourself. I don't get how you can just dismiss a relationship without even trying.'

'Because I've seen them go wrong so many times.'

'Only because of your job. You see the worst-case scenarios. That doesn't mean there aren't thousands more people out there in happy, committed relationships. I come from a family with plenty of breakups and divorces, but I still believe. If anyone should have a messed-up view of relationships, it's me. My parents are hardly great adverts for a long, happy marriage, but that doesn't mean I'll turn out like that. I want to get married and be with Genevieve. If we argue, then we work things out. We don't always agree, but we compromise and do what we can. Sure, it means letting go of some things we did when we were single, but so what? Life doesn't stand still.'

Hayley moved her head closer to the door and heard Oliver letting out a sigh.

'Maybe you're right. I just don't know how to move forward with this. I've only just got this job. It's not something I can give up on so soon.'

'What does she do? Can't she move to London?'

'We've only seen each other casually. It's too soon for her to move in. That's way too risky.'

'Sometimes life involves risks. Look at me. I almost ended up in Dubai.'

'True.'

A pause followed, and Hayley itched to know what they were doing. Maybe they were about to move this way. She didn't want to be caught and, while the idea of sneaking off somewhere quiet to digest Oliver's words looked quite appealing, she didn't have the luxury of time.

'Hey, guys.' She bounced in, putting on her biggest smile. She focused on Finlay because when she looked at Oliver her brain received signals that sent her crazy. Inwardly, she cringed, thinking about how she'd thrown herself at him that morning, but she'd been so desperate to see him. She was letting emotion take over, and that was stupid, because he kept telling her – and everyone else – he was staying in London. She couldn't have him, not unless she wanted to move or to try long distance.

'We're just coming,' Finlay said. 'We got talking.'

'Genevieve wants you.'

'On my way.'

'And I need you.' She turned to Oliver once Finlay had gone out.

'Right here? And now? Isn't that a bit risky?' Oliver said quietly.

'Far too risky. I need you to hang a flower garland at the front door.'

'Wow. I thought you'd never ask.'

She folded her arms and pulled a face. 'Well, I'm asking now, so get to it.'

He followed her out, and she showed him what she needed him to do. Watching him stretch up and hook the vine around part of the decorative door frame that jutted out was strangely hot. Perhaps it was the forearms on display. His were especially attractive, shown off by his black leather and gold watch. Or maybe it was his overall masculine shape or the woody scent he gave off as he raised his arms.

'I have a confession to make,' Hayley said as Oliver jumped down from the bench after hooking up the other end of the garland. He dusted his hands together.

'Yeah? Well, you're in the right place.' He glanced around. 'This is a Church of Scotland place though, so no confessional.'

'Not that kind of confession.' She flicked his arm.

'No? Because I know just how naughty you can be.'

'Indeed you do, but I also know about you.' She raised her eyebrow.

'Touché. So what's the confession?'

'I overheard you talking to Finlay.'

'About what?'

'About meeting a woman.'

He slowly closed his eyes, then opened them again. 'You realise I was talking about you? I don't have anyone else, if that's what you're thinking.'

'No. I wasn't thinking that.'

'Then what? I don't think I said anything I haven't already told you.'

'Not exactly.' She wrapped her arms around herself. 'But it sounded like you were considering acting on those feelings you told me you weren't going to act on.'

'Yes, that's true. Of course it's crossed my mind. I'm not an idiot. What I've had with you is like nothing I've had with anyone. Part of me is ready to give it a go. But the problem is that every part of me is living in London.'

Hayley sucked on her lip. 'I don't know what to say. I like London, I really do, but not to live in. It's just not the place for me. This is my home and I don't want to leave. My hopes, my dreams and my family are here. Moving to London would stress me out too much. I'm not made to commute and work long hours in a big city. I like being close to my mum, to Finlay and Genevieve, and working at the salon.'

'I get that and I wouldn't want you to be unhappy because of me. It would be totally unfair. Which leaves us back pretty much where we were before.'

'Stalemate.'

'Exactly.'

'Look… I'll think about it.' Her heart thudded in her chest, but it was painful. Should she give up everything to chase a man who was afraid of commitment all the way to London? She loved being with him, but he didn't want the same things as her. What if he never wanted to get married? Maybe he didn't want kids.

'Don't,' he said. 'I couldn't stand it if you gave everything up for me. Life has no guarantees. I'd be gutted if you moved to London and were unhappy.'

'Do you ever…' She swallowed, not sure if she could say the words.

'Ever what?'

'Ever think you would get married… have a family?'

He looked away with a sigh and shook his head. 'I don't know.'

She nodded and put her hand on his arm. 'I know, and I'm pretty certain you do too.' Letting out a long slow breath, she turned away and headed towards her family, leaving Oliver alone. She had nothing more to say to him just now.

CHAPTER TWENTY-SIX

Oliver

Oliver's lip twitched as he watched Genevieve and Finlay crack up laughing. They'd returned to the church for a brief rehearsal. Neither the bride nor groom seemed able to keep it together. Maybe it was nerves or just Finlay's jokey personality, but they just kept laughing, then hugging. The minister seemed to be enjoying the fun and insisted it would all go fine the next day.

'What's got into them?' Hayley whispered.

'I hope the rest of their marriage is this happy,' Oliver said.

'I just love them,' Hayley's mum said from her seat behind. She'd turned up to help decorate the church and been present for the rehearsal, but Hayley's dad hadn't. No one seemed bothered though.

'This is where the best man hands over the ring,' the minister said.

Oliver stepped forward and handed over the box. Finlay grinned and nodded. His expression said, *I knew you wouldn't let me down.*

It wasn't Oliver's way to make a joke out of something like this, like ninety per cent of best men would. He wouldn't pretend to have lost or forgotten the ring. He'd been given a job to do and do it he would. No nonsense.

When the rehearsal was done, they hung about outside chatting. The bridal party was meeting in the afternoon for a run-down of the following day's events with Genevieve's family. Her parents owned Greenacres, a large eco-mansion just outside the town, and were hosting the reception there in marquees. Oliver listened rather than joining in the chat, hyperaware of Hayley's proximity. He ran his hand around his perfectly shaven jaw. She'd come home with him yesterday after they'd decorated the church and worked her magic on him again, shaving him and trimming his hair. Then they'd spent the night together, making love, and Jesus, it had been good.

This couldn't go on, but how could he let go?

Finlay was coming over to stay that night with Oliver, and Hayley was staying with the Harringtons. Probably for the best, but the ache in Oliver's chest intensified at the thought.

'Do you know how to get there?' Finlay said and Oliver tuned back into the conversation.

'To Greenacres?'

'Yes.'

'You showed it to me on a cycle run once, remember?'

'So I did. Good. Well, let's meet there about two, ok?'

'Sure.' Oliver wanted to turn to Hayley and work out what she was doing, but she had already turned to Genevieve and they were deep in conversation. He could do this on his own. He'd had enough practise.

Greenacres was a stunning, purpose-built eco-house in extensive grounds. Oliver wandered around like a spare part, his mind rewinding to the dinner party at Nimbus 9 in London when he'd gone along with Hayley and felt on top of the world. Without her, something was missing. He wanted her by his side. When she was there talking to people, it was easier and a lot pleasanter.

Why the hell was he letting this happen? His career had always been the most important thing to him. Why all the doubt? Surely this infatuation would die eventually. Just like the initial passion in a relationship fizzled out, and either expired or evolved. He wouldn't feel this way about Hayley forever and once he was back in London, he could distance himself from these complicated emotions.

Or could he? The niggles he'd discussed with Finlay the day before hadn't gone away. What if his friend was right? Was Hayley the missing piece? Did his job never feel quite right because he was missing a special person in his life?

Hayley's laughter drew his attention, and he spotted her near the wall of glass doors, chatting with a small group of people. One of them was a tall and very handsome young man. Hayley seemed to know him and looked like she was almost swooning in his presence. Oliver ground his teeth. What else could he do? If he didn't want Hayley, he had to accept that other men would. How was she even single? She was so perfect he couldn't see her staying that way long. He moved towards the buffet table, not because he was hungry, but he couldn't bear to watch Hayley with anyone else.

'Christ on a bike.' Finlay came up behind him. 'I really could do with just having the wedding now.' He loaded his plate with food. 'Honestly, all this stuff is nice, but I just want to get married.'

'Not long to wait,' Oliver said. 'Who are all these people?' He frowned towards the man Hayley was talking to.

'Genevieve's relatives. Some of them are staying here. That's Cressida, her sister, over there with her partner, Tina, and their baby. They're talking to her cousins, who I can't remember all the names of. Don't tell her I said that. I'm pretending I know who everyone is. That's some other cousins chatting with Hayley, names of Lucy and Erica...' He pulled a face. 'I think. And the guy is Genevieve's brother, Rafe.'

Oliver picked up some crisps and nibbled them. 'And is he a single man in possession of a good fortune who happens to be in want of a wife?'

Finlay sniggered. 'Definitely the first two, but I'm not sure about the third. He's divorced and I don't think he's in any rush to go down that path again.'

'Ha. You see what I mean?' Oliver pointed a crisp at Finlay.

'About what?'

'About how common divorce is. You sure you want to go through with this?'

'Shut it,' Finlay said. 'Stop being a wedding-Scrooge.'

'Is that even a thing?'

'It is now.'

Oliver continued to watch Hayley chatting to Rafe. He may not be a man looking for a wife, but he struck Oliver as someone who wouldn't mind a hookup. He definitely seemed to be putting on the charm. Oliver crunched hard on a crisp, half wondering if he was really much different. In his head, he was busy telling Hayley to watch out; it was obvious the guy was after nothing but a fling. But Hayley could work that out for herself. She had with him.

Christ, she deserved better.

'Are you ok?' Finlay frowned.

'Fine. Why?'

'You're giving Rafe the evils. Is it because he didn't use you as his divorce lawyer? In his defence, he doesn't live here anymore, so he probably used someone in Glasgow. And I think it was a while ago.'

'Nope. I wasn't thinking about that at all. I wasn't even looking at him... Not intentionally. Something else caught my eye. I was just thinking, that's all.'

'Penny for them.'

'No, really. I don't want to share.'

'Ok, mate.' Finlay clapped him on the back. 'Let's join the others.'

Oliver followed Finlay, who unfortunately was making a bee-line for Rafe Harrington and Hayley. She beamed at them as they joined the group.

'This is going to be a stunning venue tomorrow,' she said. 'And it's so exciting that it's also the place Finlay proposed.'

'It certainly is,' Finlay said with a wry smirk. The story was the stuff of legend now. Somehow, it had worked out for them, but it was such a wild story, Oliver wasn't sure how it hadn't ended in disaster.

'Are you the best man?' Rafe asked Oliver.

'I am. Oliver Wright.' He put out his hand.

Rafe shook it. 'Rafe Harrington, brother of the bride.'

'Oliver's not just the best man.' Hayley said. 'He's also Mr Wright. Sometimes known as Mr Always Right.'

Rafe, Finlay, and the cousins laughed. Oliver frowned at Hayley. She pulled an all-innocent face.

'Whereas Hayley is sometimes known as Miss McBride, though Miss McBridesmaid is more apt.' Oliver raised an eyebrow.

Hayley shook her head, still smiling, but a flash of irritation sparked in her eyes. She slow clapped. 'It wasn't funny the first time, and this time isn't any better.'

'How many times have you pulled the *always Wright* joke? I suppose you think it just gets funnier and funnier.'

'Which, of course, it does. Never gets old.'

Rafe chuckled and gave Finlay a funny look. 'You picked a right pair for the best man and chief bridesmaid. Have these two been this in love from the start?'

He was clearly being ironic, but the phrase shut Hayley up and Oliver's jaw stiffened.

'Oh, god yes.' Finlay continued the sardonic tone. 'It'll be them announcing their engagement next.'

'Good luck with that.' Rafe toasted Oliver, then Hayley. 'You're a lawyer, aren't you?'

Oliver nodded.

'Hopefully you specialise in divorce, because it looks like you'll need it.'

'Actually, I do.'

'Ah, ok.' Rafe half laughed and took a sip of his drink.

'But we're not getting married,' Hayley said. 'There's no chance of that, is there, Oliver?'

'None.'

They locked eyes with each other, and, for a moment, that urge to take her in his arms returned. He almost didn't care people were watching.

Understanding crackled along an invisible wire. The attraction and desire hadn't gone anywhere but it wouldn't be going further.

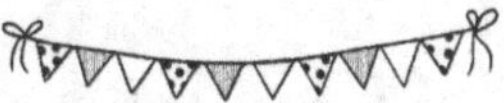

Finlay went to Oliver's house that evening after the party. Oliver was glad to be away from so many people, but missed Hayley already. He and Finlay had both eaten enough at the buffet to not want dinner, though he'd bought pizzas just in case.

'Beer?' He opened the fridge and took out a bottle.

'Yeah, but not too much. I don't want to be the groom with a hangover. My reputation is already thin after how we got engaged in the first place.' Finlay took the bottle from Oliver and searched the drawer for the bottle opener. Once he'd cracked open the bottle, he passed it to him.

Oliver held it up. 'To the groom to be.'

'Thanks.' Finlay took a drink. 'I hope your speech isn't going to be all doom and gloom and about divorce tomorrow.'

Oliver gave him a small smile. 'I'm not that cruel.'

'Thank god.'

They headed into the living area.

'This is the kind of house I need,' Finlay said. 'I love my riverside apartment, but if we have kids, it won't really be practical. When you sell this place, I might buy it.'

'I could do you an inside deal. We could cut out the middleman if you're serious.'

'Obviously I'd have to speak to Genevieve, but it's definitely the type of place we want.' He looked around like he was already imagining it being filled with his children. 'Are the neighbours nice?'

'Yeah.' Oliver gave a little shrug. 'I don't really know them, but they seem pleasant enough.'

'Perfect.' Finlay lounged back, adjusting the purple cushions, then sat up again and pulled something out from behind him. 'Nice scarf. Is this yours?' He held up some scrunched up grey fabric with white flowers on it.

The heat drained from Oliver's face. That was Hayley's scarf. Shit, shit, shit. 'Erm...'

'It looks like Hayley's.' Finlay held it to his nose. 'Smells like hers too.'

'What? You just smelt that?'

'Yeah. Remember, we used to do that at school. We always knew whose jumper was whose.'

'I'm not sure sniffing people's clothes was ever my thing.'

'This is definitely Hayley's perfume. What's it doing here?'

'No idea.' Oliver gave a nonchalant shrug. He hated lying, but the truth involved admitting the scarf had been wrenched off, along with several other items of clothing, and thrown aside to allow for a passionate encounter last night. He was pretty sure Finlay didn't want to hear about that.

Finlay tilted his head and gave Oliver a look laden with scepticism. 'Seriously? Come on. Has she been here?'

'Yeah.' Why did he keep shrugging like a teenager with a nervous tick? 'She's been here.'

'Why?'

'To tell me stuff about the wedding.'

Finlay raised an eyebrow. 'That she couldn't tell you over the phone? And that involved coming in here and taking off her scarf.'

'It was a warm day. You know what she's like.' Oliver was decidedly warm himself. 'She likes to chat.'

'Yeah, that's true. I just didn't imagine her wanting to come round and chat with you. You're not exactly her favourite person.'

'True.' He'd never be that now. No matter how much they desired each other, he wouldn't ever be the man she wanted... or needed.

Finlay tossed the scarf at him and laughed. 'You had me going for a minute.'

Oliver lifted it to move it to the side, and he caught the scent of her perfume too. So many memories flooded his brain. All of them made him want to smile, but also cry at the pain of not being able to repeat them. He didn't put the scarf down immediately and as he held it, staring at his minimalistic living room, a vision of his own started in his mind. It wasn't Finlay's children playing in the house, it was his. They were jumping on the sofas, making cushion forts and causing mayhem. A baby bounced in a little seat. Noise and chaos ruled, but also happiness and love. A home his mum would approve of. One she'd have loved to have visited as a grandmother. Why shouldn't that life be his? Maybe this time, instead of running from the fear, he had to face it head on.

'Are you sure you're ok?' Finlay was looking at him with concern in his eyes. 'You seem totally distracted. You've been like that all afternoon. Has your office been hassling you to get back?'

'My boss definitely thinks being off for a week is too long with the current caseload.' Oliver laid the scarf aside, grateful for the change of subject.

The longer he could keep Finlay away from chatting about Hayley, the better.

Finlay wanted to go to bed early, but not too early in case he couldn't sleep. Oliver was happy to go along with whatever he decided. This was his wedding, after all.

Eventually, they went upstairs at ten. Finlay man-hugged Oliver and together they stood in an embrace at the top of the stairs for a long moment.

'Thanks for choosing me,' Oliver said. 'I know I haven't always been enthusiastic, but I'm truly honoured to do this for you. You helped me through dark times and you've always been there for me when I had no one else.'

'Nae bother, mate.' Finlay clapped his back, his voice cracking a little. 'I'll never see you stuck. Remember that. No matter what changes in our lives, I'll always be here for you.'

Oliver tightened his embrace for a moment, then let go. 'Thanks. Now bugger off to bed and get some sleep.'

Finlay laughed and saluted. 'On it, mate.'

CHAPTER TWENTY-SEVEN

Hayley

The morning sun peeked through the large, energy-efficient windows of the Harrington's eco mansion, lighting up the wedding chaos that had taken over in Genevieve's bedroom. Hayley took a deep breath, very glad she'd enlisted Amber to help with this. She was happy to do Genevieve's hair for the big day. That seemed fitting, but it was too much to do everyone else's and her own.

Amber had Genevieve's sister sitting in front of the fold-out mirror she'd brought with her and was gently pulling the straighteners through her long hair.

Genevieve, in her fluffy white robe with *bride* on the back, looked amazingly calm. Her mum, Hilary, was dotting about like she wasn't sure what to do next. 'Deep breaths, Genevieve. Inhale peace, exhale bridezilla.'

'What?' Genevieve laughed and Hayley joined in. 'I haven't been a bridezilla, have I?'

'No,' Hayley said. 'You've actually been really calm about the whole thing.'

'She's been wonderful.' Lisa brought her hands together in front of her chest, looking on almost as fondly as if Genevieve were her own daughter. Well, her mum had known her since they were kids.

'That's the Finlay factor wearing off,' Hilary said. 'He's so laid back.'

'He is indeed,' Lisa agreed. 'Always has been.'

'He's probably the nicest guy you could marry,' Cressida said. 'He's always very pleasant, not to mention handsome and fit. Plus, I hear his bank balance is pretty good too.'

'Yeah, I did well, didn't I?' Genevieve said.

'You did,' Hilary agreed.

'But please stop talking about my brother as fit and handsome.' Hayley pulled a face. 'There are some images I could really do without.'

'That's tame compared to what I could be telling you.' Genevieve grinned.

'Oh stop.' Hayley held up her hand. 'Mum's listening.'

Lisa laughed. 'Doesn't bother me.'

Her mum had always enjoyed joining in the girl chat, and Hayley loved that.

Amber sprayed Cressida's hair, and the hairspray scent hung in the air. Hayley pinned a neat curl at the back of Genevieve's head.

'Stay still. This is a tricky bit.' Hayley bent down, pressing the pin into the curl to keep it in place.

Genevieve held steady until Hayley straightened up. 'I really hope I don't freeze during the ceremony or say something stupid.'

'Like what?' Hayley lifted the curling wand.

'I don't know. I'm just nervous.'

'You'll be fine,' Lisa said. 'You're so fantastic on camera.'

'Exactly,' Hilary agreed. 'Now that I've finally got with the programme and watched too, I can't imagine you messing up. You speak so beautifully on film.'

'Just make sure you say the right name during the vows,' another voice said, and the door opened. Genevieve's grandma came in with her sticks. 'This one is desperate to see what's going on.' Mitzi, the French bulldog, came toddling in, sniffing around.

'Aw my baby,' Genevieve said, and Mitzi ran to her.

'Just don't move suddenly,' Hayley said.

Hilary dashed over and caught Mitzi. 'Come on, you little rascal, let's keep you out of trouble.'

'Did anyone check the forecast with Willow?' Lisa asked.

'It's meant to be good,' Hayley replied.

'Looks like a lovely day.' Genevieve's grandma checked out the window.

'Ooh, guess what?' Genevieve said. 'Finlay messaged last night to say Oliver will sell his house to us when he gets a place in London.'

'What?' Hayley almost dropped the curling wand.

Why did that sound so final? Those dreams she'd had of pushing a buggy around that estate wouldn't come true. They would play out for her brother and Genevieve. Genevieve and Finlay would be the ones with the ideal home in the country. Sometimes life was unfair. But Hayley wasn't about to spoil their day because of a dream that was never likely to come true.

'That's great.'

'I know. It's exactly where we want to be. Houses hardly ever come up there, so we're definitely going for it.'

The door swung open and Rafe Harrington strolled in, holding a tray.

'Get out, brother dear,' Cressida said. 'What if we'd been in a state of undress?'

'Do people normally get their hair done naked?'

She rolled her eyes.

'I bring snacks. The caterers have provided kale chips, avocado toast bites, and these other things...' He picked up a bite-sized cracker and ate it, chewing like it was the most delicious and sexy thing he'd ever had. 'Can't remember what they said these were, but they're seriously good. All low in calories too.'

'Oh, Rafe.' Hilary took the tray from him. 'Off you go. No need to remind us of how lucky men are when it comes to metabolism.'

He raised an eyebrow and caught Hayley's gaze in the mirror. His smile was disarming and ever-so charming. He had that kind of face that was impossible to find fault with. All his features worked well together, and his eyes had a twinkle that was inviting, but a little naughty too. She imagined he had no trouble attracting women, but if he was thinking she was one of them, he'd got it all wrong. She just didn't fancy him – liked him, yes. Maybe if she dated him, she might grow to like him, but she didn't get anywhere near Oliver-level heat vibes from him.

Hilary sighed, gazing at Genevieve. 'I can't believe my baby is getting married.'

'Don't make me emotional, Mum,' she said. 'I need my make-up to last.'

'It is emotional though.' Lisa dabbed her eyes.

Cressida sipped her tea. 'Are you getting your hair done too, grandma?'

'Indeed, I am. Just say when.'

'I'll do you next,' Amber said.

Hayley carried on, setting Genevieve's hair in a half updo with loose curls. She had a pretty clip with roses and diamonds to fit into it too. Roses were the wedding theme and were special to Finlay and Genevieve. Finlay had proposed in a rose garden and it had become something of an emblem for them. Hayley looped another curl around the wand and her mind strolled off down speculation street. *Will I have an emblem or a theme for my wedding?* Assuming she ever had one, and right now it was looking as unlikely as ever.

'Sorry about Rafe, by the way,' Genevieve said.

'Why?' Hayley frowned at her in the mirror.

'For being flirty.'

'Hmm,' Hilary muttered. 'Not sure what he's up to. He told me he was bringing a partner but whoever she is, she's not here.'

'I don't know how he finds time to date,' Cressida said. 'He's a workaholic.'

'Yeah,' Genevieve agreed. 'I'd steer clear of him,' she added to Hayley. 'If you date him, you'll never see him.'

'Thanks for the heads up.'

But she wanted someone who lived here. Not a workaholic who lived in a big city. Like Oliver. Why had she let herself fall so hard? Couldn't she just have fallen for someone nice and available? Someone who was happy living and working locally? *Ugh.*

'Ouch.' Genevieve flinched.

'Sorry.' Hayley hadn't meant to stick in the pin quite so hard, but thoughts about Oliver came with a stab of annoyance. Taking it out on her friend wasn't her intent though. 'Are you ok?'

'Fine. Are you? You looked far away for a moment.'

'I'm just delighted you're getting married to my brother.'

Genevieve raised her hand and patted Hayley's. 'Your time will come. Just wait and see.'

'Ah, don't worry about that just now.'

Oliver had made his choice, career over love, and Hayley had to either suck it up or give up her life here. Could she do that? The idea of living in an apartment in London did not appeal. She'd love to do it for a week or so but not forever. If she did that and

Oliver agreed to marry her and have kids, the reality would be so different from the one she'd always wanted. Raising children in London wasn't like doing it here. Here everything was familiar, friends and family weren't far away.

Was she just sweating the small stuff? Was love really all that mattered? Maybe she should take control. Her heart hammered as her mind worked. People adjusted to change all the time. Could she do that? Maybe if she had Oliver, life in London would be ok.

The sleek, ivory-coloured wedding cars sat ready to whisk the bridal party to the church. Hayley bit back her own tears as Genevieve shared a teary-eyed moment with her father. Her long satin dress with a sweetheart neckline and an A-line skirt was just beautiful. Genevieve was simply the most stunning bride Hayley could imagine. The red roses in her bouquet matched the one in her hair and contrasted with the perfect white of the gown. Finlay was marrying his princess. Hayley welled up, imagining how he would feel when he turned around and saw her gliding down the aisle.

As Genevieve and her dad approached the car, a gust of wind caught the veil. It billowed around her father's head like a lacy blindfold.

'Oh god.' Hayley rushed forward and put it back in place.

'Disaster averted,' Cressida said. 'Let's hope that's the only one.'

Genevieve and her dad got into the bridal car and the chauffeur closed the door.

Hayley and Cressida gave them a wave before getting into the other car. The seats were plush cream leather, but the classic car wasn't as spacious as modern vehicles and there wasn't a lot of leg room.

Cressida gave her a look. 'I'm surprised Dad didn't insist on electric vehicles.'

The car crunched over the gravel, following the bridal car up the main driveway towards the road. Hayley smoothed her cerise chiffon dress, nerves growing in her stomach. Why was she feeling nervous? It wasn't her wedding, but she wanted everything to be perfect.

The vintage car glided smoothly along the back road towards Glenbriar. Cressida turned to her and smiled. 'This is surreal, isn't it? You have all the rehearsals and then—'

With a deafening bang, the car jolted violently, sending Hayley careening into the seat in front. Her eyes widened as she grabbed onto the armrest. 'What the hell?'

The driver swore under his breath and opened the door.

'What's happened?' Cressida said.

'Hit a pothole,' the driver muttered.

Hayley exchanged a glance with Cressida as the driver walked around the car, rubbing his forehead and frowning.

'Is the car ok?' Cressida leaned forward and called out the open door.

'It's buggered the tyre.' The driver bent over. 'And it might have knackered the axle. You better get out, ladies. It's not safe to sit in a car when we're stopped like this, even on a quiet road. I'll call for backup. The other car can come back for you.'

'That'll mess everything up,' Hayley muttered. 'That car is supposed to circle around until the last minute.'

'Maybe we should call someone to come get us. I'll see if Tina can come back, or Rafe.' Cressida pulled out her phone. 'I've only got one bar of reception here. We're in a bit of a dead spot. Let's see if it's enough to call.'

The driver didn't appear to be having much luck, judging from his frown and the way he was mussing up his hair. Hayley got her phone out too. She tried calling her mum, then her dad, but neither call connected. They'd be too busy to be looking at phones even if she did get enough reception. Maybe she should walk back towards the house. They hadn't gone that far and she could send a message once she was in range of the Wi-Fi, but would anyone look at them either?

'I'll walk along a bit and see if I can get reception,' the driver said. 'You ladies wait there and stand off the road. We don't want any accidents.'

Hayley looked at Cressida and pulled a face. This was definitely not in the plans. What on earth were they going to do?

Chapter Twenty-Eight

Oliver

People chatted around the church as Oliver and Finlay took their seats, their knees jutting out from beneath their kilts. Soft organ music drifted in the background and Oliver caught Finlay's eye. They both drew in a bracing breath, and Oliver leaned over adjusted the large pin on Finlay's shoulder that held his long tartan sash in place. They both looked the part, if nothing else. The moment was upon them. Nerves thrummed in Oliver's gut. How the heck must Finlay feel?

'What are we supposed to do?' Finlay said. 'Just sit here?'

'Yup. Keep smiling. Not long now.' Oliver turned around and leaned his arm along the back of the pew. At the top of the aisle near the entrance, Rafe Harrington stood handing out orders of service and chatting with new arrivals. Oliver narrowed his eyes and frowned when Hilary Harrington burst in, holding little Mitzi on a lead. Mitzi had a giant bow on her collar and was sniffing around people's feet. Hilary seemed to be having an anxious chat with her son. What was going on? She glanced towards Finlay, caught Oliver's eye and beckoned to him.

'Wait here,' Oliver said to Finlay. 'I need to find out what's happening.'

'What do you mean?'

'Nothing to worry about, I'm sure, just a last-minute problem with the flower arrangements or something. Don't worry, I'll sort it.' Adjusting his cuffs, he headed for the doors. He spotted Lisa close by. 'Can you sit with Finlay for a moment?' he asked her. 'I need to see what's happening here.'

'Sure.'

He didn't give her a chance to say more. Despite the assurances he'd just given Finlay, a tightness formed in his gut. Something wasn't right about this.

'There's a problem,' Hilary began, her expression fraught with concern. Mitzi scrabbled about at his shoes, trying to get his attention. 'Genevieve and Geoff are here, but the car with the bridesmaids hasn't arrived. We don't know where they are.'

Oliver's heart rate increased. Rationally, there was no need to panic. His mind was trained by years of navigating divorce cases, and he pushed himself to stay positive, though his brain had already leapt to the worst-case scenario. Images of accidents and irrevocable loss played inside his head even as he spoke, forcing his voice to stay calm.

'Weren't the two cars together?'

Hilary frowned. 'They were, but that road is very twisty, and the driver lost sight of the other one. He thought they'd got separated and the other car would catch up when they got here, but that's been almost ten minutes and he can't get the other driver on the phone.'

'I'm going to drive up there and see what's happened.'

'You can't,' Rafe said. 'You're the best man. You better stay here. I'll go.'

'We should ask Lisa if she's had a message,' Hilary said.

'Do that if you want, but I'm going anyway.' Oliver didn't wait for anymore arguing. 'Tell Finlay where I am, and I'll be back as soon as I can.'

'But—'

Whatever Rafe was about to say, Oliver didn't hear it. He was already out and running to his car. Latecomers would probably steal the great space he had in the car park, but that didn't matter. Getting back with Hayley was all that mattered.

As he started the engine, he reminded himself to keep breathing. His palms were clammy, and his pulse throbbed. Haunting memories threatened to overpower him, and he knew he wasn't the best person to be doing this. Rafe would have done the job fine. But if anything had happened to Hayley, he needed to be there. *Please god let nothing have happened to her.*

The road seemed to go on forever until eventually Oliver rounded a corner and saw the ivory car stopped on a bad bend, leaning unhealthily to one side. He slammed the car into the side and jumped out. Where were the passengers? Well, they must be alive, at least.

He searched around, rubbing his forehead. Where were they? They couldn't be walking as he hadn't passed them – unless someone else had picked them up. He jumped back in his car and checked his phone. The reception was poor.

Ok. Think.

Maybe they'd gone back to the house to get Hayley's car. He started the engine and put his foot down. As he got close to the driveway, he saw two figures walking along the side of the road – the driver and Hayley. Hayley. The tension left his shoulders, and he exhaled with a puff. Slamming on the brakes, he opened the window.

'Hey!'

Hayley turned at the sound of his voice, and he suddenly registered that Cressida was missing.

'What are you doing here?' she said.

'Looking for you and Cressida. What happened?'

'Cressida got a lift in with some latecomers, but they only had room for one person. She was going to get someone to come for me. But why you? You're supposed to be with Finlay.'

'Listen, get in and let's go. I'll explain in the car. Do you need a lift too?' he asked the driver.

'No. I'm going to walk back to the house and use the Wi-Fi to call the breakdown truck.'

'Ok.' Oliver waited as Hayley jumped in, then he turned the car and headed back to Glenbriar. 'As soon as you have reception, call someone and tell them I've picked you up, otherwise we'll have more people out here looking for you.'

'I still don't get why you're here.'

'When the car didn't show up, I panicked.'

'Why?'

'Why do you think? I care about you. I thought something awful had happened.'

'Wow...'

'I can't stand the thought of losing you. That's what'll happen though. This is what I meant about love. Love doesn't last. One way or another, it'll be stolen away. How can I live like this? How can I live panicking every second I can't see you that something terrible has happened and I'll be left alone?'

'Oliver... It's ok.' She reached out and touched his arm. 'Nothing happened.'

'But it could have done. What if a truck had come around that bend and crushed the car when you were in it? What if a car came off the road and hit you as you walked along the side?'

She shook her head. 'You can't control everything. That could happen to anyone.'

'I know. And it *has* happened to *me*. That's why I can't put myself through this.'

'Through what?'

'Hayley... I love you. I've loved you for a long time. But I can't stand it. I can't live with that fear hanging over me all the time. It's not about going to London or a fear of commitment. It's the fear of losing the person I love the most in the world and I just can't...'

Hayley shook her head and stared ahead, but whatever was on her mind, she didn't voice it. They were close to the church now and Oliver pulled in, double parking behind someone and getting out.

'Come on, we need to hurry. We're cutting it neat as it is.'

Hayley teetered along behind him. As they got closer, he took her hand, worried she might fall in her heels. If she did, she couldn't fall as hard as he'd done for her. Together, they dashed up the steps. Hilary, Rafe and Cressida were hanging about in the entrance hall with the minister.

'There you are,' Hilary said. 'Goodness me, we were all getting panicky.'

'The organist is going through the repertoire,' the minister said. 'If you go in, Oliver, and take your place, we'll get started shortly.'

Oliver glanced at Hayley and realised he was still clinging to her hand. She gaped at him like she'd been stunned and still said nothing. He adjusted his kilt jacket and made his way down the aisle, aware of many eyes on him and lots of whispering.

'Where the hell did you go?' Finlay muttered.

'Didn't Rafe tell you?'

'Yes, but why wouldn't you let him go? I was utterly freaked out.'

'Sorry.' He put his hand on Finlay's shoulder. 'Just doing my best man duties and making sure the bridesmaids were ok.'

'And did you find Hayley?' Lisa asked.

'Yes. She's here.'

Finlay let out a sigh. 'What is it with you and her?'

'Nothing. Just relax. This is your day. Smile. It's ok. Everyone is here; everyone is fine.' The last words came out like a mantra, more to himself than Finlay.

'I love you, son.' Lisa leaned over and kissed Finlay, then shifted into the pew behind.

'Your bride awaits,' Oliver whispered.

Finlay's lips quirked up, and Oliver grinned along. No way would he ruin his best friend's wedding by telling him he'd fallen for his sister but was leaving her because he couldn't bear to lose her. Even in his head the logic failed, but only someone who'd been through what he had could understand.

This was Finlay's day and Oliver would damn well smile, even if it killed him. Plastering it onto his face, he got to his feet and Finlay did the same. The music started and the minister walked down the aisle. He shook hands with Finlay and Oliver before taking his place. When the doors opened again, Genevieve entered with Geoff to a collective gasp. She looked stunning, and Oliver saw Finlay struggling to keep his emotions in check. He was such a big softy.

When Oliver caught sight of Hayley walking behind, his heart tumbled down a flight of stairs. She was gorgeous and so poised, smiling brightly but when she caught his eye, it faded slightly and she stared forward, not maintaining eye-contact.

When he sat down, she followed, taking the space next to him, but she still didn't look at him. How could he blame her? He hadn't ruined Finlay's day, but he'd probably just ruined hers.

The ceremony went without a hitch and exactly to plan. Even Mitzi sat perfectly on her ivory velvet cushion. But Oliver didn't want to let what he'd said to Hayley spoil it. He had to make sure no one looking at photos in years to come would know the best man had done anything but behave impeccably on the big day.

Outside, he posed for a few pictures with Genevieve and Finlay and one with Hayley and Cressida. When the photographer was done, he took Hayley's arm. 'Can we talk?'

'What about?' she said, her expression cold. 'This isn't exactly appropriate.'

He steered her around the side of the church, where the graveyard stretched out to meet a little stream. 'Listen, I'm sorry about what I said. Or at least *how* I said it. Please let's not allow it to spoil this for Finlay and Genevieve.'

'Who do you think you are?' She gaped at him. 'I have no intention of spoiling my brother's wedding. You, on the other hand, have been indifferent to it from the start. We would have done nothing for the sten if it was left to you. You didn't help

Finlay choose an outfit or assist with any of the admin. Then, on the day, you leave him alone to come running after me. And why? To tell me you love me but never want to be with me. God only knows what's going on in your head because I sure as hell have given up trying to understand it. So don't you dare lecture me or try to make out that something *I* might do will spoil this wedding.' She spun around and stalked off. Oliver took a deep breath and straightened the lapels of his kilt suit.

Right. That was comprehensive enough, and I probably deserved it.

His instinct was to go after her and argue his case, but he didn't. Because she was right, and he didn't want to make a scene.

He made his own way back to the Harrington's house. The wedding car was no longer at the side of the road, so he assumed a breakdown truck had picked it up. Inside, people were milling about and he was a spare part again. Lots of people were surrounding Finlay and Genevieve and Oliver joined the group, pretending he had a purpose, though he didn't know what it was.

'We're getting photos taken shortly,' Genevieve said. 'We need to go with the photographer to the garden. Has anyone seen my bridesmaids?'

A few people looked around.

Finlay caught Oliver's eye and Oliver thought for a second Finlay was going to ask him to go and look for them, but he didn't. He made his way over and embraced Oliver. 'It's finally done.'

'Congratulations.' Oliver clapped Finlay on the back. 'And I apologise if I haven't pulled my weight as best man.'

'Nonsense. You paid for the sten. I wasn't expecting that and I still feel bad about it. That was a lot of money.'

'Really. I don't mind. If it makes up for everything else.'

'There's nothing to make up.' Finlay looked him up and down. 'Why are you saying that?'

'If you're happy, that's all that matters.'

His gaze swept the room, searching for Hayley. She'd vanished again, but why should that worry him? He'd done what he could to protect his heart and now he could go on living as he'd always done... Only it didn't seem to be working that well.

CHAPTER TWENTY-NINE

Hayley

Hayley shut the door behind her, and let out a long, slow breath. Thank god for the peace and quiet. The Harrington's house had several spare bedrooms, and this one was all hers. She couldn't stay for long, but she needed a moment. The muffled sounds of the wedding reception downstairs were a constant reminder of what she was missing. Hopefully no one was missing her.

Just ten minutes and she'd be fine. Once she'd collected her thoughts, she moved towards the mirror and peered at her reflection. *Come on, Hayley! Why the long face?* This wasn't her at all and to come over so sullen on Finlay's wedding day was beyond cruel. No matter what Oliver may or may not have done to cause this pain.

Oliver! That bastard. How could he? How dare he! Why did he think it was ok to confess that he loved her only to inform her he never wanted to be with her?

'Well, screw you,' she told her reflection. Her dark eyes were tinged with a hint of red. So? People cried at weddings. She could pass it off as that. Or better still, cover it up. She took a steadying breath, and opened her make-up bag, locating the magic veil tube. This stuff worked wonders. She blinked a little and dabbed away the remaining tears. That man didn't deserve them. He was selfish. All he cared about was himself. His heart was so well protected no one would ever get to it. He'd die alone, never knowing what it was like to have loved and been loved in return. Maybe when he was a lonely old man, he'd look back and wish he'd done things differently, but there was no telling him that now. He'd made up his mind.

She ran the veil pen under her eyes and patted it on with her fingertip. The result was instant. She reapplied a little eyeliner and touched up her mascara. No one would ever know anything was wrong.

'Hayley,' someone said with an accompanying knock on the door. 'Are you in there?'

Shit. Genevieve.

'Just coming. I need to fix my make-up. Have I missed anything?'

Genevieve opened the door. 'No, you haven't missed anything.' She slumped onto the end of the bed. 'It's nice and quiet up here. Can you sort this curl before the photos? It's escaping a bit.'

'Sure. No problem.' Hayley got her hair bag and re-pinned the curl, though it was only a tiny bit loose.

'Is everything ok?' Genevieve said. 'You're very quiet. Is this really hard for you? I mean me getting married first and to your brother...'

'No, no, none of that. I don't mind that you're getting married first and I'm delighted it's to Finlay.' She closed her eyes for a second. 'Listen, I don't want to spoil your day by making this about me. Let's go down and get the pictures taken.'

'Hang on. What do you mean by making this about you? Has something happened? Because if it has, I insist you tell me. I'm still your friend, wedding day or not.'

'I'm just annoyed with Oliver, but don't worry. He'll be back in London before we know it and then we'll never see him again... And... oh god, I hate him.' She got to her feet and balled her fists.

'Bloody hell. What's he done that's this bad?'

'You won't even believe me if I tell you, so let's just forget about it and go back downstairs.'

Genevieve stood up. 'I will believe you. Now tell me.'

'Fine. Here's the short version. We've been seeing each other on and off since we started as best man and bridesmaid.'

'What?'

'Yes. Nothing serious... Well, you know. But anyway, he decided today to tell me that...' She looked away. 'I can't say it. It sounds so stupid.'

'Just say it. What did he tell you? I'm freaking out here.'

'He said he loved me, but he didn't want to see me again because he's terrified of getting into a relationship in case he loses me.' Hayley covered her mouth, willing the tears not to make a reappearance.

'Bloody hell.' Genevieve let out a low whistle. 'Ok. That's unexpected. And how do you feel about him?'

'I hate him.'

'Really? It doesn't look like that to me.'

Finlay's voice accompanied another knock on the door, 'Hayley, are you in there? Have you seen Genevieve?'

'We're both here.' Genevieve opened the door.

'Are you coming?' he asked. 'Did you get your hair fixed?'

'Yes. It's done. Listen, come in here a minute.' Genevieve pulled Finlay in the door.

'What's going on?'

'Can I tell him?' Genevieve said.

'Please, no.' Hayley let out a groan. 'Can we just go and get the photos done?'

'Tell me what?'

'Fine, tell him, but I don't want to listen. I'll see you downstairs.' Hayley left the room and almost put her fingers in her ears and la-la-la-ed. How cringy. What would Finlay make of it all?

She spotted Cressida and joined her and her partner, Tina, with their tiny baby, Alexander. 'Genevieve's just coming,' Hayley said. 'I was fixing a loose curl.'

A few minutes later, Genevieve and Finlay came in and people cheered, clapped and wolf whistled. Everyone crowded around them, chatting and offering congratulations.

Hayley made her way forward until she was close to them. Where was Oliver? Conspicuous by his absence. Well, should she be surprised?

'That was an interesting story Genevieve told me up there,' Finlay muttered in Hayley's ear and she exhaled sharply. 'What are you going to do about it?'

'Nothing. What can I do? He's a pig-headed, arrogant, self-loving—'

'Actually, he's just a very lonely, very unhappy man, who's never really got over the trauma in his past. He thinks love is the last thing he needs, but actually it's the only thing he needs.' Finlay put his arm around her shoulder.

'Ha.' She almost spat the word. 'And you think I'm going to give it to him after what he said to me?'

'That's not up to me,' Finlay said. 'But I'm pretty sure you're the only woman he's ever said those three little words to. And if you feel the same, you've got to convince him.'

'No way. That's his problem, not mine.'

'Suit yourself. But he doesn't know how to change. You, on the other hand... Well, you're the mistress when it comes to people.'

She gave him a sharp look. 'I've already tried. I'm not his therapist.'

'But you're probably the only person apart from me that he's ever really talked to.' He let out a sigh. 'I know it shouldn't all fall on you, but if it's important to you, please try. He told me some stuff when we were decorating the church and I guess now he was talking about you. I don't think his life is working out for him, but it's got nothing to do with his career. That's what he'll say it is, but he's lonely. Now he's found someone he cares about, and he doesn't know what to do.'

'But what's the point if he just keeps saying no?'

Finlay kissed the top of her head. 'Yeah. You're right. Maybe it's just not meant to be.'

'Where's Oliver?' Genevieve asked. 'We need him for the photos. And I don't see my mum and dad either. Or yours.'

'I saw Dad a minute ago.' Hayley glanced around. 'With Liz.' She was hard to miss in the garish leopard print dress she'd teamed with a fuchsia hat and shoes. 'Hang on. I'll ask Mum if she's seen them, and I'll start rounding people up.'

She made her way over to her mum, who had opted for a more subdued and sensible look in her lilac dress and matching jacket.

'Have you seen Dad and Liz?' Hayley asked. 'We need them for the photos.'

'She's about somewhere terrorising the men. I saw Marcus Bowman practically running away from her.'

Hayley covered her mouth to stopper a laugh. 'She's some woman.'

'I'm more worried about Oliver though.'

'Why?' Hayley furrowed her brow.

'I saw him leaving, and he's never come back in. He didn't look good. Do you know if he's ill or something?'

'Um... no. But.' She scanned around the crowd. 'Which way did he go?'

'Into the garden. I hope he's ok. Should I go and look for him?'

'I'll go.' With a deep breath, she flicked her hair over her shoulders and headed outside.

CHAPTER THIRTY

Oliver

Almost every part of Oliver was telling him to leave. But somehow, he had to find a smile and not ruin this for his best friend. He clenched his fists and turned to walk back to the house. His eyes connected with the one person he both wanted to see and couldn't bear to. But Hayley's face, normally so cheerful and full of joy, was icy. She glared at him as she marched forward.

'It's nearly photo time,' she said. 'You need to be there.'

Yes, he did. He had to do what was right, not what was easy. Surely that wouldn't be too difficult for Mr Wright or Mr Always Right. That nickname didn't fit, not really. He'd always made what he deemed the correct decisions at work and for his career, but when it came to relationships, he was woefully wrong. He'd had the opportunity for something special with a wonderful woman and he'd failed.

His help leading up to the wedding had been negligible, and he couldn't refuse this.

'Listen, can we talk? Later, if not now.'

'You think I want to talk to you?'

'No. I imagine you want to kick me in the nuts and slap my face, but that might not look too good. If we can get through the photos without a black eye that would be best.'

'Since when have you cared about any of this?'

'I care about my friend. This didn't matter as much as it should in the beginning. You've borne the brunt of it, and I'm sorry.'

'I feel like we've already ruined it. This is meant to be a happy day, but I feel completely shit.'

Oliver glanced over Hayley's shoulder and saw Finlay and Genevieve exiting the main house. Finlay smiled over at him. If he hoped anything would happen between his best friend and his sister, then his hopes would be dashed.

'I'm sorry,' Oliver said again.

'Me too.' Hayley turned and walked away. Oliver stood rigid and alone for a few seconds. A crushing sense of loss over-whelmed him and, stupidly, completely uncharacteristically, he almost cried. What the hell was wrong with him? Clearing his throat and adjusting his lapels, he made to follow, but he couldn't.

Hayley had reached the bridal party and was chatting to Rafe Harrington. He was gesticulating and laughing. Hayley grinned at him. This was who she was: an outgoing, fun woman, who wouldn't stay single for long.

Oliver wandered into the rose garden and along the trellis-lined paths until he came to a place with a little pond and a bench. He'd seen this place before on social media. Finlay had initially proposed to Genevieve here. He sat on the bench and put his head in his hands. What was happening to him? Everything he'd done made sense in his mind, so why did he feel so bad? Why was he always so empty? No matter what he did, a constant ache lingered in his heart. Originally, he'd put it down to losing his mum, but now it seemed more than that. Like he'd lost a bit of himself. Or maybe a bit of himself was still undiscovered. How could he find it? Would he ever? Where was the missing piece? He needed it.

'Oliver,' a woman's voice said.

He started, his hands falling from his face, and for a heart-stopping moment, he thought he would look up and see the ghost of his mum. He blinked. But it wasn't a spectre. It was Hayley. 'Oh... Hi.' He dropped his hands to lean them on his knees.

'Are you coming for the photos or what? Finlay sent me to look for you.'

'Oh god. Yes.' He went to stand, but Hayley put up her hand.

'The photographer is doing Finlay and Genevieve on their own first, so now's your chance.'

She sat beside him, but still with some distance between them.

'I'm not sure what to say.'

'Well, you better think fast.' Hayley stared forward at the pond. 'Because we don't have long.'

'I know you're mad at me, and I don't blame you. It's—'

'Actually, before you say anything, let me tell you something. Before your big confession earlier, I'd been thinking about giving up my life here and going to London with you. It wasn't exactly the life I'd planned in my head, but you know what, relationships need compromise sometimes.'

'That wouldn't be fair, you'd—'

'Let me finish. I was considering it because I love you.' Her voice cracked slightly.

'Hayley... You know that I do too but—'

'But you're too scared. I know. And there's no point in me giving up my life here because no matter where I am, it wouldn't take away the fear. If we lived together in London, you would still panic I would die in a tube accident every time I left the house.'

'Exactly.'

'But Oliver, if you're so afraid of losing me, why are you so willing to give me up?'

'What do you mean?'

'If you go back to London, you'll lose me anyway. I love you, but I won't wait forever. I can't. I have things I want to do with my life. Maybe I'll never find someone I love as much as you, but I'll try.' She held her hand to her lips. 'And you know what? I could still get knocked down or have a car accident. These things might happen whether you're with me or not. I get that you're trying to protect your heart, but what if you spend your life doing that and nothing ever happens? Isn't it worth the risk for the chance of happiness in between? Happiness is the journey, not the destination, because you may never arrive. Or you may be there already, but don't realise it. Do you have to wait until all your ducks are in a row before you do anything? Or can you accept that sometimes a couple of wonky ducks are ok? By the time they're all lined up, you might have forgotten what you were lining them up for in the first place.'

A lump worked its way up Oliver's throat and his eyes prickled. He forced himself to nod because he wasn't sure he could get words out. She was so right. He'd spent his life trying to create perfection without leaving room for happiness.

'I'm going back,' she said. 'You should come too. You're needed for the photos. I've put my cards on the table, and I can't do any more.' She got to her feet and waited for a moment. He didn't move. How could he? With a little shrug, she walked away.

Go after her! The voice in his head shouted, but his heart trembled, and he stayed put. This was the moment. He had to decide. He could plough on like he'd always done, trying to avoid sadness, but it might come anyway, or he could be brave and take this opportunity before Hayley found someone else.

He closed his eyes tight and opened them again. The fountain tinkled incessantly, and his eyes landed on the statue in the middle of it. A stone woman with long flowing hair danced with a little boy who was cherub-like with curly hair and a pudgy little tummy. Marks and weather blemishes stained the woman's face, but she was smiling. *At me?*

He'd never really believed in beyond the grave type messages or signs from another world, but words formed inside his head, and he wasn't sure where they were coming from.

What really matters is not what we bought, but what we built; not what we have, but what we shared; not what we lost, but what we loved.

How could he let this fear of loss carry on? Hayley was right. What if he spent his whole life worrying about something that may never happen? Life was going on right now and with every second he remained static, he was missing it, and he couldn't let that happen.

CHAPTER THIRTY-ONE

Hayley

With a deep breath, Hayley approached the crowd at the door, ignoring the thumping pain in her chest. The agony of knowing Oliver was alone stabbed her almost as thoroughly as if Finlay and Genevieve had run the cake knife through her instead of their magnificent three-tiered cake.

'How are you?' a deep voice said, and she turned to see Brann smiling beside her.

'Good. You?' She brushed down her dress, composing herself. 'You still on your own?' She checked around.

'As ever.' He gave her a shrug with that crooked grin of his.

'Aw.' She patted his arm. 'I take it Finlay and Genevieve are still having their pictures done?'

'Apparently there's a stile somewhere, and the photographer wants her to sit on it.'

'You're very knowledgeable about it.' Hayley eyed him over.

'I was listening in.' He winked, then scanned around. 'Are you here on your own too? Or are you and the best man hooking up? He looked like he had his eye on you.'

'It's not happening.'

'Oh dear.' Brann's smile faded. 'Why not?'

'He's got a job in London.'

'Ah. I see. A career man.' His eyes travelled over her shoulder.

'Most definitely. His career is what matters, and it's a lot more important than—'

Brann coughed and raised his eyebrows, nudging her to look behind. Hayley spun around. Oliver stood close, but his eyes were on Brann. 'Do you mind if I have a word with Hayley... in private?'

'Go right ahead.' Brann winked at her. 'I got a good feeling about this.' He did a funny shake of his kilt and moved away.

Hayley let out a little laugh, then turned to Oliver and put her hands on her hips. 'What do you want? I've said everything there is to say.'

'Come with me, just for a moment, please.'

She sighed and glanced at her feet. For a few seconds, she breathed slowly then looked back at him. 'Why? I'm not sure I want to.'

'Ok... Then I'll say it here.'

She'd never been any good at holding a grudge. 'Oh fine. Let's go over there where it's quieter.'

His hand touched her lower back as they moved, and it felt so good. So right, but she had to remember this was just temporary.

'I heard what you said to him about my career.' He stopped beside a bush close to one of the large windows. No one was about to hear, but people inside must be able to see out. Were they watching this?

'Good, because it's true.'

'No, it's not. There's always been something missing from my life. For years, I thought it was my mum. But as I got older, it changed. I've never been great at talking about my feelings or even thinking about them. It's been easier to bury them away.'

'Yeah, you're good at that.'

'I am. But that needs to stop. I'll do what I need to. It might mean going back to counselling. It might mean just talking more to my friends. Because it's you, Hayley.'

'What's me?'

'You're what's missing. The love...' His voice faltered, and he took a deep breath. 'The love you've given me is what's missing. My work isn't the most important thing in my life. You are.'

She pressed her lips together, barely able to look at him. These were noble words, but did they mean anything?

'I'm so sorry.' He took hold of her arms and leant his forehead on hers. 'I've been an idiot.'

She tried to nod but couldn't move her head. Tears welled at the corners of her eyes. 'You're far from being an idiot.' She forced out the words. 'You just don't know what it's like to be loved.'

'I want to.' His voice was hoarse, and he looked at her like he was trying to smile, but his eyes glistened. 'I really do. It terrifies me. But ever since I've got to know you, it's been what I wanted. It took me a long time to recognise it or admit it.'

'But what does it mean? I want different things from you. I want to get married and to have a family. You don't.'

'I didn't. But that was before you. It was easier not to want these things and kid myself life was better on my own, but I'm not. When I'm with you, that's when I feel most alive.'

'Oh god, Oliver.' She reached up and took his face in her hands. 'Do you really mean all this?'

'Every word. I swear.' His eyes shone.

She wrapped her arms around him, and he pulled her tight against him. 'You know I can't promise everything will be ok all the time.'

'I know. But together we can be strong.'

'Yes. We can.' She peered up at him.

He clutched her face in his hands, then kissed her with his wonderfully soft lips. 'I want you so badly. I can't bear the thought of being apart. Who was I kidding thinking going back to London without you would make everything better?'

'Just yourself.' She rubbed her hand over his back, and he increased his hold on her. 'But the fact is, you *are* going back to London.' Her heart squeezed. 'I want to be with you, but—'

'I don't want you to come to London.'

'Why not?' She frowned.

'Because I'll come back here.'

'But what about your job?'

'I'll find one here. This is where I really belong.'

'What about London and—'

'All of that is replaceable, but you're not. Your life is here, so that's where my life needs to be. I told you. You're the missing piece. The thing that's been missing from my life forever. There's nothing more important. We have a life ahead of us together, one with a wedding, a house in the suburbs and kids to make lots of noise and mess.'

A smile nudged her weary muscles and light and sparkle returned to the world.

A tapping on the glass caught her attention, and she saw Brann through the window. He gave her the thumbs up, and she laughed.

'There's Finlay and Genevieve.' Oliver pointed back to the main door. 'We should go and get our pictures taken.'

Hayley smiled, and warmth filled every chamber in her heart. 'Will you manage a smile?'

'I definitely will.'

They joined the bridal party and followed the photographer back into the rose garden.

'This is where it all started,' Finlay said with a grin. Genevieve beamed at him and led little Mitzi along the path on a diamante lead, which was super cute.

Hayley's mum caught up and took her arm. 'I'm not looking forward to having my photo taken with your dad,' she muttered, then glanced at Oliver. 'Are you ok?'

He was smiling so broadly, Hayley almost laughed. No one was used to seeing him so cheerful – no wonder her mum couldn't work it out.

'Never better.'

'Oh... That's great.' Lisa smiled back, though her brow was a little furrowed.

'Parents first,' the photographer called.

'Great,' her mum muttered, but she pulled out her best smile.

'She's doing a good job keeping it real,' Oliver said.

'She's the best.'

When she returned to Hayley, she said, 'I'm sure Liz is a lovely woman, but she gets on my nerves.'

'She's best in small doses,' Hayley admitted.

'Bridesmaids and best man!' The photographer called. 'Gorgeous.' He gently nudged Oliver's arm. 'If you ladies could stand on either side of him and maybe you could link arms.' He pointed to Hayley. 'You're nice and tall. And you' – he directed Cressida slightly in front of Oliver's arm – 'perfect.'

Hayley loved how good it felt to be on his arm again, and she couldn't stop smiling.

'Lovely,' the photographer said. 'Now, just the two bridesmaids. Then we'll get the best man and the chief bridesmaid together.'

Hayley posed with Cressida, catching Oliver's eye, and smiling even more.

When it was their turn together, Hayley's heart raced a little faster than normal. This was oddly like it could be their own wedding. Everyone was watching. The poses seemed a little stiff. Then Oliver took both Hayley's hands in his and turned her to face him. Before anyone could say anything, he leaned in and kissed her on the lips.

'Oh my god,' Genevieve squealed, and someone wolf whistled.

'I bloody knew it,' Finlay said.

'Aw,' her mum cooed, and the photographer's camera clicked.

But Hayley couldn't focus on any of it. She was too busy enjoying the heat of Oliver's lips on hers. When he pulled back, he was still smiling. 'I love you.'

'I love you too,' she said.

'Aw, you two.' Genevieve stepped up and hugged them. 'I never thought today could get any better, but it just did.'

'Explain yourselves.' Finlay joined the hug.

'Yes, do,' Lisa added.

'Oh, this is intriguing.' Liz nudged Hayley's dad, and he looked on, totally bemused.

'Oliver's coming back to live in Glenbriar,' Hayley said.

'And we're getting together.' Oliver kept his hand tight on Hayley's shoulder.

'Are you serious?' Finlay looked between the two of them.

'Always,' Oliver said.

'That's his name, after all.' Hayley beamed at him.

'What will you do?' Finlay ran his fingers through his hair.

'Nothing right now,' Oliver said. 'Except kiss your sister and maybe some other things that you don't need to know.'

'Damn right. Keep that to yourself.' Finlay smiled at them both, then at Genevieve.

'This is so great.' She wrestled them all into another group hug, and Hayley laughed.

At the meal, Hayley was at the top table beside Oliver, and she just couldn't stop smiling.

'What are you going to say in your speech?' she asked.

'Wait and see.' He winked.

Finlay and Genevieve had elected for the speeches to be before the meal. Geoff Harrington went first with a humorous and affectionate speech about Genevieve.

Finlay went next, getting a huge round of applause when he announced, 'My wife and I would like to thank you all...' No one missed his joke about third time lucky... He'd already been engaged twice before Genevieve.

'He did well to keep it together,' Hayley said. 'You know how emotional he can get.'

'Yeah, I do.' Oliver squeezed her hand. His turn next.

He stood up and adjusted his tie, his eyes landing on Finlay. He smiled, and it was infectious, lighting up his whole face. He'd always been handsome, but now he was beyond gorgeous. Hayley rested her chin on her hand, gazing up at him like a dreamy-eyed puppy. How could she help herself?

'I promise to keep this short,' he said. 'Like my patience for Finlay's jokes.'

Finlay slow clapped as everyone else laughed.

'I'm sure Genevieve understands what I mean, though I'm not sure she's grasped just how many years of those jokes she's signed up for. I hope you know a good divorce lawyer.'

Finlay pulled a face.

'That's the only divorce lawyer joke, I swear. Today, we gather to celebrate the union of two wonderful people – Finlay and Genevieve. I've known Finlay for what feels like an eternity, and believe me, it's been an adventure. We've been through highs and lows, but amid all the chaos, there's one constant – his loyalty and unwavering friendship.

'Finlay, you've always been the kind of guy who jumps head-first into whatever life throws at you. Sometimes that's meant dragging me along for the ride, quite literally when it involves a cycle run, and other times it's led to questionable fashion choic-es... again I return to the cycling. I'd never even touched a piece of Lycra before we met and now it's my go-to weekend wear.'

Hayley covered her face to laugh. *Oh god, the Lycra!*

'But hey, it's been a blast. Today, you've embarked on a new adventure, one that I hope will be filled with magic moments. I can't offer enough congratulations or put into words how happy I am for you both.

'Genevieve, I don't know you as well as Finlay, but since you and he got engaged, I've never seen him so happy. You're the perfect match for him and I'm delighted you found each other, even if it all started with a very unusual proposal.'

Genevieve nodded and she and Finlay exchanged a look.

'I doubt there's anyone in this room who doesn't know the story and it's definitely one to tell the grandkids… though maybe wait until they're over sixteen.'

Oh yes. Her brother's drunken proposal that Genevieve inadvertently caught on film was the stuff of legend.

'So, let's raise our glasses to this beautiful couple. To Finlay and Genevieve. May your days be filled with laughter, your nights with beautiful dreams, and your marriage blessed with happiness. Cheers!'

Everyone raised their glasses and clinked them on others nearby, mumbling, 'Cheers' or 'Sláinte.

Hayley drained her own glass as Oliver sat back down.

'Was that ok?' he said.

'More than. I'd say you've made up for your lack of assistance before the wedding with that.'

'Thanks.' He pulled her in for a side hug. 'Just one more duty for us to do.'

'What's that?'

'The dance. We've got to lead the way after their first dance.'

'Well, we've had lots of practise and we're hot, remember?'

'One of us certainly is.' He ran his fingers around her chin, gently raising it. 'You're so beautiful.'

'And you've turned into a sap.'

'It's your fault. You're so hot, you've melted me.'

She burst out laughing. 'How cheesy are you?'

'Very, apparently.'

By the time the dance came around, Hayley was so drugged up on love hormones that she and Oliver might have been the only people in the room. And the best bit was, everyone was too busy watching Finlay and Genevieve to care what she and Oliver were doing.

'Thank you.' Oliver slipped his arms around her.

'What for?' She placed her hands on his wide shoulders. He was so smart and sexy in his kilt ensemble, and he drew her close, pinning her against his sporran.

'For giving me a chance after I messed up.'

'What changed your mind?'

'I was looking at that fountain and... Well, I started thinking about things, my life, what I'd lost and what I'd achieved. Then I realised I could change things if I stopped dwelling on those things. All the stuff you tried to tell me made sense. The counsellor I had at school after Mum died told me grief wasn't a straight line but a messy scribble – kind of like what you said about the journey to happiness. She said there would be good days, bad days and everything in between. My life has been so focused on trying to achieve what I thought were good days that most of them have become bad days. Now I need to focus on the mess in the middle. But instead of trying to unravel it, I'll run with it.'

'Really?'

'Yeah. Why not? You can help me.'

'Sounds like something I'd be good at.'

'Because you know how to seize the day and live.'

She leaned up and kissed his cheek. 'I do. And I'm ready for whatever life throws at us.'

'Me too.' He pulled her close, and slowly they revolved on the spot. Hayley sighed and closed her eyes, enjoying the heat of Oliver's hand on her back. This was the perfect end to a beautiful day and the start of something new and wonderful.

EPILOGUE

Hayley

Hayley still couldn't stop smiling when she arrived at the salon on Wednesday morning.

'I guess the wedding was good,' Amber said.

'The best.' Hayley sat down at the reception desk. She wasn't ready to tell everyone about Oliver yet. They'd spent the past two days together in a haze, but in between snuggles, he'd paid a visit to his old job and spoken to his former boss about connections. His plan was to resign from his London job and set up his own practice. To his surprise, his boss had offered him a partnership starting immediately if he was up for it. Oliver was on his way back to London to hand in his notice. It wouldn't be long before he'd be back for good, and their new life could start.

'Are Finlay and Genevieve on their honeymoon?' Amber asked, leaning on the reception desk.

'They flew to the Maldives on Monday morning. Genevieve loves beaches. I think she was freaking out about leaving her dog, but they've posted some pics on the socials, and they look so happy. Here.' Hayley pulled out her phone and handed it to Amber. She scrolled through the smiling photos of the newlyweds on the beach with the bright blue ocean behind. Both Finlay and Genevieve were delighted about the development between Oliver and Hayley, though a little disappointed they wouldn't get to buy Oliver's house. Hayley was praying so hard that another house on the Fairways Estate came up for sale. How cool would it be to live that close to her brother and Genevieve? Her imagination sped ahead at the thought of them all a few years down the line, raising kids, the baby cousins all playing together. Her mum would be a granny and was already ecstatic at the thought.

Amber handed the phone back to Hayley. 'Your first customer looks like a tricky fish.'

'Oh? Why?' Hayley opened the booking system and checked the name. Ophelia Chattan-Blythe. 'That's quite a mouthful. Who is she?'

'Not sure,' Amber said. 'Colette and I looked her up on the socials. All her accounts are private, but she's on LinkedIn as a design consultant in Edinburgh at a place called Timeless Butterfly Interiors. Looks very upmarket. And she's gorgeous, you should see her phot—'

The bell on the salon door tinkled and the stunning woman arrived in person. Amber stopped talking, straightened up, and gaped at her. Hayley knew why. She looked like a model crossed with a member of the royal family. Hayley got up from the desk as Amber bustled off.

'Hello.' Hayley greeted her with a smile. 'Are you Ophelia Chattan-Blythe?'

'Yes.' She ran her fingers through long blonde hair that was so perfect Hayley wasn't sure she could do anything to improve it. Hayley was five foot eight and usually felt reasonably tall around other women, but Ophelia Chattan-Blythe was taller. Her clothes sang money and were the epitome of country chic with her white belted jeans, high boots and well-fitted tweed jacket.

'I can take your jacket and, if you take a seat just here, we can discuss what you want to do with your hair.'

Ophelia took off her jacket, handed it to Hayley, and sat down, leaving a cloud of expensive perfume in the air. 'I'd just like a little trim and some styling around the front. It's got too long.'

Her accent was 'posh', and nerves prickled in Hayley's tummy. She was suddenly responsible for attending to a woman who seemed like an aristocrat. Getting nervous doing hair hadn't happened for a long time. She settled Ophelia in the chair and went to put her jacket away and collect a gown.

'I hope I don't mess her up,' she muttered to Colette as she got to the backroom.

'She's bloody beautiful,' Colette whispered. 'I wish I had hair like that.'

Hayley returned to Ophelia and draped the gown over her. 'Are you just visiting the town?'

'Kind of. My family live nearby and I'm visiting them for a while.'

Hayley combed through Ophelia's hair, wondering who her family was. A family with a name like Chattan-Blythe would be easy to find out about. The salon bell rang again, and Hayley glanced around, expecting another client, but it wasn't. A woman with short dark hair and glasses came in with a large bag. Amber went to chat to her. The woman looked like she was delivering something, and Hayley recognised her from somewhere. Wasn't she the florist from the wedding? Maybe she'd come in to book an appointment and just happened to be carrying a bag. But when she left, she handed it to Amber.

Amber brought it towards the back of the salon. As she passed Hayley, she mumbled, 'It's for you from the flower shop. You got a secret admirer?'

Hayley caught herself blushing in the mirror. Ophelia was also watching and listening.

'I don't know,' Hayley said.

'I think you should find out,' Ophelia said. 'It's not every day a girl gets sent flowers out of the blue. Not in my experience anyway.'

'I should finish your hair first.'

'You've hardly started yet and I'm curious.'

'Well, ok.' Hayley put the comb away in her pouch and pulled open the box. Inside was an enormous bouquet of roses and a card.

'Shall I read this?' Amber pulled it out.

'Seriously?' Hayley stared at her.

Amber handed it to her and smiled. Hayley read.

Hayley, my love.

I miss you already. Of course, I'm ever so slightly freaked out that I'll crash the car and not make it back to you, but I'm doing my best not to think about things like that. Can't wait to see you again. You truly are the love of my life.

Oliver

XXX

Hayley sucked on her lip and smiled. He was crazy, but also wonderful.

'Well?' Ophelia said. 'Do you know how invested I am in this?'

Hayley giggled and passed her the card.

'Wow. Sounds like you're onto a winner.' She handed it to Amber.

Amber read with her mouth open. 'Oliver? Isn't he that grumpy divorce lawyer guy you hate?'

'The very same.'

'You hate him?' Ophelia said.

'We used to not get on so well.'

'Oh my god,' Amber clutched her face. 'This is hilarious. Are you dating him?'

'Yep.'

'Good for you,' Ophelia said. 'And he's a divorce lawyer?'

'Yes, but I'm trying not to hold it against him.'

'Does he do prenups?'

'I don't know.' Hayley frowned at Ophelia in the mirror. 'I could ask him. Do you need one?'

'If my father has his way, then I might.'

It all sounded very intriguing, but Hayley couldn't properly focus her mind on anything but being back with Oliver.

He'd suggested she stayed at his house until he got back. She hoped she'd be staying there quite a lot longer. Maybe forever. The roses were perfect on the dining room table, and she brought some of her favourite candle holders and set them around the room, making it instantly more homely. Oliver was due back on Saturday, which seemed like an age away, with only calls and messages to keep her going. Better than nothing, but it helped her realise that long distance would never have worked.

On Saturday night, when Hayley got back from work, she cracked open a bottle of Prosecco and messaged Oliver.

HAYLEY: Not long now. Xxx

Or she hoped so. In fact, she thought he'd be back by now.

He didn't reply straight away, and the message stayed unread for another hour as she watched TV. When she checked again, she saw one and opened it immediately.

OLIVER: Just over the border. See you soon. Love you so much xxx

The border. That was still hours away. She yawned. It had been a long and tiring day.

She went up to bed at nine-thirty. If she read for a bit, she could wait up. Her brain had other ideas though, and she woke disorientated, her Kindle flat on her chest and the room dark.

She blinked her eyes fully open. How long had she slept? She fumbled for the on switch at the side of the Kindle but froze. A thudding sound came from somewhere nearby... in the hall, or maybe downstairs. What was it? Were they being burgled? Glenbriar had a low crime rate but that didn't mean it never happened. Her heart hammered in her chest and her pulse drummed in her ears. She needed a weapon. The lamp?

The door opened, and Hayley's temperature hit burning point. She scrabbled for the lamp.

'Are you awake?' Oliver said.

'Holy shit,' she said. 'You terrified the life out of me. I thought you were a burglar.'

She switched on the lamp to see his smiling face. He crossed the room, sat on the bed, leaned over and kissed her. 'Sorry. I didn't mean to scare you. I had no idea it would take me this long.'

'Thank god you're here now. And is everything sorted in London?'

'Yeah, all sorted. My boss was actually quite understanding, all things considered. He said I can work out my notice from here. I think he's glad to get rid of me. After I took a week off for a wedding, I'm not his favourite person. I left early this morning, handed in the keys to the flat, and drove back. There are so many roadworks though.'

She tugged him close. 'I missed you so much.' He fell on top of her, laughing.

'I thought I'd be here hours ago.'

'You're here now and that's made my night, my week, my year, my life!'

'I really missed you.' He kissed her again, and she tugged his t-shirt out of his jeans, slipping her hands around his waist.

'Come and cuddle me,' she said. 'I want to ask you something.'

'What's that?' He got up, pulled off his t-shirt and jeans and slipped into the bed beside her. His hot slab of a chest was heavenly to lean on. His arm looped around her shoulder, holding her close.

'You know we discussed having kids?'

'Yes?' He stroked her hair and placed a kiss on the top of her head. 'Are you pregnant?'

'No.' She pinged his chest. 'I want to have a wedding first. I just wondered how many you were thinking.'

'I had a vision once about this house being filled with our kids. Let's make it come true.'

'Really?' She cocked an eyebrow. 'You don't think that two is fine?'

'Two sounds perfect and a lot easier than a house-full, though I imagine even two can be a riot.'

She leaned up and kissed his cheek. 'Miss McBride has found her Mr Wright.'

'I wonder if Miss McBride would consider updating her status to match her personality.'

'Meaning what?'

'Perhaps you'd like to become Mrs Wright? Then we could rename *you* "Always" which seems to fit a lot better than it does with me.'

Hayley twisted her neck so she could look at him. 'Excuse me? Is that a proposal?'

He quirked a grin. 'I suppose it is.'

'Well, let me tell you, that has got to be the worst proposal ever. What happened to the Eiffel Tower, champagne, rings? All the things I've dreamed of since I was twelve.'

'You can still have all those things… But only if you have me.'

She chuckled and leaned her head on him. 'That's all I really want. And actually, the proposal maybe wasn't as bad as all that. I might upgrade it to an eight out of ten if you go down on one knee.'

He shuffled out of the bed and onto the floor, one knee on the carpet. 'Will you marry me?'

She leaned out of the bed, laughing, and held her hand to her mouth. 'I suppose so.'

'You suppose so?' He pushed himself up and got back into the bed. 'Well, how about you let me upgrade it to a nine and we'll see what you say after that?'

'How will you do that?'

'Like this.' He leaned over and placed a long, slow lingering kiss on her lips.

Hayley moaned, opening her mouth to him.

'I'm going to ask you the same question an hour from now.'

She smiled into his dark eyes and saw herself reflected in them. 'There's no need for a third proposal, you dafty. My answer will still be yes. Of course, I'll marry you, but how will you upgrade to a ten?'

'The tickets to Paris are already booked for proposal number four.'

'Seriously? You're as bad as Finlay. Worse even. But you're also everything I want and then some. You'll always be my Mr Wright and I can't wait to be Mrs Wright.'

He kissed her softly on her cheek. 'You're exactly "right" for me and what I've needed for so long. My special person. The one I love, and I know loves me. Whatever the future holds, I'll always love you, Miss McBride.'

'And I'll always love you, Mr Wright.' She tugged him closer. 'Now stop talking and kiss me some more.'

The End

More Books by Margaret Amatt

Scottish Island Escapes

1. A Winter Haven

2. A Spring Retreat

3. A Summer Sanctuary

4. An Autumn Hideaway

5. A Christmas Bluff

6. A Flight of Fancy

7. A Hidden Gem

8. A Striking Result

9. A Perfect Discovery

10. A Festive Surprise

The Glenbriar Series

1. Stolen Kisses at the Loch View Hotel

2. Just Friends at Thistle Lodge

3. Pitching up at Heather Glen

4. Two's Company at the Forest Light Show

5. Highland Fling on the Whisky Trail

6. Snowdown at the Old Schoolhouse

7. Starting Over at the Crafty Bee Barn

8. A Surprise Proposal in the Rose Garden

9. Cutting it Neat for the Wedding

10. A Classy Affair in the Country

11. Mix Up under the Mistletoe

12. A Fresh Start on the Bridle Path

13. Last First Kiss at the Village Church

14. Fight or Flirt on the Scenic Route

15. Love Match on the Road Home

ACKNOWLEDGMENTS

Thanks goes to my adorable husband for supporting my dreams and putting up with my writing talk 24/7. Also to my son, whose interest in my writing always makes me smile. It's precious to know I've passed the bug to him – he's currently writing his own fantasy novel and instruction books on how to build Lego!

Throughout the writing process, I have gleaned help from many sources and met some fabulous people. I'd like to give a special mention to Stéphanie Ronckier, my beta reader extraordinaire. Stéphanie's continued support with my writing is invaluable and I love the fact that I need someone French to correct my grammar! Stéphanie, you rock. To my lovely friend, Lyn Williamson, thank you for your continued support and encouragement with all my projects. And to my fellow authors, Evie Alexander and Lyndsey Gallagher – you girls are the best! I love it that you always have my back and are there to help when I need you.

Also, a thanks to the editors at Leannan Press for their work on this novel.

Of course a huge thank you goes to the readers who continue to support me in so many ways. I appreciate each and every one of you and hope that I can keep bringing you more books to enjoy! Big love.

Margaret XX